A Match Made in London

THE TWICE
SHY SERIES

CHRISTINA BRITTON

everafter ROMANCE

EverAfter Romance
A division of Diversion Publishing Corp.
443 Park Avenue South, Suite 1004
New York, New York 10016
www.EverAfterRomance.com

For more information, email info@everafterromance.com

First EverAfter Romance edition May 2019.
Paperback ISBN: 978-1-63576-615-8
eBook ISBN: 978-1-63576-618-9

This book is dedicated with love to my mom, Vickie Jetté.

Thank you, Moppy, for never censoring my reading, even when I was thirteen and bringing home steamy romances by the dozen. Who knew it would lead to this?

I love you.

Chapter 1

Miss Rosalind Merriweather surveyed the lords and ladies gathered before her with trepidation. Of all the places she had never expected—or wanted—to be, a London drawing room had certainly topped the list.

Distaste roiled in her already unsettled stomach. London. The place of her sister's ruin, the beginning of the end of her family.

She touched the locket at her throat, more out of habit than any real comfort, her fingers gliding over the worn filigreed gold and turquoise cabochons. A reminder of what happened the last time a Merriweather stepped foot inside the borders of this illustrious city. A somber lesson on the vagaries of men…and how easy it was for a young woman to lose everything on the whim of a moment.

Not that she was all that young. Or anyone worth noticing in the first place. Even so, she would be a fool to let down her guard. Especially as her charge, Miss Sarah Gladstow, was one of those young, impressionable things who *was* fair game to rakes and libertines.

"Miss Merriweather, attend me," a shrill voice called close by.

Rosalind heaved a sigh and hurried to Mrs. Gladstow, the girl's mother. As her current employer, the woman was last in a long line of them and by far the worst. Truly, the collection of aging spinsters and elderly widows that had come before her, all fussy and difficult to a one, seemed the most generous and kind collection of patrons ever assembled compared to Mrs. Gladstow.

"Yes, ma'am?" Rosalind asked.

The older woman scowled. It was her perpetual expression, one that had left deep grooves around her thin lips and between her hard eyes. Yet the expression seemed even fiercer than usual. "Remember what I told you, girl," she hissed. "You are to stay close to my daughter's side, help her to engage in conversation with others, but under no circumstance are you to overshadow her. We are here to find Sarah a husband, not to stroke that ego of yours. Is that understood?"

"I hardly think I possess an ego, ma'am. I would think nine years as a companion would have effectively banished that particular sentiment, if I ever had one—"

Like lightning the woman's hand shot out, her skeletal fingers digging like talons into Rosalind's arm. Too stunned to react, Rosalind could do no more than stumble along as she was pulled to the side of the vast room.

"You have been with us how long, Miss Merriweather?" Mrs. Gladstow's voice had gone silky as custard. And as hard to stomach as a spoiled one.

"Five months, ma'am."

"And before that, where were you?"

Like the woman didn't know. "With your Great-Aunt Lavinia, ma'am. For three years," she added before the woman could ask that as well. And before that with Mrs. Kester, Aunt Lavinia's closest friend. Preceded by her first post, with Mrs. Kester's niece by marriage and Rosalind's own distant cousin, Mrs. Harper. She had been passed around as a companion to those ladies like a plate of particularly unappetizing food at a party.

Only to wind up here, with a woman who had never wanted to take her on in the first place. It all seemed like some horrible comedic play. If it wasn't her life, she might laugh.

Mrs. Gladstow pursed her lips as she considered her. "I don't believe you're stupid. You don't look stupid. And yet, time and again, you run off at the mouth in the rudest manner possible. How, I wonder, did my great aunt stand it?"

"She was deaf."

"Yes, she was," Mrs. Gladstow mused. "And yet I did not question her when she asked me, practically on her death bed, to take you on after she passed. That was quite noble of me, I think."

The woman looked at Rosalind in expectation, no doubt waiting for her to burst forth with undying gratitude. When none came she frowned mightily.

"I'll have no more out of you, Miss Merriweather," she hissed. "I have no qualms about throwing you out on your ear, deathbed promise to my aunt or no."

It was not anything Rosalind had not heard before. Mrs. Gladstow wielded threats the way an artist might wield paints and brushes; she was a master. Yet that did not stop the twinge of fear that slithered up Rosalind's spine. For she knew—as did Mrs. Gladstow, damn her—that Rosalind had no place to go if she lost this position. There was no post waiting in the wings this time. And Mrs. Gladstow would assure that there would be no reference to help Rosalind find that new post on her own.

The older woman's eyes narrowed, no doubt seeing the fear that Rosalind strove to hide. She flapped her hands in the air as if shooing a fly. "I've no more time for you, girl. Do as you're told." With that she pasted a wide smile on her face—a frightening expression, truly—and glided away.

Rosalind took a steadying breath. *And so it starts.* The next few months in London would be like swimming in shark-infested waters, a fan and her wits as her only weapons. She gazed about the room, making a mental note of the men that appeared the most dangerous to a young woman of virtue. Her eyes lit on one blond Adonis in the corner. Ludicrously attractive, with a sparkling smile that would positively draw one in, he was the epitome of a London libertine. A heartbreaker of the first order. Here was the exact creature she should be wary of. The type of person her sister, romantic that she was, would have been defenseless against.

Guinevere's face floated into her mind then, happy and vibrant. But it was too ephemeral. For, as it always did, that long-ago memory transformed into the sister Rosalind had gotten back after that fateful trip to the capital, when grief had sapped all the life from the beautiful girl she had been.

Yes, Rosalind thought as her eyes narrowed on the rake again, it was imperative she guard against men such as him. For she would be damned if she, or anyone in her care, would be duped as her sister had been.

• • •

Although, she learned some time later, smiling and nodding woodenly to some pompous lord as he prattled on about his incredibly large kennel of hounds, it was quite possible that a debonair rake was the least of her problems.

Miss Sarah Gladstow, for her part, stood like the famed biblical pillar of salt at Rosalind's side, not even attempting to respond to the man, just as she'd done for the three who had come before him. Rosalind had come to learn something of the girl in the past five months, chiefly that she was painfully shy. Now she was being forced into conversation with strangers, surely her worst nightmare come true. Rosalind might have felt pity for her if she was not so annoyed that the brunt of the effort to keep Miss Gladstow appearing interesting fell to her shoulders.

"You were blessed with a litter of fifteen puppies?" she said to the man now—a Lord Something-or-other with wobbling jowls that Rosalind was hard-pressed not to stare at in fascination. He nodded, and they danced about as if possessing a mind of their own.

Tearing her eyes from the sight, she turned to Miss Gladstow. "Isn't that fascinating, Miss Gladstow? You are a great lover of canines, are you not?"

Please, she silently begged as she watched the girl swallow hard, *please respond to the man and relieve me from this hell.* But Miss Gladstow darted one quick look up to Lord Jowls, blushed mightily, and dropped her eyes to the floor again, giving only a quick nod as she did so.

Rosalind just managed to fight back a groan. At this rate she would be out on her ear in a fortnight. Even worse, Lord Jowls was completely ignoring Miss Gladstow. Instead an interested gleam entered his eyes as he considered Rosalind. She had already learned in the five minutes they'd been in conversation that the man was widowed and without issue. No doubt he was on the lookout for a wife. He could not possibly be interested in her, a penniless companion. He would be wanting a wife of good standing, a wife with a dowry.

Yet Rosalind did not want to take any chances.

She looked to some spot behind him, widening her eyes in what she hoped was a believably surprised manner. "Oh! But Mrs. Gladstow requires her daughter. Do forgive us, my lord."

Without waiting for the man's response, Rosalind took hold of Miss Gladstow's arm and hauled her away. The girl came without protest, years of being browbeaten by her mother making her docile to a fault. Surely Mrs. Gladstow would have another less jowly man for her daughter to "charm."

Mrs. Gladstow, however, was not pleased with their return. "You have left Lord Ullerton already?" she hissed. "He is highly eligible, Sarah, and an earl. You could do worse."

Not by much, Rosalind thought. By the look on Miss Gladstow's face, she was of the same opinion. Besides, this was the girl's first true foray into society. Would her mother have her land a husband already?

The older woman shook her head. "Never mind. For I've a family I want you to meet." She leaned in closer to her daughter, her lips mere inches from the girl's ear. Even so, Rosalind could hear the hiss of a whisper as she said, low and fierce, "Get in good with them, Sarah, and you are golden."

Soon they were being propelled through the crowd—heading right for the blond Adonis. Rosalind stared in disbelief, praying Mrs. Gladstow would change course. She could not possibly mean to introduce her daughter to that man. But no, she headed right for him and his party, her steps determined, never faltering.

Mrs. Gladstow dropped into a deep curtsy when they reached them. "Pardon me for intruding once more," she said, her voice sickeningly sweet, "but I did so want to introduce my daughter. This is

Miss Sarah Gladstow, light of my life. Her father and I quite dote on her." She smiled beatifically at the younger girl.

She then went into a rambling introduction of the other party. Rosalind's mind spun as name after name was spoken. First Lord Willbridge, a handsome marquess with copper hair and twinkling gray eyes, followed by his pretty, bespectacled bride. Next was the dowager Lady Willbridge with her daughter Lady Daphne Masters, a ravishing beauty of a girl out for her first Season. Beside her was Miss Mariah Duncan, younger sister to the young Lady Willbridge and, with her flaxen hair and cornflower eyes, even more stunning than Lady Daphne.

And of course, last of the bunch was Sir Tristan Crosby, the blond Adonis. He grinned with a disgusting amount of confidence as his name was spoken.

The group smiled at them and murmured warm greetings. "Curtsy, dear," Mrs. Gladstow hissed through her smile when her daughter continued to stand stupidly staring at her toes.

The young Lady Willbridge gave her a small, commiserating look and stepped forward, taking up her hands. Miss Gladstow jumped, looking up with wide eyes into the woman's kind face.

"It is a pleasure to meet you," Lady Willbridge said, her voice melodic and sweet. She smiled in encouragement.

The effect on Miss Gladstow was instantaneous. A tentative answering smile spread over her face. "The pleasure is mine, my lady," she whispered.

Lady Willbridge smiled in delight. Something in Rosalind's chest loosened. She had come to care for Miss Gladstow in the past five months, despite the fact that she could hardly tease a word out of her. That this woman was being kind to her, as so few had been before, touched her deeply.

A deep voice interrupted. "But you have forgotten someone, Mrs. Gladstow."

Rosalind sucked in her breath, her eyes flying to the blond Adonis, the one she now knew as Sir Tristan Crosby. He eyed her with interest, his blue eyes amazingly warm for all their icy color.

Her mind seemed to fly off for an instant. She forgot her position, her purpose in London, even her own name. For a single, frozen second she was merely a young woman staring back at the most devastatingly handsome man she had ever seen.

Which was as she feared would happen. Instant fury boiled through her veins. Granted, some of it was for him. He no doubt knew what he was doing with those intimate looks and melting smiles, the cur. But most of her anger was reserved for herself alone. She had known to be on her guard. And yet here she was, practically a drooling mess over one glance.

She would not—could not—be caught off guard again.

Mrs. Gladstow's voice thankfully dragged her back from the island of self-reprimanding disgust where she had marooned herself.

"Her? Oh, she is my daughter's companion, Miss Rosalind Merriweather."

Sir Tristan grinned. "It is a pleasure, Miss Merriweather."

She might have rolled her eyes. If she had not been too busy fighting the flock of butterflies that had taken up residence in her stomach. Blessedly her mind was not so overtaken that she forgot to curtsy. The rest of the group greeted her before Mrs. Gladstow claimed their attention again. As Rosalind made to blend back in with the scenery, Sir Tristan stepped toward her. She looked at him in suspicion as he bent his head in an attempt at conversing privately with her.

"Are you new to town, Miss Merriweather?"

She briefly considered turning her back and ignoring the man entirely. But she had her position to think about. Mrs. Gladstow would surely not like her giving the cut direct. She said, in as clipped a manner as possible, "Yes."

"And how do you like London?"

So this was to be a conversation, was it? She drew herself up to her full height—not very impressive, considering she did not even reach his chin—and leveled a cool stare on him. "As well as can be expected."

He grinned, flashing disgustingly straight teeth. "And what is it you expected?"

"Do you truly wish me to answer that, sir?" she gritted.

"Certainly. As it can run the gamut anywhere from a veritable paradise to the very bowels of hell itself, you can be assured my curiosity is piqued."

"If you truly wish to know."

His grin widened. "Oh, I do."

"Very well." She looked to Mrs. Gladstow, ensuring the woman was still deep in conversation with the rest of the group before returning her attention to Sir Tristan. She cleared her throat. "It is in my very decided opinion that London is full of men who think only of their own pleasure and do not care who gets hurt in its pursuit. It is full of spoiled people with nothing better to do than to preen and gloat before others. It is a place of heartache and vice. And I wish I never had to come."

The man's smile did not falter. But there was something deep in his eyes that changed, sobering. She might not have seen it had she not been watching him so closely. "That *is* a very decided opinion, Miss Merriweather. And do you think there is nothing that might change your mind?"

"No, nothing. And if I may be so bold, Sir Tristan?"

"I do not think I could stop you if I wanted to, but I find I am most anxious to hear what you have to say."

"Very well. To be honest, everything I have seen thus far has only cemented those opinions."

For a single moment his expression altered. And she felt she could see to the depths of him. Before she could process it his debonair smile was back in place, his eyes twinkling merrily again.

"That is such a shame. For I think you would find there is much to recommend London—and its people—if you only open yourself up to it."

Before she could think of how to reply to that the butler entered, announcing dinner. Sir Tristan gave her a polite nod, stepping past her and offering Miss Gladstow his arm.

"I hope you are not opposed to my escort into dinner, Miss Gladstow?" To Rosalind's surprise, the girl placed her hand readily enough on his arm—it must be that smile, damn him—and they walked off toward the massive double doors, leaving Rosalind to look after him with not a small amount of confusion.

Chapter 2

If there was anything Tristan was good at, it was charming even the most irascible dame. Which was how he found himself seated next to Miss Sarah Gladstow during dinner, their hostess turning to warm butter in his hands at the mere mention of more informal seating.

Never say he didn't have his talents.

He turned to Miss Gladstow. "How do you like London?"

The answer was always the same with the shy ones, of course. And so he was not in the least surprised when she said, "It's all a bit...overwhelming."

He nodded in understanding. "You have not been here long?"

"This is my first social event."

Well, at least her mother had not shoved her immediately into a crowded ballroom full to bursting with hundreds of noble elite. The woman was a social climber if he ever saw one, but hopefully this small mercy on her part showed love for her daughter.

But, as he had learned in the past, talking about London only increased anxiety in women such as Miss Gladstow. And right now, her fingers were wrapped so tight about her spoon he thought she might bend the metal. She had not looked at him once, her eyes quite firmly fixed on her soup, which sat untouched in all its creamy splendor.

No, there was only one thing that would bring her out of the cocoon of anxiety she was currently wrapped in.

"Tell me of your home."

Her eyes glazed with longing, as he knew they would, though doubt that he was genuinely curious kept her silent. He smiled in encouragement. In the next moment she began to speak, the words issuing with amazing rapidity from her lips. Within the space of ten minutes he learned the color of her sitting room, where her favorite shady grove was located, even the name of her horse. He encouraged her unexpected volubility with *mmms* and *ahhhs* of interest and questions designed to draw out even the most reserved lady. He may be rubbish in most aspects of his life, but never say he did not excel in this.

As they conversed, however, he could not fail to be aware of one particular set of eyes directed unwaveringly their way. Not Miss Gladstow's mother, of course. That woman was currently gushing over whatever Lord Ullerton was spewing—*egad*, but he hoped the woman wasn't planning to pair her daughter off with that damned reprobate. No, the eyes in question were a warm cinnamon brown, and set in a pixie-like face that had struck him to his core the moment he'd spied her.

Miss Merriweather.

Quite against his will, his eyes drifted over Miss Gladstow's shoulder to settle on that woman, blessedly far down the table. As it had been the last half dozen times he'd looked her way, her direct, suspicious gaze was settled unnervingly on him. And as before his whole being reacted, tensing, awareness coursing through him.

There was no earthly reason for it, of course. Yes, she was lovely in a quiet way. And yes, he'd felt an instant pull to her. But this reaction to her had nothing to do with her appearance and everything to do with the way she looked at him: as if she knew his every secret shame and saw to his true self, to the pathetic, useless person within.

His smile must have faltered, for Miss Gladstow, sensitive girl that she was, tripped over her words, her eyes going dull with uncertainty.

Taking a deep breath, he grinned and held out a plate of blanched asparagus to her. "You were saying something about your dearest childhood friend?"

As he hoped, her expression cleared and she was off again, taking a small portion of the vegetable as she launched into a story of her friend, a young man whom Tristan was beginning to suspect was a bit more than a friend. As she talked he got the distinct feeling that this was the first time anyone had truly listened to her in a long while.

Enough of his imagined worry over Miss Merriweather and her too-sharp eyes. Miss Gladstow, shy, lonely, and miserable in her new position as debutante, was exactly what he had been searching for.

He managed to do splendidly the rest of the meal. And when the men left the dining room later on that evening to rejoin the ladies in the drawing room, he fully intended to seek Miss Gladstow out once more and continue where they had left off. Until, that was, a small hand on his arms waylaid his plans.

"Sir Tristan, may I have a word?"

He just managed to bite back the groan that threatened. Instead he gifted Miss Merriweather with his most charming smile, hoping to blind her into forgoing whatever mad notion she may have gotten into her head. He was not a vain creature, but he was not stupid, either. Well, not unduly so. He knew women found him pleasing to look at, had even used it to his advantage quite often.

But his efforts were wasted now, as they had been before. Miss Merriweather's eyelashes didn't so much as flicker as she gazed up at him in what he assumed was her typically forthright manner. With that stubborn little chin of hers and the small line that seemed to perpetually indent the space between her eyebrows, she seemed formidable indeed. Despite the fact that she didn't even reach his chin.

Mayhap if he feigned stupidity he could put the girl off. For he had a feeling that, as before, whatever she had to say would not be pleasant in the least. He tilted his head in a quizzical manner. "It was Miss Merriweather, wasn't it?"

She scowled, further deepening that maddening little groove. "Yes, as I'm sure you remember quite well."

"Now what would make you say that?"

She looked him up and down, and he had the disturbing sense that he'd been weighed and measured and found wanting. "Oh, you have the look of someone who never forgets a face."

A startled laugh burst from him. "Do I?"

"Oh, yes."

"I don't know whether I have just been complimented or insulted."

"You may take it as you wish, of course. But I can assure you, I did not mean it in a complimentary manner. If you were curious."

He stared at her. "You are most singular, Miss Merriweather."

"Yes," she mused, "it has gotten me more in trouble than not."

"I can imagine," he replied with what he thought was an impressive lack of humor, though inside he felt the first true stirrings of real amusement. And intrigue. Goodness, but he'd never met a woman like her. "I suppose it is hard to hold on to a position when one is so very outspoken."

"You've no idea," she muttered, shooting a look across the room and flushing.

He followed her gaze. As expected, Mrs. Gladstow was glaring their way. He had nothing to fear from the woman, yet still he shivered in apprehension from the furious fire in her gaze.

"Mayhap you'd best see to your charge," he said. As much as he wished to escape Miss Merriweather's presence, he was more concerned about the repercussions she might reap after talking to him.

She turned back to him then. "I'm sure I can handle my employer, sir, though I thank you for your concern. Now, then, about why I pulled you aside." She cleared her throat. "You and Miss Gladstow were in close conversation during dinner."

He quirked an eyebrow, not quite sure where she was going with this. "Yes?"

"Do you not think you were a bit too focused on her?"

He laughed. "You accuse me of giving the girl too much attention?"

"Certainly. It will not fail to have been noted. I would not have Miss Gladstow talked of."

For the first time in the exchange, Tristan felt a true smile lift his lips. "You are to be commended for your concern. Miss Gladstow is lucky to have such a champion."

But his praise only had her scowling more. "You think to patronize me?"

He blinked, the smile falling away. "Of course not. I merely meant to compliment you on your fierce defense of her."

"You mean because I am in their employ, why would I care, do you not?"

Tristan stared at her, utterly flummoxed. Truly, why was it he could not seem to say the right thing to this woman? "You mistake me, madam."

"Hmm," was her only response. That, and the suspicious look she gave him, as if she expected him to sprout devil horns and spit fire and brimstone at her.

But if kindness and levity would not do the trick with this woman, perhaps having a strong offensive attitude would. He leaned over her, so she had to crane her neck to look at him. "Miss Merriweather," he said, letting his voice dip to silkiness, "I get the distinct impression that you do not like me."

"Whatever gave you that idea?"

He very nearly laughed, she surprised him so with her sarcastic drawl. Blessedly he managed to hold onto his serious mien. "I do believe, though please correct me if I'm wrong, that you are on the cusp of accusing me of nefarious purposes with your charge."

"Aren't you?" she shot back.

"Not in the least. I happen to like Miss Gladstow. She is a lovely young woman, who is in a strange city and not at all happy about it. I had hoped to give her some comfort by lending a sympathetic ear. Do you condemn me for that?"

For the first time in the exchange, uncertainty clouded her eyes. "Of course not."

"Then please give me the benefit of the doubt. I do not appreciate my honor being questioned, especially when the one questioning it has no basis for their suspicions."

That seemed to stun the words from her. She bit down on her lower lip.

A punch to the gut could not have taken the breath from his body so effectively. His eyes zeroed in on the small movement, fairly devouring the way her small teeth dug into the plump pink lip. He had the strangest desire to bend down, to replace her teeth with his own, to taste of those lips.

Mrs. Gladstow's voice, too close to his side, yanked him back from the precipice of desire.

"Miss Merriweather, might I remind you of your position."

Stunned, feeling as if he'd taken a plunge in an icy lake, Tristan stumbled back a step. What the devil was wrong with him? He was in a roomful of people, at the home of one of the premier hostesses in London. And he had been damn near to kissing Miss Merriweather.

He was going mad, that must be it.

Apparently unaware of his turmoil, Mrs. Gladstow took Miss Merriweather's arm in what looked to be a punishing grip and whispered fiercely in her ear. Miss Merriweather, for her part, looked completely unfazed. All but for the slight flicker of what looked to be fear in her eyes, and the barely perceptible tightening around her mouth that resembled nothing so much as a wince of pain.

Fury coursed through him, hot and swift. "Mrs. Gladstow, I suggest you unhand Miss Merriweather this instant."

The woman froze, turning shocked eyes his way. "I beg your pardon?"

"You should, though Miss Merriweather deserves it far more than me." He looked pointedly at her fingers, which were digging into the tender skin of the younger woman's arm.

Mrs. Gladstow released Miss Merriweather as if she'd been burned. "My apologies, Sir Tristan," she said stiffly. "I was merely letting the girl know her place. She should not have been bothering you as she was."

"She was not bothering me, I assure you. I merely asked her if she enjoyed her first foray into a true London dining experience and she was indulging me."

Miss Merriweather looked at him sharply, no doubt surprised at the small fib. Blessedly, she was smart enough to keep silent. Mrs. Gladstow, for her part, looked only slightly mollified. To further distract from her annoyance at her companion, he said, "By the way, your daughter is a lovely dinner companion, Mrs. Gladstow. I was so happy to have secured a seat beside her. She charmed me quite completely."

As expected, the woman's expression—and attention, thank goodness—changed in an instant. Her meager chest puffed up with pride. "I am so happy to hear you say so, Sir Tristan. As I have told my Sarah repeatedly, she need only apply herself and she will turn heads."

As the woman rambled on, listing her daughter's attributes as if she were trotting out a broodmare for sale, Tristan was aware of the long, considering look Miss Merriweather gave him. *Escape, you daft thing*, he thought. At long last she did just that, moving off silently to join Miss Gladstow across the room.

As he listened with a rapt expression to Mrs. Gladstow, however, his mind stayed with Miss Merriweather. The woman was such an unexpected creature. He'd never known another like her. He was utterly surprised by her. But, more than that, his physical reaction to her left him not a little dazed.

He was sure it had been the heat of the moment. And his lack of female companionship for—what was it, several months now? Egad, he'd best see to that, and soon. Surely then his strange desire for the very outspoken Miss Merriweather would be completely eradicated. Yes, that was it. He would visit one of his willing widows with all haste. And he would think no more of Miss Merriweather and her delectable mouth.

Chapter 3

Over the next fortnight, Sir Tristan was not the only male who haunted the Gladstows' drawing room. But he was by far the most palatable. Rosalind should be nothing but happy for Miss Gladstow, that she had a suitor who treated her with such respect, who made the shy girl laugh.

But she found she could not be. For despite his protestations that first night that he was not up to nefarious purposes, Rosalind could not trust him. Not one bit.

A better woman would have taken a gentleman at his word, of course. Especially after that gentleman had been so kind as to save her from the terror that was Mrs. Gladstow. But even with him coming gallantly to her rescue like a knight of old—granted one wearing a cravat and embroidered waistcoat instead of a shining suit of armor—she had a deep mistrust in the veracity of his words.

That mistrust had grown considerably in the two weeks since.

Rosalind swatted at a bug that was buzzing about her ear, returning her gaze to the back of Sir Tristan's gilded head. He was twenty paces in front of her, Miss Gladstow's hand tucked into the crook of his arm as they meandered down a shaded path in Hyde Park. As she watched he said something to the girl, causing her to give a quiet laugh.

Miss Gladstow was never so relaxed as when she was in Sir Tristan's presence. Rosalind might have thought the girl was falling in love with him.

Except there was nothing remotely romantic about their interactions.

As if to prove her point, Miss Gladstow gave Sir Tristan a playful swat on the arm. It was something a sister would do to a brother. Certainly not the actions of an infatuated woman, a woman hoping to be wooed and wed.

Rosalind's eyes narrowed as Sir Tristan chuckled, then turned to greet a couple passing by. The baronet seemed an open book, friendly and engaging with everyone he came across. Yet to Rosalind he was an enigma. For why was the most popular man in town—truly, he was Society's darling—pursuing Miss Gladstow, who could easily be the shyest girl in the kingdom?

It could be Miss Gladstow's dowry, of course. Her parents had put it about that she would come with a tidy sum upon her marriage. Rosalind may have been ignorant of most of Society's quirks, but she was fully aware of one glaring fact: men born into great houses were not necessarily born into the wealth required to keep up their lifestyles. More often than not a sacrifice had to be made, in the form of some poor bait of a girl who was dangled with her father's money like a lure about her neck. If Sir Tristan was in dire straits and after the girl for a relief from his financial woes, he would certainly not be the first.

But something deep inside Rosalind told her this was not the case now. If he was so desperate he surely would be pulling out every trick in his arsenal to secure Miss Gladstow. He would be courting her, not sharing this strange, platonic friendship with her. And as men of his ilk did not have mere friendships with girls like Miss Gladstow, and he did not look as if he was planning to marry her, she was back to her original assumption regarding his unexpected interest in the girl, the only other assumption she could fathom.

He meant to ruin her.

Well, she'd be damned if she would let him take advantage of Miss Gladstow in such a way. Yes, Rosalind had been ordered by Mrs. Gladstow to keep her distance from the couple, all the better to promote Sir Tristan's interest.

But when had Rosalind ever been good at following orders?

Her legs, though short, quickly ate up the space between her and the couple. "Pardon me for intruding," she said as she pushed between the pair, effectively separating them. "But it has gotten quite lonesome back there. I don't suppose you would be so kind as to let me join you?"

Miss Gladstow looked thoroughly startled, though she quickly acquiesced. Sir Tristan, however, appeared suspicious. Amused, yes, but suspicious all the same. And no wonder. For she hadn't exactly hid her dislike of him over the past two weeks, yet here she was, practically begging to be in his presence.

"I do beg your pardon," he said with a small bow. "We would, of course, be delighted if you joined us."

She bobbed a quick curtsy of thanks. But instead of going around him to take his other arm, as he no doubt intended, she grabbed onto the arm closest to her, then proceeded to link her other arm through Miss Gladstow's. If the girl's mother ever caught wind of this, Rosalind would surely be let go on the spot. But Miss Gladstow would not be bringing home tales, that she knew. The girl barely spoke a word to her mother as it was. She was certainly not about to incur the woman's wrath herself by letting it be known she'd let their companion run roughshod over her.

"So," Rosalind said brightly when they started down the path again, now tucked safely between them, "what was it you were discussing when I interrupted you?"

"Miss Gladstow was just telling me of some of the places she would like to visit while here in town."

"Such as?"

Sir Tristan smiled across Rosalind to Miss Gladstow. "May I?"

The girl gave a shy nod, her cheeks flaming, stuck back in the painful shyness that she was typically mired in now that Rosalind had intruded.

"Miss Gladstow is quite anxious to see Madame Catalini perform at the King's Concert."

"Really?" Rosalind looked to Miss Gladstow. This was the first she'd heard of this very particular desire. The girl had never given any indication of having interest in a select performer before, much less in music in general.

To her surprise Miss Gladstow was nodding away, her eyes bright on Sir Tristan. "Oh yes. I have heard such incredible things about her performance. Did you know, they completely exclude all modern music there? It is quite intriguing, don't you agree?"

"Certainly," Sir Tristan replied, leaning farther over Rosalind. "And, as you are such a lover of music, you really must not miss hearing the new Philharmonic Society play in the Queen's Concert Rooms. They have only recently begun putting on performances, yet already their talent is remarked upon."

And once again Rosalind was ignored, as effectively as if she'd remained twenty paces behind. The two continued to converse, one on either side of her. Frustrated, Rosalind cut in again.

"That sounds lovely. You are kind to tell her of it. Miss Gladstow, you must tell your mother about your wishes."

Once again the girl seemed to deflate before her eyes. "Oh, I'm not sure Mama would care for it at all."

"She could not deny you. Not if you told her how passionate you are about such things."

But she heard how ridiculous that sounded the moment the words were out of her mouth. She did not need Miss Gladstow's disbelieving expression to tell her that. Mrs. Gladstow had one goal for their time in London, and that was to see her only daughter married well. Anything that did not promote such a venture would be summarily squashed.

An uncomfortable silence fell. Sir Tristan, ever the gallant, spoke into the tense void. "I do believe it is time to return you home, Miss Gladstow. I would not have your parents think I am monopolizing your time. Where are you for tonight?"

"Lord and Lady Jasper's, I think."

He grinned. "What a coincidence. I am as well."

"Some coincidence," Rosalind muttered.

Once again thick silence reigned. When would she learn to hold her tongue? She shot a glance up at Sir Tristan. His gaze was hooded, leaving no hint as to his thoughts. He opened his mouth, no doubt to give her a proper set-down. Or, more likely, to smooth over the great gaping hole of discomfort her words had brought about.

Presently a figure approached them, effectively cutting off whatever the baronet had been about to say. "Miss Gladstow," the newcomer said in somber tones.

Beside her, Miss Gladstow squeaked. "What on earth are you doing in London?"

The level of alarm in the girl's voice surprised Rosalind. She looked closely at the man. Oh, but of course, he was Miss Gladstow's friend from back home. Rosalind had met him several times in the months she'd been with the Gladstows.

"Mr. Marlow," she said, "how lovely to see you."

The man, who had up until that moment not taken his eyes from Miss Gladstow, blinked and looked at her. "Ah, Miss Merriweather wasn't it? How d' you do?"

Before she could answer, he turned back to the other girl. "How have you been?"

She flushed. "Fine, thank you."

The two of them stood staring at one another. Rosalind looked back and forth between the two, utterly flummoxed. They had never shown such a degree of tension between them. Back home they had always appeared at ease with each other, the very picture of old friends.

She opened her mouth to say something, anything to break them from the strange tableau they were frozen in, when Miss Gladstow started. "Oh! But I'm being rude. Mr. Marlow, this is Sir Tristan Crosby. Sir Tristan, this is Mr. David Marlow, the friend I was telling you about."

Making the situation more bizarre than it already was, Sir Tristan's typically carefree countenance went cold. He considered Mr. Marlow, seeming to size him up before offering his hand. "Marlow."

Mr. Marlow's attitude was equally baffling. He glared at Sir Tristan's hand before, with great reluctance, he took it, then released it as if burned. He turned to Miss Gladstow.

"Would you be so kind as to walk with me a bit?"

Miss Gladstow looked to Sir Tristan. The baronet smiled, his surliness of a moment ago gone in the blink of an eye. "Do go on. I'm sure you wish a few moments with your friend. Miss Merriweather and I shall follow presently."

Miss Gladstow, looking as dazed as Rosalind had ever seen her, swallowed hard and nodded, turning to Mr. Marlow and placing trembling fingers on his proffered arm.

Rosalind watched the young couple in confusion as they started down the path. Frowning, she made to go after them.

Her arm, however, was still linked with Sir Tristan's. And he did not seem inclined to let her go.

She returned her attention to him, to demand he release her at once. He spoke first, cutting her off.

"You have been with the Gladstows how long?"

Rosalind blinked. Whatever he'd been about to say, it certainly wasn't that. "Er, five months now. Nearly six."

"And you have gotten to know Mr. Marlow in that time?"

"A bit. Not well."

"Would you say he is a good man?"

"I suppose. He seems decent enough."

"And are they close?"

Rosalind stared at him. Where was he was going with this? The man looked as serious as she had ever seen him. He watched the other couple, a small frown on his face. Why, he looked almost concerned.

In a flash she recalled his peculiar tension with Mr. Marlow mere minutes ago, and she knew. Of course he would be concerned. If he had nefarious plans for Miss Gladstow, wouldn't he see the sudden appearance of a new male in town, one who had a previous connection to Miss Gladstow, as a threat?

"You are jealous," she blurted.

"What? No! Why on earth would I be jealous?"

"Please, Sir Tristan," she scoffed, even as she tugged on his arm to get him moving again. Blessedly he did not balk, and they were soon following the other couple. "You needn't play games with me. I know you mean to have your way with Miss Gladstow."

"Have my way with her?" The words no doubt came out much louder than he planned, for he colored and glanced around before returning his attention to Rosalind. "Are you mad? What put such an outlandish idea into your head?"

She gave him a disgusted glance. "You must think me simple. Why else would you wish to seek Miss Gladstow out at every turn?"

"Miss Merriweather," he chided softly, "that is positively unkind of you."

It was Rosalind's turn to flush. "I did not mean to imply that Miss Gladstow is unworthy of your attentions."

"Didn't you?"

"No! I like Miss Gladstow very much. She is a sweet girl."

"Yet you do not think enough of her to believe I could wish to be in her company for honorable reasons."

Rosalind dug her fingers into the wool sleeve of his leaf green coat and gave a small, unladylike growl. "You are putting words in my mouth."

"You are doing a fine enough job of that, Miss Merriweather," he murmured. "You certainly don't need my help."

Was that amusement in his voice? She shot a disgruntled look up at him. Sure enough, his lips were tight at the corners, as if he were fighting back a smile. "You are playing with me, sir," she accused.

"I would never."

"That is utter rubbish. I know men like you, Sir Tristan. Rather, I know *of* men like you. Playing with people's emotions to make yourself feel superior, taking advantage of those less fortunate than you. Ruining lives along the way and not caring who you hurt."

The amusement fell from his face as if she had struck him. His eyes turned somber and cold. "That is the second time you have disparaged my honor, madam, by implying I would hurt an innocent. That is not at all who I am and I would thank you to never again insinuate it."

A trickle of trepidation worked up her spine. He was no longer the carefree rake, but a formidable man. She had never before noticed how large he was.

But, being Rosalind, she could not let the entire thing go because he happened to grow angry with her. "You realize, of course, why I must question your intentions."

The most aggravated sigh she had ever heard issued from Sir Tristan's chiseled lips. And that was saying something, as she had heard her fair share of sighs, of all types. He closed his eyes, his face tipping to the sky as if he were praying for divine help, before he leveled a weary look on her. "You really are not going to let it go, are you?"

"I'm afraid not," she said with utter candor.

"Is that why you made your comment earlier about it being a 'coincidence' that I happen to be going to Lord and Lady Jasper's ball tonight?"

Damn it, but she had forgotten about that ill-advised slip of the tongue. And of course the man would not let it go. She sighed in resignation. "Oh, I'm sure you heard me right. It is me, after all, with a tongue like a runaway horse." She waved a hand in front of her mouth. "Nothing to block what comes out, I'm afraid. My lips are apparently utterly useless in that regard."

It was several seconds before she became aware that he was uncommonly silent, and more seconds after that before she noticed that his gaze had gone intent and hot. And centered on her mouth.

Her entire body went warm, aching in the strangest places. Unnerved, she quickly looked away. There had been something in his eyes that had at once confused and excited her.

His arm was tense under her suddenly sensitive fingers. He cleared his throat several times before speaking again, though when he did his voice was oddly hoarse.

"You were saying about coincidences?"

As much as she didn't want to get into this again, the odd mood that had come over them made her grasp it readily. Anything to distract her from her body's completely unexpected reaction. "Yes, coincidences," she said in what she thought was an impressively businesslike manner. "You have managed to seek Miss Gladstow out every day for the past fortnight."

"Yes? And?"

"Does that not seem suspect, sir?"

He shrugged. "What is so suspect about it? Being from the country, of course, you may think London is an endless pit of humanity. But I have lived here since I came of age and I can assure you, our circle in society is not all that large. You are bound to run into all manner of people time and again when you are invited to the same events."

Which, she reluctantly—if silently—acknowledged, was too true. She could attest to the fact that she had seen the same people over and over again in the past weeks.

"I see you agree with me," he murmured.

She scowled at him. "I never said I agree with you."

"That frustrated little line between your brows tells me otherwise."

"Line? What line?" She reached up, smoothing her fingers over the small divot she found between her brows. Which, of course, only made her scowl deepen. "If I am frowning, it is because you are being utterly absurd."

"*I* am absurd?"

"Certainly."

"Pray, how am I being absurd?"

But, to her consternation, an answer didn't readily come to her. For he swung his piercing gaze down to her again and she completely forgot what they were talking about.

She might have stayed that way for an eternity, held captive by his eyes, stumbling blindly down the path. If Miss Gladstow didn't in that moment approach.

"Miss Merriweather, I do believe we need to return home immediately," she said. Her voice was tight, and there were unshed tears in the girl's eyes.

Rosalind released Sir Tristan immediately, reaching out to grab hold of the other girl's hands. "My dear, are you unwell? Where is Mr. Marlow?"

Miss Gladstow did not meet her eyes. "He has left. And it grows late. Mama will be wanting us to ready ourselves for the evening's entertainments."

"Of course." She turned to Sir Tristan. "Until tonight."

He inclined his head. "I look forward to it Miss Merriweather, Miss Gladstow."

The two women hurried off, leaving him far behind. Rosalind found, however, that she could not leave her strange reaction to him, no matter how far she walked.

Chapter 4

It did not take Tristan long to locate Mr. Marlow. The man stood out on the fashionable paths of Hyde Park, more for his complete disregard for fashion than for anything else about him. His coat, while neat and clean, had seen many years of use if the slight sheen at the elbows was any indication. His hat, too, while a finely made beaver, was several seasons out of style. These facts were made all the more glaring as he weaved through the thickening throngs of fashionable elite in their bright colors and expertly cut outerwear. Was the man poor? Or was he simply frugal? Miss Gladstow had told him (on several occasions—the girl did like to talk about her particular friend) that he was the son of a local landowner. Yet while it told him the man was a gentleman, it gave nothing away regarding the financial aspects of the family.

Tristan fell in behind him, making sure to keep far enough back to remain unobserved should the man happen to turn and cast his gaze his way. He had an idea what to do. All it took now was to see what the man's mettle was.

They exited the park at Hyde Park Gate, heading west along Knightsbridge toward Kensington Road, turning left at Sloane Street. Mr. Marlow kept up a brisk pace, never faltering in his apparently single-minded quest to get to wherever the blazes he needed to be. Tristan sent up a silent prayer of thanks for the hours of boxing and fencing and riding and whatever other physical activity had taken his fancy over the years. For it quickly became apparent to him that, no matter the distance he needed to traverse, the man wasn't planning on hailing a hackney. Which was all well and good;

Tristan would have a hell of a time following him if he took to the streets in a carriage.

At last, far down Sloane Street, Mr. Marlow turned into the yard of a small but respectable-looking hotel. It was certainly not Grenier's or the Clarendon, or the newly built Mivart's, but it was elegant and clean, with a freshly washed façade and friendly-looking grooms helping the other patrons.

So Mr. Marlow had some blunt. Not much, granted, if he had chosen to stay in such a place, but enough to be well-off. He might still be after Miss Gladstow's money, but at least he did not appear to be in dire straits. For desperate men often turned to desperate measures to get their way. And Tristan would not see Miss Gladstow harmed.

But despite the reassurance that the man was comfortably situated, Tristan was smart enough to know that money alone did not make for a good man. No, there were plenty of men who encompassed all that was cruel and heartless in the world yet were rich as Midas.

His father had been chief among them.

Tristan pressed his lips together, banishing the jarring memory back to the pits of hell where it belonged. He had a purpose, and he would not be sidetracked. All it took now was to see where Mr. Marlow's morals lay.

The man disappeared inside the hotel. Tristan took up a post across the street, weighing his options. There was no telling how long Mr. Marlow would be within. It could be minutes, it could be hours. Should he wait for him to emerge, to follow him again?

Or should he head within the establishment and ask about, to see what impression the people working there had gotten of the man thus far? For Tristan had learned over the years there was no better judge of character than a person in service. To most they were invisible, and thus saw much more than they were meant.

Finally, after fifteen minutes of prevaricating, he started off across the street. Best to take the bull by the horns, so to speak.

He entered the establishment, his boots clicking on the polished floor of the foyer, when a man stepped into his path. Stumbling to a halt, Tristan found himself looking into the hard, spare face of Mr. Marlow.

"Why are you following me?" the man demanded.

Either Tristan was an appalling spy, or Mr. Marlow was far cleverer than he had given him credit for. Tristan eyed him cautiously. He had certainly not meant to be seen.

Perhaps, though, he could work this to his advantage.

He assumed an expression of bored insolence. "You spent a good deal of time with Miss Gladstow this afternoon."

The man's eyes narrowed. "And you have spent a good portion of the past fortnight in her company. Or so I've heard."

Tristan allowed his lips to kick up in a self-satisfied smile. He adjusted a cuff. "You are surprisingly well-informed for a country bumpkin."

"We get the paper in Baswich, you know. Despite your contempt for those of us who live far away from the vice of London life, I assure you I can read. And I have come to some conclusions while perusing the London papers."

"Have you?" Tristan murmured.

"Yes. You are after Sarah's dowry."

Tristan laughed. "So what if I am? It is none of your concern."

Mr. Marlow took a menacing step forward. "It is my concern. I won't have her taken advantage of."

"I am not taking advantage of her, dear boy. It is expected I marry for money, as much as it is expected she marry for a title. If there is anyone taking advantage, it is mutual."

"But you don't love her!"

"Of course I don't. But that is hardly ever the case in these situations. Which you would know if you were a man of the world. Which," Tristan looked Mr. Marlow up and down, letting amusement mingle with the repugnance currently gracing his face, "you most certainly are not."

The man's hands squeezed into fists at his sides, outrage twisting his features. "How can you marry a woman you do not love?"

"Oh, easily, I assure you. Especially when there is a fortune involved. My lifestyle does not come cheap. And I do have a presence in society to keep up. Besides, there are other avenues one may find love. Outside of the marriage bed." He chuckled.

Tristan expected any manner of responses to that, from a fist to the jaw to being outright called out. What he did not expect, though, was the tightly controlled rage.

Mr. Marlow stepped up close to him, until Tristan could fairly feel the fury radiating in waves from him. "I give you fair warning. Stay. Away. From. Sarah. Or I swear to you, on the affection I have for her, I will destroy you."

The man was on the point of breaking. Yet he held back. It spoke well of him and the control he had of the baser side of himself. Tristan cheered within, even as without he took on a haughty expression. "You would not dare to threaten me, sir."

"I would. Sarah is kind, and good. She is the most wonderful girl I have ever known. And you are a snake who would destroy her."

"Then perhaps you should have secured her for yourself," Tristan sneered.

At the stunned look on the man's face, Tristan touched his brim in a vaguely mocking manner and left.

He strolled down the street, forcing his posture and steps to remain casual even as the back of his neck burned. Any minute he expected the man to come at him and beat him to a bloody pulp. And he wouldn't blame him one bit if he did. For he had acted reprehensibly. Even thinking of it now, at the horrible things he had let slip from his mouth, he felt a horrified shame so profound he was surprised he did not melt right into the pavement. But, he told himself, it was all for the greater good.

After a time he felt he was far enough away that he was safe from the man's wrath. At least for now. Yet what to do? He pursed his lips as he made his way back up Sloane Street. Things were progressing with Miss Gladstow much faster than he had planned. Not to mention his increasingly disturbing—and arousing—reactions to the outrageous and much too tempting Miss Merriweather.

At thoughts of that lady, he stumbled. Frowning mightily, he took firm control of himself and hurried on. He was far too affected by her for his peace of mind. He could only be glad that his close interactions with the maddening woman would soon be at an end. At least, that was what he told himself. He would ignore the pang of regret that accompanied it, as well as the rebellious salute his body gave whenever he thought of the chit.

Yes, it was a good thing this whole debacle was soon at an end. Now with Mr. Marlow's presence in London, it provided him the impetus he needed to bring the whole plan to the next stage.

It was time, he decided, for a little pre-ball visit to Lord and Lady Jasper's. For tonight things would be settled, for good or ill.

• • •

"You are back."

Rosalind started. The echoing sound of Mrs. Gladstow's voice seemed to come from everywhere and nowhere at once, the cavernous front hall of the ostentatious townhouse the family had let for the Season carrying the biting tone into every recess.

Beside her, Miss Gladstow faltered in removing her bonnet, her fingers becoming hopelessly tangled in the ribbons. Rosalind hurried to her, working at the knot. The girl's skin was pale, her hands trembling. "Thank you," she whispered as Rosalind freed the bonnet from her head and handed it over to the waiting butler.

Sharp steps sounded. Soon Mrs. Gladstow was before them. Her face was composed, if chill. Her eyes, however, blazed.

"And where, may I ask, is Sir Tristan?"

A strangled sound issued from Miss Gladstow's throat.

"He had an appointment he could not miss," Rosalind was quick to say. "He sends his regards, and his apologies, and says he will see us this evening at Lord and Lady Jasper's ball."

She had meant to deflect the woman from Miss Gladstow. Her plan of mercy, however, backfired splendidly. Mrs. Gladstow spun on her. "I do not believe I asked you, Miss Merriweather." Her eyes narrowed in suspicion. "I do hope you were not monopolizing the good baronet's attentions. Such a complete disregard for the very explicit instructions I gave you would be unforgivable."

"No, ma'am. Of course not. I would never be so idiotic as to do something that would endanger my position. I followed your instructions to the letter. You can be assured, I take them very seriously—"

The older woman held up a hand. "Enough," she snapped, before closing her eyes and letting out a sharp breath as if pained. "Dear me, but your babbling would try the patience of a saint."

She remained that way for a time, her mouth working. Rosalind could have sworn she was counting. She looked to Miss Gladstow in confusion. Should they continue to stand there, waiting for the woman to acknowledge them again? Should they escape?

Miss Gladstow seemed equally uncertain. She stared in horrified fascination at her mother, as if she were watching a dragon egg and expected the beast to pop out and burn her to a cinder.

Mrs. Gladstow seemed to recover in an instant. "Sarah!" she barked.

The poor girl jumped nearly a foot. "Yes, Mama?"

"You will go to your room now. Call for Betty. She can begin readying you for Lord and Lady Jasper's ball this evening."

The girl did as she was bid with alacrity. She was not quick enough to escape the remnants of her mother's wrath, however.

Mrs. Gladstow's hand shot out, capturing her daughter's wrist in a punishing grip. The girl did not so much as cry out. That did not stop Rosalind from wincing as she eyed the pointed tips of the woman's fingers pressing into Miss Gladstow's tender flesh. She had been the recipient of that cruel manacle herself more than once.

"You will encourage Sir Tristan Crosby tonight, do you hear me, girl?" she hissed.

Miss Gladstow gaped at her mother, her eyes wide and horrified. "Sir Tristan doesn't care about me in such a manner, Mama."

"Mayhap not," Mrs. Gladstow said, her lip curling. "But you are a woman, and Sir Tristan a man. One of the more impressive examples of the species, but a man all the same. You will use that fact to your advantage this evening."

Her daughter's mouth worked silently for a time before she cried, "I don't know the first thing about using such wiles."

"You will find a way," Mrs. Gladstow grit out. She released the girl, who wasted no time in escaping, spinning on the ball of her foot and rushing up the great curving staircase.

And that is my cue to exit, Rosalind thought, desperate to get away from her still-seething employer. Mrs. Gladstow's voice rang out before she could take a step.

"Miss Merriweather, this is your last chance."

Dread washed over Rosalind. "My last chance, ma'am?"

"You will assist my daughter in capturing Sir Tristan's attention this evening."

Frantic to prevent the woman's plans from coming to fruition, Rosalind cast about for a valid argument. For she was not such a fool that she thought the woman would listen to her if she spewed her theories of Sir Tristan's nefarious intentions. And even if she did believe her, would she care? She was cold enough that she would probably see it as a boon, and use the man's interest, honorable or not, to trick him into marriage with her daughter.

Rosalind refused to see that happen.

Finally, she stumbled upon the only fact she could think of that would appeal to Mrs. Gladstow's high-reaching aspirations. "But Sir Tristan is not even a peer, ma'am. I was under the assumption you wanted a noble title for your daughter."

Mrs. Gladstow's eyes narrowed. "Like I said before, you're not stupid, are you? I don't expect the man to propose to my daughter, nor do I want him to. You think I would settle for a mere baronet when my husband has promised such a dowry on her that it should attract even the most discerning nobleman? Hardly." She let loose a harsh laugh. "But men are basically animals at heart, Miss Merriweather. His attentions will only whet the already-increasing interest of a more appropriate suitor."

Rosalind frowned. For the woman looked far too smug for this to be a vague kind of thing. She thought quickly back along the past fortnight, searching through memories, trying to single out any one man the woman might have set her sights on for her future son-in-law.

Lord Ullerton's face rose up in her mind then, his jowls jiggling about like so much cream jelly.

Rosalind felt a chill down to her bones. "You cannot mean to marry her off to Lord Ullerton," she blurted.

The self-satisfied look on the woman's face was replaced in an instant by a fury so hot and fierce Rosalind was surprised she wasn't scorched by it.

"You think to tell me what to do? You, a mere companion, the daughter of some country nobody who gambled away every penny he owned, then proceeded to drink himself to death?"

She advanced. Rosalind, shocked to her core at the venom spewing from her mouth, backed up until her spine rammed into a small end table, nearly toppling the cut glass vase of roses that topped it.

"I do not care for you, Miss Merriweather," the woman continued, towering over her. "I never have, and I daresay I never shall. And so I say it again. This is your last chance. Lord Ullerton, important man that he is, must return to his country seat for the next month. Before he leaves, you will help my daughter secure his hand. She will be a countess by the Season's end. If she fails, I will have no compunction throwing you out on your ear, deathbed promise or no."

A sick feeling swirled and bucked in Rosalind's stomach. Not only for Miss Gladstow, who was nothing but a pawn to her parents' desires to join the ranks of England's best families, but for herself as well. For though she had dealt with a daily barrage of threats to her position, this had the awful ring of truth to it, the woman's voice holding all the finality of a death knell.

And so she had no choice. If she wished to survive, she would have to fall in with the woman's plans.

"Yes, ma'am," she whispered, the words bitter as laudanum on her tongue.

Mrs. Gladstow smiled, a slow and cruel thing that only increased Rosalind's disgust with herself. "Good. Now go and help my daughter ready herself. We've a baronet to use and an earl to capture."

Chapter 5

Rosalind fidgeted in her chair, her bottom having gone numb on the hard wood long ago. She and Miss Gladstow had been seated in the wallflower line at Lord and Lady Jasper's ball for what seemed hours now, though in reality it could not have been above a half-hour at the most. With each second that passed, however, she felt the noose of expectation tightening about her throat. That sensation was only underscored each time Rosalind caught sight of the girl's mother. For Mrs. Gladstow had not changed her mind regarding the instructions she had set forth for Rosalind, if her furious head jerks were anything to go by. She would have her daughter lay claim to the earl before anyone else did, come hell or high water.

Not that Rosalind thought the woman had anything to worry about. It certainly did not appear as if Lord Jowls was in any great demand by the debutantes of London. But reason Mrs. Gladstow would not listen to, as Rosalind had learned to her detriment.

She caught sight of Lord Jowls in that moment. He was some distance away and talking to another gentleman, his jowls undulating with each expressive cast of his meaty hands. He caught her looking. With a smile and a dip of his head in her direction he returned to his conversation.

A prickle of guilt settled within her. The man had never been anything but unfailingly polite to both her and Miss Gladstow. Yes, he was not the most attractive man in London, and had to be old enough to be Miss Gladstow's father. But was that any reason to think ill of him? Were her innate prejudices blinding her to the fact that he might actually be a good choice for Miss Gladstow? Surely the girl wished for security and status, and by all accounts the earl could provide them. Would she deny Miss Gladstow these things because of her own unreasonable dislike of the man?

She let loose a mournful sigh. She had best get to it then. But where the devil was Sir Tristan? She cast about, looking over the crowded ballroom. Yet there was no sign of his blond head towering over the masses—something she had grown quite adept at locating in the past fortnight, to her disgust. Despite his devil-may-care attitude, she knew he was not typically tardy to these affairs. And once arrived, he never failed to search out Miss Gladstow. Perhaps his absence now meant he wasn't coming at all?

But no, he had promised he would see them. Mayhap he was here, and had been waylaid by friends. All Rosalind knew was, for every second that ticked by that Sir Tristan was not in Miss Gladstow's orbit, doing his bit to unknowingly pique Lord Jowls's interest, the better chance Rosalind had of being thrown out before the evening was through.

It seemed she would have to take matters into her own hands. As disturbing as that was.

She turned to Miss Gladstow. "Are you overheated, miss?"

The girl gave her a distracted smile. "No, I'm comfortable," she replied in her quiet voice.

"Are you certain? Perhaps we can take a turn about the room. Doesn't that sound nice?"

"Not particularly."

Rosalind fiddled with her fan a moment, blowing out a small puff of air. Miss Gladstow seemed determined to stay put in her seat. Not that Rosalind had any particular desire to dive into the crowd herself. But one could not very well find someone in a mass of people if one were stuck to one's seat like the proverbial barnacle. That, along with the daggers Mrs. Gladstow shot her way as Rosalind unconsciously glanced at her again, made Rosalind more nervous by the second.

"Mayhap you would like a bit of punch," she blurted.

"I'm not thirsty, thank you," Miss Gladstow said.

The girl appeared composed enough. Yet there was something off about her tonight. Her fingers, resting in her lap, were wrapped so tightly about themselves it appeared as if she were going to snap the delicate bones with the force of it.

Now that she thought of it, Miss Gladstow had been out of sorts since their walk in the park that afternoon. Rosalind had been so preoccupied, first with her quarrel with Sir Tristan, followed by the horror of Mrs. Gladstow's threats, she had not paid the proper attention to the girl. Now that she was, however, it seemed glaringly obvious.

"Did Sir Tristan do something to upset you?" she blurted.

"Pardon?" the girl looked at her as if she'd grown another head. "No. No, of course not. He is never anything but kind."

"Are you certain? You have seemed upset since our outing." Then a thought sparked. She frowned. "Was it Mr. Marlow?"

A furious blush spread over the girl's cheeks. "You know, Miss Merriweather, I do believe I am horribly parched. Would you be willing to fetch us some punch?"

"Oh! Certainly." Rosalind fairly bolted from her chair. Granted, she had not managed to pry the girl from the side of the room. But at least she could search out Sir Tristan herself.

She hurried through the crowd, weaving in and out of the swell of people, doing her best to locate Sir Tristan. She soon found, however, that being several inches shorter than the great majority of guests present put her at a distinct disadvantage. She could see even less from this angle than she had been able to while seated against the wall. For a moment she looked longingly at the orchestra balcony, stretched on one side of the vast room. Surely no one would notice if she snuck up and peeked out.

Before she could think better of it she was off, working toward the far side of the room. There must be a door there somewhere that led to the upper reaches. After a bit of searching she found it, hidden behind a heavy red velvet curtain. She ducked behind the fabric and made to open the door there.

A low conversation on the other side of the curtain snagged her attention, halting her progress.

"And have you any prospects for brides, Ullerton?"

"Several. There is a fine contingent of young misses out this year. Though I admit there is one lady I have my eye on."

"And who might that be?"

Rosalind blanched. Lord Ullerton was on the other side of the curtain? She turned the handle, intending to slip into the passage beyond. She certainly had no wish to overhear what the man had to say.

But his next words once again stalled her.

"Miss Gladstow seems a fine choice."

"Miss Gladstow?" There seemed honest confusion in the other man's tone. "I know of her father, of course, but cannot remember the chit. Which one is she?"

"You know, plain little thing, dark hair, painfully shy."

A sharp bark of laughter. "Why the devil would you want to chain yourself to the likes of her?"

Rosalind expected Lord Ullerton to come to Miss Gladstow's defense. He had seemed kind, after all, and if he was interested in her for a wife he would certainly not want anyone disparaging her.

Instead, as if he were Mrs. Gladstow's puppet, he said, "Sir Tristan Crosby has been sniffing after her, and I admit his interest has only piqued my own. Besides," he added, to Rosalind's horror, "the girl comes with the means I need to stay afloat."

A knowing chuckle answered that. "Ah, yes. One could certainly put up with a boring mouse of a wife for such a thing. And it is not as if you need live with her year-round. Get a child or two on her and you shall be free and clear."

Rosalind's hand, still clasped around the door handle, clenched tight on the metal in an effort not to bolt from her hiding place and give the other man a piece of her mind. Surely Lord Ullerton could not let that go, as disappointing as he had been up until now.

"True," he mused instead, stunning Rosalind. But what came next was worse. Much worse.

"Though I may keep her around for a long time. For she'll come with a delicious little companion that I've a mind to get to know better."

"Miss Merriweather, isn't it? I don't know, Ullerton, she seems a veritable termagant. Never knows when to shut that mouth of hers."

Lord Ullerton chuckled low, the sound sending a frisson of disgust down Rosalind's spine. "Oh, I'm not concerned about that in the least. For I'm planning on putting her mouth to other more interesting uses."

"She doesn't seem as if she'd be easy to tame."

"That will make it all the more interesting. I do like a bit of a fight when breaking a new girl in, after all."

They both chuckled, the sound growing fainter as they moved off.

Rosalind stood frozen, stunned. Her disgust of a moment ago had fled, to be replaced by a fear so acute she could taste it. It soured her stomach, clouded her mind, seized her muscles.

The heavy curtain that had hidden her from Lord Ullerton but a moment ago now felt like it was closing her in. Her lungs struggled, as if she were drowning. Needing to escape the confines of the small space, she hurriedly pushed the curtain aside and stumbled back into the brightness of the ballroom. Surely she would find safety in the glittering mass of people, would find comfort in their numbers.

Instead all she found was a strange dreamland. For people still laughed and talked and danced. How was it life still went on, as if something monumental and life altering had not occurred? As if she had not been made fully aware of how defenseless she was in the space of a moment.

She stumbled along, not knowing where to go, what to do. Her shoulder connected with one man and she lost her balance. The room swirled around her.

A strong hand reached out, grabbed at her arm, a familiar voice sounding in her ear. "Miss Merriweather, are you well?"

"Sir Tristan?" She blinked and her confusion fell away as his face came into focus.

He frowned down at her. "You do not look well at all. Let me help you to a chair."

"I'm fine, truly."

"You most certainly are not. Has something happened?" Suspicion tightened his features. "Has someone harmed you?"

"Of course not." She had been indirectly and unknowingly threatened, as well as frightened nearly witless. But she had not been harmed. Yet.

But he did not look mollified in the least. Wanting to distract him, she said, "If you'll excuse me, Sir Tristan. I need to get back to Miss Gladstow. I am fetching her some punch." At that she frowned, looking down at her empty hands. Goodness, but she had forgotten all about that. Sudden exhaustion overtook her. The very thought of returning to her charge, of acting normal, was almost too much to bear.

The concern in his eyes doubled. "I will make you a deal. I will fetch Miss Gladstow punch, and you will find a place to sit and rest."

Too tired to fight him, wanting only to take a moment for herself, she nodded. Giving her one last long look, he bowed and was off through the crowd.

Rosalind watched him go, grateful for his intervention. She moved off to the side of the room, intending to do as he had bid her.

Until she recalled Lord Ullerton.

The whole point of ensuring that Sir Tristan and Miss Gladstow remained in each other's orbit tonight was to ensure the earl's interest in her was sufficiently piqued to make the girl an offer. Miss Gladstow would get a husband of good standing, Mrs. Gladstow would see her daughter marry into the nobility, and Rosalind would remain employed. Everyone would get what they wanted.

But now that she knew the extent of the man's perfidy, she knew in her heart she could not do it. She could not sell Miss Gladstow in marriage to such a man. Nor could she enter that man's home knowing what he had planned for her. No, she would rather die.

Which, she admitted ruefully, she just might if Mrs. Gladstow made good on her threats.

But that was something she would have to deal with when the time came. She was strong; she could handle whatever life threw at her. In the meantime, she would warn Miss Gladstow immediately of the danger. And pray she had the strength to fight against her mother's dictates.

The thought should have filled her with panic. Instead she felt a strange type of freedom. There was nothing stopping her from protecting Miss Gladstow. Granted, she didn't know how she was going to keep a roof over her own head. But there was nothing she could do about that now. No, now was the time for dealing with wrongs she could right. Filled with a new determination and purpose, she hurried back to Miss Gladstow. Surely if she explained things to the girl, if they put their heads together, they could come up with some way to prevent the union.

But by the time she neared the wallflower line Sir Tristan—how the blazes had she forgotten him?—was already seated with Miss Gladstow. The two were in close conversation, Miss Gladstow's lips moving at an impressive rate. Sir Tristan, for his part, looked incredibly serious and intent. They leaned toward one another, the intimacy of their conversation left in no doubt.

Just then a particularly loud group of young people stepped in her path. They surrounded her, hemmed her in, blocking her way to Miss Gladstow. It took Rosalind some seconds to work free of the press of bodies. Free of that tight knot of humanity she took a cleansing breath, turned her gaze the way of her prey...

And froze.

The two chairs, formerly occupied by Miss Gladstow and Sir Tristan, were empty.

Rosalind hurried forward, scanning the area, panic quickly setting in. Where had they gone? If it had been physically possible she would have kicked herself. For in her altered state of mind after Lord Ullerton's unexpected revelation and Sir Tristan's subsequent kindness, she had forgotten her very real reservations about the baronet—and Miss Gladstow's orders from her mother that she should encourage him. The man *had* to be bent on seduction. And she had led him to Miss Gladstow, like a wolf to a lamb. She bit back a frustrated growl. To be so close to saving the girl from a reprobate, only to lose her to the machinations of a practiced rake? Devil take it, if anything happened to Miss Gladstow she would never forgive herself.

As she made to dive into the depths of the great room in search of them, a brush of wind caressed her flushed face, dragging her attention to the open doors leading to the terrace. Rosalind's heart dropped. The chair Miss Gladstow had occupied was positioned dangerously close to those doors. In this crush, the promise of a cool evening breeze would be an easy way for a libertine to get an overheated lady off alone. It mattered not that there were doubtless other couples meandering the garden paths. A determined man could find a private spot in even the most crowded of spaces. And quite often, such a scenario led to ruin.

She hurried for the doors, was nearly to them when a hearty laugh reached her ears. Immediately she froze. She had heard that laugh often during her time in London. No one showed their mirth in such an open, joyous way, no other man was capable of such an infectious sound. Stopping in her tracks, she spun about. Sure enough, there was Sir Tristan, towering above the other dancers on the floor. He guided Miss Gladstow in a two-hand turn. Even from this distance she could discern the happiness in the lady's eyes.

Rosalind blew out a breath. She would have to wait then, at least until the song was done. Finding an unobtrusive spot beside a towering pillar, she craned her neck as Sir Tristan led Miss Gladstow into a promenade, making certain this time she did not lose sight of him.

"Who, I wonder, has caught your attention?" A voice drawled in her ear.

Rosalind yelped, jumping back. Her elbow cracked against the pillar, shooting bright pain up her arm. She winced and cradled her abused limb against her torso.

"I'm terribly sorry," the newcomer said. "I didn't mean to frighten you. And I certainly did not intend to injure you."

Rosalind turned, and spied through her watering eyes a stunning woman, one of those seemingly ageless creatures that could be anywhere from five and twenty to fifty. She exuded sultry confidence. Nothing at all was left to the imagination, most of all her generous bosom, which fairly spilled from her nearly nonexistent bodice. Her entire form (save her bosom, of course) was draped in a brilliant green satin that shimmered with each play of light, showcasing her curves.

Rosalind forced her gaze to the woman's face. It certainly would not do to be caught staring at the woman's endowments, no matter how displayed they were. "I wasn't frightened," she said. "Merely surprised. Most people don't notice me, much less talk to me."

The stranger's ruby lips turned up in a smile. "One could hardly fail to notice you, the way you were fairly glowering at the dancers on the floor. I would have thought you someone's outraged mother if it didn't appear you were fresh out of the school room."

A startled laugh burst from her. "Then you need spectacles, ma'am, for I am five and twenty, certainly not some young miss."

The woman's face twisted. "Oh, don't call me ma'am, please. It puts me in mind of elderly women tottering about with steel gray hair and walking sticks."

"No one could mistake you for such a person," Rosalind answered.

The woman laughed gaily. "I do like you. But I forget, I have not introduced myself, and people do so like to know who they're talking to. I am Lady Belham."

"Lady Belham? I haven't heard of you." The minute the words left her mouth Rosalind wanted nothing more than to sink into the floor.

Blessedly Lady Belham did not seem the least bit offended by her rudeness. She laughed. "Should you have? Or do you know everyone in London?"

"No! That is, the Gladstows do. I don't. Though I do know *of* most people in town. Through the Gladstows, of course. As their companion. Though my father was a country gentleman, I have no connections to speak of. That is, I have no reason to know all of these people. I'm of no importance, after all."

The more her mouth ran on, the hotter her face became. Yet she couldn't seem to still her lips. At last she ran out of words and fell silent, staring at her toes. She expected any number of reactions from Lady Belham, from indignation to amusement. At the very least the woman would say her goodbyes now that she was aware of Rosalind's lowered status.

"Well, now, that can't be true," the lady said quietly.

Rosalind chanced a look up. The other woman looked kindly at her. She frowned in confusion. "What can't be true? That the Gladstows know everyone?"

"Not at all. Though I've been out of society, nay even the country, for nearly half my life, even I have heard of Mr. Gladstow and his fortune in shipping. Anyone with that much money would know any number of people. Or, rather, those people would wish to know him, though they may pretend not to. What I meant was I don't believe you're unimportant."

Rosalind stared at her. It was then she felt it, the most peculiar warmth spreading through her chest.

It was something she had not felt since before her sister died.

She might have made an utter fool of herself and hugged Lady Belham on the spot. Thankfully the woman continued.

"But I digress. You were right, in that I'm quite new to town. I arrived not a week ago from Haddington, in Scotland, and am staying with my cousin until I secure a house of my own."

"You don't sound Scottish."

"No. My husband, however, had property there, and preferred to spend his time at that remote estate and far away from London life. He passed away a little more than a year ago."

"I am sorry," Rosalind said.

"He was a good man," the woman said stoutly. "But he was con-siderably older than me, and it was his time."

Before Rosalind could react to that blunt statement, Lady Belham continued. "But you haven't told me your name yet."

Rosalind jumped, dipping into a curtsy. "Miss Rosalind Merriweather, my lady."

"What a beautifully melodic name. Full of so many dips and turns. It quite delights the tongue. Rosalind is the daughter of the exiled duke in *As You Like It*, is she not?"

"Yes, she is that," Rosalind's lips lifted in a wry smile. "I'm afraid my parents were dreamers of the worst sort. They thought that by giving me a whimsical name, it would help to inspire all manner of artistic endeavors in me."

"And did it work?"

"Not a bit." Rosalind held up her hands. "All thumbs."

Lady Belham's eyes sparkled with amusement. "And what of poetry?"

"Completely beyond me. If I had a suitor, one stanza from me would see them right off."

"Well, I do suppose you could make a new career for yourself if you wish, writing bad verse for the women of the *ton* who are eager to put off unwanted beaus," she drawled.

Rosalind laughed. "I could at that. Unfortunately I haven't the time to pen poorly written poems for debutantes."

"Pity that," the woman said. "But is that who you were watching then? Miss Gladstow?"

Recalling herself and her self-appointed job as protector to the girl, Rosalind turned her gaze back to the crowd on the floor. It took what felt an eternity before she located Sir Tristan and Miss Gladstow. Both were laughing as they did a promenade. Rosalind let out the breath she was holding.

"Yes," she replied.

"I notice she's partnered with Sir Tristan Crosby," Lady Belham said with interest. Too much interest.

Rosalind turned to her. "You know of the gentleman then?"

Lady Belham gave a small laugh. "Of course I do."

Before Rosalind could wonder at the woman's strange answer the music came to a flourishing close. Startled, she peered over the dancers, but they were already exiting the floor. To her frustration and alarm, she could not discern Sir Tristan in the crowd.

"Blast it," she muttered. "I've lost them."

Lady Belham gave a startled laugh. "If you mean Miss Gladstow and Sir Tristan, I do believe I see them heading to the doors leading to the front hall."

Rosalind went cold. She could not let them escape. Before she could hurry away, however, Lady Belham spoke, stalling her.

"I like you, Miss Merriweather. I haven't many friends in town. If you're ever up for a visit, please do stop by an afternoon. I would so love to continue our exchange." So saying, she held out a thick, creamy card. A hand-written address graced one side.

"Thank you so much, my lady," Rosalind said hastily, stuffing the card into her own bag. "I would like that." Dipping into a quick curtsy, she bounded away, following in Sir Tristan and Miss Gladstow's wake.

Chapter 6

Rosalind was motivated enough that she should have been able to cut her way through the crowd like a powerful ship through calm ocean waters, throwing partygoers this way and that like flotsam. Instead she felt more like an awkward sea bird fighting against a high wind. With every second that passed the anxiety clawing at her grew, making her more and more frantic. At long last she made it to the other side of the room. She took a quick look about, fully expecting to have to search the rest of the house where no doubt Sir Tristan already had Miss Gladstow in an amorous embrace. What she did not expect to see was that gentleman in plain view.

Nor did she expect to see him being accosted by...Mr. Marlow?

What in the world was Mr. Marlow doing here? There was no way she would believe that the son of a minor landowner had been invited to Lord and Lady Jasper's exclusive ball. Yet here the man was, standing nearly nose to nose with Sir Tristan. Outrage seized the muscles of his face, making his normally placid countenance appear positively forbidding. Miss Gladstow stood behind him, her hands clasped to her chest, her eyes wide with...joy?

"You don't care for anything but her fortune," Mr. Marlow said. "You cannot marry her."

Standing behind Sir Tristan as Rosalind was, she could not see his face. When he laughed, though, the sound was mocking, and quite unlike anything Rosalind had ever heard from him.

"Who will stop me if I wish it, pup? You?"

Mr. Marlow drew himself up to his full height. "Yes."

"Want her for her dowry, do you?"

"Say such a thing again, sir, and I shall be forced to call you out," Mr. Marlow growled. "I love Miss Gladstow. She is the creature of my heart. I was a fool not to see it before, but I'll be damned if I'll let her go now. I don't care if she comes to me penniless. If she will have me I will be the happiest of men."

Miss Gladstow hurried forward. "Oh, David. Do you truly love me?" she breathed.

The man's countenance changed in an instant. He turned to Miss Gladstow, his face relaxing into something almost handsome for all the emotion that overtook it. "With all my heart, Sarah."

Rosalind watched, stunned, as the couple fell into a passionate embrace. Their corner of the room went silent, the only sound the occasional gasp as someone new caught sight of the display. After a time the lovers broke apart, linking arms and hurrying off together, oblivious to the crowd that had gathered to gawk. As conversation erupted about her, she looked to Sir Tristan. How must he feel, after being made a fool of in such a public manner?

He turned for the door then, no doubt intending to escape the ballroom and the scene of his embarrassment. But instead of frustration or anger twisting his face, the man was…smiling?

She blinked. *What the blazes?*

He might have passed her by then if his gaze had not unexpectedly tripped to her. The change in him was instantaneous. His step slowed, his expression sobering. And then he did the most incredible thing. His eyes scanned her from her head to her toes. Before she could speak, he slipped around her; in the blink of an eye, he was gone.

Rosalind stared at the space he had been, completely flummoxed. She knew she should feel relief. Miss Gladstow was safe. She had not fallen under Sir Tristan's spell, nor would she marry Lord Jowls. No, after that display her parents would not be able to force a match on her again. Miss Gladstow would marry someone who would love and care for her, who would treat her with all the respect she deserved.

Yet Rosalind could not help feeling a deep-seated suspicion that she had been completely fooled by a rake with azure eyes.

• • •

After witnessing the pretty picture Miss Gladstow and her Mr. Marlow had made while declaring their undying—and, if he had to be honest, frightfully overdue—love for one another, Tristan knew he should be celebrating. All his planning had panned out, after all. Today, especially, his talents had been put to the test. It had taken more than a bit of maneuvering—and a good amount of flirting with Lady Jasper—to secure an invitation for Mr. Marlow to the ball, along with a note from Lady Jasper herself indicating her wishes for the dear friend of Miss Gladstow to attend. Even after it had been sent off, Tristan had not been at all sure the man had come to his senses enough to realize he loved the girl. Nor did he think Mr. Marlow would be able to put aside his pride to come and claim her. And he did seem the prideful sort, those who let it control them to a fault.

But, thank the heavens, the man had come. And had responded splendidly to Tristan's attentions to Miss Gladstow. There was nothing like a bit of competition to make a man realize where his heart truly lay.

Really, the night had been a smashing success. Tristan, however, was far too distracted to enjoy his little victory. For instead of reveling in the memory of Mr. Marlow's declarations and the moment when he claimed Miss Gladstow for his own, he saw only Miss Merriweather's troubled brown eyes.

His carriage pulled up to the curb outside Lord and Lady Jasper's then. He gave his directions to the driver before vaulting inside. As he settled back against the squabs, he prayed his club would provide him with the distraction he needed to forget Miss Merriweather. But he was fairly positive nothing on God's green earth would help him in that.

What had happened to her to haunt her so? What had affected her to the degree that she had nearly lost her composure right there in the middle of the ballroom? He had come to know something of the woman in the last two weeks. One thing he could safely say about her (despite her frustrating propensity to speak her mind on any and every occasion) was she was no wilting blossom. No, despite her diminutive stature and delicate appearance, she had a will of steel. He could think of nothing that would have laid the lady low to such a degree.

The carriage pulled up to his club. Tucking Miss Merriweather to the back of his mind, he descended to the pavement and strode in. She was not his concern, after all. And she had appeared well when he'd left, had seemed back to her normal, suspicious self.

In fact, she had seemed even more suspicious than usual. He frowned as he climbed the stairs. Surely she had not seen what he had been about with Miss Gladstow and her beau. A moment later and he shrugged the concern away. Even if she had, he needn't see her again in such close quarters. No, his time with Miss Merriweather, of him squirming under that too-knowing gaze of hers, was at an end. He would put all thoughts of her from his head and thoroughly enjoy his success from that evening. What better way than to find some of his friends and get thoroughly drunk?

"Ho there, Crosby," a jovial voice called out as he entered the Coffee Room. Tristan turned to spy a contingent of his friends crowded about a table. By the looks of it they had not only made their way through a goodly amount of fine food, but were pleasantly inebriated, and well on their way to becoming stinking drunk if the waiter delivering a full bottle of liquor to them was any indication.

Tristan grinned. Seek and ye shall find, and all that.

"I didn't expect to come across you lot still here," he remarked as he sank into an empty chair. "Shouldn't you be out finding some pleasant females to cozy up to?"

Lord Fergus let out a snort and threw back his drink. "I'm on the lookout for a new mistress m'self." He gave Tristan a considering look. "Though it looks like you might be ready for something more."

Tristan accepted a glass of whiskey from one of his friends and raised an eyebrow at Fergus. "And here I thought you were still sober enough to make sense."

"Oh, I'm plenty sober," Fergus replied, a crafty glint entering his eyes. "I've seen the way you've been panting after those wallflowers lately, Crosby. You've managed to become close to Miss Gladstow of late. She's, what, the third or fourth debutante to catch your eye since the fall?" He grinned. "Any luck there then?"

"She's a friend and nothing more," he said, taking a sip of his drink. His eyes scanned the other men as he did so, not surprised to see the amusement on their faces. He mentally shrugged. He knew he was seen as a flighty sort of fellow, that his quicksilver changes in attention would not be seen as out of character. As long as the women he was helping didn't suffer for it, he didn't give a good damn that people chuckled over his seemingly changeable affections.

"Pretend all you want," Fergus said knowingly.

Tristan rolled his eyes. "You're an ass. If you had been at the Jaspers' ball tonight, you would have seen that Mr. David Marlow declared himself to Miss Gladstow not an hour ago." He looked at Fergus over the rim of his glass and said clearly and distinctly, so the matter would not be questioned in the future. "She seems to reciprocate his feelings. And I am very happy for her."

"Tough luck for you," Fergus replied, undaunted. "Though the gal is homely as hell, she's got a tidy little sum attached to her. A man could put up with a bit of ugly for that."

Fury, a rare emotion for Tristan, boiled up fierce and hot. He placed his glass down hard on the table and leaned forward. In an instant the men in the surrounding area went silent. Fergus's eyes widened in alarm.

"I will not hear you speak ill of Miss Gladstow, or any other female, in my hearing again. Is that clear?"

Fergus swallowed audibly. "Y-yes. Of course. My apologies."

Tristan eyed him severely for a moment before, with a nod of his head, he sat back and took up his drink again. The change in the atmosphere was instantaneous, the tension gone as quickly as it had come.

"So," he said to the table at large, "what were you all discussing before I came along?"

"Women, what else?" Lord Kingston, Rafe to his nearest and dearest, said with a grin. "Denby here has got his eye on someone and won't tell us who."

Denby, younger than the rest and still a bit in awe of the whole London scene, blushed scarlet. "There's nothing to tell, for she won't give me the time of day."

Rafe turned to Tristan. "We've gone through all the popular actresses, courtesans, and singers. The lad isn't showing his hand."

"I begin to think his lady love is respectable," Fergus said in mock horror. When Denby's blush deepened, Fergus let out a surprised bark of laughter. "What ho! Have we struck a nerve Denby? Never say you're thinking of pursuing a virgin. That way lies only ruin and despair in the guise of holy matrimony."

"You're an ass, Fergus," Denby muttered into his drink.

Tristan held up a hand. "She needn't be a virgin, you know. She could be married?" He eyed the boy for a moment, seeking a tell. When none came a sly grin spread over his face. "Or a widow."

There it was, that furious flush of blood to the cheeks, the small smile. The rest of the men broke into peals of laughter. Several older gentlemen in the adjoining tables, enjoying late dinners, sent glares their way.

"A widow, eh?" Rafe drawled. "Nothing wrong with that, m'boy. There's no better tumble in my opinion."

"Who is she though?" Fergus narrowed his eyes as he considered the now squirming Denby.

"Lady Truvel," one man called out.

"Mrs. Umbridge," another cried.

"Lady Kendal," said a third.

"Please," Denby scoffed, though it was clear as day the lad was enjoying himself. "She's old enough to be my mother."

Tristan chuckled as the banter went back and forth, each suggestion more outrageous than the last. Yes, this was what he had needed. No more Miss Merriweather and that sweet face and sharp tongue of hers. Life would get back to normal, and he could put her and his unnatural desires for her behind him once and for all.

Chapter 7

Rosalind delayed emerging from her room as long as she could without it seeming suspect. Though the rest of the house should be abed until at least noon, there was no sense in taking unnecessary chances.

The revelries of the evening before had gone on until the small hours of the morning. Once the announcement had been made of Miss Gladstow and Mr. Marlow's unexpected engagement, every person present at the ball had insisted on wishing them well. Whether those congratulations had been heartfelt or done out of malicious glee was questionable at best. That didn't seem to matter to the lady. Rosalind had never seen her so happy. Miss Gladstow shone like the sun at midday. Mr. Marlow, too, had looked proud enough to burst, holding tight to Miss Gladstow's hand the remainder of the evening.

Rosalind was happy for the girl. She truly was. No one deserved happiness as much as Miss Gladstow. And no one deserved to escape from her domineering mother like that young lady, either. Which, of course, brought Rosalind to the one damper on expressing her joy.

Mrs. Gladstow.

That woman had appeared happy for her daughter, of course. It would have been noted by all and sundry if she hadn't, for it was no secret that the woman, and her portly husband as well, had wanted a title for their only daughter, and a lofty one at that. She had not even been content with Sir Tristan Crosby's possible suit; goodness knows her thoughts on a mere *mister*.

Yet Rosalind had seen the truth of it, simmering away beneath the surface. It was never more apparent than when the woman turned her blazing eyes to Rosalind. In those moments Rosalind knew, regardless of her complete lack of fault in the situation—though it was not for lack of trying on her part—she would be made to pay for the fruits of this night.

Finally she could delay no longer. Sucking in a deep breath she straightened her shoulders and marched purposely below stairs. Mayhap her fears were unfounded. Mrs. Gladstow would be too busy today preparing for her daughter's unexpected future to give her companion much thought.

That hope died a swift but brutal death as she made to pass the drawing room door.

"Miss Merriweather," Mrs. Gladstow called from the depths of the room, "a moment of your time, please."

Rosalind's blood froze in her veins. There was a calm chill in the woman's voice that bode ill. She had the feeling that, as bad as her imaginings had been, she had not begun to understand the depths of the woman's anger. No doubt Mrs. Gladstow intended to extract considerably more than her pound of flesh.

Mrs. Gladstow sat in her seat of choice, a high-backed chair covered in gold damask, giving it all the appearance of a throne. Her back was straight, her head held high, her hands draped casually over the arms. Yet her eyes burned as brightly, if not more so, as they had the evening before. As Rosalind crossed the threshold they narrowed.

"Close the door."

Had Mrs. Gladstow yelled and stormed, Rosalind might have gone in with some semblance of ease. Instead her fingers shook as she did what she was bid. When she returned her attention to Mrs. Gladstow she made sure to grip her hands tight before her. No good could come of showing this woman any weakness. She sent up a silent prayer, that whatever punishment she received would be doled out quickly.

Ironically, fear over losing her position had guided her every action for months. Now that the end was near, all she wanted was to have it over and done with.

Mrs. Gladstow, however, must have had her training during the Spanish Inquisition. She stared at Rosalind, drumming her fingers on the arms of the chair, letting the moment drag out until Rosalind thought she would scream from the uncertainty of it. After what seemed an eternity the woman spoke.

"I assume you have an explanation as to why my daughter was so unexpectedly and unceremoniously engaged last night, and to a man we had no intention of allowing her to marry?"

Rosalind swallowed hard. "In my defense, ma'am, I did as I was told. I encouraged Sir Tristan to seek out your daughter."

"Do you think that negates your fault in this? The fact of the matter is, Miss Merriweather, you should have kept a better eye on Sarah."

"I was as surprised as you must have been when Mr. Marlow declared himself to Miss Gladstow."

"Surprised?" The woman's nostrils flared. "You think I was surprised? That my husband, who has promised such a hefty dowry on his only daughter, was surprised? That word does not even begin to explain the level of disbelief that bowled us over last night. We wanted a title for our daughter, Miss Merriweather, as you well knew."

"But surely her future happiness means much more, in the grand scheme of things," Rosalind suggested a bit sickly, knowing the second the words were out of her mouth that they were the wrong ones as far as the woman seated before her was concerned. As if to prove the validity of her thoughts, Mrs. Gladstow's lips thinned to nonexistence and Rosalind's heart sank. Any stray tendrils of hope she may have retained that she would actually walk away from this unscathed—much less retain her position—was snuffed out as completely as a weak flame in the face of a furious wind.

"You think I don't wish for my own daughter's happiness?" the woman snapped.

"Of course you do," Rosalind hastened to assure her. Yet the damage had been done. Mrs. Gladstow rose, towering over Rosalind.

"I care very much for my only daughter's happiness. And part of that was to secure her proper place in the world. My husband is a powerful man. He needed a husband for his daughter that would enhance that, not drag our family back into the muck from which we rose. Sarah should have been a fine lady, with all the good things in life she has been brought up to expect. Now she will be a mere Mrs. Marlow." Mrs. Gladstow shuddered delicately.

Never one to know when to retreat, Rosalind said with utter seriousness, "I think you have proven, ma'am, that being a mere missus can bring with it a goodly amount of position and prestige."

If it was possible, Mrs. Gladstow's face twisted even further in outrage. "You think to patronize me?" she hissed.

Rosalind flinched. "No," she stammered in horror, "I merely meant to point out that—"

"There is nothing prestigious about my daughter and her thirty thousand pounds marrying some country nobody," the woman plowed on, fury bringing splotches of color to her normally pale cheeks. "He has no position, no respect among the *ton*. He is barely gentry."

"I would think being a landowner is highly respected. And she will be very happy with him, as in love with him as she is. I know he is not an earl, but surely you must see that he is the best possible thing for her."

"You know nothing, nothing at all, of the world we live in," Mrs. Gladstow bit out. "Position is everything. You have seen for yourself that being some unimportant landowner does not come with any security, any prestige. Look where such a life has gotten you. Your own father, minor gentry as he was, was a wastrel and a drunk, who lost everything on a single hand of cards. It is a blessing the rest of your family died, that they do not pollute the land with more small people with small ideals and no honor to speak of."

Fury exploded in Rosalind's veins. She took a menacing step toward Mrs. Gladstow. "Don't you ever speak of my family in such a manner again," she spat. "Regardless of our lack of fortune, despite how far I have fallen in the world, my family was a sight better than you. And much better than that horrible reprobate you had planned on selling your own daughter to. I, for one, am overjoyed she escaped him."

Mrs. Gladstow gaped. "You dare to disparage me? You dare to disparage Lord Ullerton, an earl, a peer of the realm?"

"I do dare it," Rosalind shot back. "Earl or not, he is a horrible man. Your daughter is well rid of him. And that you were willing to sell her to him, all for a title, reflects poorly on you, madam."

Mrs. Gladstow gaped at her. "How dare you talk to me in such a way?"

"I dare very well, thank you," Rosalind replied, feeling the return of her spine now that her tongue had been given free rein. "You should be happy for your daughter. She is kind, and wonderful, and deserves every happiness in the world. She is in love and had the very great luck to fall in love with a man who adores her as well. Yes, she may never claim the status of a countess. She may never have a gilt carriage, or castles spread across Britain, or people fawning over her. But she will be loved, and she will be happy. You, with your small mind, cannot see that. You choose to lash out at me, a paid companion, because I did not somehow see into the future, to see into their hearts and prevent them from coming together. I will tell you, here and now, if I had seen what joy it would bring your daughter, I would have pushed for the match myself, you and your lauded ideas of status be damned."

Mrs. Gladstow turned fuchsia. Rosalind thought she might keel over on the spot.

"You will get out of my home this instant," the older woman hissed.

She was glad of it, Rosalind told herself fiercely. She could not stand to stay under this woman's roof one moment longer. She could not wait to be free of her and her cruelty.

Even so, Rosalind felt her world tilt on its axis. For, despite her brave thoughts, utter helplessness seeped through her bones, and a fear so potent she could taste it.

But she would be damned if she would let Mrs. Gladstow see how it affected her. Drawing on every ounce of pride she possessed, she straightened her shoulders and raised her chin. "With pleasure," she pronounced, and turned for the door.

Before she could reach it, however, it opened. The housekeeper stood there, her face a blank mask. In her hands was Rosalind's bag.

"Miss Merriweather's things," the woman mumbled, "as you requested, ma'am."

Rosalind turned to Mrs. Gladstow, who looked as if she'd swallowed a lemon. "You have had my things fetched," Rosalind murmured, sarcasm heavy in her voice. "How kind of you, for you have saved me a trip. Please do extend my farewell and good wishes to your daughter. I'm sure she will understand my abrupt leave-taking. Now, if you will excuse me, I shall see myself out."

Without another look at her employer she marched for the door, stopping only to take her bag from the housekeeper. Before she could quite understand what was happening she was on the street, the door slamming behind her with a dark finality.

There was a horrible moment of true panic then. What had she done? Why couldn't she have shut her mouth, dropped to her knees, and begged forgiveness? But she silenced those poisonous thoughts with brutal will, drawing on that small part of her that was still perfectly lucid, the voice of reason she had drawn on in the most difficult times of her life. Mrs. Gladstow had chosen her to blame, had already made the decision to cast her out. The outcome had been set in stone before Rosalind had even opened her eyes that morning. Drawing her shredded pride around her like a cloak, she pulled her shoulders back, gripped her bag all the tighter, and strode forward down the busy Mayfair street. The household might very well be watching her departure; she would give them nothing to gossip about. Or, at least, nothing more than they already had.

She drew in a shaky breath to relieve the tightness in her chest, hefting her bag higher in her arms. First thing first, she should head to the registry office. The sooner she put her name down as available to work, the sooner she would find a position to support herself. Governess, lady's maid, even chamber maid, she didn't really care at this point, as long as she had a roof over her head and food in her belly.

Which meant, of course, she would have to hail a hansom cab. Something that would require her to dip into the meager funds she had managed to squirrel away over the years.

A cold feeling settled in the pit of her stomach. Even as she turned the corner, her steps faltered. What if, in the packing of her belongings, the housekeeper had "conveniently" forgotten to pack her savings? It would not be the first time she had been stolen from, and she doubted it would be the last. Even so, before she got too far she'd best take a look in her bag.

Heaving a disgusted sigh, she propped her bag on an obliging fence and opened it, rummaging through the hastily packed items, her only belongings in the world. She found the bag she kept her funds in, the one usually hidden at the bottom of her unmentionables. A quick shake of the purse told her coins were present. Even so, she yanked it open, taking a quick peek inside to determine all was as it should be.

Relief flowed through her. It appeared all was in order. Even so, she could not be too careful. She would see to it that the coins in her reticule had not been disturbed, either. For in her dire straits, every penny counted.

The small embroidered reticule, one of her mother's things she had been able to salvage after her father had lost even the clothes on their backs, was at the very bottom of the bag. She dragged it through the tangle of stockings and dresses and chemises, pulled at the drawstring opening, reached inside.

Yes, the coins were there, clinking merrily in the bottom. But as she extracted her hand, her fingers brushed against something hard. Frowning, she reached for the unknown object, pulling it out of bag. It was a small ivory card, covered in elegant script.

Grace, Lady Belham.

Ah, yes. The woman from the ball the night before.

She was about to drop it back into her reticule when a faint recollection of the woman's parting remarks swirled in her brain.

I like you, Miss Merriweather. I haven't many friends in town. If you're ever up for a visit, please do stop by an afternoon. I would so love to continue our exchange.

Rosalind had been much too distracted at the time to give the suggestion the proper attention it deserved. Now it struck her more for the strangeness of it than anything. The woman was of the upper echelons of society. She was nobility. Yet she had asked a mere companion to visit her. Rosalind fought to remember Lady Belham's face when she had made her peculiar request. The woman had kept her smile in place. Yet hadn't there been something lost, perhaps lonely in her eyes?

And didn't lonely women need companions?

In an instant she had her bag put back together and was walking down the street at a brisk pace, the card clutched tight in her fist. The hand-written address indicated the woman was currently staying in Upper Grosvenor Street, only a short walk away. She could be there in no time at all.

As she crossed the street, dodging a fast-moving carriage, the creeping thought intruded that perhaps the woman would not welcome her begging at her door for a position. Mayhap she had read the woman wrong. Perhaps Lady Belham had been in her cups the evening before and regretted now that she had ever asked someone as low as Rosalind to visit her.

But she couldn't think of that. She had to take this chance. For she had nothing to lose and everything to gain.

Even if she was humiliated in the process.

In no time she turned the corner at Grosvenor Square and into Upper Grosvenor Street. She waited for an elegant town coach and four beautifully matched bays to pass before hurrying across the street to the townhouse indicated on the card.

She purposely ignored the elegant surroundings, the size of the house, the way it fairly reeked of old wealth and grandeur even to where she stood on the pavement. If she concentrated on these things, she would never find the courage to approach. Hers had been a life of genteel poverty up until that point, and until the Gladstows she had worked for women who had been no better off than her father before he'd lost it all and had the bad sense to die and leave his daughter a pauper. Even with the Gladstows, there had been something gaudy about their wealth, as if the sheer amount of gilded objects in their homes could take away from the fact that theirs was a new fortune, something Mrs. Gladstow seemed to find the worst kind of embarrassment.

But this was something altogether different. It spoke of blue blood, and elegance, and a deep-seated belonging. It reminded her of those homes she had gone to with the Gladstows where she had been afraid to even brush against a wall for fear of ruining something. Thus, she would focus on the door, and the knocker, and assure her expression was confident enough that even the most discerning butler would not question her appearance.

It appeared, however, that was not something she had to worry about. For as she reached for the knocker the door swung open to reveal Lady Belham herself. The woman was adjusting her gloves, dressed for an outing in an elegant deep blue walking gown and wide-brimmed bonnet, when she looked up and spotted Rosalind.

"Miss Merriweather? Is that you?" She smiled in delight. "Ah yes, I can see it is. How lovely to see you. I admit, when I issued my invitation, I did not expect you to take me up on it. But Miss Merriweather," she continued, her expression sobering as she took Rosalind in, "is something amiss?"

Rosalind raised her chin, holding her bag to her chest, knowing she must look odd standing on the woman's doorstep with all of her belongings and not even a cloak or bonnet on.

"I wonder, my lady," she said with as much confidence as she could muster, "if you would be opposed to sitting with me a moment while I propose a business venture?"

Lady Belham blinked in surprise. "But of course. Danielson," she said to the butler that was hovering in the shadows inside the door, "my walk will be delayed this morning. Please see to it that a tray is brought into the drawing room."

"Of course, my lady."

Lady Belham led the way through the front hall, up the sweeping staircase. Rosalind did her best to appear unfazed by the surroundings. But though she kept her gaze fixed to the other woman's back, she could not fail to be aware of the soaring, hand-painted ceilings, the gleaming marble floor, the intricately-carved railing beneath her hand. She had thought the outside impressive. Yet it was nothing to the splendor of the interior.

What kind of person was Lady Belham's cousin? Rosalind darted quick glances to the walls, hoping for some insight into the woman. Yet there were no portraits at all. Not one. She frowned, wondering at the complete lack of personal paintings. Didn't people of rank like to showcase their long, prestigious lines? Didn't they like to flaunt their histories? Yet there was not a single portrait in the place.

They entered the drawing room then, and Lady Belham sat, indicating a comfortable chair close by for Rosalind. "Now," she said with a kind smile as Rosalind settled herself, "what was this about a business proposition?"

Despite not having practiced what she would say to this woman when the time came to ask for a position as her companion, Rosalind had no doubts she could make a case for herself.

Now, however, the strain of the past hour caught up with her. She held her bag tight to her chest, feeling like, if she let it go, she might very well unravel.

Lady Belham seemed to sense her troubled thoughts. She tilted her head in concern. "First, though, perhaps you'd best tell me what has you so out of sorts."

Rosalind gave a short bark of surprised laughter. "Do you know me so well then that you know what I'm like when I'm *in* sorts?"

The woman's lips quirked. "You're right on that score. I can hardly claim to know you well after a five minute conversation at a ball. Though I think that, any time a person comes to my doorstep carrying what looks to be the entirety of their possessions, there is something wrong. Now tell me, does this have anything to do with Miss Gladstow's engagement last night?"

Sudden exhaustion laid waste to Rosalind's hard-won poise. She slumped back in her seat, eyeing Lady Belham wearily. "You are quick, aren't you?" she muttered. When the woman merely waited patiently, she sighed. "I'm afraid Mrs. Gladstow was not pleased with the outcome of the evening."

One perfectly manicured brow rose high up Lady Belham's forehead. "One of those women, is she?"

"Oh no, I'm quite certain Mrs. Gladstow is an original," Rosalind said, bitterness coloring the words.

"Don't be fooled, darling," Lady Belham drawled. "Sadly enough, women like her are not rare in society. Though I cannot understand why she would let you go, simply because her daughter is marrying a man not of her choosing."

Rosalind shrugged, beyond trying to make sense of what her life had become. She would like nothing better than to reverse time to yesterday morning, to have never stepped foot outside her bedchamber. She would still have been miserable in her position as companion to the unhappiest woman in creation. But at least she would not now be wondering where she would find her next meal.

As if to underscore that last point, her stomach gave a mighty growl, reminding her she had not made it to the breakfast room before Mrs. Gladstow's tirade. She flushed, pressing a fist to her traitorous stomach to quiet its rumblings.

Lady Belham gave her an amused look. "Well then, we'd best get you something to eat. But first, we must locate you a room."

Rosalind looked at her uncomprehendingly. "A room?"

"Certainly. It is why you came here, wasn't it? To secure a position?"

The woman rose. Rosalind scrambled to her feet, flushing under the woman's kind gaze. "I know this is most unusual. And I would not dream of imposing. Only you appeared so lonely last night, and I assumed perhaps you might benefit from a companion." Her skin heated all the more. "That is, you looked like you could use a friend. Not that you don't have any friends. And your cousin, of course, who you mentioned you live with. And so you cannot be completely devoid of companionship. Yet I remember you said you are new to town, and it is never easy making new acquaintances, and we seemed to get along so wonderfully. So I thought I would give it a try, and see if you would hire me on." She smiled, a sickly thing that must have been more grimace than anything. "And so here I am."

Lady Belham laughed, a throaty sound that was nevertheless pure delight. "And I am so very glad you came. For I did not realize how much I would like a companion until you showed up at my door. Now, about that room."

In a daze Rosalind followed Lady Belham as she went in search of the butler. She must be dreaming. It could not be this easy to obtain a position. She shifted her bag, took the skin of one arm in between her fingers, and gave a vicious pinch.

To her utter shock she remained where she was. There was no sudden awakening in the narrow bed and dingy room at Mrs. Gladstow's, no crashing back to sad reality. No, she was still here, with Lady Belham, in the elegant townhouse in Upper Grosvenor Street. She had done it, she thought with mounting excitement. She had started a new life for herself, a better life.

But even as hope burned like a newly kindled flame in Rosalind's breast, a small voice of reason whispered in her ear.

Warning her that her luck, ever capricious, could not possibly hold.

Chapter 8

Even after a night of heavy drinking—and fleecing his friends of a goodly portion of their yearly income—the next morning found Miss Merriweather still firmly entrenched in Tristan's thoughts.

Of all the women in London to capture his interest, why did it have to be her?

But no, he reminded himself brutally as he gazed out the window of his carriage, he was most certainly not attracted to Miss Merriweather. It had been that vulnerable look in her eyes the evening before and nothing more. She had been upset about something, and it had snagged on his intrinsic protective instincts. There was nothing more to it than that.

Even as the thought crossed his mind, though, he knew he was merely fooling himself. There was something about her that pulled at him, like a moth to a flame.

He had been drawn to other women, of course. Some he had even fancied himself in love with. Yet this was different. It was like a bright and glowing light just out of the corner of his eye, constantly snagging his attention, making him turn his head in search of her. He might believe his thoughts had been successfully detoured elsewhere. Eventually, however, there was that light again, almost out of view, sending his thoughts clattering back to her.

He frowned as the carriage pulled up in front of his townhouse. He needn't worry about her presence today, thank goodness. The timing could not be better for Mr. Marlow to declare himself to Miss Gladstow. For Tristan did not think he could take one more day of Miss Merriweather's company without either losing his willpower or his sanity.

It was time, he decided, to reclaim his life, and his wandering mind right along with it. He would fall back into his old habits and pursuits with passion, and it would soon be as if Miss Rosalind Merriweather had never encroached upon his time. With that thought in mind he eschewed going inside, instead starting off for his friend Lord Willbridge's townhouse with a determined gait. If anyone could drag Tristan from his doldrums it would be the delightful company that could be found at his friend's home.

He made it to the townhouse on Brook Street in record time, letting himself into the front hall as was his custom, calling out heartily as he strode across the gleaming parquet floor, "Good morning, Masters family!"

Willbridge's youngest sister, Lady Daphne Masters, poked her head out from the sitting room. "I shall forgive you your blatant disregard for the time of day, as I have the distinct feeling you were quite inebriated after your splendid victory last night."

Tristan grinned, striding forward to buff Daphne on the cheek. "You could help next time, you know. I've seen for myself how brilliant you are at a bit of matchmaking."

She rolled her eyes. "Caleb would have both our heads if he heard you suggest such a thing," she whispered, indicating with a jerk of her chin her brother's presence in the room behind her. "Not only would he be utterly shocked that you have taken up matchmaking as a hobby, but he's still not forgiven us our part in Emily's marriage."

Which was nothing but the truth. Oh, Tristan knew Willbridge was happy enough with it now, having seen his sister, the former Lady Emily Masters, positively bloom in her new position as Lady Morley. That did not mean that he was ready and willing to forget that it had been largely in part to Tristan and Daphne's meddling that had brought the union into being.

He supposed a man would feel that way, when one of his best friends went and married his little sister.

Of course, Willbridge's feelings on the matter might be a bit skewed. Ever since he'd gone and married, he'd shed his libertine ways—quite blissfully, Tristan might have added—and taken up the mantle of familial duty with a vengeance. That sense of honor had only increased in the last week, since learning that his bride, Imogen, was in the family way.

At the thought Tristan smiled. He had not believed a man could be more besotted with his wife. Until said wife announced the eventual arrival of the man's heir. Now there was no standing the couple, who more often than not were making cow eyes at one another.

It was a glorious sight, indeed.

"And how are the soon-to-be parents?" he asked.

"How do you think?" she said in a purposely carrying voice. "Sickening to be about."

Willbridge's voice called from within. "I heard that, you harridan. Why don't you remove yourself from the doorway and let the man in?"

"You're only jealous that he prefers my company to yours now," Daphne quipped, skipping back into the room. Choking on a laugh, Tristan followed.

The private sitting room in the Masters household was a hodgepodge of styles and colors. From dainty rosewood furniture to overstuffed couches piled high with pillows to amateur watercolor paintings of every subject and level of talent, the room was centered on comfort rather than fashion. In the midst of this cacophony of tastes sat Willbridge in a heavy, scuffed leather chair, his long legs stretched before him. Imogen was beside him, reclining comfortably in a pale blue damask seat, her feet propped up on a cushion, one slender hand resting lovingly over her still flat stomach. They both greeted him warmly as he entered.

Nothing had ever looked so gloriously welcoming.

"Tristan," Imogen said with a concerned look, "how are you doing today?"

He gave her a puzzled smile as he bent over her, kissing her on the cheek before taking a seat close by. "I'm well, thank you. As I ever am."

She peered closely at him. "Are you certain?"

"Of course." He looked to Willbridge. "What is this all about?"

His friend's lips quirked. "Imogen is worried you are nursing a broken heart after Miss Gladstow's unexpected engagement last night."

Goodness, he must have done a better job at playacting for Miss Gladstow's beau than he had thought. Chuckling, he leaned back and crossed one booted foot over the opposite knee. "Now, Imogen, I know you want me happily settled. But I assure you, my feelings for Miss Gladstow were purely platonic. She is a wonderful girl and I enjoyed her friendship, but nothing more."

"You are certain?" Imogen asked, frowning.

"Of course. Don't worry your pretty head over me, my dear."

"Well, I must say I'm relieved." She gave him a smile. "And now I may express my joy that Miss Gladstow is settled, and with a man who appears to love her deeply. She is a sweet girl and deserves every happiness."

"Meaning," her husband said, reaching for her hand and linking fingers with her, "you are glad to see another woman escape the nefarious clutches of a scheming, overbearing mother, such as you did."

"Hush," she said to Willbridge, a smile nonetheless lighting her eyes behind the lenses of her spectacles. She turned back to Tristan. "You are too late for breakfast, I'm afraid, though I'm sure there's something we can offer you. Would you like me to have a tray brought up?"

Tristan grinned. "You positively spoil me, Imogen."

She made to rise. Daphne sprang forward. "I'll do it," she declared as she hurried across the room to the bell pull.

Imogen heaved a sigh and settled back. "I'm having a baby, not made of glass," she grumbled. "I am not even far enough along to make rising a difficulty yet. Besides, people do this every day."

"We don't care about other people," Willbridge declared. "We care about you."

Imogen tried to remain bland to his comment. Tristan could see it in the way her brows drew together, as if she were trying mightily to hide whatever it was she was thinking. Yet the faint flush that stained her cheeks, the way her lips twitched told him everything he needed to know. She was pleased. Ridiculously so.

Not for the first time Tristan felt a spurt of envy for Willbridge's great luck. Imogen was a glittering diamond amongst paste gems. Thank God his friend had the good sense to see it and snap her up. Women like them should not be overlooked. For they had much more heart to them than the great majority of those in society.

He looked to Daphne as she settled back down into her seat. "Not out with Mariah this afternoon?" he teased, referring to Imogen's younger sister and Daphne's closest friend. "I must say, I'm surprised. You two have been fairly joined at the hip since your arrival in London nearly a month ago."

"We're meeting later this afternoon for a bit of shopping," she replied, tucking her legs beneath her. She flashed him an arch smile. "And so the hip joining commences."

"And what are you shopping for today? New gowns? Bonnets? Husbands?"

She rolled her eyes. "Just for that, I shall not tell you what we received in the post this morning."

"As you think I would care about what came in the post, I am going to assume it is from Emily. And as there is more than one way to skin a cat…" He turned to Imogen, who was in quiet conversation with her husband. "What news from Emily and Morley?"

Beside him Daphne let loose a growl of frustration. He grinned.

Imogen smiled in delight. "Emily is doing splendidly. You may read her letter for yourself if you like." She reached into her skirt pocket and pulled out an envelope.

"You would have known earlier had you been here for breakfast," Daphne piped up.

"Quiet, you virago," Tristan said good-naturedly before reaching for the letter. He quickly unfolded it, more excited than he would have realized he could be for word from his friends.

He smiled as he read over Emily's neat, precise scrawl. "She sounds as if she is settling into her home nicely," he commented. Shooting a sly look at Willbridge, he added, "I daresay she has never been happier. What a fortuitous turn of events that she should marry someone who loves her so well."

As expected, Willbridge's smile fell. "Fortuitous my foot," he grumbled. Yet the glimmer of pleasure in his eyes told Tristan all he needed to know: the man was holding on to the illusion of anger over his dearest friend marrying his younger sister, but he could not be happier that she was so well-settled.

Fighting back a knowing chuckle, Tristan returned the letter to Imogen. "She mentions a visit you plan to make. Surely that will wait until after the Season is through?"

"Not according to my husband," she answered.

Tristan shot Willbridge a questioning look.

"Imogen and I plan to leave within the sennight," his friend said. "Imogen has a mind to visit with Emily to see her new home."

"Translation: he is being protective and wants me out of London," Imogen whispered in a loud aside.

"Well, there is that as well," Willbridge said somewhat sheepishly, not at all put out by his wife's teasing. "London puts too much of a strain on you, my love. Besides, Daphne is settling into London life. There's no reason for us to remain any longer."

"Don't tell me you want me to help keep an eye on Daphne for you?" Tristan asked in mock horror.

Willbridge's horror, however, was not feigned. "Gad, no. For one, you're an absolute libertine, and would only influence her in the worst way." He smirked before sobering. "Secondly, I've no wish to see another sister married off to a friend who was only supposed to be looking out for her best interests."

"Oh, I don't know," Tristan mused, "I think Emily is more than happy with the outcome." He chuckled as Willbridge's expression turned stormy. "Oh, very well. I shan't tease you any more about it. Would it help if I tell you that the idea of marrying Daphne is completely repugnant to me?" He looked to Daphne and dipped his head. "No offense, of course."

"None taken," she replied with a cheeky grin, "for I certainly have no wish to marry you, either."

Willbridge groaned. "The both of you shall send me to an early grave."

Imogen patted his hand. "All the better to prepare you for fatherhood, Caleb. Our son will be as incorrigible as you, so you'd best get used to such talk."

"You mean our daughter," Willbridge declared officiously, with a superior look that let Tristan know this argument was a familiar one, even at this early stage. "And she shall be as sweet-tempered as her mother." He brought Imogen's hand to his mouth and kissed it.

Daphne made a gagging sound. "What did I tell you?" she muttered to Tristan. "Absolutely sickening." He could not fail to see the misty light in her eyes, however, as she gazed on her brother and his wife.

"Says the woman who has been in love not once, but twice already this Season," he muttered back.

"Quiet you," she hissed as Willbridge and Imogen continued to murmur lovingly to one another. "I told you that in the strictest confidence."

He smirked, only saved from her wrath by the arrival of the tea tray. Blessedly the Masters' cook did not skimp on heartier sustenance in addition to the small cakes and biscuits that were the typical fare. He wasted no time, helping himself to a heaping plate of sandwiches. "I shall miss this once you're out of town, Willbridge," he said in between bites. "My cook isn't nearly so talented."

"You may come over any time you wish after Caleb is gone, you know," Daphne said, pouring out the tea. "Mama will adore having you here."

"You know I can't, imp," he said, reaching for a biscuit. "With your brother gone, it will seem suspect if I visit too often. They'll be thinking I'm after you for more than friendship."

"So let them," Daphne grumbled. "All these rules are ridiculous, anyway."

"I don't care what your opinion is on the matter," Willbridge said severely. "Those rules are in place for a reason, and I will not see you break them."

"Says the man who made a name for himself by doing as he pleased," Daphne muttered.

"Daphne," Willbridge warned.

Imogen quieted him with a gentle hand on his arm. "Caleb, Daphne is a bright girl. She will not make a spectacle of herself." She turned her wide turquoise eyes to her sister-in-law. "Isn't that right, dearest?"

It was amazing, the power in those gentle words. For Daphne was all meek sweetness as she said, "Of course."

"How will we ever keep her in line while you're gone, Imogen?" Tristan drawled, only half-joking.

Imogen smiled as she accepted a cup from Daphne. "Goodness knows."

The rest of the afternoon passed pleasantly. But Daphne was a popular lady and Tristan knew he'd best become scarce before a barrage of admirers descended. He made his farewells and headed for home, whistling a jaunty tune. The sun was warm on his back, the breeze light. And while London air was never the most fragrant, with the blue sky above and birds chirping merrily in the trees, he could almost forget that faint attack on his senses.

As he had forgotten Miss Merriweather.

Tristan stumbled to a halt, the whistle dying on a sputter. *Well, damnation.* And here he had been doing so well.

He made for his house then and bounded up the front steps, letting himself inside. Wasn't there someplace he needed to be? Some shy miss he needed to visit, some friends he could meet in Hyde Park? It didn't much matter where he went, really. Calling to his butler to have his horse readied for him he marched across the marbled front hall, taking the stairs two at a time to the upper floors. He could be changed into his riding gear and out of the house in a thrice.

He was nearly to his bedchamber, could see the door. Suddenly, out of nowhere, a small female came barreling out of the bedroom in front of him. His first thought was that his cousin Grace, staying with him until she found a place of her own, certainly didn't possess such nondescript brown hair. Then the woman's elfin face came into view, and Tristan groaned.

He blinked, hoping it had been a figment of his imagination. But no, there she was, staring at him with outraged cinnamon eyes.

"Miss Merriweather," he ground out, "what in blazes are you doing here?"

Chapter 9

"What am *I* doing here? I could ask the same of you, sir." Really, the cheek of the man. And what was Sir Tristan Crosby doing in the family quarters? Granted, this was not Lady Belham's home but her cousin's. She supposed Sir Tristan could be known to the owner of the house. It seemed Sir Tristan knew anyone and everyone in London, after all. But the intimacy could not be so great as to merit him exploring the house at will.

He continued to stare in disbelief at her. No, not disbelief, she amended. More like patent horror, as if he could not believe his bad luck.

That made two of them, she thought darkly.

"If you are here to visit Lady Belham or her cousin, I must insist you await them in the drawing room."

Sir Tristan's mouth dropped open. "Lady Belham's *cousin*?"

"Yes."

"Her *cousin*."

"Yes," she said, slowly and distinctly. Truly, was the man simpleminded?

"Do you know her cousin then?"

"I have not had the pleasure to meet her yet. I arrived a short time ago, and she has not returned from her outing."

"*Her* outing."

Rosalind very nearly rolled her eyes. "Yes."

He frowned. "But you are companion to the Gladstows. What are you doing here with Gra—er, I mean Lady Belham?"

"I am no longer employed by the Gladstows," she said stiffly. "Not that it is any of your business, but I was relieved of my post this morning. Lady Belham was kind enough to take me on." But she was letting her tongue get away from her again. She drew herself up. "That is neither here nor there. You should not be in this part of the house. I insist you accompany me back to the drawing room and I will fetch Lady Belham straight away."

To Rosalind's consternation, the confusion in Sir Tristan's face was quickly being replaced by…levity? "By all means, Miss Merriweather," he said, grinning, "let us go to the drawing room."

Flummoxed by such a change in demeanor, Rosalind peered closely at him. His eyes sparkled with what looked suspiciously like mischief, his mouth tightening at the corners as if he were holding in a laugh.

He swept his hand before him. "Shall we then?"

Rosalind narrowed her eyes and started off down the hall. He was a ridiculous man, no doubt having a good laugh at her expense for some unfathomable reason. All men like him were cut from the same cloth, after all: trampling others in pursuit of their own pleasure, thinking nothing of those beneath them. Well, he would soon see she was not one to be cowed easily.

She hurried down to the first floor, walking blindly, eager to see the man get his comeuppance. As she turned left at the bottom of the staircase, Sir Tristan cleared his throat.

Stopping, she turned to glare at him. "Yes?"

"Ah, I do believe the drawing room is this way, Miss Merriweather," he murmured, indicating the hall behind them.

Rosalind's face went hot. "Erm, yes. As I said, I was just taken on this morning. Still learning the house and all."

She moved to pass him. His hand on her arm stopped her in her tracks.

Heat shot through her body at the contact. She sucked in her breath, staring dumbly at his bare fingers on her skin.

"What, no thanks?" he murmured. He was not scandalously close, yet his warm breath fanned the stray tendrils of hair at her temple, making her shiver.

Her reaction to him shook her. Frowning, she yanked her arm from his loose grip with much more force than was warranted. "Do not presume to touch me, sir," she gritted. Without waiting for his response, she stormed off.

As luck would have it, the butler, Danielson, reached the first floor and headed her way. "I have distressing news," she called as he came closer. "It seems Sir Tristan has lost his way and was wandering the family apartments. Would you be so good as to show him the drawing room where he can await Lady Belham at her pleasure?"

The butler froze, his eyes going wide, darting from her to Sir Tristan. Rosalind smiled smugly. Surely their interloper would not fail to see the utter brass of his actions now. But instead of a proper level of dismay, the man's amused grin had returned tenfold.

"I'm sorry, Miss Merriweather," Danielson said, drawing her attention back, "I don't quite understand."

She scarcely managed to hold back her growl of frustration. Was every male being deliberately stupid today? "Sir Tristan was in a part of the house he ought not to have been."

The butler was looking more confused by the second. "And why should Sir Tristan not have been in the family quarters, miss?"

Why could the man not understand? It was then it hit her. He was showing similarities in confusion to her second employer, who had been slowly losing her faculties, becoming increasingly senile. Was the man troubled by a mental deficiency? Oh dear, Lady Belham had not warned her of this. No doubt it was kind of her cousin to keep the man on, impaired as he was. Yet something should have been said.

She smiled and said in a gentle manner, "Sir Tristan does not live here, and so should not have been in that part of the house."

The man only seemed more dismayed. He looked to Sir Tristan, who chuckled.

"Ah Danielson, forgive me. I was having a bit of sport at Miss Merriweather's expense. It seemed she was not informed that I am Lady Belham's cousin, much less the owner of this house."

A ringing started up in Rosalind's ears. She gaped at him. "That cannot possibly be true."

"I assure you, it is. Though I must commend you on your protection of my cousin. You were fierce indeed and I am glad to see she has someone as loyal as you to keep her company." He turned to the butler. "Please inform the groom to hold my horse for me. I shall be a few moments longer than expected."

"Very good, Sir Tristan." Danielson gave her a hooded glance before, with a smart bow, he was off.

Rosalind swallowed hard, watching the man go. If the ground opened up into a great gaping hole in that moment she would have cheerfully jumped in. How long, she wondered as she kept her eyes averted from Sir Tristan, would she be forced to ignore his presence before the baronet turned around and left.

"So my cousin has hired you on, has she?" he murmured.

Rosalind pulled a face. Apparently the man had not gotten the hint that she didn't wish to speak with him. Heaving a sigh, she faced him. His smug, amused look dragged at her frown all the more.

"Lady Belham was kind enough to do so, yes," she said through stiff lips.

He cocked an eyebrow. "You don't sound pleased at the prospect."

"I like Lady Belham very much," she said, training her eyes on Sir Tristan's chin. Which might be a mistake. His chin was incredibly strong, after all. And all too close to his mouth.

He grinned, those disturbingly straight teeth flashing, snagging her attention. "Then I can only assume your dislike of the situation has to do with my presence."

"You are astute, Sir Tristan," she snapped without thinking. No, no, this wouldn't do. For, though the man was not her employer, as Lady Belham's cousin and the owner of the house she now resided in, he had sway over her future.

The idea left a bitter taste in her mouth. That a man such as he, the very kind of creature she abhorred above all others, had power over her life was lowering indeed. At least at the Gladstows' she merely had to deal with a social-climbing harridan. Now she had to bow and scrape to a libertine, a man she could not like and did not trust.

A man who affected her far more than she was willing to admit.

But life was not always fair, was it? She found the locket at her throat, the pads of her fingers pressing forcefully into the stones as if to impress its message into her very bones. She had learned that nine long years ago, when her belief that life was fair and good had been cruelly ripped from her. Swallowing what was left of her pride, she focused on his cravat—much safer, in her opinion, than any part of his face—and said, "Forgive me, I am out of sorts and didn't mean to offend."

He was silent for a time. She barely managed to keep herself from sneaking a glance up. Finally he said, his voice quiet, "You do not have to apologize for speaking your mind, Miss Merriweather. You are entitled to your opinion. And I did tease you, after all."

She stiffened. No doubt he meant it as a comfort. But Rosalind knew that, the first chance he got, he would be back to making her life hell. "Am I excused now, Sir Tristan?"

Again that thick silence. "You do not need to ask my permission to leave. You are free to do as you wish here."

There he was, playing at being nice once more. Like a cat toying with a mouse, no doubt. Managing a jerky nod and curtsy, she spun about and hurried from the room. Feeling the burn of his eyes in her back—and the remnants of heat from his fingers on her skin—long after she was safe in her room.

· · ·

Tristan rapped his knuckles on his cousin's bedroom door.

"Come in," she sang.

He grinned. Grace was his favorite blood relation by far. No one had been there for him, had supported him through the trials and troubles of his life as she had. When he had learned of her husband going to his heavenly reward, and that she intended to find a house in London after her period of mourning, he had leapt at the chance to help out in whatever way he could.

He let himself in. Grace sat at her dressing table, peering at her reflection with all the intensity of the most discerning critic. Her eyes met his in the mirror and she waved him forward.

"Tell me," she demanded as he sauntered closer, "do you see a white hair there?" She pointed to her temple, where, as far as Tristan could tell, there was nothing but inky black strands.

Tristan pretended to look concerned as he studied her. "Hmm, I do. In fact," he continued, roving his gaze over her coiffure, "I believe I see several."

Grace's eyes grew wide with dismay, her hands going to her hair. "No!" she gasped, tilting her head, attempting to see the back of her hair in the looking glass. When that proved impossible she took up a silver hand mirror and angled it behind her. "Show me where," she demanded.

Tristan could not contain his laughter a moment longer. It broke free, shaking his body.

Grace's eyes narrowed and she spun in her seat to face him. "You beast. You would tease me?"

"You are so vain, Grace," he said between chuckles. "You make it an easy feat indeed."

"Arse," she grumbled, though it lacked even an ounce of bite to it.

"You do not deny it I see," he drawled, propping a hip against her dressing table and crossing his arms.

She shrugged, turning back to the looking glass. "Why deny the truth? I am nearly five and thirty. It would seem odd if I do not fear a small bit the very physical aspects of aging. Especially as I never once had my London Season, and it seems all the other women here for the first time are hardly women at all, but mere infants." She used two fingers to gently pull back at the skin by her eyes before sending him a cautious sideways look. "Have you seen Danielson yet? He mentioned that a letter arrived from Sainsly."

Immediately Tristan's muscles seized. He had expressly instructed that all correspondence from his ancestral home in Lincolnshire be conveyed through his solicitors. But when had his stepmother ever heeded his wishes in that regard?

For a brief moment he was that boy again, fighting for his father's approval. And forever destined to fail.

He set his jaw, fighting down those feelings he had worked so hard at burying. Yet another feat at which he'd failed, for they cropped up powerfully, and often. "I'll tell him to burn it. As I have the others."

Grace looked troubled. "It could be important, Tristan."

"If it was important, my solicitor would have contacted me with all haste. No, this is merely Josephine's attempt to manipulate me again, nothing more."

She seemed to sense, as she always did, when he was done discussing it. For after a long look she directed her gaze to her dressing table. She selected a small pot from the assortment of containers there while asking, "Are you just returning home then?"

"Yes." Relief at being freed from the subject of his stepmother was quickly replaced by concern as he watched her open the pot and apply some rouge to her cheeks. "Are you certain you wouldn't rather I stayed in more? I hate that you are alone so much."

She waved a slender hand in the air, rolling her eyes. "I told you, I do not need a keeper, Tristan. I am not here to upend your life in any way. You may go about your days as if I am not even here, and before you know it, I shall be out of your hair completely."

"You must know I love having you," he said, his frown deepening. "It's been too long since you were in England at all. I've missed you."

She tilted her head, smiling up at him. "I have missed you, as well. But that does not mean I have any wish to be in your pocket at all hours of the day."

"Yet you hire a companion to keep you company?"

His voice was sharper than intended, ringing out through the room. Grace laid the pot down on the gleaming top of her dressing table and faced him. "Are you upset I have hired Miss Merriweather?"

"Of course I'm not upset," he scoffed. Yet her gaze remained intent on his face. He pushed away from the table, unable to look her in the eye. His cousin was taken aback, and rightly so. He had sounded a churlish bore.

"You do a fairly poor job of making that sound at all believable, Tristan."

"Do I? I cannot imagine why." He walked to the window, looking down into the small, square garden that backed the property.

She came up behind him. "Don't lie to me, darling. What is it about my hiring on a companion that has turned you surly?"

He could not very well tell her it had nothing at all to do with her hiring a companion and everything to do with the identity of said companion. If he voiced such a thought either she would let the girl go without a *by your leave*, or she would read much too much into it.

He broke into a cold sweat. The very idea of Grace thinking he felt more for Miss Merriweather than he did was inconceivable.

He eventually said, with utmost honesty, "The very fact that you feel you need a companion tells me I should not be leaving you to your own devices quite so much."

"Nonsense," she scoffed. "I'm much used to my own company, especially in the past year since Hubert died. But I happen to like Miss Merriweather. And she was in need of a position. What else could I do, send her back out into the streets to starve?" Her face grew hard. "Can you believe, Tristan, that those horrible Gladstows threw her out of the house without even a reference, carrying everything she owned in one small bag?"

A vague sense of unease worked its way across his shoulders. "They tossed her out?"

Grace nodded. "And it was not as if the girl was neglecting her charge. If you had only seen her last night, watching over Miss Gladstow. Such concern, such care for the girl."

"You don't say," he muttered. The vague unease was turning into a tingle that set the very hairs on his arms on end.

She nodded, her eyes fierce. "From my understanding, it was Miss Gladstow's unexpected engagement that prompted Miss Merriweather's termination. Though I cannot understand it. It is one thing to be unhappy with your child's choice in husband. It is quite another to punish the girl's companion for it when she was doing her best."

Tristan's stomach lurched with the bitterness of guilt. *Well, hell.* This was something he had not expected. But Grace was peering suspiciously at him.

"You were dancing with Miss Gladstow shortly before her engagement was announced. You wouldn't have any insight into the matter, would you?"

"Of course not," he scoffed. He may love his cousin, would entrust her with his life. But there was something about his little matchmaking venture that made him want to protect it, to hide it from the world. He only hoped she would take him at his word, that her curiosity would not prompt her to probe for more.

His acting skills must have been exceptional, for Grace nodded and turned her gaze to the window. She heaved a sigh. "Poor girl. I am thankful I passed her my card last night, that she had the sense to seek me out for a position. Heaven knows what would have happened to Miss Merriweather if she had not."

It did not take much of an imagination to deduce. There was only one place for women to go when they had no home, no family, no money. The thought of Miss Merriweather on the streets, begging for coin to survive—or worse—slammed through him. Horror and fury at Mrs. Gladstow's unfeeling actions boiled up. But with it was mixed a healthy dose of disgust in himself, for he had equal fault in the whole debacle. Seeing Miss Gladstow happily settled was cold comfort now, as a young woman's life had nearly been destroyed because of his interference.

It was more proof that he was nothing special, that it would only take the smallest misstep on his part to reveal to the world what a fraud he was.

"Tristan? Tristan, are you well? You appear ill."

Grace's voice shocked him back to himself. He looked at her, quite unable to dredge up his typical carefree smile. "I'm happy she came to you, is all," he rasped.

Though what the repercussions would be for him, he thought with no small amount of trepidation as Miss Merriweather's face flashed in his mind, he hadn't a clue.

Chapter 10

By the time Rosalind prepared to set out for a brisk walk with Lady Belham later that afternoon she was determined to make the best of her situation. Surely Sir Tristan was a minor snag in this new chapter of her life. Her employer would soon acquire a house of her own. Once that occurred, she could put the man and his sick sense of humor behind her.

"You will come to find," the other lady said as they marched down the hall, "that I am not one to sit idly by all day, reading and stitching and such. I much prefer to be out and about. I hope you don't find such a life distasteful."

"It sounds divine," Rosalind replied with utter truth. How many hours had she spent reading dusty tomes to drowsy old women, or embroidering intricate designs on things she would never use or wear? How many times had she sat with nothing to do but watch others talk as if she were invisible?

But being out of doors, and with a woman who already felt more of a friend than an employer, was like being in the most beautiful dream. And she never wanted to wake up.

Sir Tristan chose that moment to exit the room they were passing. He stepped in their path with a jaunty grin. "Going somewhere, ladies?"

Then again, no dream was perfect, Rosalind thought sourly.

"We're off on a walk," Lady Belham answered cheerfully. "The day is much too glorious to stay indoors."

"I don't suppose your party could handle one more?"

And there went Rosalind's good mood, right out the window. "I thought you were going out for a ride," she blurted.

Sir Tristan turned to her then. The effect those clear blue eyes had on her was instantaneous, making her hot and itchy all at once.

"That is," she continued hurriedly, needing a distraction from her body's perplexing reaction, "you mentioned to Danielson when we met earlier that he should hold your horse. I assumed you had meant to go on a ride." *Shut your mouth, Rosalind.* "Not that it has anything to do with me." *For the love of all that is holy, be quiet.* "You may do as you wish. I certainly don't care." At long last her mouth heeded her and stilled. Though it was much too late for her to come away from it with any semblance of grace.

"I find I could not pass up the promise of such company," he drawled, a slow grin stretching over his face.

Rosalind flushed. Despite his flirtatiousness—Sir Tristan's typical way of conversing with females, she knew, and thus no reflection at all on her—his eyes were strangely sober. No doubt he had seen the rudeness of her little run of the mouth. She may as well have declared in clear and ringing tones that she didn't care for his presence. Granted, it was true. But it was not generally something you said to someone, deserved or no. Especially when they might have sway over your future security.

"That is pure poppycock, Tristan," Lady Belham said. "I do hope your change in plans is not due to our conversation from earlier. I told you that you are not required to entertain me. I am more than capable of seeing to my own comfort. And now that I have Miss Merriweather's company you need feel no guilt that I am lonely."

"You both wound me," Sir Tristan declared, laying a hand over his heart. "I would think you have no wish to have me join you."

"Silly man," his cousin said with a mix of exasperation and fondness. "Very well, you may join us. But," she said as his grin returned, "you must promise me, no more flirting with Miss Merriweather. I'll not have you scaring her off when I have just found her."

"I would not dream of offending Miss Merriweather," he pronounced. He inserted himself between them, winging out both arms. "Shall we?"

The very last thing in the world Rosalind wanted to do was to take this man's arm. Yet he gave her no choice. Pressing her lips tight, she gingerly placed her fingers on the cobalt wool of his coat.

He tensed beneath her hand, a sudden and jarring movement she felt even through the layers of his fine clothes, right through her gloves. She cast a sharp glance up at him.

The breath left her body. Again. He was staring down at her, the bright blue of his eyes disturbingly direct and intent. Damnation, what was it about his gaze that affected her so? She could not be attracted to the man. If there was anything Guinevere's tragedy had taught her, it was that men such as he could only lead to ruin and heartache. Surely she was much too smart to fall for his charms.

Wasn't she?

Mayhap not. For she could not help the way her knees weakened, making her sway as his gaze settled on her lips. Nor could she help the way her tongue darted out to wet her suddenly dry lips.

His eyes widened before he hastily looked away. "Ready then?" he asked his cousin. Was it Rosalind, or did his voice crack?

They set off, heading out of the house and west on Upper Grosvenor Street toward Hyde Park. As the cousins chatted amicably, Rosalind stayed silent, her thoughts troubled. She could no longer ignore the fact that Sir Tristan was a danger to her. Despite her better sense, despite not even liking the man, her traitorous body continued to react in the most worrisome way to him. She forcefully brought to mind her sister's face as it had been after that fateful London trip. She had been drawn and haggard, her eyes haunted. And so much worse all those months later, when the fruits of her ruination had killed her. Would she forget the lesson to be learned there?

With luck Lady Belham would soon find a place to let of her own. Until then, Rosalind would have to be on guard. Surely she could manage herself for a few more weeks. It was not as if the man reciprocated her desires, after all.

• • •

Tristan had spent far too little time with Grace since her return to town nearly a week ago. As they walked the shaded paths of Hyde Park, conversing as they had not in too long, he was reminded of how much he had missed her. It would have been an ideal afternoon.

If he was not achingly aware of Miss Merriweather at his side.

Damnation, but he had to get control of himself where that woman was concerned. No easy feat now that she was staying in his home. But he could manage it.

He had to.

But he and Grace had been discussing something. What had it been? Oh, yes.

"Has the house agent contacted you with any new properties to let?"

"Nothing I would think of taking."

He grinned. "Too small for you and your grand tastes?"

Grace made a face. "You truly have a lofty opinion of me, don't you? No, they're much too large. What would I possibly need with eight bedrooms? Or a ballroom? I like a good ball as well as the next person, but I certainly don't intend to throw one. Besides, if I ever change my mind I can make use of your house. What you've been doing in that monstrosity, a lonely bachelor, is beyond me." She peered around him. "Miss Merriweather, do you have any ideas as to good neighborhoods I may take a house in? For I am having no luck thus far."

"I don't know London very well, I'm afraid," Miss Merriweather replied. "I have only been here since the start of the Season."

"Where were you before that?"

Tristan thought for a moment she would not answer his cousin. She ducked her head, but not before he saw the tightening of her features. Her words carried a faint tension when she spoke. "In

Lancashire for three years. And before that Shropshire. Preceded by Derbyshire. But before taking on the position of companion, my home county was Durham."

"Durham? My goodness, that is far north. You are a long way from home, then," Grace exclaimed on his other side. "And so much movement at such a young age. It must have been difficult."

"Difficult is not the word for it," Miss Merriweather said, her voice low and tight.

She'd had a hard life, it seemed. But so had many people. Her troubles were not his concern. Yet even though he told himself to stay out of the conversation, he found himself saying, "You must have been quite young when you became a companion."

"I was seventeen. About eight years now."

Tristan waited for more, but for once she was surprisingly quiet. Ironic, as he would dearly love to hear the story behind those simple words. Even so, he was transfixed. Her face was so expressive, like seeing a story played out. Her whole history was there in the cinnamon depths of her eyes. Not the details, no, but the heart of it. All the grief and anxiety and strain of the past years was there in vivid color.

But the mood was turning much too serious. He didn't do serious. Not if he could help it. He schooled his features to the easy-going, lopsided grin he was renowned for. "You are in luck with my cousin if a life of moving about was not to your liking," he quipped. "Unless she remarries. Then goodness knows where life may take her, or where you will end up. When she married Belham nearly eighteen years ago she wound up in the wilds of Scotland."

That small line deepened between Miss Merriweather's brows and she opened her mouth, no doubt ready to let loose with some unexpected remark that would throw him completely off guard. Before she could, however, a lone gentleman approached, calling out cheerfully to his cousin.

"Why, if it isn't the beauteous Grace."

The frustration he felt at being denied access to Miss Merriweather's thoughts was swift and utterly surprising.

Thankfully Grace quickly distracted him from his troubling reaction.

She released his arm and hurried forward, taking the newcomer's outstretched hands in hers. "Hugh Carlisle, is that you? Goodness, but it's been an age." She stepped back a pace, taking the man in with disbelieving eyes. "My, how you have changed from that rascal who tormented me so."

He grinned. "How could I not torment the absolutely gorgeous thing who went and married my cousin right under my nose?"

"Please, I was five years your senior, much too old for a youth not even out of school," she said with a chuckle. "But forgive my rudeness. Allow me to introduce my cousin, Sir Tristan Crosby. Tristan, this is Lord Belham's cousin, Hugh Carlisle."

Tristan took the man's hand. "It's a pleasure. Have you been in London long?"

"Not long at all. I've been situated in the country for some time now, as I've taken over the management of several of my father's properties and have only just returned. My father spends his time in London, you see, but has recently taken ill and there is no one else to care for him."

"I'm sorry to hear that," Tristan answered.

The man nodded in thanks, then looked to Miss Merriweather in expectation. Something shifted in his gaze, an interest sparking that was a bit too strong to be construed as mere friendly curiosity.

Tristan's body tightened. He had the mad urge to place himself between Carlisle and Miss Merriweather. A reaction that had him nearly blanching. What the devil was wrong with him?

He really had better rein in his obsession with the girl before he made an utter arse of himself.

Grace spoke again. "Hugh, this is Miss Rosalind Merriweather. Miss Merriweather, Mr. Carlisle," Grace said.

"It is a pleasure." Miss Merriweather smiled and curtsied. Carlisle, however, looked as if he'd seen a ghost.

"Miss Merriweather, you say?"

Tristan stared at the man, utterly flummoxed as to his reaction. Miss Merriweather, however, seemed to know what the man's reaction meant. Her eyes grew bright, an almost feverish excitement lighting them. "Yes. Did you know my sister, Miss Guinevere Merriweather? She would have been here in London nine years ago."

Carlisle was quick to recover. He smiled warmly, no hint of the shock that had drained his face so completely just seconds ago. "Yes, yes I did. Such a sweet girl. So kind to all us young bucks who vied for a dance with her. How is your sister? I daresay she captured the heart of some lucky fellow and is living out her life in marital bliss."

A sister? This was the first Tristan had heard of any relations of Miss Merriweather's. Immediately a haunted look passed over her face. And her next words told him all he needed to know why he had never heard a whisper of the girl before.

"She died shortly after that trip, I'm afraid. She contracted an infection of the lungs upon her return and never recovered."

Carlisle appeared stunned. "I am so sorry."

Miss Merriweather nodded in thanks. "Did you know my sister well?"

"Somewhat. Though as there were so many of us who made it a point to stay in her orbit it was difficult to get close."

"Do you recall a Mister Lester? Mister Gregory Lester?"

The question was pointed, intense in the execution. Tristan glanced sharply at Miss Merriweather. She was peering closely at Carlisle, her fingers at the locket at her throat, a seemingly nervous reaction he had noticed several times before.

Carlisle smiled. "Certainly. He was a popular fellow, lively and well-liked by all. We were quite close. Of course," he continued, his happy look faltering, "mayhap you are not aware that he was killed in action in the Battle of Vimeiro in oh-eight."

"Yes, I had heard."

Tristan started at the strange tension in her voice, as if she were wound so tight she might snap.

Carlisle, however, seemed utterly oblivious of her darkened mood, for his happy look returned. "Lester was a good man. Never knew one who could hold his drink so well. But we grow morose. And I refuse to be sad in the company of such beautiful women." He turned to Grace, bowed. "We have much catching up to do, you and I. Do you think Sir Tristan and Miss Merriweather would mind if I walk on ahead with you a bit?"

"Oh, it matters not what Tristan minds," Grace drawled with a teasing look his way. "But I would not foist this great lummox off on my companion if she has a dislike of the plan. Miss Merriweather, do you mind keeping my cousin company?"

"Not at all, my lady," Miss Merriweather replied. "I would be happy to."

Tristan peered at her as Grace and Carlisle moved off. The tone of her voice troubled him. For there was a decided lack of emotion in it. If there was anything he knew about this woman, it was that she was vocal about those things she disliked. And he knew for a fact she didn't care for him in the least. When they had been forced to walk together in this very same park yesterday—*goodness, could it have really been a mere day ago?*—she had held her own against him. Yet now she appeared utterly defeated.

It must have been the mention of her sister and that old beau of hers. So tragic, that both young people were now in their graves.

But he could not stand to see her like this, as if all the life had been drained from her. He leaned in close. "And here I thought you spoke your mind in all things, Miss Merriweather," he murmured into her ear.

Miss Merriweather gave a small yelp and jumped. It set her off balance and she stumbled into him. Her hand gripped tight to his arm, her fingers biting into his bicep. Instinctively he reached out to steady her.

And immediately saw his error. The new angle brought her body flush to his. She was small and slight and yet utterly feminine, the faint curves of her small breasts pressing into his side. Her scent assaulted him, some combination of roses and lavender that was mouthwatering. He swallowed hard and hastily set her away from him.

Her eyes still appeared clouded. Yet now confusion—and a bit of annoyance—shone in their depths, like a light through the densest fog. "Pardon me?"

"You are not one to hide your true feelings, I think," he replied with an impressive display of unconcern. At least it was impressive considering his frame of mind at that moment, for his body had not yet recovered from their little stumble. "Yet you blatantly lied to my cousin when you told her you would be happy to keep me company."

She scowled. "And what was I to say? That I have no wish to be in your company?"

"Is it the truth?"

"Of course it is," she snapped, then immediately turned scarlet, the remainder of her grief falling away like dead leaves from a tree.

He chuckled, knowing it would only increase her ire. Did he enjoy baiting her? Of course he did. But it was also necessary. For look at the change in her. There was color to her cheeks again, and a spark in her gaze. He offered his arm. After looking at it blankly she took it and they started along the path after Grace and Carlisle.

"Forgive me," she said, her voice—and her hand on his arm— stiff as whalebone. "I should not have said such a thing."

"Oh, don't curb your tongue on my account," he said.

She only looked more furious. He just managed to stop a grin from showing. He truly was a beast, to enjoy her discomfort so. But it was so much better than the downtrodden look that had pulled at her. That expression had troubled him more than any bit of fury she could blast him with.

"Why is it," she said through gritted teeth, "that I constantly find myself alone in your company in this park?

"You're lucky, I suppose."

"Luck? You call this luck?"

"Oh, most definitely. There are many women who would love to trade places with you."

Seemingly against her will, a laugh broke free from her lips. "You must be joking."

"No, I am utterly serious. Why, look right there," he said, pointing to a young girl gaping at him. "That lady cannot keep her eyes off of me."

Miss Merriweather's lips twitched. Tristan could not tell if she was annoyed or fighting down mirth. "She is not even out of the schoolroom. She hardly counts."

"Picky are we? Very well, there is an entire group of ladies down the lane there that is quite envious of your place at my side," he declared, inclining his head in said group's direction.

She did laugh then as she eyed the gaggle of elderly women blatantly staring at them. "And they are old enough to be your grandmother."

He shrugged, even as he fought the urge to grin in triumph at having gotten her to laugh. It was the first he had ever heard her react in amusement in the weeks he had known her. "Flattery is flattery, Miss Merriweather, and I shall take it where I can get it. If they wish to ogle me, I give them my blessing."

"You are horribly vain. Has anyone ever told you that?"

"Often, and loudly."

She laughed again. The sound was so wonderful, so free, he was stunned by the strange joy it gave him. It seemed Miss Merriweather did not often allow herself to let loose in such a manner.

"You should laugh more often, you know."

The look on her face changed in an instant, transforming to careful distrust. The typical expression she used when looking at him.

Damn and blast. He and his big mouth.

"I do not often laugh because there is not much worth laughing at," she said in faintly censorious tones.

"Come now, Miss Merriweather. Surely there is something that gives you joy."

She stopped in the middle of the path and faced him. Anger colored her cheeks, turned her eyes feverish. "Do not presume to tell me how to react, sir. You do not know what I have lost."

"You refer to the sister Carlisle mentioned."

He didn't know what prompted him to say it. But he immediately saw his error, for she looked as if he'd struck her.

"Forgive me," he mumbled. "It is only that I was not aware you even had a sister."

"Why would you have had cause to know it?"

It was on the tip of his tongue to quip that he'd been in her company daily for more than a fortnight so he should know something of her by now. But realization struck, making his mouth close with a snap. For he didn't know a blasted thing about her. He had conversed with her about inane things, of course. And had talked with Miss Gladstow in her company often.

But he had never once tried to draw Miss Merriweather into a meaningful conversation, had never asked her about herself, or her life, or her thoughts on more than the weather.

"You're right, of course," he murmured. "That was not well done of me. Won't you tell me of your sister now?"

She appeared struck dumb, confusion marring her brow. He took the chance to offer his arm again, and they were soon making their way along the path.

"You wish to know of Guinevere?" she asked after a painfully long silence.

"If you're willing to speak of her."

"Oh, I'm always willing to speak of her. But that is difficult to do when everyone who knew her is gone."

He nodded. "Which is why you were so stunned to meet with Carlisle."

She peered up at him. "You are quite observant, did you know that?"

Only with you, he nearly said. Blessedly he stopped himself in time. "She was older than you, I assume?" he asked instead.

"By three years." A small smile lifted her lips. "Funny enough, I was the responsible one. She and my father were dreamers, you see. I had to keep them both in line." She gave a little laugh. "They always said that without me they would be lost."

A cloud seemed to move across her face then. All the joy fled, to be replaced with an unbearable sadness. "Then she died, and my father followed soon after. And I was left with no one."

"And that is when you became a companion," he deduced.

"Yes. A distant cousin took pity on me and hired me on."

"It must have been difficult for you."

"More than you know."

He paused at the darkness in her voice. He should change the subject. It appeared to give her only pain, keeping on in this vein. But he could not ignore the injustice that had been dealt her earlier that day, apparently only the last in a long line of it. "It was not fair of Mrs. Gladstow to let you go over her daughter's engagement. It seems to me Mr. Marlow will make Miss Gladstow a fine husband. I am sorry you were caught up in the whole mess, that you suffered because of it."

She pursed her lips, her sharp eyes cutting to him. "Are you taking blame then?"

He blinked, nearly stumbling at the sudden change in her. "Pardon?"

Her voice dropped. "I know you were responsible for Miss Gladstow's engagement."

Speared by the accusation and certainty in her eyes, Tristan took a moment to consider his options. He could either feign anger or laugh it off and declare her mad.

Or he could admit it all.

The last held a surprising amount of appeal. And besides, she would not believe him if he denied any involvement in it. He saw it in her eyes. For the briefest of seconds he was tempted to tell her all.

But no, she would never understand, would only look on him with more disgust than she did now. It was the very reason he refused to tell others of his endeavors. No one would be able to comprehend the importance of such a venture to him. How it made him feel that, for the first time in his life, he was worthy, and useful, and more than what society perceived him to be. Daphne was the only one who knew, and that was because she was the one who had aided him on that very first matchmaking scheme, when he had realized there was something more to him than an empty smile and a handsome face.

In the end, he merely asked, "If I was responsible for helping Miss Gladstow find her happiness, would you blame me?"

The self-righteous anger that had settled hard over her gaze like a lacquer cracked at his soft tone. "No," she admitted reluctantly.

"Well then, there is nothing more to say on the subject, is there?" He looked down the path, toward Grace and Carlisle. They had fallen behind quite a ways. And he found himself desperate to get to them. "We should hurry."

To his surprise she stopped, letting her hand fall from his arm. "No," she answered slowly, "I don't think I shall join you."

"Are we to stand and glare at one another then? For though you are a lovely vision and I wouldn't mind it in the least, I would like a bit more exercise before we return to the house. One does not get this trim form by standing idle."

Instead of lightening the mood as he had hoped, his comments only served to deepen the line between her brows. "I think it is best if we part here."

"Part?"

"Yes. I think we can agree, Sir Tristan, that we are better off not getting friendly with one another."

He frowned. "I should not let you go off on your own, Miss Merriweather."

She laughed at that. But it was not the light-hearted mirth she had shown earlier. No, this was a dark thing. "And what will happen to me, Sir Tristan? I am not a young lady of good breeding that must be coddled. I have been forced to make my way in the world for too long. And I assure you, with how I feel now, no one would dare presume to accost me. Good day."

Tristan could only watch helplessly as she strode away, knowing he was partly to blame and not able to do a blasted thing to help.

Chapter 11

Three days had passed but things had not improved between Rosalind and Sir Tristan.

Not that she was actively trying to improve things. No, for all she cared he could go jump in the Thames. Being drenched from head to toe might make the man a little less physically appealing, after all, thus helping her out considerably in squashing her completely irrational desires for him.

She paused on her way down to the ground floor as an image came to her: Sir Tristan dripping wet, hair slicked back, clothes clinging to him.

Then again, she thought as she hurried downstairs, going hot with mortification—and something altogether different—mayhap not.

But why was she even thinking of him? And why had it only grown worse in the past few days? Granted, she was seeing him much more often than before. Which was only to be expected, seeing as she was staying in his home. But it was more than that. For more often than not her mind wandered to their conversation in the park, when he had brought her out of her melancholy spirits, then had proceeded to ask her about her sister.

No one had been willing to talk about Guinevere in ages. It had loosened that bit of herself that she had bundled up in a protected ball in the pit of her stomach, hiding it away from the harshness of the world. That vulnerable bit of herself that she had never wanted to see the light of day again, yet was now clamoring to get out.

And it frightened her witless.

Which was, of course, why she had attacked him as she had. It had been more for self-preservation than true anger at the man, confronting him with her suspicions regarding Miss Gladstow. She had needed it to be said aloud, to remember why she distrusted him so. For she could not open up to him. Ever.

But she was growing agitated thinking of it. And as Lady Belham did not need her presently, she refused to waste her precious time thinking about Sir Tristan and the danger he posed to her. She would instead find a private spot to mull over the other issue that had taken up a good portion of her waking thoughts.

Mr. Hugh Carlisle.

It had been a shock to meet someone who remembered Guinevere. Her sister had not travelled in exalted circles during her time in London, after all. And it had been some time since that ill-fated trip.

Mr. Carlisle's fond recollections of Mr. Lester, however, were altogether different. Mr. Lester had always played the part of a monster of the worst kind in her imaginings. The man who had ruined her sister, who had broken her spirit, could not be anything but. To hear him being spoken of as if he had been a good man had been a blow.

She made the ground floor then and stood for a moment undecided, unsure where to go. A book would not do her any good now. Her mind was in too much of a tangle to wrap it around prose. No, what she needed was mindless relaxation. And in a place she could be fairly confident she would not run into a certain libertine.

Decided, she spun about and hurried for the back of the house. The garden it was, then. Sir Tristan did not appear to be the sort to sit among the flowers and daydream. She would be safe there.

She stepped out into the warm afternoon air and let her gaze rove over the vegetation. Blessedly there was nothing overly formal about the space. There were no severely clipped hedges, no heavily trimmed trees, no sterile paths. It was not that it was unkempt. Not in the least. She was sure a warning must have been given to each weed and fallen leaf, for there was not a one in sight. Yet there was something wonderfully natural about it all, as if the plants had been given leave to grow at will and had thus thrived.

It did not take her long to find what she needed: a wide bench tucked in the natural alcove between two shrubs. She sank down on the cool stone, arranging the skirts of her gown, and gave a small, relieved sigh. Being on a side path and thus out of sight of the house, with plants hugging her from behind, it felt like the most private place in London.

Until she heard the unmistakable sound of boots on the path. Boots she knew would be encasing strong calves, leading up to the most wickedly handsome man in existence.

Rosalind gave a little sigh. For the first time she understood a little of what had prodded her sister off the path of chastity. If Mr. Lester had looked anything like Sir Tristan then her sister, a romantic of the first order, would have been defenseless indeed.

But he was headed her way. She could hear it in the way the sound of the ground beneath his feet changed from paved brick to the gravel of the side path she was on.

Rosalind bit back a groan and sent up a prayer instead. *Please let him pass by without seeing me. I'll be good, I swear it, if you'll only grant me this.*

And for a moment it seemed her prayers had been answered. He came into view, head down, hurrying along the path. She tucked farther back in her bower; if she could only remain still enough, he would continue on blissfully unaware of her presence and she could continue to brood in peace.

But then his steps slowed. And he turned in her direction.

It was only when he was nearly on top of her that he noticed her at all. He started in surprise, his boots skidding to a stop barely a foot from the hem of her gown.

"Miss Merriweather," he said, belatedly dipping into a small bow.

"Sir Tristan." She thought that would be that. Yet the man simply stood there, staring down at her. She frowned. "I'm sorry, did you need me for something?"

For a split second his eyes appeared to go molten. Something deep in her responded, turning liquid. Then he blinked, and it was gone.

At least, the strange look in his eyes was. The unexpected warmth in her belly was not so easily discarded.

"Ah, no," he said. "Though it appears you and I have the same idea when it comes to relaxation." He indicated the bench with a wry tilt of his head.

"Oh! I'm sorry, is this where you come to relax, then?"

"On occasion. But please," he continued, holding out a hand when she would have risen, "don't leave on my account."

Rosalind had no choice but to fall back to the bench. His close proximity, as well as the abrupt movement of his hand, ensured that.

But after her body's strange reaction mere seconds ago, she was in no hurry to remain close to the man.

"I never meant to usurp your bench," she said. "Please let me up and you can rest at your leisure."

He smiled, his eyes crinkling at the corners. "Hardly usurping. I am not some king bent on ruling all in my purview. Besides, there is more than enough room for the both of us."

Rosalind froze. "You cannot be serious."

One eyebrow rose. "I assure you, I am."

"I am not sharing a bench with you," she blurted.

A relieved chuckle escaped him. "Ah, I am glad we are past the cool politeness and you are back to telling me what you think."

He proceeded to sink down onto the bench beside her. Seeing her chance to escape, Rosalind rose with alacrity.

"I did not think you a coward, Miss Merriweather," Sir Tristan murmured.

She spun to face him. Her hands balled at her sides. "I am no coward, sir."

He looked her straight in the eye—no hard task; she was not tall to begin with, and even when he was sitting she did not have many inches on him—and said, clearly and distinctly, "Prove it."

Rosalind fought it with everything she had in her. She was not so stupid that she would respond to a taunt. She would turn and march away and that would be that.

Only apparently her pride was out in full force today. And she really was that stupid.

She sat.

He smiled, a wide thing that used every muscle in his face. She might almost think he was proud of her. "Now," he said as she arranged her skirts so that not a fiber of them touched his leg, "that wasn't so hard, was it?"

She would not answer him. He would only tease her more. Surely she could manage to ignore him, to simply go about whatever it was she had been doing before he arrived. Though they shared a bench and the same small alcove, they needn't converse.

Sir Tristan, however, was of a different mind.

"It's a lovely day, isn't it?"

"Mmm," she answered noncommittally.

"Overcast, of course. But most days are in London."

She nodded, keeping her gaze fastened on the lazy buzzing of a bee among the rose bushes across the path. Bees didn't have to worry about distracting rakes with clear blue eyes and beguiling smiles. Lucky things.

"I had planned on taking a ride later," he continued, completely undaunted by her non-answers.

The bee drifted toward her, hovering over her knee before flying off. Her eyes followed it as it disappeared over the garden wall. If she were a bee she would do the same. Instead she was stuck here, pride holding her to this bench as she tried her damnedest to ignore the heated presence of the very large, very male person beside her.

"Will you go out with my cousin later to walk or ride?"

"I hardly know," she replied in as cool a voice as she could manage. Which, she was pleased to find, was quite cool indeed.

Still the man did not catch on to the fact that she wished to be left alone. "I am heading to Lady Harper's ball this evening. And you?"

Accepting the fact that the man was either too dense or too stubborn to understand her wish to sit silently and enjoy the small space of freedom she was allowed each day—though Lady Belham was no horrible taskmaster, Rosalind was here to work—she let out an exaggerated breath of frustration and pivoted in her seat to face him. "We are not attending Lady Harper's."

He did not so much as blink an eye at her surly tone. If anything, his smile widened. "Where are you for, then?"

Patience, Rosalind. "I do believe we shall attend Lord Grover's dinner."

"Splendid. I hear he provides quite a spread. His cook is from France, you know."

Her patience melted away like a lump of sugar in tea. "Are you quite through, sir?"

"Oh! You'll be wanting some quiet, then. I'm terribly sorry, you must be wishing me to the devil." The twinkle in his eyes, however, belied any truth to those words.

"You are an astute man," she replied scathingly, turning her face away and plucking at the material of her gown with agitated fingers.

His pause implied he considered her words. "Astute. Hmm. That is not a word often applied to me."

She shot him a disgusted look. "I cannot imagine why. For you are far too clever for your own good."

The surprise that flashed across his face appeared genuine. "Clever?" He gave a sharp laugh. "That is a word even more rarely used in regard to me."

She scowled. "You are fishing for compliments, sir."

He shifted so his body more fully faced her. "I assure you, that is the last thing I am about."

"Please," she scoffed, turning her own body. "Men like you are always after compliments. You like nothing better than to hear yourself speak, or to hear others speak well of you."

Aggravation tightened his features. "You have a very decided view of men. It really is too bad you have no idea what you are talking about."

"Don't I?" She shifted in her seat. Her leg pressed against his but she didn't care at that moment, the anger boiling up in her was so great. "If I have a decided view then you may be assured I have a reason for it."

A heavy silence fell. *Stupid, stupid girl*, she thought as the frustration cleared from Sir Tristan's face to be replaced with a horrible curiosity. A question formed in his eyes.

Before he could voice it, she burst forth, letting every ounce of her frustration with him color her words. "Why are you doing this to me? Why can you not leave me alone?"

He frowned, no doubt taken aback by her outburst. But when he spoke, it was not the censure she expected to hear.

"I don't care for strife in my home, Miss Merriweather. I see no reason we cannot be civil with one another."

"I was already being civil."

"Barely," he scoffed.

She raised her chin. "I was being as civil as anyone in my position is expected to be."

"So cold and taciturn is a requirement for being a companion?"

"You expect me to shower you with smiles and cheerful greetings?"

He let out a frustrated breath. "Of course not."

"You think as I am a female, I am good for nothing more than to stare at you with eyes as blank as a child's doll, that I should only giggle and simper and not show a bit of my true feelings? That I am to cater to your ego when all I want to do is wring your neck?"

He gaped at her, his eyes as clouded as the sky above their heads. As she glared back at him a realization dawned. Rosalind looked at him with a new understanding. "But you need more, don't you?" she murmured.

Her questions seemed to snap him from his stunned stupor. "What are you talking about?"

"You need more than cool civility. You need me to *like* you. You need *everyone* to like you."

"That is ridiculous," he sputtered.

But she was already warming to her idea. "No, it's true! You charm everyone you meet. It's like a compulsion. And people respond unfailingly. It's your special gift, your talent. It must gall you to deal with someone who wants nothing whatsoever to do with you."

Instead of lashing out in anger—he was her employer's cousin, after all, and she should not have talked to him as she had—a sly look crossed his face. "Come now, Miss Merriweather. I think you're protesting a bit too loudly, don't you?"

She blinked. "I'm sorry?"

"You seem very determined to tell me in every way, shape, and form just how much you despise me. It's a bit overdone. All bluster and smoke. And if I have learned one thing over the years, it's that where there is smoke there is often fire." He paused and waggled his eyebrows at her. "And I am not referring to fire as a hateful emotion. For hate is cold. And your feelings for me are decidedly not cold. Quite the opposite, I think."

Rosalind's jaw dropped. "You think that because I proclaim how much I dislike you that I actually do not dislike you, but desire you?"

A slow smile lifted his lips. "You said it, not I."

The gall of the man! Rosalind sputtered for a moment, unable to anchor a coherent thought. Finally she found the words needed. "You are mad!"

Very well, they were not the best of words. But they certainly conveyed everything she wanted to say.

Sir Tristan, however, only found them humorous. "You do not deny it, I see."

"I do not deny it because it should not have to be said. But as you are too thick-skulled to understand me, I shall say it regardless. I do not desire you. As a matter of fact, if you were to kiss me this very instant, I would feel nothing. Nothing at all."

Which perhaps had not been the smartest thing to say. For as soon as the gauntlet was thrown, his eyes warmed and found her mouth. No, that wasn't quite right. She swallowed hard, her mouth going dry. For his eyes did not simply warm, they burst into flames.

"Do you care to test that theory?" he purred before his arms came about her, dragging her against the long length of him. And then, with the buzzing of the bees in her ear and the faint spice from his skin permeating her senses, he lowered his head to hers.

The first touch of his lips stunned her. For she did not only feel it where they touched, but in every fiber of her being. It bounced along her nerves, heating her blood, pimpling her skin. And it overrode any protests she might have made after the initial shock of it. Instead of the curses that should have poured from her, a low moan rose up in her chest.

She had dreamt of this, though she had done her best to deny it, had longed for it though it was never freely admitted. She was forced to face it now. For her body cried out in joy, responding in ways she never knew it was capable. She arched into him, her arms going around his neck. His response was immediate, his hands grabbing at her dress, the bands of his arms dragging her closer.

It was not close enough.

As if he heard her desperate thoughts, his tongue pushed between her lips. The intimacy of it stunned her. For a second she was frozen, unsure what to do. Until his tongue touched her own. It was then she tasted the essence of him, all maleness and spice and warmth. He was delicious. And she could not get enough. Her tongue reached out, twined with his own. Beneath her hands he shuddered. The realization that he was as affected as she hit her then. She had power here.

Fire raced through her limbs, settling in a molten pool in her belly. And lower. Oh yes, it was there, too. She gasped at the feel of it, opening herself to him further. He took advantage, tilting his head, deepening the kiss—dragging her further into the abyss of desire.

His hands were everywhere, roaming her body, bringing her to even greater heights. Strong fingers skimmed down her spine, over her hips, up her ribs until they trailed, feather-light, over the sides of her breasts. And there they stayed. She held her breath as he circled the straining tip. At long last they curved around her, and she was filling his palm.

Undone by the sheer exquisite feel of it, she tore her mouth free, her head falling back in supplication. He followed, his mouth finding the long column of her throat, his lips and tongue laving her sensitive skin. Her breath came in shudders, her hands clutching at the incredible breadth of his shoulders. "Tristan," she whispered.

As if through the haze of a dream she felt him start, sensed him pause. And then he pulled back, the warmth of him leaving her.

She opened her eyes, dazed, the haze of desire slowing her brain. She expected gentleness and smiles. What she did not expect was the look of horror overtaking his face.

"Rosalind, I am so sorry," he rasped. Before she knew what he was about, he rose. With one last long look at her, he turned and disappeared into the lush vegetation. The throbbing of Rosalind's body—and heart—the only proof he had been there at all.

Chapter 12

What had he done? What the hell had he done?

Tristan escaped the house as if the hounds of hell were at his heels. He forgot everything in his haste; hat, gloves, coat…pride. He only knew he had to get as far away from Rosalind Merriweather as he could.

Rosalind. Damn, he had never thought of her in such terms, had always held tight to Miss Merriweather. As if it were a lifeline to sanity. Now her name wound its way around and through him like a creeping vine, twining around his heart, forcing its way into his soul.

He ran a hand through his hair, walking blindly. Damn and blast, what had he been thinking? Had he actually thought kissing her would be a good idea? But she had gotten under his skin, and then had thrown that damn gauntlet, and he had been unable to resist teasing her. Then teasing had turned to daring, had turned to something quite different entirely.

But he was being a coward, to blame her for what happened. For while she had infuriated him, it had been he and he alone that had pushed at the end. He was the one who had not been able to let her comments go, who had brought it to the next level. She had certainly never asked to be kissed. She had been very vocal that she did not want it at all.

But she had responded in the most delicious way, a voice whispered in his head. And with that came a vision of her, head thrown back, skin flushed pink, her little bow of a mouth swollen from his kisses and opened on a gasp.

He groaned and stopped dead in the middle of the pavement. Scrubbing his hands over his face, he fought to erase the image from his mind. But nothing could banish the sweetness of it, nor the remembrance of the breathy sound of her voice moaning his name.

He had to find something to distract him, for it would not do to walk down the street in the aroused state he was in. He peered around, hoping for inspiration. To his surprise he saw he was on Brook Street. And Willbridge's house was two houses down.

In that moment he knew he had never needed his friend more. Willbridge would know what to do about this debacle he had gotten himself into. Or, at least, he would have a stiff brandy he could imbibe to help make the memories of Rosalind and her too smooth skin and delicious mouth a fuzzy memory instead of the active torture it currently was.

And Willbridge's home would provide a safe haven for him for the foreseeable future. The less time he spent at his own home the saner he would be.

But when he entered the house minutes later he found utter chaos. He spied two footmen carrying a heavy trunk down the stairs and knew with a sinking heart that there would be no easy escape from Rosalind and her tempting mouth. For Willbridge was leaving town much sooner than planned.

The man himself appeared then. His face was tense, his copper hair tousled, his cravat askew. He saw Tristan and started.

"You must be a mind reader, for I was about to send you a note," Willbridge said.

"Well, now you have saved yourself a bit of correspondence." Tristan looked up as two maids came hurrying down the stairs, their arms full of hat boxes. "You are leaving town ahead of schedule, I assume? Though," he continued, taking in Willbridge's strange somberness with cautious eyes, "it does not appear to be a pleasure trip."

"No, I'm afraid our visit to Emily and Morley must be postponed. For we have just received word from Frances, Imogen's sister."

"Lady Sumner?" He knew of the woman, of course. Imogen's sister had married the Earl of Sumner years ago, had an infant daughter, and lived a stone's throw from Willbridge's Northamptonshire estate, Willowhaven.

She was also one of the unhappiest women in existence.

It was no wonder. Her husband was a selfish blackguard who was not above using people to get what he wanted, his wife included.

Willbridge nodded. "Yes, I'm afraid we've word from Northamptonshire."

"Their babe is not sick, I hope?"

"No, it is Lord Sumner. The damn fool has gone and hurt himself in a carriage accident."

"Not gravely?"

"Banged up a bit, but nothing serious from all accounts."

Tristan quirked a brow. "Hardly cause for you to go flying back home, then."

Willbridge's lips twisted, though not with amusement. "Unfortunately it seems there is more to the story. Much more." He paused, as if to find the right words. Then, seeing no other way around it, he shrugged and said, "It seems the man was not alone. He was with a woman who was most decidedly not Lady Sumner."

Instantly Tristan understood. "His mistress, eh?"

"Yes. And to make matters worse, the woman did not survive the crash."

"Damn me," Tristan said low. "As if the bastard has not caused enough grief to Lady Sumner."

"Needless to say, Imogen wishes to get to her sister with all haste. Though," Willbridge said, a spark of humor lighting pale gray eyes, "she's more furious than aggrieved over the scandal. I do believe I will have quite a job keeping her from beating the man over the head with one of those gothic novels she's taken a liking to lately. At the very least she will have strong words for him. And coming from Imogen, you can be assured that, quiet as she is, they will be all the more potent for it."

Tristan chuckled. "Have I told you what a brilliant decision it was on your part to marry Imogen?"

"Yes," Willbridge grinned, satisfaction evident in every line of his face, "but you may say it again as many times as you please, for I happen to agree with you wholeheartedly."

Daphne appeared at the top of the stairs then. "Caleb, you are needed upstairs. Oh, Tristan! We did not expect to see you until tonight at Lady Harper's."

"Are you staying in London, then?" he asked as she descended the stairs.

"Of course, silly man. Imogen would not have it any other way, though I did offer to return home with my darling brother."

"Oh yes," Caleb drawled as Daphne joined them, "you were so insistent."

Daphne shrugged. "Do you blame me for wishing to stay? Even though my dearest Mariah will be traveling with Imogen and Caleb, and so I will be quite lonely. Still, I'm certain Lord Poncy will offer for me any day, and I do not want that horrid Glynis Cowper getting the jump on me."

Willbridge rolled his eyes, then turned to Tristan. "I know I told you I don't wish you to keep an eye on her when I leave town, but can you at least see that my sister does not cause too large a scandal?"

Tristan grinned. "I'll do my best. But you know Daphne."

"Yes, I do that," Willbridge muttered darkly before, a rueful smile lightening his face, he shook Tristan's hand and hurried off.

Tristan raised a brow at Daphne as Willbridge strode away. "Lord Poncy now, is it? I thought you had your heart set on Barnaby Noble."

Her lips pushed out in a pout. "Mr. Noble offered for Viola Thorpe two days ago, or haven't you heard? I was quite heartbroken, though you did not notice. But Lord Poncy…" She sighed, her eyes going hazy. "Oh, I'm sure he is the one. So handsome, so attentive."

"So rich and titled," Tristan teased.

"Oh, stop it, you." She slapped at his arm. "But I know you did not come here to tease me, though you do enjoy it so. Tell me, what drove you from your home that you could not even remember to don your outerwear?"

The imp was much too observant. "How do you know the butler did not take them when I arrived?"

"Because the butler is currently upstairs overseeing the packing, you dolt. Out with it, then, for you know I shall not let it go until you spill all."

"Yes, I know," he grumbled. "Fine, I shall tell you. But not here."

Triumph gleamed in Daphne's pale green eyes. "Come into the sitting room. It is empty presently, and you may regale me with whatever spectacular mistake you have made."

Tristan grumbled but followed. It was to her credit that she did not pester him until they were comfortably ensconced. Once he settled his posterior on the settee's plush cushions, however, Daphne was ready for him.

"So tell me, what female has you so turned around?"

He scowled. "How can you be sure it's a female?"

"Because I know you. You have a look about you, all feverish and cold at once. And as far as I know, there is only one thing that causes such a look in a person, and that is thwarted desires."

Tristan gaped at her. "You are barely eighteen and have only just come out. What the devil do you know about thwarted desires?"

"Never mind that," she said in lofty tones. When he continued to gape at her, his expression no doubt colored by the outrage that was quickly overtaking him, she rolled her eyes. "Please, you know me better than that. Do you honestly think I have been promiscuous?"

"Do you mean to tell me you haven't been kissing all these men you have fallen for?"

"Oh, I've kissed a fair few," she said, waving a slender hand in the air in dismissal.

"Daphne!"

"What? Why are you surprised? Especially since you were the first of the bunch to kiss me?"

His face flamed. It was too true, he had fancied her last summer. And he had kissed her. But they had blessedly come to their senses and seen there was nothing between them, nipping it in the proverbial bud.

Besides, if Willbridge heard them talking of it, he'd have his head. Again.

"Anyway," Daphne went on, "kissing is a mere flirtation. It doesn't mean anything."

His mind flew to the kiss he'd shared with Rosalind. He squirmed in his seat. "Or it may mean a whole lot of something," he muttered.

She speared him with a knowing eye. "Is that what has you all feverish then? A kiss that meant something?" When he groaned and put a hand over his face, disgusted that he had let the small tell show, she crowed in triumph, "I knew it! It is a woman. Tell me who."

"Enough, you harpy," he gritted. "I will most certainly not tell you who."

But he could tell by her grin that his refusal would not deter her. "Let me see if I can deduce it. It's more fun that way anyway. You came from somewhere, sans hat, coat, and gloves. And you were close enough to arrive on foot, as I did not hear your horse or carriage arrive. As I know you're a slugabed, and it is still quite early in the afternoon, I don't believe you had time to go anywhere yet. Therefore you came here straight from home. Which means the woman in question was at said home. Was she a visitor of your cousin's?" Before he could so much as open his mouth to beg her to stop, she was off again. "No, I don't believe so. For whoever it was has you quite flustered. Which means she is someone you should *not* have kissed. Which means—" Here she stopped. Her eyes opened wide, her mouth forming a little oval of surprise. "Oh. Oh my goodness, Tristan. Never say it is Miss Merriweather!"

As if his guilt wasn't potent enough, the horror on her face made him feel about an inch tall. Immediately his defenses came to the fore. "I assure you, it was not intentional."

She rolled her eyes. "Oh, so what happened? Did you trip and your lips happened to fall onto hers?"

"I really don't need this right now," he snapped. He rose from his seat.

Her hand on his sleeve stopped him. "I'm sorry. That was not well done of me. Especially as you no doubt came to talk to Caleb about it, and instead you get me and my judgment. Sit and I promise to listen with as unbiased a view as possible."

He scowled but sat all the same. For the truth was, he truly did need someone to talk to. Only now that he had a willing ear, he didn't know what to say.

She seemed to sense his uncertainty. She smiled brilliantly at him. "So," she prompted cheerfully, "you and Miss Merriweather?"

He heaved an exasperated sigh. "No, Daphne, there is no me and Miss Merriweather. Like I said, it was a mistake." He groaned and scrubbed at his face. "A huge, blundering, asinine mistake."

"But if you kissed her, you must feel something for her."

"No." The word came out much too loud. "No," he repeated at a much more normal volume. "There is nothing between us at all. It was done in the spur of the moment." After dreaming of kissing her for more nights than he cared to remember. He flushed and cleared his throat. "Besides, she has been very vocal in her dislike of me."

Daphne pursed her lips thoughtfully. "You know, dislike can be a cover for deeper emotions."

Which was what he had teased Rosalind with. Before he'd gone and kissed her. *Idiot.*

"No," he said, "I'm quite certain she does not have any of the softer emotions for me."

"Did she kiss you back?"

He opened his mouth to respond with a resounding *no*. The word, however, would not come. For she *had* kissed him back. With a surprising amount of passion.

Merely thinking about it was affecting him in the worst way. He shifted in his seat.

Daphne grinned. "I thought so."

"There is nothing between Miss Merriweather and me," he repeated with what he hoped was a goodly amount of force, accompanied by the sternest scowl he could muster.

She only grinned wider.

"Enough," he growled. "Damnation, could this day get any worse?"

"I'm sorry," she said, instantly contrite. "I'm being horrid, and after promising to be completely unbiased. But you must understand my surprise. She isn't at all your type."

"May we please change the subject," he begged.

Daphne seemed to deflate a bit at that. "Very well. I won't say another word." She sat in morose silence for a moment, her fingers picking idly at the brocade cushions, before she straightened, brightening. "But I have just the thing to get your mind off of...ahem, things," she finished lamely when he glared at her. "I know you must be at loose ends seeing Miss Gladstow so happily settled and must be in want of another project. Well, I have one for you, in the form of Miss Henrietta Weeton. She is a shy thing, and from what I hear out for her third Season. If she has not secured an engagement by the summer, I've been told she will be married off to some distant cousin, no doubt a horrible old man with a hump and a wart." She smiled in triumph. "She's exactly what you need to lift you out of your doldrums."

It sounded ideal. Helping Miss Weeton would no doubt take up a good portion of his time, thus helping to distract him from his completely unwelcome desire for Rosalind.

So why did the familiar thrill of the prospect elude him?

He mentally shook himself. Never mind. "I'll do it," he declared to a beaming Daphne.

And hopefully by the time he raised his head from his efforts to pair off Miss Weeton happily, Rosalind and her tempting little mouth would be long gone.

Chapter 13

Rosalind was still in a daze that evening as she hurried to Lady Belham's rooms. She had been unable to look the woman in the eye all afternoon. What had she been thinking? To allow Tristan, her employer's cousin and a rake of the first order, to kiss her?

Her cheeks burned as she remembered the encounter with shocking clarity. Was it any wonder she had avoided Lady Belham?

Now, however, it was time for them to go to Lord Grover's. And she could avoid the woman no longer. Would her employer somehow know what had happened? Would she turn her out on the street?

But no, she told herself fiercely as she knocked on Lady Belham's door, the woman would not see it. Her actions were not printed across her forehead in blazing scarlet. Nor would Tristan have told his cousin. The horror in his eyes had told Rosalind all she needed to know about his feelings on the subject. He had been no more pleased than she had been.

She would not look too closely on why that particular fact was so lowering.

Lady Belham bid her enter then, saving her from further mental torture. "My lady," Rosalind said in as cheerful a voice as she could muster, "are you ready for Lord Grover's party?"

Lady Belham was seated at her dressing table, adjusting a glistening comb of rubies and pearls in her dark locks. She smiled at Rosalind in the glass. "I'm afraid we will be attending quite a different event tonight. I have decided to accept Lady Harper's invitation instead."

How Rosalind managed to keep her smile in place she would never know. Especially as her heart thudded with a disturbing degree of anticipation. For hadn't Tristan told her just that afternoon that he was headed to Lady Harper's himself? "Is that so?" she asked with impressive unconcern.

"Yes. I'm feeling the need for something less tame than Lord Grover's promises to be." She grinned, tugging her bodice down a fraction lower and sitting back to admire the effect.

Rosalind hardly registered the precarious position of the woman's bosom, barely held in by the thin strip of crimson silk and black lace that formed her bodice. All she could see was the heat in Tristan's eyes immediately before he'd claimed her mouth. She could not see him. She was still not in control of her faculties; if she came face to face with him she might very well melt into the floorboards.

Not that she would be able to avoid him forever. Still, every second counted in making sure she held tight to the slippery thing her sanity had become.

"Oh, I don't know that Lord Grover's will be all that tame," Rosalind said as Lady Belham fiddled with her rouge pot. "I hear he has a French chef. That in itself is exciting, don't you agree?"

"My palate is not so sophisticated that I would know the difference, I daresay." Lady Belham applied a bit of rouge to her cleavage, then sat back and looked it over with a critical eye before, nodding with satisfaction, she rose and turned to face Rosalind. "I need some dancing, and some flirting, and what better place is there than a grand London ball?"

How could Rosalind argue that? Still, she could not go down without a fight. "But I am not attired for a ball." It was a flimsy attempt, she knew, yet still she had to try.

Exactly as she knew would happen, Lady Belham quickly laid waste to the excuse. "Oh, pooh. You are perfect. That old gown of mine looks wonderful on you, darling. That shade of violet does wonders for your coloring. Or," she said, pausing, a small frown marring her brow, "don't you care for it?"

Rosalind blanched. "I love it," she hurried to say, aghast that it may have seemed she disliked the dress. "Truly, it is the most glorious gown I have ever owned, and far too generous a gift."

"Nonsense," Lady Belham said with a wave and a smile. "I never wore it, I assure you. It wasn't daring enough for the likes of me." She laughed.

That Rosalind could believe. Even so, it had taken her three nights of sewing to take the gown in and make it presentable. Especially in the bust.

Which, of course, made her think of other things. Such as Tristan's hand cupping her breast, the warmth of his large palm like a brand through the material of her dress that afternoon. She shivered, a strange reaction indeed considering how overheated she suddenly was. No, she thought as she clenched her hands in her skirts, she was definitely not ready to see him just yet.

But did she have a choice? Lady Belham's maid arrived then, and the next few minutes were a whirlwind of preparation as Tessa helped their employer with the rest of her ensemble. All too soon she was done, and they were hurrying downstairs to the waiting carriage.

The time it took to get to Lady Harper's should have been arduously long. Arriving at the most popular events was never an easy thing, and this particular ball was no exception. Yet the time passed as if accelerated. Why was it, Rosalind thought, that the minutes passed by so much quicker when the thing awaiting you at the end of a journey was dreaded? For too soon they entered the Berkeley Square mansion. And the time of her courage was at an end.

They approached the double doors leading to the ballroom. Hundreds of voices reached them then, a wave of sound that made Rosalind's steps falter on the polished parquet floor. The trepidation she had been prisoner to since leaving the house bloomed then into panic. In a last gasp attempt to stall, she blurted, "Wouldn't you like to visit the card room, my lady? Wearing that gown, I'm sure you could easily fleece half the men in London."

Lady Belham laughed. "That's not the type of victory I'm looking for right now, darling. And you needn't worry you will need to play mother hen to me as you did Miss Gladstow. I assure you, I'll be more than fine, no matter what comes of tonight."

"Then I should return home," Rosalind said, a hint of desperation coloring the words. "For surely you will have a much better time if you do not have me to worry about leaving behind."

Lady Belham linked arms with her, dragging her on, securing her fate. "Nonsense, for I quite adore you. Besides," she said, her voice dropping, "it will be nice to have a friend at my side."

The words stunned Rosalind mute for a moment. No, not only the words, though they themselves told all she needed to know about her employer. It was the tone as well. For there was a pain there she had not expected.

Beyond their first meeting, when Rosalind had gotten an inkling of Lady Belham's loneliness, no hint had been given of the woman's lack of confidence. Indeed, she seemed to exude nothing but.

Now Rosalind thought back on the past three days in her employ and realized that the woman didn't have a friend in the world. Oh, she had Tristan. And she had the admiration of more men than Rosalind could count.

But the woman did not have a single female friend. No one to lean on, to talk to, to gain comfort from. Did Lady Belham truly see her as a friend?

Her heart swelled. It had been too many years since she'd had someone to care for. She thought of Guinevere then—of the brilliant, kind, vivacious girl she had been. And it stunned her to realize that there was an amazing number of similarities between her sister and Lady Belham. Both were beautiful, vibrant, dazzling in their exuberance for life. Each like a brilliant shooting star, lighting up the darkness.

Only Guinevere, like that shooting star, had quickly burnt out, swallowed by the darkness when she'd tried to cut her shining path through the world.

She could not bear it if Lady Belham suffered the same fate. Oh, she knew the woman was stronger than Guinevere. She had suffered the death of her husband, after all, had her life uprooted. Still she was here, head held high, ready to jump back into life.

Yet she had let a bit of her vulnerability show tonight, revealing the pain beneath the surface. And now that Rosalind had seen it, she could not possibly ignore it. As implausible as it was, the woman needed her. And if she needed Rosalind to accompany her into a ballroom, where right this minute a particular someone to be avoided at all costs was surely holding court, then so be it.

Squeezing Lady Belham's arm, Rosalind straightened her shoulders and raised her chin. She could do this. She would face Tristan and overcome this strange longing she had for him, then move on. She was stronger than she gave herself credit for. She was no romantic lady, no milk-and-water miss so overcome by emotions that she couldn't see straight. She was Rosalind Merriweather, a level-headed female with common sense in abundance. No man, no matter how devilishly handsome he happened to be, would get the best of her.

They entered the ballroom, and with unfailing accuracy her gaze found Tristan's blond locks. Immediately the butterflies that had taken up residence in her belly fluttered about like mad. She swallowed hard, fear and longing and anticipation tightening her shoulders. Yes, she could do this. But it would not be easy.

· · ·

She is here.

The realization hit Tristan like a punch to the gut. He had thought perhaps he could avoid Rosalind until tomorrow, when he could be assured of a decent night's sleep between him and the massive mistake he had made in kissing her. Or at least, several hours of his typical pursuits to remind him of what life was supposed to be. For it was most assuredly not mooning after a woman who despised him. A woman who made him feel as if his every flaw had been laid bare.

Only now there she was, a veritable vision in a pale purple gown. It hugged her form, the bodice caressing the slight swell of her small breasts, the soft tone setting off the pale porcelain of her skin to perfection.

He recalled then with painful clarity the feel of those breasts in his palm, the warmth and faint weight of them. He groaned.

"Tristan, what in the world is wrong with you?"

He started, looking sheepishly to Daphne. She stared at him in horror, as if he was about to cast up his accounts at her feet. "Sorry," he mumbled.

"That was the most distressing sound I've ever heard from a human." She pursed her lips as she contemplated him. "You aren't ill, are you? Because if you soil my new gown I shall never forgive you."

"No, I am not ill. Now, what were you saying about Miss Weeton?"

"Never mind that." A gleam entered her eye. "You weren't thinking of that little peccadillo with you-know-who, were you?"

He growled. "Daphne…"

"I know you told me never to mention it, but really, you know me better than that."

Rosalind came into view then as she and Grace walked the perimeter of the room. He did his best not to look her way. But Daphne was anything but stupid.

"Ah," she said, her voice a knowing purr, "now I understand."

"If you understand it so well, perhaps you might enlighten me. For I haven't a clue what the devil is going on," he snapped.

Daphne started, her eyes going wide. Instantly he felt an utter arse. She was his friend, and certainly didn't deserve such treatment from him. No matter how annoying her little innuendos might be.

"Damn it, I'm sorry," he muttered. "I'm out of sorts."

"She truly has gotten under your skin, hasn't she?" she said in disbelief.

"It isn't like that," he grumbled.

"But it is. I've never seen you in such a state."

"What you've never seen is me in the throes of guilt after accosting someone in my cousin's employ."

"Then why did you kiss her?"

The very same question had been haunting him since said kiss that afternoon. Why indeed?

"It doesn't matter why."

"But it does," she insisted. "Perhaps..." She seemed to lose courage, but in typical Daphne fashion quickly found it again and plowed on like a runaway carriage, heedless of what damage she might cause. "Perhaps you feel more for her than you're letting on."

He gaped at her. "You think I am coming to care for Miss Merriweather?"

She shrugged. "Why not? Granted, she isn't at all conventional—"

"Conventional?" he let lose a bark of laughter. "No, she isn't that."

"And she doesn't seem the type to capture your interest," she went on as if he had never interrupted her. "Miss Merriweather is a serious kind of creature. I had assumed you would be attracted to a woman with your same spirit."

"I told you before, I am not attracted to Miss Merriweather."

"Tristan," she said, and from the look in her cunning eyes she was about to launch on again. And without Imogen in town to keep her in check, he wasn't at all confident he would be able to rein her in once she started.

"Enough," he said firmly. "I have taken you into my confidence quite against my better judgment. If you continue on, I am never telling you anything ever again. Besides, hadn't you planned on introducing me to Miss Weeton this evening for the express purpose of taking my mind off of...certain things? You are not helping matters at all by being so annoyingly inquisitive."

Her face fell. "Very well," she grumbled. "And I am sorry. I can't seem to help myself. I've never seen you so affected." She held up her hands as he leveled a stern look at her. "Sorry! My lips shall remain sealed on the subject. I swear it. Now, let me fetch Miss Weeton straight away and we shall get you started on your new project."

"You say 'fetch' as if she were a dog bone. Let's go find her together, shall we? That way we may begin my little project all the sooner."

For the sooner he was distracted the better he would be. Though as they wove through the thickening crowd Tristan wasn't convinced there was a distraction on earth capable of helping him forget what Rosalind Merriweather was quickly becoming to him.

Chapter 14

Rosalind's intentions to provide Lady Belham with the companionship she so desperately craved worked beautifully in keeping her occupied. She saw Tristan, but from a distance, and had no trouble focusing on her very important job.

Until, that was, a debonair younger man—who could not keep his eyes from her bosom—approached her employer.

The instant attraction between the two fairly permeated the air with a tangible energy. Lady Belham appeared fifteen years younger. She flirted coyly with the man, tapping him on the shoulder with her fan when he gave her a compliment, used that same fan to draw the man's attention to her endowments. Really, it was fascinating to watch, a veritable art form. And the man responded. When he asked Lady Belham to dance, she accepted readily enough. Before she went off, however, she turned to Rosalind and whispered in her ear, "Best not wait for me, darling. Head on home when you tire of the place and send the carriage back for me later." And with a wink and a grin, she was off through the crowd, clinging tightly to her gentleman's arm.

Rosalind worried her lip as she watched them go, a twinge of disquiet deep in her gut. Lady Belham needed a friend, not an affair.

A moment later and she shook her head. Lady Belham was a grown woman. She knew what she was about. Who was Rosalind to judge her? She was nothing, a mere companion. Yes, the man looked a rake. Yes, Rosalind despised all men like him. But Lady Belham was not some young debutante out on the marriage mart needing to worry over her chaste reputation. She was a widow, with all the freedoms that entailed.

Rosalind buried her disquiet as she watched them dance a touch closer than was proper on the floor and did what she had been bid. Though she certainly didn't need time to tire of the place before leaving. For she hadn't wanted to come in the first place.

Forcing her attention from her employer, she turned for the door. And was fairly slapped with the vision of Tristan across the room, giving a plain young woman The Look.

She had seen the expression before, of course. It was the same he'd used on Miss Gladstow. And it made distrust—and a fair amount of jealousy, though she wouldn't focus on that—swell up in her breast. The man was up to something. Again.

She should head home as she had planned. It was no business of hers what Tristan did with the young woman. But Rosalind found she could not let it go. If something were to happen with that girl, and Rosalind suspected and did nothing to prevent it, she would never forgive herself. Letting loose a long sigh of disgust, she looked around, finding a quiet corner to hide in while she watched the couple. She would stay a short while, ensure Tristan had not planned anything nefarious for the girl, and be on her way. He didn't even know she was here, after all. He would be none the wiser, and she could at least sleep easier tonight.

What she had not taken into account, however, was the assault on her senses as she stared at Tristan. She had spent so much of the evening *not* looking at him, she hadn't realized what it would do to her when she did. The man had the same effect he always did on her, sending her good sense right out the window. Only now she found it had grown much worse in the last hours. For now she knew what it was to be held by him, to be kissed by him. And her body responded. Goodness, but it responded.

She took up her fan, snapping it open and plying it vigorously over her face and bosom. *I am strong*, she repeated silently to herself, a repetition of words she fully believed would sink in if said enough. *I am not a ninny. I am strong. And he is just a man.*

She turned the words over and over in her mind as he fetched the lady a punch. She repeated it fiercely as he smiled, his eyes crinkling and teeth flashing. And she very nearly said it out loud as he gallantly bowed to the woman and led her to the floor for a dance.

She had seen him dance before, of course, in the half dozen times he had taken Miss Gladstow out onto the floor. For a tall man he was ridiculously graceful, the moves of the dance showcasing his trim form to perfection.

But that was before she knew what said body felt like pressed to hers. Now she could admire it in a completely different manner. She plied her fan faster.

The dance was quickly over, the couples dispersing. Rosalind kept her gaze on Tristan, determined not to lose sight of him. He brought the lady to the side of the room and into the company of a young woman Rosalind remembered as being Lady Daphne Masters. After some minutes of polite conversation he was off.

…Leaving Rosalind feeling not a little deflated. She blew out a breath. She had been so sure he was up to no good. Yet his actions bespoke nothing of the sort.

Which was preposterous. She frowned, starting around the perimeter of the room. He was not a benevolent person. He was a rake. Men like him used people, women in particular. They did not cater to the lonely and the shy. They ate them up.

Which, of course, led to thoughts of mouths, and tongues, and other delicious bits that she had recently become acquainted with.

If she hadn't been fairly blinded by such recollections, perhaps she might have seen the man in question lurking by the doors leading to the garden. And perhaps she might have been able to avoid him.

But, through perverse fate, she did not. A hand on her arm jerked her back to the glaring present. "We need to talk," Tristan growled. Without waiting for her to agree, he dragged her out the doors and into the darkness of the night beyond.

The air was cool. Which was a blessing, as Rosalind's skin was decidedly and unexpectedly warm. Especially where Tristan's hand clasped her arm. She pulled from his grasp, before that heat flared into the dangerous inferno from the afternoon.

"You have been watching me."

The accusation came hurtling at her from the shadows. Rosalind's eyes were not yet adjusted to the dimmer light of the balcony. Even so she could see the tense line of Tristan's jaw. "Yes, I have."

He started, having not expected candor. "Why?" he demanded.

"Well, it is certainly not because I wished for more kisses," she snapped, then immediately wished for the ground to open up and swallow her whole.

Through her embarrassment, however, his features were quickly becoming clearer in the indirect light from the ballroom. An unmistakable guilt twisted his lips. "Ah, yes. That." He cleared his throat. "Please allow me to apologize for my actions. I fear I wasn't myself."

That made two of them. But she could not admit that. Instead, face burning, she mumbled, "Please, don't mention it again. We shall forget it ever happened."

"Yes, certainly." He stood awkwardly for a time. Rosalind, seeing it as the ideal opportunity to escape and slink back home, where she could wallow in her embarrassment in peace, gave a jerky kind of curtsy and turned to go. His voice held her back.

"You have not answered my question."

"No, I have not."

Frustration tightened his mouth. "Rosalind," he growled.

The sound of her name on his lips, said in that animalistic way, stole the breath from her body. Furious at herself for her reaction, she went on the attack. "You wish to know why I watched you? You truly wish to know?"

He seemed uncertain in the face of her ire. But he gave a sharp nod, thus unknowingly sealing his fate.

She stalked forward, pointing a finger into his chest. "I know you're up to no good with that young lady. And I won't stand for it."

"Miss Weeton?" He let loose a surprised bark of laughter. "What the devil do you think I'm about?"

"Please," she scoffed. "I know of men like you."

Anger flared, erasing the stunned look in his eyes. "Once again you imply such. I am getting heartily sick of being lumped in with the despicable creatures you liken me to."

"Are you saying you do not have ulterior motives in mind with Miss Weeton?"

He faltered. Triumph—and a surprising amount of disappointment—filled her. "Just as I thought."

He held up a hand. "You have the wrong idea about it all."

"Ha!"

The sound was surprisingly loud. Rosalind glanced around furtively. It was then she noticed how close they were to the open doors of the balcony. And in full view of the glittering throng within.

Grabbing his sleeve, she dragged him farther into the shadows, down the steps leading into the garden, along the side of the house. When she was certain they would not be seen, she rounded on him again.

Only he had followed incredibly close to her. And his body was much too warm, much too large, much too...*Tristan*...in the darkness.

She gasped and stepped back. But her mind was in a tangle now. What had they been talking about? *Ah yes, Miss Weeton.*

"I don't trust you, Sir Tristan. I won't stand by and see that girl ruined."

"I seem to recall you saying something similar about Miss Gladstow."

She ignored the slightly strangled tone of his voice, instead focusing on her outrage. "Yes, I did."

"And what happened with Miss Gladstow? I don't seem to recall any ruination that took place. The opposite, in fact."

It was her turn to falter. Had she forgotten so quickly that Miss Gladstow and Mr. Marlow had become engaged? Tristan had not ruined the girl. Quite the opposite, in fact. For he seemed to have had some part in their engagement coming about.

She stilled. An idea had come to her, but she could not countenance it. No. Surely not. He could not be...matchmaking?

In the faint moonlight Tristan's eyes glittered, shock making him transparent. It was then she realized she had spoken aloud.

And that she was right.

"You are a matchmaker?" she asked, stunned.

He did not answer. But the sudden defensive angle of his chin told her all she needed to know.

Her jaw dropped. "You are. You're playing matchmaker."

His brows lowered. "You make it sound dirty."

"Isn't it?"

"No!" He growled low in his throat. "I swear, you are so stubborn and misguided you would make even a saint's actions seem nefarious."

She laughed, a harsh sound even to her own ears. "Are you likening yourself to a saint then?"

He stared at her in disbelief. "How is it that I can never say the right thing to you, that you can turn even the most innocuous things offensive?"

"I do not think playing with women's lives is innocuous," she retorted.

"I am not playing with them!"

"Is this a hobby for you?" she demanded. "A way to pass the time? You think to use these women to relieve your ennui?"

"No!" he ran a hand over his face. "You don't understand."

"Oh, I assure you, I do," she snapped. "You probably think yourself some benevolent philanthropist, helping the plain and unwanted women of London find their happily ever afters. You cannot begin to think that a woman might find happiness without a man in her life; that she might prefer to be without one of the selfish, entitled males that think nothing of using a woman at will and then discarding her at the first opportunity to heartache and ruin."

He gaped at her. Her anger dissolved instantly to horror. Why had she said so much? He must know now that there was something much deeper at work than a mere dislike of overbearing men. She steeled herself for the questions that must surely come after such an outburst.

But either he was too thick-skulled to put two and two together—complete poppycock—or he chose to overlook it. For he said, his eyes going serious, "I swear to you, I am not playing with these women."

"We shall see about that."

He stilled. "What the devil does that mean?"

"It means," she said, advancing on him, "that I will stick to your side and see that Miss Weeton—or any other woman who comes into your orbit—remains safe, and is not pushed into anything against their will. It means," she said, poking at his chest again, craning her neck to glare up at him, "that you will not be free of me until I see that you do not mean to cause mischief for the sake of merely relieving your boredom—"

He grabbed at her arms. She gasped, suddenly incredibly aware of how close they were, how large and warm his body was in the cool night air. She flattened her palms on his chest, intending to push him away. Instead her fingers curled around the material of his evening jacket, unintentionally strengthening the tether between them.

"Are you certain," he rasped, his breath fanning over her face, "that is something you wish to do?"

Her heart pounded like a drum against her ribs, the strangest lethargy taking over her limbs even as her mind became incredibly attuned to every move he made. She scrambled to make a sensible argument. Instead, all she could manage was, "You won't frighten me away."

"You need to be frightened."

"And you think this is the way to do it?"

His mouth lowered, hovering over hers. Their breaths mingled, rasping, drowning out the faint sounds of music and laughter drifting to them from the ballroom. "I know you liked my kisses, Rosalind," he whispered, and she could almost taste the punch—and something stronger, champagne?—on his breath. "You wanted me. You want me now. I can feel it in the way you tremble beneath my touch, in the way you strain up to meet my lips."

She almost closed the distance between them then. She very nearly pushed up on her toes, pressed her lips to his, answered the deep, primal call that he had awakened in her.

Instead, with incredible will, she released him, tore from his grip, and stumbled back. There she stood, panting, staring with a fair dose of defiance at him.

Not the smartest move, for bathed in pale blue moonlight, he looked like a Greek god of old, caught in stunning marble. Granted one clothed in exceptionally-cut clothing and not a sheet. Which only seemed to enhance his beauty. Drat it.

But she was losing her focus, something she needed in abundance when it came to Tristan.

"I am well able to refuse your advances, as you can see."

He stared at her with growing respect before tugging on his forelock in salute. "So you can."

"And you have not remotely managed to frighten me away. I am stronger than you think, Sir Tristan."

"No, you are just as strong as I think you are," he murmured.

It took Rosalind an amazing bit of effort to ignore the glow of pleasure that undeniable compliment gave her. "If that is true, then you know I have no choice in the matter."

He narrowed his eyes. "I think you forget, Miss Merriweather, that you are employed by my own dear cousin. I daresay you will not have the time to follow me about."

The smug look on his face made her long to slap him. Instead she smiled. "Put nothing past me, sir."

Chapter 15

Put nothing past me, sir.

No, Tristan recalled ruefully as he helped Grace and Rosalind into his carriage the following evening, he certainly wouldn't.

Grace adjusted her skirts, smiling at him as he vaulted inside and closed the door. "I am so glad I changed my plans tonight. Lord Avery's musicale sounds much more diverting than the little dinner party we had planned on attending. Miss Merriweather made it sound quite exciting."

"Did she now?" he murmured, shooting that woman a look. She smiled smugly at him. He tipped his head slightly in acknowledgement of her abilities. He should be furious, of course, should denounce her to Grace as a scheming baggage. But he could not help feeling a grudging admiration. The woman was not one to be trifled with, that was certain.

"So tell me," Grace went on, clearly oblivious to the roiling tension filling the carriage, "is it true Lord Avery is notorious for his singers?"

"Yes." Tristan cleared his throat, focusing with all his might on Grace, doing his best to ignore Rosalind and her self-satisfied grin. "They are all brilliant to a one, of course. His ear for all things musical is exceptional, which is the main draw of his events. His ear for accents, however, is deplorable. It seems anyone can convince him they're from Italy."

Grace chuckled. "Well, if anything the evening shall prove to be enjoyable." She launched into a list of the entertainments she had managed to see during her years in Scotland. Tristan did his best to focus on his cousin and remain unfazed by the watchful miss across from him. No easy task. Rosalind was entirely too pleased with herself. He was now positive that her threats from the past night had not been empty. She would stick to his side like a burr.

The irony of the situation did not elude him. In attempting to find something to distract himself from Rosalind, he had ensured he would be in her company for the foreseeable future.

He briefly considered abandoning the whole project. Miss Weeton was not the only young lady in London, after all, who could use his help. But he knew in his heart he would not. For one, Rosalind's attentions were not limited to Miss Weeton; she had stated quite emphatically that she planned to look out for *any* female he paid attention to. But also, after the short conversation with Miss Weeton last night, he was drawn to her cause. She was sweet and sensitive. And the dreaded cousin her parents were considering marrying her off to should she fail this Season—a distant relation she had met but once as a child—sounded a taciturn brute who would drain all life from her. The girl needed help. He pressed his lips tight. And he would not let Rosalind and her misplaced honor interfere.

They arrived then and, after descending to the pavement, made their way into the brightly-lit townhome. As luck would have it, Miss Weeton and her family were milling about the front hall.

No, he would not give up on the girl. But he did not want to intentionally place her in Rosalind's path. Tristan put his head down, planning on forging ahead straight to the music room and securing their seats. There were enough guests between them and the Weetons that it would not seem suspect to bypass them. Hopefully Rosalind would be too distracted to notice the young lady.

But luck, that faithless hussy, was not with Tristan that night. For Rosalind stopped dead in the middle of the cavernous hall and remarked, in a carrying voice, "Sir Tristan, is that not Miss Weeton, the lady you met last night?"

Several conversations faltered, numerous sets of eyes swinging their way. Miss Weeton's among them.

Seeing no way out of greeting the lady, Tristan forced a smile and guided Grace and Rosalind over. Before they reached the young lady and her family, however, he dipped slightly in Rosalind's direction, saying through gritted teeth in a low, tense voice, "I know what you're about, you minx."

"I know you do," she whispered back. "I also know you absolutely hate it. Which is an added bonus, really."

He choked on a laugh. Really, the woman never failed to surprise him. Granted, most of her surprises were unwelcome in the extreme. Still, he had to give her credit for creativity.

"Miss Weeton," he said with a bow, "it is an absolute pleasure to see you again."

The young woman, a tall, thin creature with severely styled hair pulled back from her pale face, smiled and dipped into a curtsy. "Sir Tristan, the pleasure is mine. I did not know I would see you this evening."

"Oh yes, I never miss Lord Avery's musicales. For though the singer he chooses is always a draw, I never fail to find something else to recommend the occasion to me."

She blushed, her smile widening. In the next moment her mother's elbow connected with her side. She jumped, giving a squawk of surprise. Her delicate blush turned to flaming mortification. "But forgive me, I'm being rude. Please allow me to introduce my parents, Mr. and Mrs. Weeton of Derbyshire. Mama, Papa, this is Sir Tristan Crosby. I met him last evening at Lady Harper's."

Tristan bowed, gifting the girl's parents with his most charming smile. "Your daughter is a lovely dance partner," he said.

Mrs. Weeton blushed and stammered, her husband smiling benignly at his daughter.

And Rosalind's small heel found his foot.

He shot her an annoyed glare. She returned it with an impatient one of her own. Did she think he would forget her? Hardly. He was painfully aware of where she was every minute of every blasted day.

"Please allow me to introduce my cousin, Lady Belham," he said, purposely turning his back on Rosalind, facing Grace on his left. He fought back a grin at the small huff of annoyance behind him.

"Grace, this is Miss Weeton and her parents. I was lucky enough to meet and dance with Miss Weeton last night."

This time Rosalind's shoe connected with his calf with a surprising amount of force. Tristan could take a bit of pain—he had been brought up by his father, after all, who had been stingy with neither the whip nor the cruelty of his words—and would have delayed acknowledging Rosalind forever if he could manage it.

But he was not an uncivilized brute. He turned to Rosalind. "And this is my cousin's companion, Miss Rosalind Merriweather," he muttered.

To his shock, Rosalind stepped forward, holding out her hand to the young lady. "It is such a pleasure to meet you, Miss Weeton. I was most anxious to make your acquaintance, you see, for Sir Tristan has nothing but praise for you."

Miss Weeton stared down at Rosalind as if she were a feral cat about to attack. Eventually she took the proffered hand. "Thank you."

Rosalind did not seem the least bit discouraged by the other girl's less than enthusiastic reaction. "Have you attended Lord Avery's musicale before? I have heard wondrous things about the performances."

"Y-yes." Miss Weeton looked to him in a panic.

"Oh? Perhaps we may sit beside one another. I am not at all gifted when it comes to music, but mayhap you are?"

Tristan couldn't take a moment more. For not only did Miss Weeton look like a startled fawn about to bolt, but he did not think he could keep a straight face were he to allow Rosalind to go on as she was.

"You know, Miss Merriweather, I think it a grand idea that our two groups combine. If Mr. and Mrs. Weeton are not opposed, of course." As the two elder Weetons stammered their delight with the idea, all the while looking cautiously at Rosalind, he flashed a smile and offered his elbow to Miss Weeton. "Shall we go ahead and secure our seats? I'm sure your parents and my cousin would love to become better acquainted. Lady Belham has only recently come from Scotland, you know, where she has lived for close to two decades now," he said, directing his attention to Mr. Weeton. "I hear you have a beautiful property there, and near Edinburgh, which is quite close to my cousin's former estate Manderly Hall, outside of Haddington."

As Mr. Weeton's eyes lit and he began to ply Grace with all manner of questions, Tristan guided Miss Weeton away. But not before he caught Rosalind's frustrated glare. Smiling in triumph at her, he turned his back and moved off through the crowd.

• • •

The man was insufferable. She knew she must have thought it before, but now she truly *meant* it, with every fiber of her being.

Rosalind sent a covert glare his way. He didn't see it, blast him, seated as he was half the row away, beside Miss Weeton. Yes, the man had taken advantage of the seating, and seen to it that not only was Lady Belham placed between them, but Mr. and Mrs. Weeton as well. Not a hard thing to do. For after discussing their Scottish properties, it had been discovered that the Weetons and Lady Belham shared several acquaintances. This led to an involved discussion that carried them beyond the front hall, through the hallways of the stately home, and into the sage and cream opulence of the music room.

Rosalind had glowered and seethed her way through the entire ordeal. For how was she to get into Miss Weeton's good graces if she could not have access to her? Yes, she had come off a bit strong upon their introduction. And yes, she had much ground to make up if she was to befriend the girl. But she could not very well do that from where she was.

As Tristan well knew.

As if she had called to him, he lifted his head and looked her way. She had the childish urge to stick her tongue out at him. Instead she speared him with a stern glare that she hoped conveyed her thoughts on his little manipulation of the seating arrangements.

Her message must have come across loud and clear. For he grinned in that unrepentant way of his that never failed to set her teeth on edge.

She didn't care how beautiful the singing was, she thought sourly, this evening could not end soon enough.

When the performance finally ended, Rosalind stood up with alacrity, ready to pounce on Miss Weeton and make her like her. Yes, she had botched things up horribly already. But really, it couldn't be that difficult. Look how easy it was for that bounder Tristan, after all.

But already he was guiding the girl away, no doubt in search of refreshments. She let loose a little growl of frustration.

"I say, Miss Merriweather, are you well?"

Rosalind gasped and spun around. "Oh! Mr. Carlisle. I did not expect to see you here. Is your father well?"

He smiled warmly at her. "He seems to be improving, thank you. And so he has sent me from the house to enjoy a night on the town. How did you like the performance?"

"It was lovely," she replied automatically. Yet she realized in that moment that she hadn't truly heard a bit of it. She knew the singing had been beautiful. She also knew the soprano, though she had made herself somehow appear young and vivacious, had to be sixty years if she was a day.

If the woman ever found it difficult to find a job singing, she could certainly make a fortune selling her beauty secrets to the women of the *ton*.

But if one were to ask her opinion beyond that, she would be hard pressed to answer with any certainty. All because of a devilish rake that seemed to enjoy making her life difficult.

But perhaps Mr. Carlisle would prove what she needed to lay waste to Tristan's plans. She lifted her fan, working it over her face until a brisk wind started up. "Is it over warm in here, do you think?"

As expected, he looked instantly concerned. "Perhaps you are in need of refreshment. Shall I fetch something for you?"

She graced him with a look that suggested he was the most brilliant man in existence. At least, she hoped that was what it conveyed.

For it certainly would not do for him to see the self-satisfied cunning she currently felt at knowing he was falling right into her plans.

"A refreshment sounds ideal. Though perhaps," she continued, taking a quick peek at Lady Belham to assure herself she was engaged, "I may join you in the search? Sitting still so long makes me anxious."

He nodded graciously, guiding her out of the row and through the busy room. "You know," he mused as they circumnavigated a group of matrons, "I cannot help noticing that you are quite different from your sister, in more ways than one. For if I remember correctly she was not so fond of exercise."

Rosalind laughed quietly, her hand going to her locket as it always did when she thought of her sister. "You are right in that. She preferred travelling in a carriage to walking any distance. I recall on one occasion we were to visit a family a mere quarter mile away. She insisted on the carriage being readied, though it took a full three quarters of an hour to prepare, rather than to walk ten minutes to our destination."

"That does sound like her." He chuckled, before sobering. "I truly am sorry she is gone, you know. She was a wonderful person and did not deserve to have her life cut so short."

The burn of tears was not from grief this time, but happiness. It stunned her. She had been focused so long on the bad, she had quite forgotten to think of the good. "Thank you," she replied with feeling.

They entered the hallway where guests were mingling. Mr. Carlisle immediately flagged down a footman, taking up two glasses of champagne. She took hers gratefully, all the while scanning the surrounding area for Tristan. Where the devil was he?

"Shall we head this way, then?" she asked her companion. Before he could answer, she started off down the hall. Mr. Carlisle she assumed trailed behind. She wasn't quite certain, for she never looked back to check. She was much too busy scanning the heads that towered above her, peering into the rooms on either side, trying with all her might to find that telltale pale hair.

When she had begun to give up and head back to the music room and her employer, she spotted him in the entrance hall. She strode across the gleaming floor, stopping not a foot from him. "Sir Tristan, Miss Weeton." She smiled and curtsied.

He looked at her as if she were demon spawn from hell. "Miss Merriweather. You are not with my cousin?"

"Very astute of you," she said archly, biting back a smile as he glowered. "As you can see, I have run into Mr. Carlisle, and he was kind enough to escort me to refreshments, for I was so very parched."

She turned to indicate the gentleman. To her surprise he was nowhere to be seen. Flushing hot, for she must have lost him in her eagerness, she was about to return her attention to Tristan when she caught sight of Mr. Carlisle pushing through the crowd and hurrying toward her.

He grinned at Tristan. "Miss Merriweather has led me on a merry chase, but I have caught up with her. Never knew a woman who moved so fast. Good to see you again, Sir Tristan."

"And you Carlisle." Tristan made introductions all around. "And this is my good friend Lord Kingston," he finished, indicating a swarthy, incredibly tall man she had previously overlooked. "We were at school together."

"Lord Kingston," Rosalind acknowledged, eyeing the newcomer with suspicion. Was Tristan planning on using his matchmaking skills to bring together Miss Weeton and this man? For he had all the indications of being the worst kind of rake.

He cemented those suspicions a moment later as he bowed over her hand and winked roguishly. "Miss Merriweather, it is a pleasure."

She scowled mightily at him, transferring that scowl to Tristan as the other man returned his flirtatious attentions to Miss Weeton.

"What?" he whispered to her as Mr. Carlisle joined in the other couple's conversation.

"You are planning on matching Miss Weeton with that...that... *libertine*." Her lip curled on the last word, as if it were the worst curse. Which to her, she supposed, it was.

"There is nothing at all wrong with Rafe."

Her mouth dropped. "Rafe? His name is *Rafe*? You cannot be serious."

He actually had the audacity to roll his eyes. "Rafe is short for Rafael, a completely normal name."

But their frantic whispering was beginning to draw odd looks from the others. She forced a smile. She did not need Miss Weeton to think any worse of her. "We will discuss this later," she hissed through gritted teeth.

"Highly doubtful," he mumbled back before redirecting his charming persona to the threesome.

"Challenge accepted," she muttered.

• • •

"We have a discussion to continue, if I remember correctly."

Tristan did not bother biting back his groan. He briefly considered turning right around and heading out of his study. He had alcohol in other rooms, after all. Rooms that did not contain the very distracting, very maddening presence of Miss Rosalind Merriweather.

But he refused to allow her to see how deeply she affected him. Without even a glance her way, he went to the small table in the corner and poured himself a drink. "You should be in bed, you know."

"As should you," she quipped. *Of course.*

He threw back the drink, feeling the burn of the whiskey straight to his gut, before pouring himself a second glass. "Would you care for some?" he asked in a casual manner, his tone a far cry from the way he truly felt.

There was a pause before she replied, with false bravado, "Yes, please."

He poured a second glass before, picking both drinks up, he turned to go to her. There was a small fire lit in the hearth, the butler being fully aware of his propensity to visit his study for a drink after a night out. It was a low-burning thing, but enough to give a golden glow to Rosalind's skin where she sat curled up in one of the overstuffed leather chairs placed before it.

It was such a homey scene. Rosalind was wrapped in a simple cotton dressing gown, her feet tucked beneath her like a child's, her dark hair in a thick plait over one shoulder. The firelight caught in the strands, giving them a burnished glow. His chest ached from looking at her.

He realized in that moment that the desire he suffered for her was nothing compared to this. For this was longing, plain and simple. Yes, he wanted her body. He'd known that for weeks. But this was so much more. He wanted *her*. In his home, waiting for him at night, in his bed in the mornings.

He started so violently he nearly lost the contents of the glasses in his hands.

Tristan was not like many of the men in his position. He was not opposed to love or marriage by any means. In fact, he would dearly love to fall for someone, to make a life with that person.

But not Rosalind. Not the one person in this world who seemed to see through him, who made him feel as if he could do no right. The one woman who saw the scared boy within that he had worked so hard over the years to bury.

He had spent years denying that child who had tried so hard to please and had failed in every way, building himself up beyond himself and into the man he was. He was not about to give his heart to a woman who made him doubt the purging of those sad memories.

She sensed his hesitation then. He could see it in the deepening of those lines between her brows, in the slight tilt to her head. To stave off the questions that were surely taking shape in that too-busy mind of hers, he hurriedly handed her one of the glasses and sat down opposite her.

"Now," he said, holding his glass before him like a talisman against the pull of her, "you were saying something about continuing our discussion?"

"Yes." She cleared her throat, swinging her feet to the ground and sitting forward. He thought it would bring him relief, the businesslike mien she had taken. To his dismay, it did the opposite. For her dressing gown gaped in the front, showing the demure nightgown beneath, making him realize how little she was wearing.

Blessedly she was completely unaware of the torture he was in. "What in the world are you thinking, trying to match Miss Weeton with Lord Kingston?"

"And what is wrong with Lord Kingston?"

She rolled her eyes so violently he was surprised they did not roll right out of her head. "Oh, please. I saw the man."

"And?"

"And? And he is a rogue. He will not think twice about ruining her, breaking her heart, destroying all the happiness in her."

He looked closely at her. For there was entirely too much passion, too much knowledge hidden in those words for them to be prompted by a mere opinion garnered from gossip and assumption. And it was not the first time she had given this tell. "What happened to make you feel this way?"

She stiffened, her fingers tightening around her glass. "Nothing," she muttered, sitting back.

Her expression was once more shuttered. He took a sip of his drink, watching her over the rim, letting the warm slide of the liquor travel down to his stomach before speaking again. "Then you have no reason to think badly of my friend."

"I have every reason to think badly of him."

"Do you know him then?"

She hesitated. "No," she admitted with reluctance.

"Have you heard rumors about him? A firsthand account of his debauchery?"

"No." This time through tightly gritted teeth.

He shrugged. "I rest my case."

She sat forward again, her eyes blazing. "You rest nothing. I know what he is."

For the first time in the exchange, anger began to stir in his breast. "Take care, for he is a friend of mine. I will not hear him disparaged."

But she was apparently too angry herself to see how close he was to losing his temper. "Speaking the truth is not disparaging. Men like him think of nothing but their own pleasure. Women are playthings to them, nothing more."

He slammed his glass down on the side table, the sound like a shot. She jumped, her eyes going wide as he sat forward. "You have said similar things of me, Rosalind. Tell me, do you think I am a beast as well? Do you think I am unable to control myself, that I would use a woman for pleasure and then abandon her to pernicious fate?"

For once, uncertainty seemed to take hold of her. And yet, being Rosalind, she would not give up her argument with any grace. "I—I couldn't say."

Damn stubborn woman. The anger that sat slumbering in his breast came roaring to life then. "If I was that creature," he snapped, "I assure you, you would not have walked away from our kiss in the garden with your innocence intact. For the very last thing I wanted to do in that moment was to stop kissing you. Even now, as maddening as you are, I want nothing more than to take you in my arms."

Too late he realized what he had let slip. Her lips, those deliciously full lips of hers, parted in shock. He closed his eyes as mortification washed over him. Surely she would rant and rave at him for that. Goodness knew he deserved it.

But she did not. Instead a disconcerting silence reigned. Finally he could take it no more. Without looking her way—for he could not bear the censure in her gaze—he rose and spun about, heading for the door.

Her voice, soft and trembling, stopped him.

"Why did you tell me that?"

He stood frozen for a moment, struggling to understand it himself. "Damned if I know," he managed before striding from the room.

Chapter 16

By the next morning Rosalind had nearly managed to convince herself that Tristan's confession had been a ruse. He wanted to distract her, she reasoned, to throw her off the scent of his plans for Miss Weeton. He was much smarter than he let on, after all. He'd seen that she would not let it go, would make his life a living hell in order to keep Lord Kingston from the girl.

Yet there was a small kernel of doubt in her, like the faintest pinprick of light on the darkest night. What if what Tristan had said had been nothing but the barest, most raw truth? What if he truly did want her?

And if so, why the devil hadn't he acted on it?

For, as appalling as the realization was, she had been deeply affected by his words. She knew that, if he had so much as touched her, she would have been lost to him. She would have given him everything he'd asked for.

It was that realization that had kept her awake all last night, that had her dodging him throughout the day. Not only because she should have been the last person to fall for a rake's charms, but because he must have seen it in her. She had always been appalling at hiding her feelings. Her loose tongue had made that a certainty. But she also knew that her eyes often gave her away on the rare occasions her mouth did not. Her father used to love to tease her on it, claiming she would never be able to make a living at the tables.

Ironic, that, considering it had been his own losses at the tables that had put her in the situation she was in now.

But if Tristan had seen how she'd wanted him, why had he not taken advantage of the situation? Isn't that what men like him did? They used women and discarded them like so much refuse.

Yet he hadn't so much as touched her. And for the life of her she couldn't figure out why. For if that small yet glowing part of her was correct, and he had voiced his true feelings on the matter, then her opinion of him thus far was wrong.

Which, of course, meant it was quite possible that everything she believed about men like him was wrong. And she could not comprehend such a thing. Not after it had ruled her life as it had for nearly a decade.

Blessedly, when she did see him later that night, he proved immediately that he could not have possibly told her the truth regarding his desires for her. For never had a man looked less thrilled to be in a woman's presence than he did when she descended the stairs with Lady Belham for their planned evening out.

"Grace," he said, all warmth and smiles as he moved forward to kiss his cousin on the cheek, "you look stunning. You will put every other lady there to shame."

As Lady Belham laughed at his flattery, he turned to Rosalind. Immediately his smile faltered, his eyes skimming over her face and coming to rest somewhere above her right ear. Rosalind fought the urge to reach up to verify she didn't have something offensive sprouting from the side of her head, so distasteful was his expression.

"Miss Merriweather," he said with unconcealed reluctance.

And that was that. He offered his arm to Lady Belham, forcing Rosalind to trail behind them as they exited the townhouse and climbed into the waiting carriage.

"I must say," Lady Belham said, adjusting her skirts to make room for Rosalind on the plush bench, "I truly enjoyed last night, Tristan. Lord Avery's musicale was wonderful, a feast for the senses. I can see why they are highly acclaimed."

"I'm glad you joined me," he replied. The carriage started forward with a gentle rocking. "I did not expect to have your company."

"Miss Merriweather does seem to have the most intuitive knowledge of what amusements I will find enjoyable," Lady Belham replied. "I'm of a mind to give her free rein with my schedule." She chuckled, patting Rosalind's hand with affection.

Rosalind pierced Tristan with a look. Surely he would not ignore that. He never seemed to be able to pass up a chance to torment her.

But beside a slight tick in the muscles of his jaw there was no reaction at all from the man. He kept his eyes focused with impressive intensity on Lady Belham. It was like his cousin had not spoken of Rosalind at all. As if Rosalind was not even there.

A small devil seemed to perch on her shoulder then. Narrowing her eyes, she said, "Sir Tristan is the one with the intuition, I think. I am merely following suit. Though you must be happy, Sir Tristan, to be in company so often with your cousin."

He did not even flick a glance her way. Instead he leveled a smile on Lady Belham. "It is true that I am happy to escort you about. It was my fondest wish when you first told me you would be joining me in London that we would be able to spend some time together. We got that chance so seldom when you were at Manderly Hall."

"And yet you will not stop hounding me about my housing prospects," she teased.

"Only because I believe you will be much happier to have a home of your own. You lived so long under Belham's watch, you must be excited to have a place where your taste and spirit can be indulged."

"That I would," she mused, a melancholy look entering her eyes. It cleared quickly enough, turned to a teasing twinkle. "That does not mean I am in a hurry to leave your glorious company. Unless you wish to be rid of me?"

Once again that small devil whispered in Rosalind's ear. "It's not you he wishes to be rid of, my lady. I do believe Sir Tristan would be happy to see me gone with all haste."

The blunt statement rang through the confines of the carriage. Finally Tristan's gaze settled on her. Yet instead of denouncing her claim, as he would typically do, he merely stared at her with those blue eyes of his that told her he agreed with her wholeheartedly.

She swallowed past the surprising lump of hurt that settled in her throat.

Lady Belham laughed. "Miss Merriweather, you do know how to lighten the mood. It is why I adore having you about so."

She went on talking, but Rosalind heard not a word. Instead she was held captive by Tristan's gaze. Finally he turned to answer his cousin, releasing Rosalind from the prison of his unnerving stare.

Rosalind's face burned so she directed her attention to the passing scenery, letting the two cousins converse. Why had she spoken? Why had she purposely drawn his attention? She should be happy he was leaving her be. She was merely a paid companion, after all, certainly not his equal in station nor circumstance. She was not here to enjoy the evening, but rather to keep her employer company.

But perhaps if she had not already been the recipient of Tristan's polite, gentlemanly ways, perhaps if she had not known what it was to be treated with deference by him, it would not sting as much as it did now. And she realized in that moment that, though he had not been required to, he had not treated her as one would a servant. No, he had treated her as if she was on the same level as him, as if she belonged to his world. It was not something she had experienced in all her time in service. And it made her homesick in the worst way.

They arrived then. Rosalind forced herself back to the present. No good could come of thinking of the past. Or of pining for the attentions of a man who she had no intentions of being friendly with in the first place. It was time to focus on her job.

She managed to do so beautifully. For all of five minutes. She stuck to Lady Belham's side like a burr, helping her with her outer things, seeing she was seated in a prime spot, securing her a drink. She might have gone on doing a proper good job for the remainder of the evening.

...Had she not spied Tristan and Lord Kingston making their rakish way toward Miss Weeton.

That was the only adjective she could think to use. She narrowed her eyes as she watched them. There was an easy grace to the way both men moved, a kind of loose-limbed surety. There was no doubt in either of their minds that they would be welcomed by the young lady, no doubt that anyone they wished to talk to in that infernal room would greet them with joy.

And, as suspected, Miss Weeton and her parents were only too happy to have them join their small group. The quintet soon fell into happy conversation and remained that way for the next quarter hour.

Rosalind seethed the entire while. Could the girl's parents not see what a danger those two men were to their daughter? Did they not comprehend what they were about? Men like them did not pursue shy debutantes without ulterior motives in mind.

"Darling," Lady Belham murmured, "I do think I'll take myself off to the ladies' retiring room."

Rosalind started guiltily. She had only given the barest attention to her employer since her watch on Tristan and his unsavory friend began. Lady Belham had fallen into conversation with an older gentleman when they'd first arrived, but the man was gone now. How long ago had he left? Damn, but she was the worst companion in the history of the world, to ignore her employer so completely.

"Do you wish for me to accompany you?" she asked, desperate to make up for her inattention.

"No need. For what I have to do does not require company." With a wink and a grin Lady Belham was off, threading through the growing crowd, disappearing out into the hall.

Rosalind sighed morosely. If she wished to keep her position she had better start focusing on her duties rather than worrying about what one handsome baronet was up to.

She clasped her hands in her lap and purposely turned her head to the side, assuring herself Tristan was nowhere in her line of sight. She would not have the man lose her a second position. Granted, it was her own fault this time, for she could not seem to put him from her mind. But still.

Time passed slowly. More than once she glanced to the small clock above the mantle. At five minutes she began to grow restless. At ten, she began shifting in her seat. And at fifteen she had to battle with herself to keep from turning her head. Her neck began to ache, her eyes to strain as she focused with all her might on the decorative carvings that adorned the massive marble fireplace beside her. She would not look at Tristan, would rather die than lose this battle.

But when the hands of the clock moved past the twenty-minute mark, concern reared its head. For it came to her in a flash that Lady Belham had still not returned.

She frowned. No, surely she could not have been gone that long. But the hands of the clock did not lie. Rosalind stood and marched for the door. Mayhap Lady Belham was in some distress. She'd best check on her straight away.

She hurried down the hall and quickly found the small room set aside for the ladies. But once within, Lady Belham was nowhere to be found.

"Excuse me," she said to the young maid stationed there, "but has Lady Belham come this way? She is tall, with black hair, wearing a sapphire blue gown."

"Yes, miss," the maid piped up with a grin, looking up from her kneeling position as she hemmed with quick fingers an elderly woman's gown. "That is, she was here, oh, about twenty minutes past. Left right quick, though."

"Thank you," Rosalind murmured, her brow puckering as she turned back toward the door. Where had Lady Belham gone?

So distracted was she, she stepped out into the hallway—and nearly ran Miss Weeton over.

"Oh! I am terribly sorry, Miss Weeton. I was not looking where I was going. I was searching for Lady Belham and have been unable to locate her."

The young lady dipped her head, an embarrassed flush spreading over her cheeks. "Please think nothing of it. And if you are looking for Lady Belham she has just returned to the drawing room."

Relief poured through Rosalind. That at least answered that, though where her employer had been for nearly half an hour was still a mystery. But as Miss Weeton made to go around her Rosalind stepped in her path, halting her. She might not get another chance like this to befriend the girl. She had better take advantage of their chance meeting.

"It is so lovely to see you again," she said with warmth. "It was such a pleasure to meet you at Lord Avery's. Are you a great fan of music?"

Miss Weeton looked at her with uncertainty. "Yes, I suppose I am."

"I love it as well, though I have no talent for instruments. Do you play?"

"Yes."

"And what is it you play?"

"The pianoforte."

Again the girl tried to go around her. Again Rosalind stepped in front of her.

"And what composer do you favor?"

She had hoped that, by giving the girl an encouraging smile and asking after her likes, she might draw her out. But if anything her expression became more closed off, tense. "I don't rightly know," Miss Weeton gritted.

Rosalind stopped herself from growling her frustration. Really, why could the girl not meet her halfway? She was being nothing but pleasant. Pasting on another bright smile, she tried again. "But surely you have a preference. Or mayhap you prefer older country tunes? Or something with a religious bent?"

"Miss Merriweather," the girl burst out, with more passion than Rosalind had ever seen from her, "would you please move. For I need to access the retiring room."

At once the folly of what she had done came crashing down on her. Goodness, here she had been intent on befriending the girl, and instead she had forced the girl to stand in discomfort. Her face going hot, she quickly stepped to the side.

Miss Weeton, polite girl that she was, nodded her thanks, and then sprinted through the door, slamming it closed behind her.

Foolish woman, Rosalind silently berated herself. For if the girl had not wanted to be friends before, she certainly would not now.

Not after that bit of embarrassment. She turned for the drawing room, feeling much like a dog scurrying back to safety with its tail between its legs, when the sight at the other end of the hall froze the very blood in her veins, then immediately heated it to boiling.

For Tristan stood there, staring at her with blatant horror.

Pulling her shoulders back, she marched forward. But that same devil that had perched on her shoulders earlier in the evening performed an encore, for she could not pass Tristan by without muttering acidly, "Are you happy, you cretin?"

"Not in the slightest, Miss Merriweather."

The answer was said so gravely, she stopped and glared at him. "Talking to me again, are you?"

Instantly his expression shuttered. "I would think you could guess why I have acted the way I have this evening."

"And I would think you could guess that your change in attitude toward me would bring up unwanted questions as to its cause. Something I have no wish to happen, as I like this position and have no wish to lose it."

She didn't know what made her say it. She was certainly better off having him ignore her. For when she received his full and direct attention she tended to make the most bumbling, idiotic mistakes imaginable. *Like letting him kiss you senseless.* She hurriedly quieted the small voice in her head. She should apologize, should let it be. For hadn't she wanted more than anything for him to leave her alone?

Before she could open her mouth, however, he spoke. "You are right, of course. I seem to forever be making mistakes where you are concerned."

The comment was so heartfelt, so genuinely frustrated, she was struck dumb. Flustered beyond bearing, knowing she only had to get away from him as soon as possible before things became even stranger between them, Rosalind ducked her head and hurried past him. Not knowing if she had won a battle or made the biggest mistake of her life.

• • •

Tristan had sent his valet off to bed and was about to shrug out of his dressing gown, climb between the sheets, and attain blessed sleep. He needed that oblivion, troubled as he was by his confrontation with Rosalind earlier in the evening.

As his hands went to the silk tie of his dressing gown, however, his eyes fell on the two small miniatures he kept on his mantle. They were the only family portraits he had in his home. The first showed a young woman barely of age, a gentle smile curving her lips. His mother. Married at sixteen, a mother at seventeen, dead a mere five years later. She had not lived long past the painting of the picture. The very sight of it brought him pain. But she had been forgotten by everyone else, his father especially, who had done everything in his power to erase every reminder of his first wife from his life after her untimely passing. Including pushing his son away, doing everything but disowning him.

The other portrait was of Grace. She too was smiling, young and innocent and eager for her life to start. That had been before she'd been married off against her wishes to a man twice her age, forced to live far from everything she'd ever known. It had not been a happy union, Tristan knew, though she had made the best of it, had even become friends of a sort with her husband after a time. He had thought her coming to London after her year of mourning was up was an ideal plan. She had always thrived in a lively, vibrant atmosphere. And they could finally spend more than a few weeks at a time with one another, out from under the stern eye of her husband. He'd thought she might find happiness here.

Now he wondered.

For though he had been focused on Rosalind and her failed attempts to befriend Miss Weeton and the muck-up he'd made— yet again—in dealing with her, he had been distantly aware of something seeming very off about Grace. She had appeared pensive most of the night, more subdued than she typically was. But now that he thought on it, there had been moments of melancholy since her arrival. And then hiring Rosalind on? His cousin was a kind woman. When Rosalind came to her asking for work she would have helped her in some way. But she seemed to genuinely need the other woman's presence, relied on her in a way he had never expected. Was she unhappier than she was letting on? Without a second thought, he retightened the sash and hurried from his room on bare feet.

His cousin answered his knock cheerfully enough. But she was not in bed as he expected her to be when he entered her room. Rather, she was at her desk, a letter smoothed open before her on the shining top. When she saw him she took it up and folded it, hiding it away in a side drawer.

"Have you come to tuck me in and kiss me on the head and bid me sweet dreams?" she teased, turning in her seat to face him.

"I might, if you were not a year older than me. And if I didn't expect you to kick me in the shins."

She chuckled as he pulled up a chair close to her and sat. "Well, I know you must have come here with a purpose in mind. Out with it, darling, for you keep me in the most acute suspense."

Nothing but the bluntest words would do for Grace. And so he said, without even the slightest pause, "Are you happy in London?"

She blinked. "Goodness, what brought this about?"

He blew out a breath. "London is a far cry from what you're used to, Grace. You have lived nearly half of your life quietly at Manderly, surrounded by picturesque moors. Before that you lived with your parents, an uneventful life in the country."

Her smile became strained. "And you know full well that was not a life I would have chosen. I have always wished for the vibrancy of a big city, the life and noise and excitement."

"What we want and what we need are often two very different things," he replied quietly.

She cut a hand through the air, her lips pressing in a thin, unforgiving line. "Enough. Where did this come from, Tristan? For something must have spurred on this particular concern."

He leaned back in his chair, crossing his arms over his chest. "We know each other better than anyone, cousin. And I know you have not seemed entirely happy since your arrival."

She arched one inky eyebrow. "I would remind you that I am a widow now, and thus have a perfectly good reason for being melancholy at times, but you are fully aware of that fact."

"And I would remind you that your husband, who you barely tolerated, died over a year ago." He peered closely at her. "But it is more than that. Over the course of the last two nights it has become more pronounced. What is it, Grace?"

She seemed to deflate before his eyes. Her gaze dropped to her lap, where her elegant fingers plucked mercilessly at her dressing gown. "Mayhap it was remembering Scotland and Manderly so clearly," she mumbled.

He frowned, thinking back, before lighting on her meaning. "You refer to the Weetons?"

She shrugged, her eyes still on her hands. "As you said, I've lived there half of my life. Talking of it with them, remembering all that was good about it, made me a touch homesick."

He leaned forward and took her hand in his. She gripped his fingers tight, her knuckles going white.

"I admit I did not give a thought to how difficult such a move must be to you. I know you went about in society as often as you could. Yet it cannot compare to what you have been thrown into since you arrived."

She frowned. "That's not it at all. It's just…different, is all."

He watched her for a time before asking quietly, "Do you want to return?"

Her eyes did meet his then, the surprise in them evident. "To Manderly?" She laughed, but there was no humor in the sound. "No, Tristan, I do not want to return there."

"Perhaps there is a part of you that truly wishes to." When she opened her mouth, no doubt to give him a proper set down for being so pig-headed, he held up a hand. "Will you promise to think on it at least? I have no wish to lose you back to the North, but I also want you to be happy, Grace. Consider it, will you?"

For a moment she tensed, and he thought she might give him a blistering set-down for presuming so much. But then she blew out a long breath and slumped in her seat. "Very well, I will think on it. I know you only want what's best for me. Though you can be assured I will not change my mind. You are stuck with me, you know."

He grinned. "I would not mind that in the least." But as he kissed her on the cheek and rose to leave, he thought about Rosalind. If Grace remained, so would her companion.

Panic filled him at the very thought of being forced into company with Rosalind for weeks, months…years, even. But liberally laced with that panic was an acute pleasure.

He had to find Grace a home of her own. And the sooner the better.

Chapter 17

Nearly a week later and Rosalind was no closer to befriending the very shy, very skittish Miss Weeton.

She had not been short on opportunities—nor the drive to succeed—but there was always something that seemed to go wrong. Such as the punch she spilled on Miss Weeton's hem during one unforgettable ball. Or the stumble she'd taken in the park, propelling her into Miss Weeton and nearly sending the poor girl arse over head into the bushes. Or when she'd suggested Miss Weeton play after dinner one evening, not knowing the paralyzing fear public performance had on her.

Really, she thought morosely as she hurried to Lady Belham's room for their afternoon walk, if awards were being given out for tormenting the poor girl, Rosalind would have received a number of medals by now.

And then there was Lady Belham herself. For she seemed to be plagued at times by low spirits. That and her growing tendency to eschew Rosalind's company had begun to prey on Rosalind's mind. What did it mean? Did Lady Belham mean to let her go?

To her relief, Lady Belham appeared in good spirits today. As Rosalind entered she gave her a glowing smile and motioned to the two pelisses her maid Tessa was holding out.

"Which one of these do you think goes with my gown, Miss Merriweather?" Lady Belham asked.

"The pale cream, I think," Rosalind answered. "It is a beautiful contrast to the amethyst of your gown and makes your dark hair even more striking."

Lady Belham smiled in delight, letting Tessa help her on with the pelisse before turning to admire herself in her looking glass. "Miss Merriweather, you are a gem. You truly have an eye for these things."

"Thank you, my lady. Are you ready? Shall we be off?"

Lady Belham's face fell. "Oh, but didn't I tell you? I had planned on a solo outing this afternoon."

Rosalind's heart dropped to her stomach. "Are you certain, my lady?"

"Oh, yes." Lady Belham tugged on her gloves, holding them out to Tessa to be secured, and sent a smile Rosalind's way. "Relax this afternoon, darling, and I'll see you when I return."

Rosalind left the room as her employer busied herself with her bonnet. She shouldn't fret over it, she told herself as she returned to her room to drop off her things. It was nothing. So the woman was enjoying some time alone. It certainly didn't mean Rosalind was not wanted.

But a creeping voice inside of her warned that it could very well mean Rosalind was no longer *needed*. Which was a death knell for companions. For if Lady Belham decided she could do without her, where did that leave Rosalind?

She had often feared losing her position in the past. And with Mrs. Gladstow that had been a daily concern, a constant ball in the pit of her stomach that could not be eased.

Now, however, it was more than the position she feared losing. It was Lady Belham herself. For Rosalind cared for the woman much more than she ever dreamed she could. It was almost like having Guinevere back.

She did not know what she would do if she lost that now.

Much soberer than before, Rosalind emerged from her room after a time and descended to the first floor. She would escape to the library and forget her troubles in a book.

But as she wandered down the hall that led to Tristan's study she heard his deep voice rumbling from its depths. Her steps slowed, then stopped. She found herself moving closer the better to hear him. She had not expected him to be home, as he often took himself off in the afternoons now. No longer did he attempt to join Lady Belham on her walks. No longer did he force his company on Rosalind. Oh, he was never anything but polite. After their talk nearly a week ago, he had been unfailingly proper with her.

Even so, Rosalind felt the loss of his easy smiles and quick, teasing wit like a blow.

"I won't need a carriage tonight, Danielson," Tristan was saying. "Lord Kingston will be here at eight with Miss Weeton and her parents, and I shall ride with them to the theatre."

Rosalind's back teeth ground together. She had tried so hard over the past week to protect Miss Weeton as best she could from Tristan and his friend. Yet nothing had worked. She felt like a bystander watching a carriage accident. She was utterly helpless, with no recourse at all to protect the girl from the attentions of such charmers.

Even worse, her own common sense seemed to be crumbling to dust where it came to the man. For her heart, traitor that it was, was pining in the worst way for the return of the attentions he had shown her before.

"Very good, Sir Tristan," the butler intoned, pulling her from her discomfiting thoughts. Just then the man's voice dropped, carrying a tension that she had never heard from him. "Another letter has arrived from Sainsly."

There was a rustling of paper followed by a thick silence. Then, to her shock, Tristan's voice, tight with some barely controlled emotion.

"Burn it," he growled. "I have told you on numerous occasions to burn anything that comes from her."

"Very good, sir," the butler said, his tone once again devoid of anything but calm deference.

There was another bit of rustling, then a crackle as the offending letter hit the fire. That sound finally snapped her back into herself. Her present position could only be construed as eavesdropping. And Danielson would no doubt be leaving the study any moment—as the approaching footsteps announced loud and clear.

Rosalind bolted for the nearest door, a seldom used sitting room, hiding herself inside. And just in time, for from her vantage she could make out the butler as he exited the study, followed not a minute later by Tristan.

Breathing a sigh of relief, Rosalind emerged from her hiding place. But as she hurried on by the study door and on to the library as she had originally planned, she caught sight of the low burning fire in the grate.

And the half-burned paper within.

Curiosity getting the better of her, she changed direction and darted inside. The letter the butler had been ordered to burn was still there, part of it having been spared from the fire. As she bent closer to get a better look, a fresh flame caught on the paper and the missive was quickly engulfed. But not before she caught a glimpse of a name.

Josephine

Who was Josephine? Why had Tristan ordered that all letters from her be burned?

And why was jealousy sitting sour in her stomach?

Furious with herself, she hurried from the room. It served her right, spying on Tristan. She was despicable.

Overwhelmed by a wave of self-disgust, she was in the front hall before she knew it. Blowing out a harsh breath, she spun about on the ball of her foot, intending to backtrack to the library, to find a book, and to hide herself away in her room so she could evade further mischief.

A knocking on the front doors, however, halted her in her tracks.

She half expected the butler to appear. He seemed to materialize at every other time he was needed, as if magicked into being. Now, however, it appeared the man was not about. She bit her lip, staring in uncertainty at the doors. Again came the knock. Shrugging, she hurried forward and pulled the heavy door open.

"Mr. Carlisle!" she exclaimed with a delighted smile. "What a pleasant surprise. Have you come to visit Lady Belham?"

Mr. Carlisle blinked at her before grinning. "Miss Merriweather, so good to see you. Are you playing at butler today?"

"It seems so." She waved him in, closing the door behind him. "I suppose I should take your outerwear then. Your hat, sir," she intoned in a deep, sonorous voice, holding out a hand imperiously.

He chuckled. "Ah, I see you have found your calling. For I never knew a butler with such impressive poise." He handed over his hat and coat, which Rosalind deposited on the hall table.

"I'm afraid Lady Belham is out. Which I suppose I should have told you before taking your hat and coat," she admitted sheepishly.

"You may have," he agreed, "though I would have quickly told you I would be glad to visit with you if you've a mind to entertain me. And so we would be in the same place we are now. Assuming you would agree to sit with me awhile."

Rosalind grinned. "That sounds absolutely lovely."

The butler arrived and took in Mr. Carlisle without his outerwear before turning to Rosalind. "Would you like a tray brought up to the drawing room, Miss Merriweather?"

"Thank you, yes please, Danielson."

Bowing, the butler moved off. Rosalind stared after him.

"I feel strangely like a child playing at being an adult," she murmured.

Mr. Carlisle chuckled. "I know exactly what you mean. When I first returned home and had to deal with my father's servants, people who had known me since I was in frocks, I felt much the same."

Rosalind started off for the stairs, Mr. Carlisle falling into step beside her with a natural ease. "And does your father continue to improve?"

"Thank God, he does," the man said with feeling. "So much so that he wants me to spend more time at social events and the like. I begin to suspect that he feigned the whole illness in order to get me to come home and secure the family line."

They entered the drawing room and found a cozy spot near the window to sit. "Do you really think that?" Rosalind asked.

He chuckled. "No, I don't. I suppose it is not well done of me to even suggest it, for he was suffering greatly when I arrived." He sobered for a moment before brightening. "But he is so improved, I have every hope he may one day return to full vigor. Now that he is well, however, I have noticed his suggestions that I marry and set up a nursery have increased. He used to mention it once a day. Now it is hourly."

Rosalind chuckled. "And how do you feel about such things?"

"Oh, I'm all for it," he said. "Though I would very much like to find someone to care for. I was in love once, you see, and would like to feel that again." His expression turned appalled. "Goodness, I don't know why I told you that."

Rosalind gave him a gentle smile. "You can be assured, I will keep your secret. I'm quite good at it." For a moment she was lost in thought. Her fingers found the locket at her throat, brushed over the smooth turquoise stones, before she forcibly dropped her hand back to her lap.

"Was that at one of your father's properties in the country?" she asked.

"No, when I was still a young man and living in London." He sat forward, suddenly earnest. "I loved her with everything in me, Miss Merriweather, would have given her the moon had she asked."

Rosalind, though taken aback by such a statement, felt all the heartache behind it. "What happened?"

"She loved another."

The words were simple, and simply said. But there was a wealth of emotion behind them.

A maid arrived then with a tray, and immediately Rosalind went to work preparing the tea.

"I always feel utterly useless waiting to be served," Mr. Carlisle said while she busied herself. "We kept a skeleton staff in the country and so I have learned to do for myself. I find I actually prefer it, keeping busy and all. Why don't I fill our plates in the meantime?"

"I would like that very much," Rosalind replied. As he went to work, stacking biscuits and bits of fruit on the small bone china plates provided, Rosalind snuck considering looks at him. Truly, the man was the most pleasant, accommodating person. He was a true gentleman. Not at all like that Lord Kingston and his wicked smiles. Would that Tristan had chosen such a person for Miss Weeton, and not a rogue of the first order.

A thought hit her then, like a lightning bolt. But wait, why couldn't Miss Weeton be paired with Mr. Carlisle? And wouldn't it be the best way to foil Tristan's plans? Goodness knows her attempts at befriending the girl had failed miserably. There was no chance she would get in the girl's confidence to warn her away from Lord Kingston.

But Miss Weeton could be given an alternative.

"Mr. Carlisle," Rosalind said as nonchalantly as she could manage, considering the excitement that was bubbling up inside her. "I think your father is right, in that you should begin looking for a bride."

He stilled, a buttery shortbread suspended from his fingers. "Do you really?"

"Certainly," she said, placing the teapot down and pouring a generous amount of milk into the cup as Mr. Carlisle had indicated he liked. "And I do believe you will find someone to care for again. It is simply a matter of putting yourself out there and making yourself available."

He passed her one of the plates, piled high with delicacies, then accepted the cup from her. "Do you really think so?"

"Oh yes, most definitely. As a matter of fact, I think it's best to start right away. To give yourself the best chance for success, of course."

He sipped at his tea, considering her. "You know, Miss Merriweather, I think you may be right. But where in the world do I start?"

"Oh, I don't know." She pretended to consider the matter deeply for a time before blurting, "Perhaps the theatre? Tonight?"

"Tonight?" His brows drew together. "Do you truly think so?"

"Certainly." She sipped at her tea as he chewed on a biscuit thoughtfully. "The theatre is the perfect place to see and be seen, you know. Or so I've heard. You do like the theatre, I presume?"

"Oh, most definitely," Mr. Carlisle replied with feeling. "I have not been in some time. It was a favorite pastime of mine before I left London. There is nothing quite like immersing oneself in the pageantry and art of a performance." He looked wistful for a moment.

Truly, she could not guide the man more easily if she tried. She might have felt guilty at manipulating him in such a way if she wasn't absolutely certain what she was doing was right. "I have every hope that I can convince Lady Belham to attend the theatre, and I'm sure she would love to have you there."

"Do you think so?"

"Oh, yes. Most definitely."

And as he declared his delight at the prospect and they made short work of the delicious spread the cook had provided, Rosalind found she was looking forward to the proposed evening with as much, if not more, excitement than her friend. It was due to thwarting Tristan's plans, she told herself. But deep inside she knew, with a kind of fatalistic dread, that she couldn't wait to see *him* again.

Chapter 18

What in blazes is Rosalind doing here?

Tristan stared across the expanse of the theatre, stunned. He perhaps should not have seen her so quickly. The performance had not yet begun, and the theatergoers were busy making sure they were seen. Every box had movement, people squawking and preening and fluttering like so many colorful parrots.

But he had seen her the moment she entered the box. She was a beacon. Even from this distance he could behold her in painful detail, her brown hair catching the light from the sconces, wearing a deep amethyst gown that was no doubt one of Grace's cast offs. The dark color had an incredible effect on her skin, turning it the palest porcelain. As he watched, transfixed by the sight of her, she was helped into a seat by…Hugh Carlisle?

What the devil was she doing with him? An uncomfortable feeling settled between his shoulder blades, making the hair of his nape stand on end. He tightened his hands into hard balls on his thighs. It took him a moment to realize what he felt was jealousy.

Damn it, he had no right to feel jealous. Even so, he could not help the question swirling around in his brain: Was Carlisle courting her? And why the hell did he care if the man was? If anything, it should be a cause for celebration. Being a companion could not be easy. She deserved happiness, a home of her own, children.

But the very thought of her with Carlisle nauseated him beyond belief. No, it wasn't that it was Carlisle in particular, for Tristan had nothing against the man. He seemed a good sort, jolly and polite to a fault. The kind of fellow ideal for matrimony, who would remain faithful and provide a good life for his family.

What had him feeling sick to his stomach was Rosalind with *anyone*. A troubling realization, indeed.

Before panic took hold, however, he spied Carlisle helping a second person to their seat. Grace.

The reason for Rosalind's presence became clear. She was there with his cousin, who was related by marriage to Carlisle. Of course that explained it. Relief such as Tristan had never known coursed through him. Which was much more worrisome than the jealousy, to be honest. Rosalind was not his, he told himself fiercely. He'd best get it through his head.

"Who are you staring at with such a glower?" Rafe asked, looking out over the crowd with a curious expression.

"No one," Tristan muttered.

But his friend was anything but dense. "I say, is that your cousin across the way? You should invite her over. My box is able to hold their party as well."

"No!"

Rafe started, looking at him in surprise. And no wonder, for in his horror at his friend's suggestion, he'd been much louder than he'd intended.

"Ah, that is," he continued, trying for an easy smile, "it is so much more pleasant with a smaller party at these kinds of things."

The surprise on Rafe's face transformed to amusement. "Where is my friend and what have you done with him? For the Crosby I know would never say such a thing. Why, I've known you to stuff a dozen or more people into this box and still look for more to join us."

Which was all too true. Yet that kind of wild socialization seemed to no longer hold the same draw for him. "It's merely the natural progression of life, I suppose," he said. "We're past those days."

"Bite your tongue," Rafe admonished. Even as he teased Tristan, however, his eyes searched for and found Miss Weeton on his other side.

The girl, talking to her mother, caught them looking at her and turned as pink as the lace of her gown. Tristan smiled to himself as Rafe began a low conversation with her. The girl was flustered as she ever was. Tristan had quickly learned that she was not easy with people, more specifically with men. Yet when she looked at Rafe there was something more, a softness in her eyes not typically present.

As for his friend, he had worried at first the man wouldn't respond to Miss Weeton. He was a lively fellow after all, always found at the center of whatever social celebration was being had.

In the past year, however, he'd appeared discontent more than not, and increasingly restless, as if he were looking for something but unable to find it. Was the man searching for a wife? Several telling remarks indicated he rather was. Then along had come Miss Weeton, with her dilemma and shyness. Put the girl before Rafe, he'd reasoned, and his friend would see her in a whole new light, would see past what society saw, to the gem within. And Miss Weeton could not fail to be enchanted by Rafe. He was not one of the darlings of London society for nothing, after all, and could put anyone at ease with his good-natured, easy-going ways.

Thus far he'd been proven correct. For in the course of the past week Rafe had grown utterly enchanted with the lady. And Miss Weeton too was responding to his friend in a wonderful way that was quite unlike her usual reticence. If things progressed as they were, Tristan would see another conquest in the form of an engagement announced within the fortnight.

He vowed then and there to pour his focus and energy into matching Miss Weeton to Rafe and ignore Rosalind's presence. Surely it couldn't be that difficult to do.

• • •

By the time intermission arrived, however, Tristan wanted to bash his pathetically optimistic past self over the head.

For no matter how he tried, he could not avert his gaze from Rosalind. She seemed bound and determined to keep her head turned his way as well.

He might have thought his eyes were playing tricks on him. Perhaps it was simply coincidence that had her looking his way every time he happened to peer across at her. Yet he could not ignore the fact that she seemed far more interested in his side of the theatre than was necessary.

Especially when he caught her peering at him through a pair of quizzing glasses, of all things.

It was a relief when intermission came. At least now he did not have to pretend interest in the stage. Sighing, he openly turned his head to look Rosalind's way.

She wasn't there.

In fact, her entire party was missing from their box. He frowned. Surely she wouldn't come over to theirs.

As if to mock his assumption, the curtain parted at the back of the box. And then she was there, and he forgot to breathe.

How was it, he thought dazedly, that one small, unassuming woman could so completely overwhelm a space?

Rafe stood, bowing with a flourish. "So good to see you all here in my humble box. Though I cannot hope you are visiting in order to see me, as I have someone much more appealing here tonight." He looked to Miss Weeton. Once again, the girl flushed. Yet Tristan did not miss the small smile that lifted her lips as she looked to her lap.

There was a nearly indiscernible sound from Rosalind's direction. He looked at her as the others exchanged greetings. She was fairly shooting daggers at Rafe before she grabbed onto Carlisle's arm and moved farther into the box, dragging him along with her.

"Miss Weeton, so good to see you again," she said, approaching the girl where she sat. "You remember Mr. Carlisle, of course?"

"Ah, yes." Miss Weeton eyed Rosalind with trepidation—and no wonder, after the long line of accidents Rosalind had tortured the girl with over the past week—and cleared her throat, her fingers twisting about each other. "Mr. Carlisle, it's a pleasure."

As the man bowed, Rosalind spoke. "Mr. Carlisle was telling me the most fascinating story of a play he saw performed in Leeds years ago. Mr. Carlisle, you should tell Miss Weeton. I'm sure she would be most interested."

"Er, of course," Carlisle said, not a little stunned, before he inclined his head toward the other lady. "If Miss Weeton is not opposed, that is."

What could the girl say? She quickly mumbled her acquiesce. Carlisle sat in the seat beside her, the one Rafe had vacated minutes ago, and started in on his story.

Tristan might have gone on wondering at that little scene had he not caught sight of the self-satisfied smirk on Rosalind's face. So that was the way of it, was it? The little minx was planning on foiling his attempts to match Miss Weeton with Rafe by acting matchmaker herself.

As she stepped back he advanced on her, taking advantage of the distraction of the rest of the group to grab her arm and drag her into the corner of the box. The cool politeness he had adopted with her over the last days would not help in the least now.

"I know what you're about, Rosalind," he growled low.

In a move that surprised him not one bit, she rolled her eyes before saying, "I would think you a simpleton if you did not."

"You've no right."

"On the contrary, I have every right in the world. And I must say," she continued smugly, giving the young couple at the front of the box a satisfied look, "they do look well together. Mr. Carlisle is much more her match. Not at all like that Lord Kingston."

Tristan bit back a sharp reply. When last he'd come to his friend's defense he had said far more than he'd intended regarding his feelings for this maddening woman. He would not make that mistake again. "You have no idea what you're doing," he growled instead.

She pursed her lips. "We shall see."

"No, we won't. You will give up this little scheme of yours immediately."

"I will not."

He let out a harsh breath. "Rosalind," he warned.

"Tristan," she came back.

The effect of his name on her tongue set his every nerve aflame. And if the look on her face was any indication, she was as deeply affected by her slip.

"I mean," she stammered, "Sir Tristan. My apologies."

He had been so very careful with her over the past week. He had needed to be. But now was not the time for that. Now he should do what he did best and tease her unmercifully until the fire was back in her eyes.

Instead his fingers, which were still on her arm, stroked the bit of bare flesh above her glove. And he found himself fairly begging her, "Please don't do this, Rosalind."

She laughed, but it was forced. Pulling her arm from his grip, she raised her chin. "Do I frighten you that much, then?"

"You don't frighten me, you harridan. But I will not watch you play with these people's lives because of a whim."

"You dare to accuse me of such a thing? You, who are doing just that?"

"I am not playing with their lives," he gritted.

"But you are."

"I am not. I am trying to show them what they normally wouldn't see, that they are ideal for one another."

"Please. You think a man such as Lord Kingston is right for Miss Weeton, a woman who can hardly talk to a man much less look him in the eye?"

"Yes."

She crossed her arms over her chest. "I would dearly love to hear how you think they could possibly suit."

"I have seen men such as Kingston find happiness in the arms of women such as Miss Weeton. My two dearest friends are such men."

She shrugged. "A mere anomaly, I'm sure."

"You stubborn woman," he growled. "Nothing I say will dissuade you from your course, will it?" How would he ever get her to lay off this mad idea of hers?

But perhaps he needn't stop her. He merely needed to make her see how serious he was about the whole thing.

And then, with a jolt, an idea came to him. He smiled slowly, taking a step closer to her. Her eyes widened, but in her typical fashion, Rosalind did not retreat.

"Would you care to place a wager on the outcome?"

"A wager?" Outrage contorted her features. "Just as I suspected. You truly are trifling with their lives."

"The wager will guarantee I'm not. For if, by some miracle, your Mr. Carlisle wins the fair Miss Weeton's heart, I promise to give up matchmaking forever."

Rosalind paused, the glint of excitement lighting her eyes. "You would give up your matchmaking? Truly?"

"Truly. But," he declared, holding up a hand as a triumphant smile curved her lips, "only if Carlisle wins her hand. And only if you don't interfere."

She pursed her lips, considering him. One hand came up to fiddle with the worn locket at her throat. Not for the first time he wondered what the small gold circle held. He was about to ask her when she released it and spoke.

"And what would you have me give up should I lose? Not that I expect that to happen," she muttered.

"Well, if I'm giving up matchmaking, I think we can come up with something equally difficult for you. Let's say…letting me match you myself?"

The very idea of Rosalind marrying another, of loving another and bearing his children, had sent him into a panic when he'd considered it earlier. Which was the very reason he suggested it now. For perhaps if she had a husband and a life outside of his cousin's employ, maybe he would be able to put her from his mind and return to the life he'd had before she'd barged her way into it.

And until then he would ignore the peculiar grief that welled up in his gut thinking of it.

Rosalind seemed to find the idea of him matching her just as abhorrent. She let loose a bark of horrified laughter.

He raised a brow. "You doubt I'm serious?"

"But…I won't do it."

He crossed his arms, mimicking her posture, and stared down his nose at her. "If you wish for the chance for me to give up my matchmaking, those are my terms. Unless," he went on with a sly smile, "you aren't as confident of Mr. Carlisle as you pretend to be."

As he expected, she drew herself up and did her best to stare him down. Well, as well as one could stare down another nearly two heads taller. "I am very certain of Mr. Carlisle, I assure you."

He leaned down, until their eyes were almost level. "Prove it."

She chewed on her bottom lip. His gaze was drawn there, to that perfectly pink lip, wanting very much to be the one to bite it so unmercifully.

He began to sweat. If anything told him he was doing the right thing with this asinine bet, it was his reaction right here. He had to free himself from this maddening woman one way or another, and the sooner the better.

"And how do I know you will play fair?" she asked, suspicion coloring every word.

It was no surprise to him now that Rosalind didn't trust him as far as she could throw him. Which, for Rosalind, wasn't far at all, considering her diminutive stature. She had been vocal enough on the subject in the past. Therefore, he knew she required more than the usual platitudes to get her to agree.

He placed a hand on his heart. "I vow I shall not promote my own candidate for the good lady's hand," he swore with utmost seriousness. "I will do everything in my power to ensure both men are on equal ground with her, and will see to it that they are all in company together as much as I can manage."

For a moment he thought she might turn her back on him and declare the whole idea preposterous. But then she held out her hand.

"Very well. I accept."

He grabbed hold of it before she could reconsider, shaking it firmly. But as she moved away to Grace's side, he couldn't help thinking he'd signed a deal with the devil.

• • •

Rosalind had known the second she'd shaken Tristan's hand she'd made a mistake. Not that she didn't believe she could win; with every fiber of her being she knew she would.

But what she'd realized in the split second their hands had met—besides the disturbing zing along her nerves, of course—was that, to see to it that Tristan dealt with the situation fairly, she would have to watch him like a hawk. Which would not be easy, for every time she looked on him she thought of him confessing that he wanted her, sending her body spiraling into molten desire.

But the draw of winning, of having him give up his matchmaking and meddling in these women's lives, was too potent a thing to ignore. For his choice in men was appalling.

She purposely ignored the fact that the man he'd matched Miss Gladstow with had been ideal for her. What had he done, after all, but clear the path for two people already in love?

Lord Kingston was another matter entirely. The man was a rake and a rogue. How Tristan could ever consider him a proper husband for the shy, nervous Miss Weeton was baffling. Why, even if the earl did marry the girl, he would make her miserable within a fortnight, for he could not be content with the quiet life that having such a wife would require. Goodness only knew how many other couples Tristan had matched in his illustrious career—and how many young women's lives he had inadvertently ruined. Even if his intentions were good, it was evident his instincts were ghastly. The man had to be stopped at all costs.

Even if it meant she would have to suffer some highly improper, unwelcome feelings for him in the meantime.

Like now. As he had promised, he had gathered them all at Mrs. Juniper's rout the following evening. And, as promised, he had seen to it that Miss Weeton and her two beaus were seated at the same card table, then had excused himself to let nature take its course. She certainly could not say he had not kept his word thus far. Which, she had to admit, she had not expected. She had spent so long thinking that men of his ilk were the devil incarnate, she could not easily let go of the natural distrust that simmered within her breast.

She had watched closely for him to break his word. Goodness, but she had watched him closely. But he had not done a single thing to awaken her suspicions. If anything, he was the perfect gentleman. *Blast him.*

But she could not stay here in the card room indefinitely. Shooting one last look Tristan's way, she walked out, making her way down the hallway to the drawing room and Lady Belham. She had a job to do, after all, one that did not include watching certain baronets to make sure they didn't cheat.

Before she reached her destination, however, she heard him behind her. No, that wasn't right, for the hallway was too populated to hear his quiet steps with any clarity. She *felt* him. Instantly her body tightened in anticipation. Furious at herself for her reaction, she hurried her steps.

"Why so rushed, Rosalind?"

She shot him an annoyed look. "I'm merely returning to my post."

He matched his steps to hers. "I must say, I'm honored you trusted me enough to leave me alone with them."

"I don't trust you, not even a bit."

To her surprise, he actually looked hurt by her snide outburst. "I do wonder what I've done to bring about this distrust."

Instant guilt overtook her. Not a welcome sensation by any means. Still, she was not an unfair person. "I must admit," she said grudgingly, "that you have not given me cause to say such things since making our bargain. You have been incredibly forthright since yesterday."

"High praise indeed," he murmured, his blue eyes twinkling with mirth.

Despite herself, she felt her mood lighten. "Yes, well, you should feel honored. I don't often give such glowing compliments."

He stopped and stared at her. She stopped as well, ignoring the people about them, and gave him a quizzical look.

"Why, Rosalind, was that a jest?"

She could not stop the inevitable curve her lips took at his mock surprise. "You know, it might have been."

"Will wonders never cease?"

As they entered the drawing room, Rosalind found herself not a little stunned. What had that little exchange been? And why did she no longer mind having him by her side? He was no different than he had been yesterday.

Yet something had changed. Watching him to ensure he kept his word to her had loosened something long held and closely kept within her.

She looked about then, determined to distract herself from such troubling thoughts by finding Lady Belham. To her surprise her employer was nowhere in sight.

"I wonder where she could be," she mumbled, frowning as she scanned the assembled guests.

"Grace? Isn't she here? She was talking to Mrs. Weeton before we left."

She was about to respond when Lady Belham appeared. She ducked into the room via the open doors that led to the garden, with a flushed, strangely flustered look about her.

Rosalind hurried to her, for with her heightened color and almost feverish eyes her employer appeared almost ill. "My lady, are you well?"

Lady Belham tried for a smile but it faded quickly. "I'm fine darling. I needed some air, is all."

Tristan was on her other side, peering at her in concern. "You don't look well. Should we return home?"

"Of course not," she scoffed. "Goodness, I am hardly fragile. There's no reason for such concern."

Lady Belham kept her voice light, yet Rosalind thought she detected a slightly strained undercurrent to it. When she studied her, she noticed there were tense lines bracketing her unsmiling mouth. She hazarded a glance at Tristan to see if he saw it as well. He shot her a hooded look, but it did not hide the banked emotion in his eyes.

He was worried as well. A jolt of anxiety shot through her, for his concern only cemented the fact that she actually had reason to worry at all. But there was also a relief, deep in her gut, warm and comforting. She was not alone. Whatever happened, she had someone to lean on.

It was a foreign feeling, something she had never thought to experience. She had the sudden urge to throw her arms around him. Instead she turned back to Lady Belham, hoping to distract her and relieve the tension that had crystalized in her like veins through marble.

"There is quite a collection of debutantes ready to regale the party with their talents I see." She pointed out a giggling group of young women gathered about the pianoforte in the corner, no doubt waiting to descend upon the instrument the moment the lady at the bench lifted her fingers from the keys. "Which do you think shall win the honor of playing the next song? As for me, I think the girl in blue shall be the victor. She has a cunning, bloodthirsty look about her."

As she'd hoped, Lady Belham gave a tinkling laugh, the strain in her eyes melting away. "I don't know, the blonde in pink looks like she has the makings of a winner in this instance."

"Surely you're joking," Rosalind said, eyeing the girl. "Why, she appears much too demure."

"The demure ones are often the ones to look out for, Miss Merri-weather," Tristan drawled.

Rosalind peered up at him, pursing her lips to keep from smiling. "Are you teaming up with Lady Belham then? Hardly fair; I am outnumbered."

"Oh, no. I would never be so ungentlemanly as to do that."

Lady Belham gave him an arch look. "I am your cousin, you ungrateful whelp, and your elder as well. I should garner your loyalty without question."

"Ah, but you see," he said officiously, "I refuse to take sides at all. For I don't believe either of you will win in your choices."

"And who do you think will be the next to descend upon the pianoforte to regale us with her playing?" Rosalind asked, unable to keep the laughter from coloring her words.

He considered the group. "I am for the dark-haired lass in white silk."

Rosalind laughed openly then. "She is not even part of the group."

"Ah, but you are not looking closely enough. If you study her, you will see she is merely biding her time. She will wait until the others are distracted and swoop in for the kill."

"Come along, you are reaching." Rosalind looked to Lady Belham. "What do you think of his choice?"

Lady Belham, to her surprise, was looking at Tristan with interest. "I think, my darling Miss Merriweather, that you will find yourself surprised by my cousin's insight into people. He is amazingly adept at such things."

The song came to a close. Rosalind, Tristan, and Lady Belham fell silent by some unspoken mutual agreement, watching closely the group of women across the room. As suspected, before the last strands of the song had even faded, the waiting girls started twittering with one another, apparently trying to decide who should take the next place at the instrument. Rosalind watched with amazement as the girl in white, sneaking behind the women, slid onto the bench and began to play before anyone had even noticed she was there.

Rosalind looked to Tristan, equal parts amazement and respect clamoring in her breast. "I did not think it possible. That is quite a talent you have."

He grinned as Grace laughed delightedly. "It is not the first time you have underestimated me, Miss Merriweather," he murmured.

She should have perhaps taken offense at that. It was a distinct dig at their little bet that was currently taking shape in the card room even as they spoke.

But she could not manage even the smallest kernel of outrage. Instead she murmured to herself as he began conversing with his cousin, "And I daresay it shall not be the last."

Chapter 19

"Well, I must say," Grace declared as the carriage returned home from a midday outing two days later, "that was one of the most enjoyable afternoons I have had in some time. Who knew that such an intimate group could provide better company than the great majority of elegant, crowded affairs of the Season?"

Tristan couldn't help but agree. Until recently, he had been more likely to gravitate toward those things that provided the greatest number of attendees, the largest mix of personalities, the most distraction in the form of music and laughter and conversation.

But over the course of the last few days, he'd found himself looking forward to their small group more than he ever had those busy parties. He wondered what the change was.

Of their own volition, his eyes found Rosalind. She sat beside Grace, looking amazingly pretty in another of his cousin's cast-offs, a rose-colored gown that lent a blush to her pale skin. As if he had called her name, she looked his way. The blush in her cheeks deepened when she saw his gaze on her. But, instead of scowling at him as she used to do, a small smile lifted her lips before she looked away.

Perhaps he should have been concerned that his heart leapt; Instead, he found himself smiling as well, looking out at the passing scenery yet seeing only the softened look in her brown eyes.

They arrived at their townhouse a short time later. Tristan leapt down, offering a hand to his cousin to help her disembark. She surprised him by waving him off. "I've somewhere to be and so won't be getting off here. You don't mind if I take the carriage out again do you?"

"Of course not," he replied. There had been a marked improvement in her spirits today; he would do anything in his power to keep her happy. He made to close the carriage door and send her and Rosalind on their way.

"Oh, Tristan," she called, "you may help Miss Merriweather down. I don't require her company this afternoon."

"Are you certain, my lady?" Rosalind asked.

"Oh yes, quite."

Tristan helped Rosalind down. Together they waved as Grace started off down the street.

And then they were alone.

Why, he thought as they stood side by side on the pavement on the busy street, did he feel as if they were the only two people in the world?

He knew they could not stand there forever, that they should move indoors, which he in his dazed state of mind seemed unable to do. Beside him, Rosalind fidgeted, moving from one foot to the other before, with a jerky motion of her hand, she said, "Shall we?"

He cleared his throat. "Ah, yes, let's."

As one they entered the house, their silence broken only by the murmurings of the butler as he took their outerwear. There was something incredibly intimate in the whole thing, as if they were a couple, returning home together.

The strangest longing overtook him at the thought. It was not abhorrent in the least; instead, it made his chest ache in the most surprising way.

"Well then," Rosalind said as the butler moved off. "I shall see you later." She turned to go.

The most intense panic overcame him then. "Wait!"

She started, looking at him uncertainly. "Yes?"

Now what? He didn't have a clue. All he knew was he didn't want to part with her. Then he hit on a brilliant idea. "I thought perhaps we could discuss the progress of our wager."

Was that relief in her eyes? But it was gone in the blink of an eye. "What a splendid idea. For I shall be able to list all the reasons why I shall be the victor."

He laughed. "We shall see about that," he murmured.

As one they started through the house. Truthfully he could hardly see where they were headed, his mind too full of visions of her momentary relief.

The last days had provided a kind of peace from the constant battles that had taken up their time together thus far. Now that she wasn't attacking him with her sharp tongue, he could see more clearly the humorous wit she possessed, the innate kindness in her. And the fierce loyalty. She truly cared for Grace and Miss Weeton. And, he realized now that he was distanced from the situation, she had cared for Miss Gladstow as well. She truly wanted what was best for these women and feared them being taken advantage of almost to the point of obsession.

What, he wondered not for the first time, had brought about such a protective instinct in her, an instinct that went well beyond normal concern?

They reached the downstairs sitting room then. But at the door Tristan paused.

She looked at him in curiosity. "Is something wrong?"

"Not at all. Only we've had such a lovely day out of doors, I thought perhaps we might take a walk in the garden?"

"Certainly." She flushed and followed him to the small garden at the back of the house.

It was a natural thing for him to lead the way then, to find the small alcove with the stone bench that he so loved to spend time in. He often retreated here, after all, in troubling times. But as they sat on the cool stone, Tristan realized the reason for Rosalind's small blush when he had suggested the garden. For it wasn't long ago that he had kissed her in this very same place, on this very same bench. Merely thinking of it now had him aching to do the very same, to take her in his arms and claim her mouth with his own.

He clenched his hands on his knees and slid across the seat to the farthest corner. They had barely begun to grow friendly. He would not ruin that blossoming friendship with a renewal of those attentions she had been so vocal in proclaiming a disgust for.

"Now," he said a touch too loudly, determined to make this as normal a situation as he could manage, "you were saying something about listing all the reasons why your Mr. Carlisle will win Miss Weeton's heart?"

She seemed to relax at the return of their playful banter. At least as much as one person could relax while nearly hugging the edge of the bench. "Yes." She cleared her throat. "First off, may I say what a brilliant idea it was to take a trip to the country for a picnic. Never have I seen Miss Weeton so relaxed."

He blinked. "Why, Rosalind, never say you are complimenting me."

She flushed again. "It would be rude of me not to say anything. As a matter of fact, I must commend you on your integrity through-out this entire affair. You have kept your word, which I certainly never thought you would do."

"You overwhelm me with your praise," he drawled.

"That is," she hurried to say, aghast, "I never believed men such as you would keep their word. I mean," she gasped, turning as red as the roses across the path, "you…I… Oh," she moaned, putting her hands over her face, "can we please forget the past minute ever occurred?"

He might have chuckled and waved it off. Instead he reached out, gripping her slender wrist in his hand, gently tugging until her face was exposed, every reddened, horrified bit of it. "Rosalind, were you or someone you loved hurt by a man like me?"

From the misery that darkened her eyes, he realized he had deduced the truth of the matter. For so many weeks she had treated him like the enemy. Now that they had begun to be friends, he realized there was something much deeper at work here. She had been hurt by a man's perfidy. And had painted all men similar to him with the same broad brush.

Had Rosalind been the one to reap the fruits of such a man's betrayal? The very idea sent a shaft of fury through him. But no, it could have been anyone she had cared about. A friend, a neighbor.

A sister.

At once he knew he was right. Especially when he saw her fingers once again at the small locket that graced her throat. It was the perfect size to contain a memento of someone she had cared for and lost. Who better than the sister she still mourned?

He wanted to question her on it. More than anything, he wanted to know the secrets deep in her heart. But looking into her eyes, he saw the fragile trust there. Trust that she was only beginning to form with him. A trust he had not realized until that very moment he wanted so badly. He would not destroy the new bud of it before it had a chance to blossom, would not destroy the chance for it to grow into a natural and lasting thing.

He smiled gently. "Well, I must say I'm glad you have decided to bestow your trust in me. But you needn't be surprised. For I vow I shall never give you cause to doubt my word."

She seemed to melt under his regard. They stared at one another for long minutes. It was only then he realized his hand had moved from her wrist, that her fingers were in his, that his thumb was drawing circles over her knuckles.

He dropped her hand as if it were a hot coal. "Now then, where were we? Ah, yes, you were proclaiming me the best of men, the most trustworthy creature in existence. You may continue."

She laughed a bit breathlessly, though he could not help but see out of the corner of his eyes how she was slow in bringing her hand back to her lap. "At least I may know that no compliment is too small for the likes of you, for you shall inflate it to suit. Now then," she continued, suddenly all business, "you wished to know why I think Mr. Carlisle will win the day?"

He inclined his head to indicate she should continue.

Rosalind cleared her throat, and he was put in mind of a barrister standing up before the courts. "You may have noticed," she said, "how at ease Miss Weeton has become with Mr. Carlisle. And though she can claim the same ease with Lord Kingston, at times she is positively flustered around him. Mr. Carlisle, however, never brings about such a malady in her."

"So let me see if I have this right, you believe that, because Miss Weeton is not as affected by Mr. Carlisle, that she prefers him?"

"Yes, quite."

He laughed. "My dear Rosalind, if that is your belief then I am heartily glad I was the one to take up matchmaking and not you. For it is precisely Miss Weeton's flustered state when dealing with Rafe that tells me he is the one she wants."

She frowned. "How so?"

"Well," he hemmed, "I'm not sure you would be at all willing to hear my excuse. For it tells of a certain knowledge of the inner workings of the human heart."

She swallowed visibly. "You have…been in love then?"

"No."

Relief flared in her eyes. His heart leapt. Was she troubled by the idea of him being in love? And why did that make his heart sing?

But she quickly frowned, banishing the softer emotion. "But if you have not been in love, how do you know how a person in love acts?"

"I've seen my fair share of couples in love. And I can tell you with certainty that when one's heart is engaged, the body responds as well. With, let's say, flushed skin." He pointed to the faint blush staining her porcelain cheeks. "Or a quickened pulse." Here he indicated the long column of her throat, where even from where he sat, he could see the beat of her heart making the fine, translucent skin beneath her jaw flutter like mad. "Or an increased sensitivity of the skin." He traced the line of her arm, his fingers a hairsbreadth from her skin, fascinated as the fine hairs there stood on end. "Mayhap," he continued hoarsely, "even trembling." He should not touch her. Yet when he saw the faint tremor in her hand he could not help brushing his fingers along it where it lay in her lap. She shook under his touch, overtaken with a gentle shudder.

"And you think Miss Weeton is affected in such a way with Lord Kingston?" she asked, her voice faint and breathy. "You can tell by observing that she feels none of those things for Mr. Carlisle?"

"I know she doesn't."

She arched an eyebrow. "Are you a mind reader then?"

"No, just incredibly observant."

"I must take care then," she said as she leaned away from his touch, her voice sounding strangled to his ears, "that you don't read me as well."

"I would never presume."

Her lips kicked up in a small, humorless smile. "Afraid of what you shall find?"

"Not at all." But wasn't he? Hadn't he shied away from her from the very beginning because she seemed to see straight to the flaws in him, to every uncertainty and fear?

She pursed her lips thoughtfully, seeing his hesitation. Then, in customary Rosalind fashion, she turned the conversation right on its head. "Lady Belham appears much happier today."

It took him a moment to reorient himself, but he could only be glad for the change. They had been swimming in dangerous waters indeed.

"Yes. I admit myself deeply relieved."

"As am I." She hesitated before launching on. "Is your cousin prone to low spirits?"

"Not typically. She is ruled by her heart, of course, though that tends not to work in her favor. She is a creature of sensibility."

"Indeed she is," Rosalind said thoughtfully, even a bit sadly. "She reminds me of my sister at times."

He thought perhaps she would tell him of her. She had been remarkably close-mouthed about her sister, considering how open she was with every other thought that crossed her mind. Instead she asked a question that was guaranteed to knock him on his arse if he'd been standing.

"Do you have siblings?"

Instantly an image of a youthful face swam in his vision, and the pride on their father's face as he paraded the boy before Tristan during one of his few visits home. Pride that had never been present when he'd talked of Tristan.

His mouth worked silently for a time before he answered. "Er, yes. That is, I used to. A half-brother, Arthur. He died, quite young."

A look of intense sadness passed over her face. "I'm so sorry to hear that. I know more than anyone the pain that losing a sibling can cause. You must miss him dreadfully."

"Not so much," he replied, his voice sounding far away to his own ears. "There was such an age difference, and I was off at school for much of his life. We were not close." Not by choice, he silently amended, their father having made sure it was so.

"That must make it doubly hard, having forever lost that opportunity," she mused, considering him with sharp eyes.

He was still reeling from that incisive response when she spoke again. "And your stepmother? Does she still live?"

"Yes, though I have not seen her in some time. Not since my father's death."

"You should visit her, for you may give one another some solace."

Already he was shaking his head. "That is not possible."

"Have you had a falling out then? For it is never too late to reconcile, you know. It must be very lonely, after all, to lose your husband and son. I'm sure she would not wish to lose you, too."

"Perhaps," he muttered vaguely, even as he knew in his heart that would never come to pass. Not ever.

But why had he told her all of this? He never talked of Arthur or his stepmother with others. They were part of his past, and best kept there.

And she was looking at him with entirely too much knowing in her gaze.

He rose so quickly she jumped in her seat.

"Well, then, I have business to attend to. Thank you for the talk. It was most enlightening."

Enlightening? He must sound an utter fool. He started down the path, trying to put distance between them.

Her voice, however, chased after him.

"Where are we for tonight then?" she called to his retreating back.

"Vauxhall," he said over his shoulder a moment before he turned the corner.

Chapter 20

Dusk had not yet fallen when Rosalind stepped gingerly into the small boat that waited to take their party across the Thames. It dipped slightly under her weight and she hurried to an empty seat on unsteady legs, desperate for stability in the precarious craft. But even seated, she could not seem to lose the panic rising in her like a floodwater. She fought to focus on the other occupants, who all seemed happy and unconcerned. Even so, her gaze was drawn against her will to the dark depths of the river. The crowd on the Westminster side of the bank and in the boats crossing the river were in high spirits, the water amplifying the sound of voices colored with anticipation of a night of pleasure. The river, though, looked menacing and forbidding. And much too close.

"Rosalind, are you well?"

Tristan's voice sounded in her ear as he settled into the boat. An instant calm settled over her, knowing he was beside her. It was an idea that should have unsettled her. She had never relied on anyone before; even when her father and sister had been living, she had more often than not been the one that others leaned on.

But Tristan was turning much of what she believed on its head. In more ways than one.

"I'm fine," she murmured, casting another careful look over the side of the boat as Lord Kingston settled into a seat, gently bobbing the craft. "I simply never cared to spend time on the water, is all."

"Never tell me the fearless Miss Rosalind Merriweather dislikes the water," he teased.

"Call it an instinct for survival."

"Did you never learn how to swim as a child? I was under the assumption you grew up in the country, and I never met a country-bred person who didn't learn to swim while still a babe in arms."

"No, I did. But it was so long ago, I don't believe I'll remember how if we should happen to find ourselves in *that*." She indicated the water sloshing against the hull of the boat with a jerk of her chin. A boat that looked smaller and less stable by the minute as they pushed from shore and started their swift way across the river.

She sucked in a quick breath, her hands tightening on the bench beneath her. Immediately Tristan's arm was around her. The warmth and strength of it seeped under her skin, relaxing the knotted muscles of her back, unclenching her teeth. It was a totally natural posture on his part. Anyone looking at him would assume he was merely laying his arm casually along the back of the bench.

Yet Rosalind felt the true meaning behind it. He was offering her his strength, giving her comfort. The protective ball in the pit of her stomach eased a bit, unfurling, letting loose part of that vulnerability she kept so closely hidden. She sent him a small, thankful smile. He returned it, his blue eyes crinkling at the corners. Her heart thumped in her chest in the most peculiar way.

Before she could countenance it, their craft came to rest against the Vauxhall Stairs at the south bank. In no time they had disembarked and found themselves at the entrance to the famed Pleasure Gardens.

Rosalind had read of this place, of course. Guinevere herself had written of it, having visited during her own trip to London. She recalled the happily-penned words she had received from her sister, telling of the elegant elite mingling with common folk, of the music and lanterns and gaiety. She had poured over that missive night after night, until it was fairly burned in her brain.

Now she was here. She took several steps away from their group, the better to take the glory of the place in. The orchestra building was front and center, the musicians hard at work above the mingling crowds. Handel's famed statue was a shining white marble beacon, peering with a relaxed kind of contentment from his perch. Lanterns swayed in anticipation of their lighting, ready to illuminate the smiling faces of the attendees.

She gave a small sigh, thinking of Guinevere. How she must have loved this. As clear as day she saw in her mind's eye her sister walking these wide lanes, dancing beneath the orchestra, dining in the supper boxes. She wished she had Guinevere here, that they could share this moment together.

Once again she felt a presence at her side. She turned with a smile, expecting to find Tristan. And was surprised to find Mr. Carlisle beside her.

"How are you enjoying the evening, Miss Merriweather?" he asked in his jolly way. "Is Vauxhall all you expected it to be?"

"Thus far it is exactly as my sister described in her letters home."

The happiness in his expression faded to something bittersweet. "Yes, I remember that night well."

She blinked in surprise, turning to more fully face him. "You were with her that night then? The night she came to Vauxhall?"

"Indeed. We were not of the same party, of course. I was a young bachelor and came with a group of friends who were determined to make mischief." He chuckled, his eyes on her, though the remnants of memory so glazed them she suspected he did not see her at all. "But then we spotted your sister and her group and quickly joined them. It was a fine night we all had, eating and dancing and walking about. I believe I even took her on a promenade at one point."

She blinked back tears. "It sounds lovely."

"It was." He was silent for some minutes, until Tristan returned to their group, lifting the pall over her and Mr. Carlisle.

"Dinner has been ordered and we will now be shown to a supper box, if you're amenable."

The group moved into The Grove. Night was beginning to fall in earnest, and the crowds were quickly thickening. Mouthwatering scents floated in the air, savory ham and sweet tarts, and the perfume of hundreds of flowers, all mingling in a wonderful decadence.

"In the three Seasons we have been to London," Mrs. Weeton said, "we have never once stepped foot in Vauxhall. Sir Tristan, your idea for this evening's outing was positively genius."

"You hear that, Rafe?" Tristan said to his friend as they entered the box and settled on the benches. "The Weetons have never visited these famed avenues. We shall have to give them an evening they shall never forget."

"I shall take that challenge, gladly," Rafe replied with a grin.

The men were true to their word. For soon a waiter brought their repast, a stunning array of cold meats and pastries, puddings and salads. The ham was amazingly thin, the punch surprisingly strong. And then a whistle blew, followed by a second, and thousands of lanterns flared to life simultaneously, illuminating the partygoers in a wash of gilded light.

Rosalind gasped and clapped with the rest, then accepted a second—or was it a third?—cup of punch from the waiter. Something had loosened in her tonight; she could not remember a time she had enjoyed herself more. Their small group was in high spirits, even shy Miss Weeton proving herself a lively member.

Tristan stood. "I propose we take a promenade. For while the food is incomparable, the sights will enthrall."

As one the group stood and moved into the mingling crowds. There was an easy pairing off. Lord Kingston offered his arm to Miss Weeton, who accepted with a blush and a smile. Mr. and Mrs. Weeton linked arms and followed after the pair. Mr. Carlisle looked to Rosalind, and she expected him to suggest they stroll together. But Lady Belham intercepted him, pulling him along behind the Weetons.

Then there was only Rosalind and Tristan.

She stared at him as he sauntered toward her, fascinated by how the lantern light gave even more depth, more fire to his gaze. His lips quirked in a small smile as he held out a hand to her.

"Walk with me, Rosalind?"

His quiet voice shivered a delicious path down her spine. She accepted with a nod, reaching out with trembling fingers. With infinite care, he tucked her hand into the crook of his elbow, holding it close to his side.

They walked in silence for a time. Perhaps she should have taken the chance to study the scenery, to watch the people and immerse herself in the experience of the place. Instead her entire focus centered on the strength of the arm beneath her fingers, at the way the corded muscles, felt even through the layers of his clothing, bunched beneath her touch.

"You looked so sad when we entered the gardens," he said, so low she could hardly hear him over the swelling music and laughter that surrounded them. "And then even more melancholy when Carlisle came to your side."

"Yes."

He remained silent, and she knew he would leave it there if she so wished it, would not press her to continue.

But she wanted to continue. She wanted to confide in this man, who had shown himself to be so kind, so fair, and quite unlike what she had first thought him to be.

Even so, it was a difficulty to get the words out, to purposely make herself vulnerable. She sucked in a slow, steady breath, heart thumping like mad in her chest. Then, before she could think better of it, "I was thinking of Guinevere."

"Your sister."

She nodded, looking out across the grounds. "As you know, she was in London many years ago. When I first entered this place, I remembered a letter she had sent me, telling me of her time here. It all sounded quite magical, and at the time I believed she embellished it for me. Even so, I cherished that letter, for never had she sounded happier."

"And now that you have been here?"

She shrugged, smiling up at him, "I realize she was telling me the truth. This place truly is as magical as she made it out to be. Even more so, really."

"And Carlisle?"

"He was here that night, when Guinevere walked these very same paths. He was kind enough to share his memories of that time with me. I perhaps shouldn't have allowed it to sadden me as it did. She spent some of the happiest hours of her life here."

"You miss her," he said simply. With an incredible amount of understanding.

They reached the end of the long line of supper-boxes, each full to bursting with ruddy-faced people, their merriment like a living thing in the air. Beyond, Rosalind caught sight of the darker paths veering off beyond the bright lights. She had a mad wish for a moment that he would continue, off the well-lit path, and find a secluded place to kiss her senseless.

Instead he guided her in a right turn, keeping to the populated area where a multitude of lanterns burned bright, like stars captured and brought down to earth.

She fought down her disappointment, a surprisingly difficult thing to do. "You have lost someone close to you." She said, remembering his eyes when she spoke of her sister. It had not been the strain he had shown that afternoon when they'd talked of his half-brother. No, this went much deeper.

"My mother."

The answer was quick, his mouth pressing in a hard line, as though he were fighting down a great pain.

She tightened her fingers on his arm in a show of comfort. "How long ago did she pass?"

"Oh, years ago. I was just a boy, five, maybe six at the time."

"I don't think it matters how much time passes after losing a loved one, there is always the hole in your heart they once occupied. That pain, while it can dull and change, never leaves you."

He looked at her, and she saw it then, that same banked pain that she felt over Guinevere, that could flare unexpectedly at a memory.

"I always felt weak for letting it affect me as it has."

"It is not weak to remember someone you loved. Rather, it is weak to forget them simply because the memory of them brings you pain." She fingered the locket at her throat.

They made another turn then, heading down the path that led through soaring stone arches and alongside the dinner boxes that lined the other side of The Grove. They were quiet for a time, each mired in their own thoughts, their own pain, their own memories.

Yet Rosalind's memories of Guinevere were softened now. Remembering her as she must have been here, as she had used to be before her return from London, had changed something in her. She had spent so long with the image of pain and grief dulling the recollection of her sister's natural joy, Rosalind had quite forgotten how much happiness she used to pull from life.

As if reading her thoughts, Tristan said, his voice infinitely gentle, "The locket, it's a reminder of your sister?"

"Yes." The answer came without hesitation. For where was the secret in that? No, the secret was in the contents themselves.

"She is the reason you have such a distrust of men like me."

It was said so matter-of-factly, so calmly, it stole Rosalind's breath. She could deny it, of course. Could claim outrage over his assumption.

Instead she said, with an ease that should have frightened her, "It was during her time in London. She fell in love, was seduced, abandoned. She returned home a veritable shell of her former self." She swallowed hard, the memory a cherry pit lodged in her throat. "She never recovered and died not long after. She simply lost the will to live. The man who left her might as well have killed her himself."

He was silent for a moment before speaking again. "I am so sorry."

"Thank you."

They came to Handel's statue then. As one they turned to look the way of the composer's gaze, to the orchestra and the dancers below. It was an odd feeling, to witness such gaiety while they were in their own bubble of sadness.

"You know," she said, "I have never told that to another living soul." She waited for panic to set in. She had revealed secrets of her sister's, ones she had sworn to never divulge to another person.

Yet all she felt was relief; her burden had been lightened. She hugged his arm to her, feeling at peace for the first time in too long.

Tristan felt the importance of Rosalind's confession to the very marrow of his bones. He was humbled by her trust in him. She had no reason to confide in him. Yet she had done just that.

He looked on as she watched the dancers twirl and dip to the lively music pouring from the orchestra. The small line between her brows was almost gone, the lines of her face softened in a way he had never seen. It was as if the telling of her pain had relieved it, as if sharing it had given her peace.

But it was more than that, really. For she had not given part of her burden to him—and mustn't that secret have been a terrible burden to carry all these years? No, she had given him a gift of incredible value. His heart squeezed with the importance of such a thing from this woman, who did not trust easily, yet had trusted in him.

And suddenly he wanted to give her something equally dear, to show her how much her faith meant to him.

How much *she* meant to him.

"You have entrusted me with knowledge that is infinitely precious," he said haltingly. "And so I will entrust you with something of my own."

She looked up at him then and laid her free hand on the dark green wool of his sleeve. "Truly, you needn't—"

"I want to," he cut in, his voice soft but firm with intention. He drew in a deep breath. "As I've told you, my mother died when I was quite young. What I have not told you was how my father hated her, and me by extension."

She sucked in a sharp breath. "Surely not, Tristan. He could not have hated his own son."

He could no longer meet her gaze, so full of disbelief and horror at his bald confession. "But that is the thing," he replied, the words ripped raw from him. "He did not believe I was his."

"Oh." The one word left her in a rush of breath.

"She had loved another, you see, and was forced into the marriage. You can imagine the hatred he felt for me. It was not something he ever hid from me but battered me with daily. If I had not found my friends Willbridge and Morley after I started school…" He paused, swallowed hard, the muscles of his throat working as he remembered those difficult days. Before he learned to hide his uncertainty and self-doubt behind false bravado, blessedly bolstered by the friendship of the two boys. "Anyway, it was something I learned to live with. And then my father remarried, and everything changed. Instead of heaping abuse upon my head, it was as if I had never been born in the first place. An improvement on what I had known before, I suppose." He tried to say the last with a touch of his typical humor, but it rang hollow in the air, a mere echo.

She was silent for a time, studying him as he had her after her own confession. He expected all manner of platitudes, not the simple question that issued from her lips.

"And your brother? Was he not treated in the same way?"

"Arthur?" An image flashed, of a boy with hair as red as their father's, his features as sharp and prominent as a proper Crosby's should be. "Not in the least. He was the wanted son, the one my father told me on numerous occasions he wished would inherit the title, the legacy."

"How incredibly cruel."

The anger in her voice surprised him. And warmed him, banishing for a moment the hurt that still festered. She was fierce when she championed someone. That she championed him, of all people, was touching indeed.

"And your stepmother allowed him to treat you so?"

"Our relationship has never been a healthy one. It could not have been easy for her, coming into a new family, knowing her beloved son would never inherit." A bitter taste entered his mouth. He swallowed it down, continued. "As I've said before, I have not seen her in years. It's easier for all involved this way, fewer hurt feelings, none of the past dredged up. Even our correspondence is handled through my solicitor. Not that Josephine follows that particular rule if it does not suit her," he finished in an aside.

She tensed, as if stunned. But when he looked down on her again her face was smooth. Though perhaps there was a deeper understanding in her eyes.

"Perhaps it is time for you to heal from the pain your father caused and reconcile with her. She could be lonely, could be wishing to make amends."

"No," he answered hurriedly. "No, I'm not sure that will ever be possible." Even as he said it, though, he felt the pain of that boy left on the outside, looking in on the happy family he should have been a part of.

Her lips quirked in wry amusement, her eyes scanning his face as if she had never seen him before.

He tilted his head. "What is it?"

"It's funny, isn't it, how we are all like paper dolls, flat, garbed carefully, only showing what we wish for others to see. But within we are books' worth of stories and dramas, heartaches and joys."

A spark of something kindled in him. "Yes." He smiled, and she smiled back. And that spark turned to a constant glow that warmed him like nothing had in far too long.

"Will you dance with me?"

The words flew from his mouth before he even knew they had taken shape in his mind. Yet the moment they came into being he knew it was quite possibly the most brilliant idea he had ever had in his life.

But this was Rosalind, the woman who quite vocally let him know how she despised men like him. Surely she would not agree, and especially in such a public setting.

Yet, to his everlasting shock and delight, she said in a sure voice, "I would love to."

He led her forward, toward the dancers already twirling about on the green before the orchestra. The delicate strains of a waltz floated through the warm evening air as he took her hand in one of his, her waist in the other, and guided her into the mass of couples.

It was as natural as breathing. Though he had never before held her in his arms like this, had never guided her in dance, they fit together, moved together as if they had been made for such a purpose. There was no elegant ballroom surrounding them, no ornate ceiling soaring high, no chandeliers heavy with candles. Instead there was the night sky above their heads and the merry lanterns lighting the trees, dancing as joyfully as the people below them. There was not a multitude of lords and ladies pressing in on them, dripping jewels and arrogance. Instead they passed by simple, happy folk: a carefully dressed lad with a wide-eyed shop girl in his arms, an elderly couple who moved with an ease that proclaimed them having danced many such sets with one another over their long lives together, a gruff dock worker with his tired but smiling wife.

Never had anything felt so right. And he never wanted this feeling to end.

• • •

Even hours after they returned home from Vauxhall and were supposed to be snug in their beds, Rosalind still felt the magic of those minutes beneath the inky black of the night sky, twirling in Tristan's arms.

Was it magic? She wondered as she stood at her window looking out over the darkened landscape. Had she been bewitched? For something had changed in her once she stepped foot inside that fabulous pleasure garden. A wonder had been revealed, a longing unlocked.

Could it have been the exchange of long-held pain with Tristan? She still did not know what had possessed her, to reveal one of the darkest secrets of her heart to him. Yet she could not regret it, especially as he had given her such an important part of himself in return.

She was overcome with the urge to see him. Which was silly, really. It was not as if he were in another house across town. She would see him with the coming of the new day.

Even so, the morning seemed an inordinately long time away.

She chewed on her lip, eyeing the door to her room. Perhaps he was up. Perhaps he was even now looking at his own door, thinking of her. Or mayhap he was out in the hall this very moment, waiting for her to look out.

The idea was preposterous, of course. What reason did he have to think of her, after all? She was nothing, a nobody.

Even so, she could not stop her feet from moving for the door, could not halt her hand, grabbing hold of the handle and turning. She would have a quick look, then duck back inside and go to sleep like a proper companion.

Taking a deep breath, she threw the door open and stepped into the hall. And immediately stumbled to a halt. For there he was, burnished gold by the faint light from the wall sconces, wrapped in a sapphire brocade robe, his feet strong and bare on the plush runner. And he was staring at her in a shock that she knew must mirror her own.

They stood that way for a time, like statues, frozen. Then he let out a breath, her name escaping his lips like a benediction.

"Rosalind."

She could not have stopped from rushing to him had she wanted to. He met her halfway, his arms coming about her, his mouth finding her own. Then there was no room to think; only feeling, and sensation, and joy. And him. Always him.

Chapter 21

Heaven. He was in heaven. Never had anything felt so right in his life. For the first time he felt a homecoming, like he belonged.

She was all eagerness, her mouth opening beneath his, her arms dragging him close. And her body. He wanted to weep for the gloriousness of her body, barely clothed in a thin cotton nightgown, without stays or layers to bar him from feeling her breasts pressed into his chest, the gentle swell of her belly against his groin, the delicate arch of her spine as he swept his hands down its length to find the flare of her hips.

He pulled his mouth free, ran his lips across her cheek to the long length of her pale throat. "I had to kiss you," he rasped, skimming his teeth along the sensitive skin below her ear, eliciting a gasp from her. "If I didn't kiss you this moment, I swear I would have gone mad."

"I hoped I would find you here," she breathed, her fingers grasping greedily onto his shoulders, bringing him closer.

The confession nearly buckled his knees. He found her lips again, plundered her mouth, drowning in the smell and taste of her until it was a part of him. She responded, matching every stroke of his tongue, every caress of his hands. He had experienced a taste of her passion before, when he had kissed her in the garden. This, though, was unlike anything he expected from her. Here was Rosalind unleashed, showing him a passion he never knew existed in her.

But even as he began to lose himself, the smaller, saner part of him took hold, reining him in. He forced himself to pull back, the soft cry of loss tumbling from her lips nearly breaking his resolve. With a shuddering breath and clenched teeth he held himself in check. Barely, but he managed it. He pressed his forehead to hers, knowing if he looked down at her, at the proof of her desire, he would be lost.

"I can't keep kissing you, Rosalind." The words were bitter on his tongue, even as her sweet breath fanned his face, further weakening his resolve. "If I do I won't be able to stop."

There was silence in the hall, broken only by the rasp of their uneven breath. Then her voice, so soft he barely heard it.

"So don't stop."

He let out a shuddering breath, the longing those words brought nearly unmanning him. He clenched his eyes all the tighter, shaking his head, her hair rasping against his. "You don't know what you're saying."

"I do." Her voice was stronger now, and unbelievably calm.

He opened his eyes. Surely she was mad to suggest such a thing. After what she had divulged to him tonight, he knew now why she would keep her distance, would hold herself away from men like him.

Yet her eyes were clear, the certainty and trust in them wrapping around his heart.

His resolve began to melt like frost after the first rays of a spring sun. Still he must make her understand what was at stake.

"I won't be able to keep myself from claiming you. You will be mine, Rosalind."

"You won't hurt me, Tristan." She laid a soft hand against his cheek and smiled. "I know you now. I trust you. Make me yours."

The remainder of his willpower vanished in an instant. With a groan he pulled her back into his arms, lowered his mouth to hers. Joy sang through his veins as a realization hit him: he loved her. By God, he loved her. Rosalind was his, and he was hers. He belonged to someone.

And he would never let her go.

• • •

Rosalind had known their kiss was getting out of hand. She was smart, after all, could take control of the situation and see that it did not go too far. She had been readying herself to pull away, to put a stop to it, to return to her lonely bed and spend the rest of the night dreaming of what might have been if she had less sense.

But then Tristan had torn his mouth from hers and dragged in that ragged breath. And the vulnerability in his warning to her had gone straight to her heart.

He was not that man she thought he was. Not even close. And she knew in that moment, despite her intentions, she had gone and fallen in love with him.

She, Miss Rosalind Merriweather, a woman of too little trust and too much sense, had gone and fallen for Sir Tristan Crosby, a London rake. She wanted to laugh. She wanted to shout it from the rooftops. Instead she pulled him closer, running her hands over the incredible breadth of his shoulders, reveling in the strength of him. In answer he swept his arms beneath her, cradling her to his chest and striding to her bedroom. As if from a distance she heard the soft click of the door as he closed it, a metallic rattle as he turned the key in the lock. And then he lowered her feet to the floor, and she was against the door, his body pressing her into the wood panel, every hard inch of him demanding surrender.

She gave it, with a joy she could not remember ever feeling before. Spearing her fingers into the silkiness of his hair, her tongue met his with wild abandon. His hands skimmed down her body, brushing over the sides of her breasts, her waist, her hips. His fingers found purchase behind her knees, hitched her legs up to settle about his hips. He pressed into the cradle there.

Rosalind's eyes rolled back in her head, her mouth tearing free on a gasp as sensation bombarded her. His lips found her throat, laving the skin there even as he pressed against her, rocking against her most tender flesh. The tension that had been coiling within her wound tighter, until she thought she might shatter. Yet with every press of him into the core of her, the feeling intensified. How was this bliss possible?

"Rosalind." His voice was deep, moving through her, a raw and primal thing. "I will stop if you wish, I swear it. For there is no turning back if we finish this. But I beg of you, tell me now while I still have the strength."

Her heart filled until she thought it might burst. She grabbed his face in her hands, forced him to look her in the eye. And said, with a certainty she felt down to the very depths of her soul, "Don't stop, Tristan. Please."

He searched her face, disbelief and desire and longing all coalescing in the blue of his eyes. Realization dawned, and a joy that seemed to match her own. He lowered her, and before her feet had even touched the floor his arms were beneath her, cradling her to his chest as if she were a precious treasure. His steps were long and sure as he carried her to the bed, his arms strong as he lowered her to the mattress, his body hard as he covered her. She opened her arms to him, eager for what was to come next now that she had gotten a taste of it.

"I need to see you." His words were hot on her skin, scorching her. His fingers found the hem of her gown then. She expected him to yank it off of her in one fluid motion; instead his fingers began a slow climb up her body, grazing her sensitive flesh, exposing her skin to the cool night—and his hot gaze—inch by inch. She lay as still as possible, watching his face the whole while, for the first time doubt creeping in. What would he think of her? She, who was too thin, too small, with hardly a curve in sight. He must be used to voluptuous, desirable women throwing themselves at him daily. She had seen it for herself, seen the beauty and the sultriness of the ladies of society, the women who looked at him with blatant invitation.

Yet his gaze only grew hotter the more she was exposed to him. And then her gown was up and over her head, and she was bared completely to him as she had never been to another. And he looked at her as if he could not believe his fortune.

"You are beautiful, Rosalind." His gaze skimmed her, over every dip and valley, and she felt it like a physical touch. "You are so damn beautiful."

She felt the hot press of tears behind her eyes. She had never felt attractive. Yet now, with him, she was the most beautiful creature in existence.

Wordlessly she reached for him. She needed him in her arms. Instead of going to her, however, he rolled from the bed. Rosalind had no time to wonder at it, for his hands immediately went to the sash of his dressing gown. Soon the silky material was falling from his shoulders, his smalls soon following. She had only a moment to drink in her fill before he rejoined her. Yet what she saw was not something she would ever be able to forget. Smooth golden skin, a broad chest tight with muscles and covered in a dusting of pale hair, all tapering down to a lean waist, hard thighs, long legs. And that most private part of him, large and strong and ready for her.

She might have faltered then. But he was covering her, his bare skin pressed close to hers. And there was no more room for doubt or fear. For never had anything felt so incredible as this.

A low moan escaped him, the sound vibrating his chest against her sensitive breasts, the combination of sound and sensation going straight to the center of her. She thought he would kiss her then. And he did. Only not where she expected.

He moved down her body, his hands large and warm on her skin, his lips following. Over her neck, her shoulder, her chest. Then he was cupping her breast, and his mouth settled warm over the nipple, drawing it into his mouth.

Rosalind cried out, her back arching off the mattress as heat speared her, shooting from her breast straight to the core of her. She writhed beneath him, pushing up into his mouth, her fingers diving into his hair, silently begging for more. He answered with tongue and teeth, heightening the pleasure until she thought she might scream.

His mouth lifted then, releasing her breast from his sweet torment. But the agony did not end there. For his lips trailed over her feverish flesh to her other breast, lavishing it with kisses, bringing her to even greater heights. His hands splayed over her abdomen, trailed lower, brushing the curls over her sex. The heat there intensified, scorching her very soul.

"Tristan." His name escaped her on a desperate breath, begging him for something though she knew not what. He answered the plea immediately, moving up her body.

"Open for me, Rosalind." His voice was raw, primal, touching something in her even as his trembling hands on her knees proved how deeply he was affected.

She did as he bid. At once he settled into the cradle of her thighs. A low hiss of pleasure escaped him, stirring the tendrils of hair at her temple, fanning the flame that was now raging in her. His hand moved between them, at once gentle and demanding as he searched out the heart of her. His fingers stroked her, working magic on her body, slick with the very essence of her desire. She cried out, pressing her face into his shoulder, pushing up against his questing fingers.

"You are so ready for me," he rasped. Then his hand was gone, and he was there, the blunt tip of him pushing into her.

A memory flashed then, of the sight of him, large and so very male. She froze, her muscles tensing as he began to fill her. There was burning, stretching…

He stopped. "Relax, love," he whispered against her lips, his hands stroking the hair back from her forehead, cradling her face. Then his mouth was covering hers. And there was no room to think as his lips made her forget her fears, as his hands on her body brought her back to that same place she had been.

He pushed forward then, until he was buried fully in her. She sucked in a shocked breath. But the pain was quickly gone, the warmth back. And then he moved. And the warmth turned to a blazing fire.

"Tristan," she gasped, digging her fingers into his sweat-slicked back. She wrapped her legs about him, the new tilt of her hips sending waves of pleasure coursing through her.

The guarded care he had shown moments ago melted away at proof of her desire. With a growl he moved inside her, his thrusts coming faster, harder. She matched every movement, her hips rising to meet his with some ancient instinct. Their breaths mingled, coming in ragged gasps. A bright white light began to burn behind Rosalind's tightly closed lids as her body tightened to an almost painful degree. She pressed her face into Tristan's shoulder, felt his hand cradle her head to his chest. And then his voice was in her ear, desperate, urging her on.

"Let go, sweetheart," he whispered brokenly. "Let go for me. Come for me."

His voice enveloping her, wrapping through and around her, she gasped and shattered. The white light behind her eyelids burst forth in brilliant color, fireworks that shot from the very top of her head to the tips of her toes. Even as her entire being floated in bliss, reaching the very heights of heaven, she was vaguely aware of his body tensing, of his shout of completion echoing in her ears. And then she was floating back to earth, and he was there, his arms tight about her as she drifted off to sleep.

Chapter 22

There was a moment of utter bliss when Rosalind first opened her eyes the next morning. How was it, she wondered as she lay wrapped in the tangled cocoon of sheets, that the sun looked to shine a bit more brightly this morning, the birds to chirp a touch more joyfully? She smiled, and stretched…

And immediately froze. For she wasn't wearing a stitch of clothing.

A scent reached her then, Tristan's own spice. It was in the very pillow her head lay on, ensnaring her senses. Filling her with memory. How she had begged him to come to her bed, had opened for him, given him everything she was. How she had taken him into her body… into her heart.

In an instant she was wide awake. But there was no magic of the night before to ease her mind. No, the coming of the day had brought the return of reality. She had gone and done what she had vowed to never do, had allowed her heart to be touched, then had allowed it to reign supreme over the better sense of her mind.

But surely he had not merely used her, she thought. A pernicious voice sounded in her ear, asking if that were so, why was he gone from her bed without even a note goodbye? And, more importantly, without any idea what their future might bring?

She fought down the encroaching panic those thoughts brought. Curling onto her side, she wrapped her arms around the pillow, pressed her face into it. There, with her eyes shut tight, darkness and Tristan's cologne her only companions, she was able to remember the feel of his arms about her, his tender words in her ear. He had made her feel so safe, so cherished. He must care about her. He would not have lain with her if he didn't. Not after what they had become to one another. He was different from other men like him, would not take advantage of her.

But as she sighed and sat up, intending to put aside her anxiety and start the day, she caught sight of something gleaming amidst the white sheets.

A gold chain.

She gasped, her fingers going to her throat even as she knew there would be nothing there. Before her the chain lay broken, the clasp twisted beyond repair. She stared at it uncomprehendingly for a moment, only realizing as she reached for it that the locket was missing.

Once again panic took hold of her. She lurched to her knees, tearing the covers back, searching frantically. At last she found it beneath the pillow. The burnished gold winked feebly up at her in the bright morning light, the brilliant turquoise dull and lifeless.

She grasped onto it, her fingers folding around the small locket so tightly the stones bit into her palm. "Guinevere," she whispered brokenly. How had she forgotten Guinevere? It was then the foolishness of what she had done hit her. Her sister had loved where she should not have, had made the mistake of surrendering her innocence for that love. And she had regretted it for what remained of her short life. All this time Rosalind had thought herself above such things. She would never be so naïve, would never make such a mistake.

Yet how different were they really? For Rosalind had done the very same thing. She had fallen in love with Tristan, had surrendered her body and her heart to him. All without the promise of tomorrows. He had never once said he loved her, had never spoken of marriage. The future had never been mentioned. And now he was gone, without a word or a note.

And she was the greatest fool that ever walked the planet. For she wanted nothing more than to find him, to surrender to his embrace again.

A sob escaped. Furious at herself now, she threw off the covers and hurried from the bed. A pitcher of chill water stood ready on the washstand. She dipped in a cloth and scrubbed herself with it, making her skin pink with protest, removing every trace of him from her body. She ignored the blood she wiped from her inner thighs, ignored the sore hidden muscles that groaned with every movement. She had made a horrible mistake. Over the course of the last few days she had allowed herself to be lulled by him, had even begun to find enjoyment in a kind of friendship with him. Then last night, with Vauxhall working its magic on her, she had been completely enchanted into giving up that which she should have protected at all costs.

She went to the wardrobe in the corner and pulled out a chemise, yanking it over her head. She wouldn't let him see what he had done to her. He would have no cause to pity her. It was a brutal lesson she had learned, but learn it she had. For she would never make such a mistake again.

* * *

Tristan whistled as he bounded up the steps to the townhouse later that day, letting himself into the front hall with a flourish that would have been impressive had anyone been about to see it. He had slipped from Rosalind's bed before dawn, leaving the warmth of her arms reluctantly. But he could not chance anyone seeing him, would not have her talked about below stairs. Besides, he'd had an important errand to run, one that could not wait a moment longer.

He had not planned for it to take as long as it had. Rosalind had to have been up for hours now, and Grace with her.

But any annoyance she might feel at his absence would surely disappear in an instant when she learned the reason for it. As a matter of fact, he thought as he patted his jacket pocket and grinned, he expected she would be so delighted that they might wind up back in her bed again before the day was through. He chuckled as he mounted the stairs to the upper floors two at a time. He would have to see to it that Grace had something to do for the remainder of the day, far away from the house.

But his cousin's room was empty when he reached the family quarters. Undaunted, he hurried down the hall to Rosalind's chamber. However it, too, was empty. The bed was made, the room neat as a pin. In his mind's eye he could see it as it had been when he had left, the bedding in complete disarray, waning moonlight bathing Rosalind as she lay amidst it all. Her eyes had been closed in a deep sleep, her face smooth from care. He recalled the fight he'd had with himself to leave her then. For he'd wanted nothing more than to return to her arms, to sink back into her welcoming warmth, to never let her go.

But his self-control would be worth it in the end.

Until then he could take the time to make his next meeting with Rosalind all the more perfect. He went to his room and to his wardrobe, digging into the very bottom until he located the simple carved wooden box hidden there. He had not looked inside the small chest for too many long years. Now was the time he made use of the contents.

An hour later, while Tristan busied himself in his study in his impatient wait for their return, he finally heard them. Grace laughed, the joyful sound carrying through the house. There was an answering murmur, Rosalind's softer voice. He straightened at that, every ounce of his attention homing in on it. He had always responded to her, had always been drawn to her. Yet now it was as if every barrier he had erected had been torn asunder, the draw to her was that much greater.

He jumped to his feet, striding from his study, and reached the front hall as the two women were about to ascend the stairs.

Grace smiled when he came into view. "There you are. I had wondered where you had got off to so early."

He hardly saw her, hardly heard her. For he could not drag his eyes from Rosalind. How had he never seen the way sunlight brought out faint red and gold highlights in her tresses, the way her eyelashes kissed her brows when her eyes opened wide, how her mouth formed a perfect bow when she pursed her lips? He noticed all that now and more.

But Grace had spoken. He fought to portray some semblance of sanity. "I had errands to run."

Grace snorted indelicately. "Errands at such an hour? You?"

He grinned, his eyes never once leaving Rosalind. "There is much you don't know about me."

"No doubt. But I have things to do, and so cannot be waylaid by your abundance of charm. I shall see the both of you later this afternoon?" Without waiting for an answer, she was off, sailing up the stairs.

Leaving him alone with Rosalind.

Tristan grinned. Never say his cousin did not have impeccable timing.

He moved closer to Rosalind where she stood on the bottom riser. "You're looking well this morning."

She said nothing. As a matter of fact, she had hardly moved at all since he had come upon them.

It was only then he noticed the pallor of her cheeks, the tight line of her lips. She was upset, deeply so.

Frowning in concern, he took up her hand in his. Even through her glove he could feel the chill of it. He removed her glove, hastily chafing her fingers between his own. All the while she stood mutely, her hand limp in his.

"Damnation, I knew I should have left word. Rosalind, I'm sorry. I did not think I would be gone so long, I swear it."

She finally reacted. But it was not with a relieved laugh and a smile. No, it was with that same disdain she used to show him, the one that made him feel he could do no right.

She pulled her hand from his. "You owe me nothing, Sir Tristan. Not your apologies, and certainly not word as to your whereabouts."

The very marrow in his bones froze as she turned from him and started up the stairs. He reached out to stay her. "Rosalind, you've got it all wrong—"

"Unhand me, sir."

Immediately he released her. Of course, he should not be talking in such a familiar way to her in such a public setting, where no doubt someone was within hearing. At least not until things were settled between them. "Come with me into the sitting room then," he murmured. When it looked as if she would deny the request he said, a touch of frustration making the word come out harsher than he intended, "Please."

She considered him with narrowed eyes, eventually nodding. Together—yet it felt as if they were worlds apart—they moved down the hall to the small private sitting room at the back of the house.

Immediately she scurried to the far corner as he closed the door, choosing an uncomfortable high-backed chair that denoted more than words her wish to have this conversation over and done with as quickly as possible. Pressing his lips tight, knowing he only had himself to blame for this debacle, he strode toward her, taking the closest possible seat, moving it even closer until their chairs touched. She stiffened but said nothing as he sat, keeping her profile to him as he turned to face her.

"I know you must be angry with me—" he began.

"You are mistaken, for I have no reason to be upset with you at all. If anything, you saved me from a very uncomfortable morning by disappearing from my bed. Which it surely would have been now that we have had our fun."

He sucked in a sharp breath. "Our fun?"

"Certainly."

"You make it sound as if that was all there was to it."

She laughed, the sound of it like sharp branches scraping windows in the dead of winter. "Ah, I see it now. You worried I would be one of those women who would expect a ring and a promise after performing such an act. Well, you may rest assured, I never wished for or needed such a thing from you."

Part of him thought she must be pushing him away on purpose. This was not the Rosalind he had come to know in the last several days. That Rosalind had been warm and giving, confiding in him things she had never told another, giving to him of herself.

But the greater part of him was louder, shouting that he should have expected as much. For if he had never been good enough for his father, his own blood, what made him think he was good enough for someone like Rosalind?

"Don't do this, Rosalind," he rasped.

"Do what? I assure you I am not doing anything."

"You are. You're pushing me away."

"Of course I'm pushing you away."

The bluntness of it, the faint way her lip curled, as if she thought him the biggest simpleton in history, was like a punch to the gut. "Why?" he managed.

"I would think it was obvious."

He ground his teeth together so brutally he thought they would shatter. But he would not win this by taking the defensive with her. He forced his jaw to relax, enough to grit out the words, "Enlighten me."

She shrugged. "You are renowned for your prowess in the bedroom. I have seen the way you charm everyone; the invitations other women give you. I admit I have been curious to experience it myself for some time. Last night in the gardens was a bit magical, I admit. I might never have had the nerve to sample what you have to offer otherwise."

His fingers dug into the arm of the chair. "You are lying," he choked.

"What reason have I to lie?"

"You are protecting yourself."

"Only in that I feel it prudent to end this now. I didn't want you to have the idea that I might be willing to continue on with the affair. It was meant to be a one-time thing, after all."

He exploded from his chair, paced the carpet in front of her. "No," he growled, his fists balling up at his sides. "No, I don't believe you're capable of such a thing. After what happened to your sister, you would never enter into a physical relationship with a man for such cold, calculating reasons."

"But you see, that's why I have."

He spun to face her. "What the devil are you talking about?"

Her eyes were flat as she considered him, as opaque as muddy pools of water. "Guinevere was foolish. She fell in love. That was what ruined her. Not the act itself, but the emotion. I made certain that I would not be tangled up in all that mess when you and I went into it."

A roaring started up in his ears. He could not have heard right. "You don't love me?"

She laughed, a horrible sound that scraped down his backbone. "Of course not. Have no fear, you needn't worry about that particular sentiment from me. And you needn't feel guilt over our tumble last night, either. For I was more than a willing participant. You have helped me to see what all the fuss is about, anyway."

Something in him broke. He reached into his pocket, felt the precious paper there. The special license he had hurried out for at the crack of dawn to secure Rosalind to him for all eternity.

His hand clenched painfully, crushing the paper. Tangling it with his mother's ring that he had picked out especially for Rosalind.

"I'm glad to hear it." His lips felt numb, letting the lie slip out. He had to get out of here, before he lost his composure. "Now, if you'll excuse me, I have somewhere to be."

With that he spun about, marching from the room. Though his broken heart remained behind with Rosalind. As it always would.

Chapter 23

"It seems we are on our own tonight," Lady Belham said as they headed out to the carriage that would take them to the evening's entertainment. A ball, from what Rosalind had been told, though she didn't have the faintest clue whose ball. Nor did she care.

She had been numb since Tristan had left her that afternoon. It was a necessity. For if she felt half of what simmered below the surface, roiling away beneath her breast, she would shatter. She had done the right thing. She was certain of it. Yet there was that small part of her that whispered of her bruised heart, telling her she had made a horrible mistake.

She had not wanted Tristan to join them this evening. As a matter of fact, she should be only relieved. He at least had the decency to see that it would not be in either of their best interests to be in one another's company tonight.

Even so, her employer's casual words were a blow.

"Sir Tristan has declined to join us?"

"Yes." Lady Belham frowned. "He declared he would be absenting himself for much of our social engagements for the foreseeable future." She looked to Rosalind. "You were with him for much of last night, my dear. Would you know anything about this sudden change?"

Rosalind blanched. Lady Belham must know what happened between them.

But the woman's eyes were kind, and full of concern, not condemnation. Rosalind drew in a steadying breath. "No, my lady."

Blessedly they reached the door and stepped out into the cool evening air. There was a bustle of activity, as they were ushered to the street and handed up into the waiting carriage.

All too soon, however, the carriage started off. And Rosalind was left in the dim quiet with Lady Belham and nothing else to occupy them.

"It's strange, his sudden shift. He has been so attentive the last few days. Now all of a sudden he is stepping back. What do you think it could be?"

Rosalind gripped the seat beneath her, digging her fingers into the plush cushion. "I hardly know," she said through stiff lips. She tensed, waiting for a bolt of lightning to hit her where she sat. Surely she would be struck down soon for her sins, not the least of which was lying to Lady Belham. The woman was concerned for her cousin, that was plain to see. Yet what could Rosalind do? Answer truthfully, that Tristan's sudden leave-taking was due to the fact that she had taken him into her bed and then had pushed him away to protect her own battered heart?

"I admit," Lady Belham went on, unaware of the torment Rosalind was in, "I have enjoyed the last several days immensely. It seems an empty evening without such wonderful company. Don't you agree?"

"Mhmm." Anything more and Rosalind thought she might loose the sob that seemed stuck in her chest. For it *had* been wonderful. For the first time in too long she had felt herself a part of something, not only a companion from the outside, brought in only when something was needed from her.

"Ah, well, we shall have to content ourselves with one another, darling." Lady Belham smiled, then launched into a long discourse on the merits of men and which would make the best dance partners for this evening. She didn't seem to mind that the conversation was decidedly one-sided.

Rosalind, for her part, knew she should attempt to respond. This was her job, after all. But she could not seem to concentrate, much less reply with any semblance of sense.

How she missed Tristan. She had not realized how much color he had given to her world, how much joy. He had become a friend in the last days, someone she had felt comfortable confiding in. He had quite stolen her heart, and the rest of her right along with it.

She fingered the locket at her throat, now held in place by a length of black ribbon. But she had been a fool for being lulled by him, and an even greater fool for giving so much of herself to him after what had happened to Guinevere. She could see that clearly now, and that the path she had taken since waking this morning was the right one. She would not be the fool her sister had been, would not allow herself to be destroyed by her love for a man.

So why did she want so badly to see him again, to laugh with him, talk with him...to love him?

She would focus on Lady Belham, she decreed as she entered the mansion beside her employer. Even so, as they passed into the front hall, as they greeted their host and they made their way into the ballroom, Rosalind found her eyes scanning the heads towering above her, looking for those telltale golden locks. Her lips twisted in disgust. It seemed her head was in full agreement with her. But her heart, that traitorous organ, would take some more convincing.

Lady Belham, thank goodness, was in high spirits. She was quickly set upon by all manner of men who would secure a dance with her. As soon as the music started up for a set, a gentleman was there to lead her off. And as soon as the music ended she was back at Rosalind's side, her eyes sparkling, her lips at Rosalind's ear as she whispered all kinds of scandalous comments, both good and bad, about her partners.

Yet Rosalind could not fail to notice that Lady Belham left the waltz open. Nor could she fail to see the sinking of the woman's spirits when that dance came and went and she remained at Rosalind's side.

It was not a blatant change of mood. She still smiled, still conversed with Rosalind. But she could see the way her employer's eyes tightened at the corners, how she scanned the room for something or someone. Had she been hoping for a particular man to claim her for the dance? Surely not, for Lady Belham had shown no favor to any of the men this evening, or any evening before this.

The dance ended, and Lady Belham's next partner arrived to claim her for the next set. As she placed her hand in his, a sudden commotion went up from the orchestra balcony. Their host stood there, looking pleased as he called for attention. The roar of conversation dwindled and as one the assembled guests turned their attention to him.

"I thank you for humoring me," he said, his voice booming over the sea of heads. "I know you wish to get back to your dancing, but I have received the most glorious news and I was given the very great honor of sharing it with you all. My very dear friend, you see, has gotten himself engaged, and I could not be more pleased. And so, without further ado, may I present Lord Bilton and his future wife, Miss Georgiana Harvey."

A roar of well-wishes erupted from the partygoers. Rosalind clapped along with them as the newly engaged couple took their places beside their host. The gentleman she recognized as having danced with Lady Belham on more than one occasion. He looked down at his future wife with a small smile, while she beamed and blushed. Such was the commotion from the announcement that Rosalind did not immediately notice Lady Belham still at her side—nor the woman's changed pallor.

It was when her employer began to sway, however, that Rosalind understood that all was not right. She hurriedly put an arm about her. "My lady, are you unwell?"

The woman did not answer. She looked to be in more distress as her eyes remained fixed to the balcony. "It can't be," she muttered weakly.

"Lady Belham?" The woman did not seem to know Rosalind was there at all. Her lips worked silently, tears pooling in her eyes. Without warning she listed to the side.

Rosalind stumbled under the shift in weight but managed to hold her ground. She looked about, desperate for help, hoping someone might see and assist. Yet no one paid them the least mind. Blessedly a footman spied them and rushed over.

"Please," she panted as Lady Belham's head lolled. "Please help me get her to a quiet place."

The man sprang into action, lifting Lady Belham as if she weighed no more than a feather, hurrying through the crowd and out of the ballroom. Rosalind followed, scurrying after him. All about them people were in high spirits, calling out congratulations, partaking of the glasses of champagne that had been brought out. Not once did a person show concern for Lady Belham. Their eyes passed over her as if she were a trivial inconvenience.

Fury pounded through Rosalind. She had begun to enjoy her time in London, had begun to look forward to outings. All because of Tristan.

Yet since she had woken, since the spell he had wound about her had fallen away, all she could see was the falseness of it all. The people in this city cared only for their own pleasure. And she was tired of it all. So damn tired.

The footman led her to a sitting room off the front hall. But as he made to move into the room he gasped, then backed out. Frustrated, only wanting to get Lady Belham to a couch where she could be revived, Rosalind peered around him.

There, in the depths of the room, a couple was in an amorous embrace. At any other time she would have hurried away. In that moment, however, she was well beyond caring what anyone thought of her. She had no more delicate sensibilities. They had fled along with her innocence the night before.

"Please leave," she called out in a strident voice, moving into the room and waving the footman in after her. "A lady has fainted and we require use of the space."

There was a scurry of movement, as clothing was put to rights. Soon the couple was hurrying out. They were passing her when she chanced to look at the man's face.

"Lord Kingston," she gasped.

He jerked, his gaze finding hers. But there was not an ounce of guilt in his eyes as he smiled sheepishly. "Ah, Miss Merriweather. What a surprise to see you here."

"No doubt," she replied coldly. She was vaguely aware of the footman moving to a settee, of him lowering Lady Belham to it. But she could not take her eyes from Lord Kingston. Here was Tristan's good friend, the man he had vouched for, saying he would be a perfect match for Miss Weeton.

Speaking of which. "That was not Miss Weeton," she remarked, narrowing her eyes.

He chuckled, and fury pounded up her spine. "You know how things are. Temptation and all." He leaned in closer in a conspiratorial manner, and Rosalind clenched her hands tight in her skirts to keep from scoring his face with her nails.

"I don't think I have to mention that it would be best if this is kept between us," he murmured meaningfully. Giving her a wink, not waiting for an answer, he sauntered off.

Rosalind stared after him. She wanted to rage. She wanted to weep. She should have known this would happen, had felt it from the start. But she had begun to believe Tristan, to hope that he was right, that a rake could be turned, that men were not evil beasts bent on exploiting and conquering...

More fool she.

But he did not deserve even a second more of her time. She had more important things to take care of. Rushing to Lady Belham's side, she immediately began to chafe her hands. "Please fetch me a vinaigrette," she said to the footman, who still stood beside the settee.

Before he had taken a step, however, Lady Belham began to rouse. Her head thrashed on the pillow, a frown marring her brow. "No," she moaned. "No, it cannot be."

"Lady Belham." When the woman only moaned the more Rosalind took hold of her arms and gave her a shake. "Lady Belham. Grace!"

The woman gasped, her eyes flying open. "Goodness, what happened?"

"You fainted." Rosalind peered at her closely, watching as confusion clouded her employer's eyes. "Do you remember what happened to put you in such a state?"

It was as if realization crashed down on her then, taking the very color from her cheeks. She sucked in a sharp breath, her eyes clouding with pain. "Rosalind, darling, I need to get home. Now."

Rosalind frowned. "It's best if you rest. You need to regain your strength—"

"What I need," the other woman said, struggling to rise to a sitting position, "is to get away from here with all haste."

Beyond the pain, beyond the strange grief that colored her employer's face, there was also a stubborn determination. Rosalind could see it in the mulish tilt of her chin, in the steely glitter in her eyes.

"Very well," she replied with reluctance. She rose, giving Lady Belham her arm to assist her in standing. She looked to the waiting footman as her employer found her balance. "Please have our carriage brought around. We'll be departing immediately."

"Very good, Miss." With evident relief, the footman hurried off.

"Lady Belham," Rosalind said as the man disappeared, leaving them blessedly alone, "what is going on? What happened in the ballroom to cause you such distress?"

A sad smile flitted across the older woman's face. "I promise to tell you all once we are safe at home," she rasped. A swell of sound was heard then, music starting, and cheers. Her eyes found the door to the hall, a look of intense pain contorting her features for a moment before she smoothed them and returned her attention to Rosalind. "And darling, don't you think you had better start calling me Grace? For I can promise you, you are the very dearest friend I have ever had."

Rosalind's throat closed. She squeezed the other woman's hand. "Very well, Grace."

Grace returned the pressure. "I am so very glad I had the good sense to hire you on, dearest," she whispered thickly.

"You saved me," Rosalind managed.

"I do believe we have saved each other," Grace whispered with a watery smile.

Chapter 24

The strength that had been roused in Grace proved temporary. The moment they arrived home and reached the seclusion of her bedchamber, the soft snick of the door announcing their privacy, the woman's composure crumbled like the thinnest pastry.

Sobs wracked her body, so violent she could hardly breathe much less stand. Rosalind supported her as best she could, guiding her to a chair, feeling more helpless than she had in nearly a decade. What kind of comfort could she give? What comfort had she been able to give Guinevere all those years ago?

She pushed down the hopelessness. Now was not the time. Grace needed her. She moved to help the other woman with her outer garments, to make her more comfortable. But Grace's hand gripped hers tight. Giving up her ministrations, she perched on the arm of the chair and pulled her into her embrace.

As the woman let loose her sorrow, shaking their bodies with the force of it, memories assailed Rosalind again, unearthing the pain of a past that too closely mirrored the present. Only once had Rosalind witnessed such grief. The night of Guinevere's return from London, well after they had all retired for the night, Rosalind had heard it: muffled wailing, as if dredged from the very depths of a person's soul.

She had found Guinevere then, curled up on the floor in her room. Rosalind had not understood the despair her sister felt, much less the cause of it. But she had held her as her sister cried herself insensible, until dawn had come and her weeping had subsided. Guinevere had been a shell after that night, walking the halls of their home as a specter. Had Rosalind known in the beginning what had caused her to grieve so, perhaps she might have been able to help. But she had given her sister space, and thereby had lost her more and more each day.

She would be damned if she'd lose Grace in the same way.

"Who is he?"

Grace's sobs hitched at the gentle question before falling away altogether. She lay quiet in Rosalind's arms then until, with a shuddering breath, she began to speak.

"I did not intend to begin an affair. Despite my outlandish, flirtatious ways, I have only ever been with one man. I am not naturally a promiscuous creature."

Rosalind remained silent, knowing that, more than anything, Grace needed the time to gather her thoughts. At length, she spoke again, weariness coating every word.

"But the moment I saw Lord Bilton I was lost. And, by some miracle, he seemed to feel the same for me. It all happened quickly, so quickly I was carried away by it all. He made me feel beautiful, and adored, and young again. I never had a Season, never came to London in my youth. The moment I was of age I was married off to Lord Belham and spirited off to Manderly. Eventually I came to care for Belham, in my own way. He was not unkind, tried to make me happy." She took a deep breath. "But I always felt I had been deprived of experiencing that which all young women were given: a chance to be young, to have admirers, to flirt and dance and be courted."

She pulled back, looked up at Rosalind as if begging her to understand. "Bilton gave me all that. He told me I was the most beautiful creature in existence. He told me he loved me, that we would be together forever." Her lips twisted, but it was an expression more of pain than humor. "I should have known he did not mean to marry me. Oh, I knew it was expected of him, that he should find a nice biddable young girl who could give him a large dowry and sons. But, fool that I am, I allowed myself to hope he meant to marry me. Even when he insisted that we meet in secret so we could revel in our new love. Even when he took me to his bed without promise of tomorrow."

The words struck to the heart of Rosalind. For they too closely mirrored her own situation, her own hurt.

"I should have known," Grace continued, her voice turning into a low moan of sound. "Why would he want me? A woman past her youth, who failed to give her husband a child in all the years of her marriage? No, I was a fool, a damned fool for believing it."

Rosalind took Grace's face in her hands. "You are the least foolish woman I know. You are kind, and strong, and brilliant. If anyone is a fool it is Lord Bilton, for not seeing the treasure he had in his grasp."

Grace collapsed against her, insensible again. Rosalind rubbed her back, murmuring soothing, nonsensical words into her hair. Were all women fools then? And were all men destined to destroy their very hearts?

She should be glad she ended things with Tristan when she had, though she had lost her innocence and her heart to him before finding the wisdom to do the right thing. Even so, as she held Grace, she wished his arms were around her, and wanted to weep for it.

. . .

It was dawn before Tristan stumbled through the front door of his house. He would have stayed away longer if he could. But even broken-hearted fools needed a shave and a change of clothes from time to time.

The house was quiet, chambermaids hurrying about, doing their work before the household awoke for the day. One spotted him, squeaking before hurrying off. As he made his way down the upper hallway leading to his bedchamber, he endeavored to keep his steps light. He did not wish to rouse Grace. Or, rather, he did not wish to field the questions she was sure to have regarding his terse words to her yesterday afternoon, his sudden abandonment of her.

But as he made to pass his cousin's door it was thrown wide. He turned sheepishly to face her, feeling like a green lad being called to the carpet.

Instead he came face to face with Rosalind.

Despite the hurt she had given him, despite his anger at her usage of him, he stood dumbly for a time, drinking her in. God, she was beautiful, her chin in that little point, her bow of a mouth. And those eyes, like warm chocolate, huge enough to drown in.

It took him several long seconds before he realized how disheveled she was, that the line between her brows was deeper than ever. He opened his mouth to question her. She spoke before the words could form in his fuzzy brain.

"Your cousin needs you."

Instantly the fog of alcohol he had cloaked himself in since yesterday afternoon lifted. "Grace? What is wrong with her?"

In answer, Rosalind stepped aside. He hurried past her, into his cousin's room. He was barely aware of the soft sound of the door closing as he rushed to Grace's bedside.

She was tucked under the blankets like a small child, her hair in an inky plait over the pillow. Her skin was pale, her eyes red-rimmed. He had never seen her looking so vulnerable and frail.

He sank with care onto the bed, taking her hand. At his touch, her eyelashes fluttered up. "You're home."

"By the looks of you I should have never left."

Her lips quirked in a ghost of a smile. "Look that hideous, do I?"

"Quite," he teased softly. But the small smile left his face as quickly as it had come. "Are you ill?"

"Only in heart." She let out a sigh before pushing herself to sitting. "I have been a fool, Tristan, though my darling Rosalind tells me otherwise."

"Tell me everything," he demanded.

"I shall not." She raised her chin, a bit of her typical fire returning. "There are some things a woman must keep, secrets of her heart that cannot be told, even to the dearest cousin. Suffice it to say, I did something incredibly stupid. I fell in love." A look of acute pain crossed her face. "Though I wanted something permanent from it, he had other ideas."

Heat raced under his skin. Stunned, it took him a moment to recognize it for what it was: fury. Toward the unknown man, yes, for hurting his cousin, for breaking her heart.

But also toward himself. How had he missed the signs? How had he completely overlooked this important thing that had been going on in his cousin's life? He hated himself then for the bastard he was, to be so wrapped up in his own troubles and pleasures that he had abandoned Grace to the machinations of a libertine.

He understood then some of the desperate hate Rosalind had felt for rakes. And he could understand more fully her refusal to open her heart to him, to use him as her sister had been used. The pitiful hope he'd unknowingly harbored in his breast that Rosalind had been lying, that she might truly love him and he might have a future with her, was snuffed out in an instant.

Rage crashed through him then, for all he had been deprived of in his childhood, for all he had lost after being foolish enough to believe he might find his place with Rosalind. He focused it on the faceless man who had caused his cousin pain, until it was all he felt. "Tell me who it is," he growled.

"I most certainly shall not. For I won't have you doing anything idiotic for my mistake."

"Tell me, Grace," he ordered again.

"No."

He let out a frustrated breath, rising, running his hand through his hair as he went to the window. "Why? Why can't I know?"

"Because, dearest cousin, I happen to like you and don't wish you to leave this world with a bullet lodged in your skull."

He let out a harsh bark of laughter. "You think I would lose?"

"Perhaps. Perhaps not. But it is not something I wish to chance. Besides, I am not some innocent, that you need to protect my honor. My heart shall be the only casualty of this fiasco."

He ground his teeth together, looking out over the back of the house and the garden below it. Dawn was lighting the sky in faint oranges and pinks, but the garden remained in shadow. Even so, he could just make out the edge of the bench where he had first kissed Rosalind.

It seemed a lifetime ago. Things had changed so much between them, first for the better, then for the worst. Did she truly not care for him? Had she truly used him? He could not believe it, not after the way she had opened to him, had given of herself, had trusted him.

Yet he could not put from his mind the cold look in her eyes when she had turned him away, the cruel certainty of her words. His own father had thought little of him; was it such a stretch to believe Rosalind did too?

"She stayed with you all night."

"Rosalind?" Grace's voice grew soft. "Yes, she did."

"And she knows who broke your heart?"

There was a pause. "She will not tell you, you know. She will keep my secret."

He snorted. "That I believe. Rosalind does not do anything she does not wish to do."

"You have had a falling out."

It was not a question. It did not deserve an answer, not after Grace's own secretive manner. Yet he answered it all the same. "Yes."

"Would you like to talk about it?"

He turned to look at her. "Men have secrets as well," he murmured, unable to keep the sorrow from his voice.

She held out her hand. He went to her, took it in his, pressed a kiss to it.

"Was it a mistake, I wonder," he mused somberly as he studied the lighter skin on the finger where her wedding band used to reside, "to invite you to London?"

"I wanted to come."

His lips twisted. "You do not answer the question."

She pressed her lips tight. "That is because, if there was a mistake, it was mine to make. You did not force me to come, Tristan."

He ignored her. For he was, once again, too far along in his self-hatred to pay any attention to any platitudes she might offer.

"You were happier at Manderly, even with that husband you did not want."

"I do not know if you can call it happiness when I was so numb I hardly felt a thing."

He squeezed her fingers once more before releasing them and stepping back. "What will you do?"

She shrugged, looking suddenly weary. "I hardly know. But I do know that I am the one who has to make the decision. As much as I hate to admit it, I am a grown woman, Tristan, and must act like one."

He gave her a small, sad smile before moving for the door.

"You are going out again."

Once more, it was not a question. And again, he felt compelled to answer it regardless. "Yes. But I will be back later. You will tell me your decision the moment it is made?"

"Of course, darling," came her soft reply.

With a nod he let himself out into the hall. *I will not look to her door*, he told himself as he strode to his bedchamber. Even so, his eyes slid along the wall until he found her room. At his door he stopped, remembering how she had looked when he had seen her that night, before she wound up in his arms. If Grace did as he suspected and returned to Scotland, would she take Rosalind with her? The idea tore into him, stealing his very breath. He hurried into his room, closing the door with as much finality as he closed the gate on his heart.

Chapter 25

Not an hour later Tristan stormed into the Coffee Room of White's. Because why not? He'd spent the better part of last night here. He might as well make it his permanent refuge. He briefly wondered what the waiters would do if he set up a makeshift cot in the corner. For he did not think he could spend another night under the same roof as Rosalind.

He caught sight of Hugh Carlisle across the room. The man was deeply immersed in his paper to the point that he remained unaware when a waiter deposited a steaming cup at his elbow. Thank the heavens, for Tristan had no wish to make conversation with the man. It was too much of a painful reminder of the past few days, and Rosalind, and what she deemed the perfect man. Here was the type of gent women would marry, not Tristan and his reputation and his rakehell ways.

So immersed was he in self-recriminations, he was nearly upon Rafe before he saw him. Without waiting for an invitation—for when had he ever needed one from his friend?—he dropped into a chair beside him.

"I had hoped I would find you here," he growled. Motioning to a waiter, he barked, "Coffee, and make it black and hot enough to scald my tongue off."

He expected all manner of teasing from his friend. Rafe had often joked about Tristan's seeming inability to be anything but cheerful, and here he was being decidedly not. But his friend looked surprisingly sober when Tristan looked his way.

"Miss Merriweather told you then, has she?"

Tristan could only stare at him. What the devil was he on about? And why had he mentioned Rosalind?

Before he could even begin to formulate a question of his own, Rafe's lips twisted. He lifted his drink—definitely not coffee, that—and took a healthy swig. "I told her it was nothing, the silly woman. Why she had to go running to you, I've no idea."

Tristan straightened, gripping the chair arms tight to keep from taking the man by the cravat and shaking him. "What did you do to Rosalind?" he said in a low, dangerous voice.

Rafe gaped at him. "What the devil has gotten into you?"

"Tell me," he demanded, leaning in close, until he could smell the whiskey on his friend's breath. "The whole of it. Before I do something we both regret."

"I don't know what she told you to set you off to such a degree, but it was only a bit of fun."

Tristan's vision went red at the edges. "I repeat, and you had best answer truthfully, what have you done to Miss Merriweather?"

"Not a blasted thing. Unless you count offending her innocent sensibilities."

"Rafe," Tristan growled in warning.

His friend—if he could still call him that—held his hands up in surrender. "So she saw me with another woman. It's nothing to her."

It took a moment for the words to sink in. When they did, Tristan stared at Rafe blankly. "So you did not proposition Miss Merriweather?"

Rafe laughed. "Gad, no. Why would I want to do that?"

Relief such as he had never known flowed through Tristan. He slumped back, accepting his coffee from a cautious-looking waiter. "Damn it, I'm sorry, man. I'm out of sorts."

Rafe leaned back with a grin. "You had me scared there for a second. I've never seen you in such a state."

Tristan lifted the coffee to his lips, taking a scalding gulp, feeling the burn of it fill him, down through his chest, into his gut. And with it came a clear-headedness.

…As well as a realization of what Rafe had unwittingly revealed.

He slowly lowered his cup, peering closely at his friend. "What do you mean, she saw you with another woman?"

But Rafe did not heed the dangerous undercurrent in the question. He crossed one booted foot over the opposite knee. "Oh, I was only having a bit of fun with Mrs. Shreeves last night and Miss Merriweather barged in. I thought she would bring fire and brimstone down on my head, with the fury that was in her eyes." He chuckled.

Tristan's eyes narrowed. "Mrs. Shreeves? But what of Miss Weeton?"

"What of her?"

"I was under the impression you were courting her?"

"Oh, I am. I fully intend to marry the girl." Rafe grinned. "But that does not mean I'm dead."

With slow, careful movements, Tristan placed his hot cup of coffee down on the table beside him. "Do you mean to tell me that you do not intend to give up your inamoratas when you marry?"

Rafe scoffed. "Course not. Would you wish to drink only one beverage for the rest of your life, partake of only one type of cake? I thought you knew me better than that, Crosby."

So did I, Tristan thought as he looked on the other man with new eyes. A pounding started up at his temples. This was a man he had trusted, someone he thought would treat Miss Weeton with all the respect she deserved.

He had been wrong. So damned wrong.

Rosalind's recriminations hit him then, nearly stealing his breath. She had seen from the beginning that Rafe would not suit, that he was a bad choice for Miss Weeton. And Tristan had fought against every one of her valid concerns.

He stood, needing to escape Rafe's presence. But first, something needed to be said.

"You will stay away from Miss Weeton."

Rafe looked up at him in surprise. "What was that?"

"You heard me. I don't want you near her."

Letting out a bark of laughter, Rafe turned his attention back to his drink. "Good joke, old man."

"It is not a joke."

But Rafe only chuckled and took a sip. Tristan knocked the glass from his hands.

Rafe surged to his feet, staring in dumbfounded outrage at Tristan. Whiskey stained his snowy white cravat, dripped from his nose. "Damn it, Crosby, what in hell are you about?"

Tristan was distantly aware of the room having grown silent, of the other occupants staring at them. He didn't give a damn. Stepping closer, he said, his voice deadly calm, "You will stay away from Miss Weeton, or you will hear from me."

"You have no right, no right at all to warn me away from anyone." Rafe pulled himself to his full height. "If I wish to court Miss Weeton I shall. It's not as if I don't care about the girl, after all."

"If you cared about her you would not be cavorting with other women. You would not be planning to betray her once wed."

"It's the way things are done with our set."

"I don't give a bloody damn how things are done. I believed you a better man than that, Rafe. Else I would not have directed your attentions to her."

"I would have found her eventually. You cannot take all the credit for it."

"Would you have?" Tristan came back hotly. "You have known the girl for two years now. Can you tell me with utmost certainty that you would have *eventually* seen the gem that she is without the fact being thrust under your nose?"

For once Rafe looked uncomfortable. His eyes slid away from Tristan's, unable to admit such a falsehood.

Tristan felt suddenly weary to his very bones. "Go look elsewhere. There are plenty of women out there who would not be utterly destroyed by your lack of devotion. But stay away from Miss Weeton. For all that is between us, please."

His defeated, heartsick tone must have finally reached something in Rafe. His friend peered at him before, releasing a harsh breath, he nodded once.

Tristan released a breath he had not realized he'd been holding. "Thank you," he said, before he turned about and left.

But even with the relief Rafe's agreement brought, the weariness did not leave him. He would have told himself it was the sleeplessness of the past two nights catching up to him. Yet he knew in his heart that was far from the reason.

He had been wrong about so many things in the past weeks. First in being blind to Grace's plight, allowing her to fall prey to a libertine. Then in being so devastatingly mistaken about Rafe.

More than anything, however, was thinking he could claim Rosalind for his own, and the fact that he was no longer furious with her, but rather with himself. He had been a fool in more ways than one, but none worse than believing he was worthy of the love of a woman such as she.

Even as he made his way to the street and his carriage, dreaming of a soft bed and the blessed oblivion of sleep, he knew there was more he had to do before he rested. First and foremost, there was a young lady in need of his apology. He only prayed Miss Weeton would not take his news regarding Rafe too hard. His soul could not bear to have her heartbreak piled onto it.

• • •

It was a mere hour later that he departed from the Weeton's townhouse. Miss Weeton had done her best to hide her hurt over Rafe's actions, but Tristan had seen it there, clouding the gentle depths of her eyes.

He did not deserve her gracious acceptance of his apology, did not deserve the emphatic way she insisted he was not at fault, that her heart, while not unscathed, was only slightly wounded and would heal in a very short time. But he would take it, and gladly.

Exhaustion weighed heavy on him. Though even the call of his bed and the oblivion of sleep was not enough to make him wish to return home, where he would see Rosalind around every corner. In the end he decided to go to the only place he knew he could find some semblance of solace: to Willbridge's Brook Street house and the friendly ear he could find in Daphne.

But even that was denied him as he was directed to the sitting room and caught what was undoubtedly the most somber look ever to cross her perpetually cheerful countenance.

"What is it now?" he groaned as he came closer.

"It is Lord Sumner."

Tristan dropped into a chair across from Daphne. "Don't tell me Imogen has done away with the man after the idiotic thing he has done."

Daphne did not even crack a smile at the pathetic attempt at a joke. "She has not. But he has died nonetheless."

Tristan gaped at her. She was jesting. By all accounts the man had barely received a scratch in the carriage accident that had taken the life of his latest mistress. But the seriousness of Daphne's face told him it was nothing but the truth.

He lurched forward, taking her hand in his. "Damn me, I'm so sorry."

"Don't apologize. You could not have known." She sighed, the weight of the world in it. "We received word not an hour past. It seems an infection set in from the minor injury he sustained. Mama says we are to leave with all haste, before the day is even done."

He squeezed her hand. How this must weigh on her. Daphne, who had so looked forward to her first London Season it had been all she could think or talk about for the year before. And too, he knew her genuine like of Lady Sumner. First, as their neighbor of many years back at the family seat, Willowhaven, but more so now through Imogen and Caleb's marriage.

"Is there anything I can do?" he asked.

She shook her head morosely. They sat in silence for a time, listening to the chaos that trickled down from above, no doubt the household being turned on end as Daphne's mother, the dowager Lady Willbridge, saw to their hasty packing. He should depart, leave the family to their preparations. Yet even faced with Daphne's grief he could not bring himself to leave.

He stilled. Why did he have to? Daphne could use a friend in the days to come. Willbridge would appreciate his sister and mother having a travelling companion on a trip that would doubtlessly be difficult for them. It would be perfectly natural for him to lend his services to them, being as close to the family as he was.

And if hying off to Willowhaven gave him time and distance to come to terms with his heartbreak over Rosalind, so much the better.

"Let me go with you," he said.

Daphne frowned at the suggestion. "I would not want to impose." He could not fail to see the glimmer of relief in her eyes.

"You silly thing, I think of your family as my own. Of course you would not impose."

Finally a hint of a smile lit her face. "Oh, Mama will be so relieved. She has been in such a state since we received word, has been in such a frenzy of activity, I feared for her nerves during the long trip home. Now we may have some comfort."

They wasted no time in locating Lady Willbridge. The dowager was directing servants in the family quarters, her graying copper hair frizzy, her clothing mussed. When Daphne apprised her of Tristan's offer, her eyes filled with tears.

"Oh, my darling boy, you cannot know what it means to me. We shall be more than happy to have your company and protection on the long trip to Willowhaven."

After quickly discussing the schedule, Tristan was off. It was necessary to pack, surely. More important than that, he must say goodbye to Grace. For he had a bone deep feeling she would be gone by the time he returned to London, headed back to Scotland.

And perhaps he would have the chance to bid farewell to Rosalind and close that painful chapter of his life for good.

• • •

"Rosalind."

Having spent the better part of an hour standing at the ground floor parlor window, watching as Tristan's gleaming black carriage was made ready for a long journey, Rosalind was unprepared for the quiet, somber voice behind her. But it did not startle her so much as steal her breath with the pain it caused.

So he had come to say goodbye. She had not expected it, not after the way things had ended between them.

Regret nearly choked her. For the way things had ended, yes, but also that they had ended at all. Such anguishing thoughts had begun to encroach on her, though better sense told her she had done the right thing to protect herself from further hurt.

Silencing the mournful voice in her head was not easy. Over the last two days it had only grown louder and more insistent. Focusing on the memory of Guinevere hanging about her neck on its borrowed ribbon, and the constant reminder of the heartache in Grace's face, she turned to face him.

"Sir Tristan."

His mouth pressed tight, his eyes flashing with what appeared to be pain. No, she told herself firmly, he was annoyed and nothing more. In the next instant his face cleared and he took on a distant, businesslike mien as he entered the room.

"I have come to say goodbye."

"Where are you going?" She cursed herself. The question had been burning in her mind the past hour, so much so that it burst forth quite without her permission. "Not that you need tell me. I am merely a paid companion."

"You were never *merely* anything, Rosalind."

His words, low and intense, stunned her silent. Before she could wrap her head around them, he spoke again, breaking the momentary spell.

"There has been an unexpected death in Lady Willbridge's family. I am accompanying Lady Daphne and her mother back to Northamptonshire." He paused, looking out the window at the carriage, searching for the right words. With effort, he said, haltingly, "I do not know when I shall be back. I expect you and Grace to have departed by then. But I wished to say goodbye before I left, as I may not see you again."

Tears, sudden and unexpected, nearly choked Rosalind. But what was this? She was not weak. This was a blessing. She need not see Tristan any longer, need not be faced with the monumental mistake she had made in opening her heart and body to him. She could silence the regret fermenting in her gut and put this all behind her.

Swallowing forcefully, she held out her hand to him. "Goodbye, Sir Tristan. I wish you safe journey."

He looked at her hand for a long moment, until her fingers began to tremble. When she thought he would not take it, he reached out, gripping it in his warm grasp.

The contact of his skin on her own, even something so innocuous as a handshake, was like an electric jolt through her body. She gasped, softly.

His eyes, as blue as the sky on a cloudless day, darted to her mouth. The clear blue darkened, turning stormy. His fingers tightened, infinitesimally, and for a moment she thought he might pull her close and bring his mouth to hers.

To her horror, she found she wanted that, with every bit of her heart.

After what seemed an eternity, he released her and stepped back. There should have been only relief, but Rosalind found herself fighting bitter disappointment.

"Farewell, Rosalind," he murmured. Then, with one final, shuttered look, he turned and left.

For long minutes she stood there, listening with greedy ears to the sounds of his departure. The sharp, staccato click of his boots as he crossed the entry hall, the timber of his voice as he spoke indecipherably to the butler, the heavy echo of the door as it shut behind him. And then the muffled closing of the carriage door, the sharp call of the driver, the clomp of the horses' hooves and the roll of the carriage wheels as the equipage started off.

It was only then Rosalind could draw a deep breath. But it was a shaky thing, filling her lungs with moans of loss that she refused to let loose. Smoothing out her skirts, patting her hair with trembling fingers, she left the room with determined steps.

By the time she reached Grace's room she had almost convinced herself that she would quickly get over his leaving, that things would now return to normal. She expected to find the other woman abed, as she had hardly left it since the previous evening's heartbreak.

To her surprise, Tessa was helping Grace on with a walking dress.

"Are we going out then?" Rosalind asked hopefully. It broke her heart to see her employer brought so low by the actions of one despicable man.

Grace gave her a bracing smile. "I am tired of lazing abed. A spot of fresh air shall do wonders for me."

In no time at all they were headed out into the fitful afternoon sunlight. Grace breathed in deeply, allowing out a sigh.

"I am so glad I decided on this. It is helping immensely." She turned her gaze to Rosalind and linked arms with her. "I suppose you know Tristan has left town."

Again, she felt starved of air. "Yes, he made sure to bid me farewell," she managed. "It was kind of him to do so."

Grace was quiet for a time, as immersed in her own thoughts as Rosalind. "I have given it much thought, and with my cousin's leave-taking I believe I have come to a monumental conclusion. Rosalind, darling, how do you feel about Scotland?"

Rosalind blinked. Of all the things Grace could have asked her, this was most unexpected. "I have to admit I have not given it much thought. It's to the north, and there are kilts. I do know you lived there for some time. Beyond that my knowledge is sadly lacking."

"Would you like to expand upon that minimal knowledge?"

Rosalind frowned, for Grace appeared positively uncertain. "I don't quite understand what you mean."

"Over the last days—no, it started before that." Grace seemed to be struggling with something. After a time she continued, her voice slow and careful. "I thought I was well and truly rid of Manderly. It had been more of a prison to me for more than half my life, you know. But when I made the Weetons' acquaintance and began reminiscing about the beauty of it all, I admit I began to grow homesick. Then, when this whole debacle with Bilton came to a head, I realized I had missed it much more than I ever expected I would. I have decided I'll leave London before the week is out and return."

Rosalind stumbled to a stop on the pavement and stared, stunned, at her employer. "Oh."

"Would you miss England so very much if you were to accompany me?"

"You wish me to go with you?"

"Of course, darling." Grace smiled at her. "I could not imagine leaving you behind. You have become much too important to me. Unless," she conceded, looking closely at Rosalind, "you have a reason to stay?"

Immediately a memory flashed, of Tristan holding her in his arms, his mouth on hers as he moved inside her. She blinked, and the image was gone. But not the feel of it, which would forever be imprinted on her heart if she did not put distance between them—and the sooner the better. "No," she said, more firmly than she thought possible. "No, nothing is holding me here."

A look of sadness passed over Grace's face before she smiled and took up Rosalind's hand. "Well then, I am glad. After our walk we shall return home and begin packing for our journey. Be ready, my dear," she said, a decided twinkle entering her tired eyes, "for a grand adventure!"

Chapter 26

The days since Tristan's arrival in Northamptonshire with Daphne and the dowager marchioness had been long. Instead of staying at Willbridge's Willowhaven home, they had moved into the late Lord Sumner's country seat within an hour's distance. Imogen would not hear of leaving her sister Lady Sumner for even a moment.

But after three days of watching his wife, wearier by the hour, scurry after her sister with mounting helplessness and frustration, Willbridge put his foot down.

Tristan and his friend, along with Imogen's younger sister Mariah, lay in wait at the front hall early in the afternoon of that third day. It had been decided that Tristan would provide brute strength should Willbridge fail to hold his wife back. Secretly Tristan hoped he wasn't needed, for if Willbridge was unable to convince Imogen to stop, he knew his own efforts would be wasted.

Eventually Lady Sumner hurried by, Imogen fast on her heels. Willbridge stepped forward and snaked an arm about Imogen's waist. "You are done for the time being, my love," he stated when she made to protest. "Your sister Mariah can do as good a job as you, without the added burden of carrying my child."

"I am fine," she argued. Even so, she went pliant in her husband's arms, her constant forward momentum having been halted.

Mariah stepped forward at Willbridge's nod, a signal they had agreed on earlier in the day when this plan had first been hatched. "You are not fine," she said with sisterly concern. "You need rest."

"But Frances—"

"Has more energy than ten of you right now, love," Willbridge said in a tone that brooked no argument.

"Have no fear, dearest," Mariah said when Imogen looked about to argue regardless. "I know you worry over Frances so. But let one of us see to her for once." Planting a quick kiss on Imogen's cheek, she was off, hurrying after Lady Sumner's retreating form.

Imogen watched her go, frustration plain on her face, before turning back to her husband. "You are a devious man," she grumbled. Yet when he pulled her to the drawing room, Tristan following, she made no protest. And when they all seated themselves on the least offensively ostentatious furniture, Willbridge and Imogen close together on the sofa, she yawned and rested her head on his shoulder.

Tristan eyed her in concern as he tried to get his long frame comfortable in a high-backed chair close by them. The woman was utterly exhausted. And no wonder, for Lady Sumner had not taken to her bed with grief nor allowed her mother—with whom she appeared to have a rather uneasy relationship—to take over a bit of her duties. Thus Imogen had been forced to run hither and thither after her in her determination to be close by should the woman succumb to emotion.

Tristan rather thought she never would, for the woman had certainly held no love for her husband. At least not in the end, when his blatant carousing had caused her so much humiliation.

"I shall only sit for a moment," Imogen declared sleepily.

"Wife, if you think I am about to let you go after I have finally secured your attentions, you are sadly mistaken."

They bantered quietly for a bit, their voices low and intimate. Imogen let loose a low chuckle and swatted his arm. Willbridge caught her hand, bringing it to his lips for a kiss.

Tristan's heart twisted. With what, he wasn't sure. Longing? Loneliness? Jealousy? But surely not, for he could not be happier for his friend. And he had determined not to think of Rosalind at all during his stay. Surely time and distance would cleanse the memory of her from his mind. By the time he returned to London again she would be gone, all trace of her swept from his home. And he could go on as if she had never barged into his life, turning it on its head.

Even so, there were times like these when he saw the utter contentment of his two closest friends Willbridge and Morley, both newly married to women they adored, when the pain of losing Rosalind hit him. It was then he knew, with a certainty that frightened him, that he would never be free of her. He would grieve over the loss of her for years to come.

As if to further underscore those dismal thoughts, Malcolm Arborn, Viscount Morley entered with his own bride, the former Lady Emily Masters and Willbridge's own sister, now Lady Morley.

When Emily saw Imogen looking so haggard she released her husband's arm and hurried to her. "Imogen, are you unwell?"

"Not a bit, my dear," Imogen hurried to say, straightening away from Willbridge. She could not hide the slight sway her body gave, however, as she fought to stay upright.

"You should retire to your room immediately," Emily said, sitting beside her and putting an arm around her. "You need rest."

"I am fine," Imogen soothed. "I shall be right as rain in a few moments."

"I must insist, dear. You are exhausting yourself."

Both their voices were as gentle as they ever were. Truly it was the politest argument Tristan had ever witnessed. "My goodness," he drawled, "what have you two reprobates done to these women? They used to be the tamest, quietest little things. Now I can hardly hear myself over their squabbling." He chuckled.

"You think they are tame, do you?" Morley murmured, looking on his wife fondly as she continued to gently insist that Imogen retire. "You may not countenance it, but Emily has a fiery temper when roused."

"Imogen, too, has been known to blister my ears on occasion," Willbridge quipped, watching his wife as she continued to calmly and affectionately counter Emily's interference. "A calm exterior does not necessarily mean there is no fire beneath the surface."

"Never tell me the two of you are in accord on something," Tristan remarked, leaning back in his chair—as far back as the blasted uncomfortable thing would allow—and stretching out his legs to cross his booted feet. "I had begun to think, Morley, that Willbridge would forever despise you for how badly you mucked up things with Emily before ultimately doing the smart thing and securing her hand."

"Oh, I have not forgiven him," Willbridge remarked flippantly. "Not in the least."

"Yes you have, you fool," Morley growled.

"Have not."

"You have."

Tristan grinned. "There seems to be some disparagement in your opinions on the subject."

Morley waved a hand in the air. "He's being a bloody stubborn imbecile. Of course he's forgiven me. Look how happy I make Emily."

"Well, I suppose that's true enough," Willbridge admitted with unconcealed reluctance.

It was then Emily rose, helping Imogen up as she did so. All three men rose as well.

"I'll be taking Imogen up to her room," Emily said to her brother.

Willbridge's hand was immediately at his wife's elbow, his head lowered close to hers. "Do you wish me to join you?"

"No, my love," she murmured. "Emily will stay with me. If, Morley, you can bear to be parted from her for so long," she teased.

"I shall endeavor to survive until her return." The look he gave Emily, however, was full of heated promise. She returned the look, a faint blush staining her face, the scar that cut across her left cheek from her temple to the corner of her mouth standing out in relief without detracting from her loveliness.

"Are you certain?" Willbridge asked.

"Very much so. I shall be fine. Besides," Imogen continued, her voice dropping meaningfully, "don't you think this is the perfect time?" Her turquoise eyes slid meaningfully to Tristan. Beside her Emily nodded.

Tristan did not miss a bit of the exchange. "The perfect time for what?" he demanded. But Imogen and Emily only gave them small smiles before leaving the room.

"The perfect time for what?" Tristan repeated as they returned to their seats.

Willbridge shot Morley a meaningful look. They both appeared exceedingly uncomfortable.

"If only we could go out riding," Willbridge grumbled.

Morley nodded. "It would make it easier, that is certain."

"Damn Lord Sumner, going and dying after such an idiotic carriage accident. If it wasn't frowned upon to speak ill of the dead, I'd be in the churchyard now, giving him a piece of my mind."

Morley chuckled darkly. "I think you would have to wait in line behind your wife, old man, for no one is as incensed by the jackass flaunting his mistress for everyone to see than Imogen."

Willbridge's expression lightened. "That is too true. Damn me, but she's glorious when incensed."

Tristan looked from one to the other in mounting frustration. "Truly? Come on, out with it you two, before I knock your skulls together. And I've truly no wish to do it, for I happen to like your wives."

Willbridge's face fell again. "Very well. But know this is not coming from us."

"It's our wives," Morley chimed in. "They've insisted we speak to you on, as they term it, a matter of immense importance."

Tristan's eyes narrowed as he considered them. "And what is this matter of *immense importance*?"

Willbridge cleared his throat and actually squirmed in his seat. Tristan knew with mounting apprehension it was not due to the uncomfortable furniture this time. "It seems they've been talking to Daphne."

Hurt exploded in his breast. He recalled the conversation he'd had with her regarding Rosalind. As well as his belief that she would keep his revelations to herself. More fool he. "Have they?" he asked coldly.

"They have," Morley confirmed, his black brows drawn together in worry. He sat forward, resting his elbows on his knees. "Won't you tell us about it?"

Tristan let out a harsh breath, exploding from his seat and pacing across the plush carpet. "It's not something I wish to discuss."

"Perhaps we can help," Willbridge suggested.

"There is nothing you can do," he growled. "It is over."

"Mayhap things are not as dour as you think," Morley replied. "It is quite possible that, by putting our heads together, we may come up with a solution."

"A solution to what?" Tristan snapped, spinning to face his friends. "Securing Rosalind's hand when she has no wish to marry me? Making her look beyond her prejudices to see we will suit?"

Both men went utterly still. But as Morley frowned in confusion, Willbridge's pale gray eyes changed with shock.

"Rosalind? Surely you don't mean Miss Merriweather."

"Of course I do," Tristan snapped. But then an inkling of suspicion settled under his skin, chilling his fury. "Wait, do you mean to tell me you didn't know a thing about Rosalind?"

The guilty looks on their faces told him the answer to that question.

"In our defense," Morley said, "we did not know our line of questioning would work quite so well."

"We had hoped it would, of course," Willbridge chimed in, "but you can be remarkably close-mouthed when you've a mind to and so we warned our wives that we might fail spectacularly, might even make you retreat back to London without learning a thing." He turned to Morley. "That did work better than I ever dreamed. Good idea of yours, old man."

"Thank you. I had hoped. But you know Tristan."

"Yes."

Tristan sliced a hand through the air, cutting off their back-and-forth with a curse. "What was that about your wives talking to Daphne? That was all a ruse?"

Morley shrugged. "It was the only thing we could think of, the only way to get you to reveal what has you so out of sorts. By her closemouthed manner we knew she was in possession of information. Feigning that she revealed that information to Emily and Imogen was our best bet to trick you into disclosing it to us."

As Tristan tried to wrap his head around this devious and convoluted way of thinking, Willbridge spoke.

"Daphne will flay us alive, I think, should she learn of this."

Morley nodded morosely. "Emily did say she had never seen her sister so reticent in her life. She figured it must be dire indeed to keep her so uncommonly secretive. But even in all our imaginings we never thought it was about a woman."

Tristan gaped at him. "What the devil did you think was wrong then?"

"Gambling?" Willbridge suggested.

"Ruin?" Morley supplied.

"You've taken to alcohol?"

"You are wanted for killing a man in a duel?"

"A secret life of crime?"

"You all think highly of me, I see," Tristan said, narrowing his eyes on each friend in turn.

"Not at all," Willbridge denied. "But you must remember it was not long ago when Morley and I were living the same lifestyle you currently are."

"And you are a flighty fellow," Morley chimed in. "There's no secret in that. Look at your brief infatuation last summer with Daphne, after all."

"Don't remind me," Willbridge growled, rising. He strode to the ornate cabinet in the corner, grabbing up a decanter of brandy and pouring out three snifters of alcohol. He brought them over and passed them out, one to each of them. "We had no wish to question you, man," he explained. "It's never been our way. We are all three of us silent support for the others. But Imogen and Emily got it in their heads that our way wasn't the way to go about it this time. And, as usual, my brilliant wife and my sister are right. Perhaps this bit of liquid courage shall help us get through the conversation that must now be had." He raised his glass, looking on Tristan and Morley in expectation.

Morley rose with alacrity, clinking his glass against Willbridge's before turning to Tristan. "Come on, man," he said, his voice gentler than Tristan had ever heard it. "You know we love you as a brother and only want what's best for you. Open up to us."

Tristan considered them cautiously. And as he looked on these two men who had been there for him unerringly since he was eleven years old and fresh from the betrayal of his father's second marriage, he saw the concern in their eyes and knew they only spoke the truth. They truly were like brothers to him.

He let out a breath, his shoulders slumping, and brought his glass to theirs. "You'd best bring over that whole damn decanter then, Willbridge," he said with a sad humor coating his words. "For we shall need it."

• • •

At the end of an hour Tristan fell silent. He felt eviscerated, laid raw. There was nothing else in him to give. He raised his glass, which had sat untouched for the whole of his speech, bringing it to his mouth with trembling fingers, letting the smooth taste of the brandy slide over his thick tongue and down his parched throat.

Morley and Willbridge were silent. Their expressions had not changed since he started talking. But he could see when he chanced a look at them something working in the depths of their eyes, like cogs in a clock whirring away.

And was it any wonder? For he had not only told them all that had happened with Rosalind—minus their love-making, of course, and any specifics regarding her sister, for he was not a cad—but also what he had failed to tell them over the years regarding his father. Every hurt, every tragedy, every insecurity he had was spread before them, like a feast of pain and suffering.

Unable to bear looking at them while they soaked in the glut of information he had poured out for them, he studied his glass, the way the late afternoon light played through the amber liquid, struggling to get through the dark, rich color. In one swallow he downed it, then brought the crystal glass back in front of his face. The light poured through, clear and unfettered.

That was what his chest felt like this moment, he realized. As much as it had pained him to reveal so much of himself to anyone, even these men whom he loved like brothers, it was freeing. It was like his soul had been wiped clean.

He wondered now if he would have ever found the strength to tell them if Rosalind had not first freed him to do so. She had loosened something in him, had given him permission to take what had shaped him and face it head on.

How would he continue to find that strength without her?

"So," Willbridge said, "you have fallen in love." He reached for the decanter at his elbow, refilling all their glasses to the brim before settling back and taking a sip.

"So it would seem," Tristan responded dryly.

Morley tapped one finger on the rim of his glass. "And you are certain she does not return your feelings?"

Tristan felt his back teeth clench as the memory of Rosalind's cold eyes and cruel words bit into him. "Quite certain," he managed. "She was most emphatic herself, and so I have no reason to doubt her."

"And you do not believe she could have been lying to you?" Willbridge asked after a long, thoughtful pause.

"What reason would she have to lie to me?" He let lose a sharp, angry laugh. "I was going to propose to her, damn it."

"And did she know that?"

Morley's quiet question stopped his anger in its tracks.

"You said her sister's life was destroyed when she gave her heart to a man who did not return her affections," his friend continued. "She may very well have seen a parallel to her own situation, would have been desperate to protect herself from the same fate."

But Tristan was already shaking his head. "No. No, that's not possible. I was going to offer for her—"

"Did she know?" Willbridge asked gently, echoing Morley's question.

Tristan frowned. "She had to have known that I would offer for her after...well," he hedged, clearing his throat.

Willbridge chuckled. "My friend, you are brilliant, from all accounts, with a woman's body. But you are rubbish when it comes to knowing the workings of their hearts."

"Hell," Morley piped up, "I'm still rubbish at it. But I'm blessed to have a woman who at least knows the workings of my heart and has chosen to overlook my many, many blunders."

"Trust me," Willbridge continued, "for I speak from painful experience. If you love a woman, for God's sake, let her know it. She is not a mind reader, man, though it seems at times they know much more than we want them to. When it comes to love, however, you must let her know exactly where your heart lies. She must have not a single doubt as to your feelings."

Was it possible? Had he mucked the whole thing up assuming she would know his intentions? Damn it, surely he had told her he would not take her to bed without doing the right thing by her. He must have said something to that effect.

But as his friends quietly talked amongst themselves, leaving him to his troubled reflections, he thought back over that night when she had given so much of herself to him. And he realized he could not recall a single time his intentions had been addressed.

Oh, his plans for a future with her had filled his mind. All through that magical night, when he had held her in his arms and felt the glorious joining of his body with the woman he had come to love so completely and unexpectedly, he had thought how wonderful it would be to wake up with her beside him each day. How marriage to her would be, how he had never been happier in his life than in that moment. How he loved her.

Yet the words had never made it past his lips. They had been present in every kiss, every caress. But perhaps what Willbridge and Morley said was true, that the words themselves were as important as his actions.

And if that was the case, he was the biggest fool in creation.

He stood with a suddenness that stunned the other men into silence. When they saw the determination on his face, however, they both broke into grins.

"Good luck, old man," Willbridge said as Morley saluted him with his glass.

Without a word Tristan left the room. They would understand his haste, he knew. And as he heard their chuckles follow him out into the hall he felt a grin tug on his own lips. He broke into a run, taking the stairs two at a time. If luck was on his side, he would get to London before Grace and Rosalind left. And he would see if fate was ready to take pity on him and grant him the love of the most maddening, wonderful woman he had ever known.

Chapter 27

Rosalind was carefully packing the dresses Grace had given her over the last weeks into a borrowed trunk when the butler came to her door.

"Mr. Hugh Carlisle is here, miss."

She had not seen him since the night at Vauxhall. When she had forgotten everything but Tristan and what he made her feel. She gripped the edge of the trunk hard. What was he doing here? But of course, he must have been informed that Grace was returning to Scotland and had come to say his farewells. He was related to her by marriage, after all.

But why was Danielson coming to her? He knew as well as she that Grace was out and would be for the better part of the afternoon, buying up all of Bond Street before leaving London. She gave the butler a distracted smile, gently lifting a tissue-wrapped gown and placing it with care into the trunk. "Please inform him that Lady Belham is not in but will return this evening."

"He is not here for Lady Belham, miss. He expressly voiced a wish to speak to you."

"Oh." Rosalind blinked several times before rising from the floor and following after the butler. At that moment she wanted nothing more than to hide herself away in her room and prepare for the long journey on the morrow. But she supposed she and Mr. Carlisle had become something of friends over the past several weeks. It would be lovely to say goodbye to him, to talk once more of Guinevere with someone who had known her.

He was standing at the window of the drawing room when she entered. He must have been deep in thought, for he did not hear her until she was directly behind him.

"Mr. Carlisle," Rosalind said, "what a pleasant surprise to have you visit."

He turned, reaching out and taking her hand, gifting her with his easy smile. But there was something off in his eyes, something somber and troubled.

"I heard you and Grace are to leave tomorrow for Scotland. I could not let you go without coming to visit first."

"I am very glad you did." She indicated a small circle of chairs close by. "Shall we have a seat?"

They moved to the chairs. While Mr. Carlisle was usually quite cheerfully chatty, today he was almost morose. He could not possibly be so upset as to their leaving that his spirits would be affected to such a degree. Yet what other reason could there be? Unless…

"Is your father well?" Rosalind asked in concern. "He has not worsened, I hope."

Her voice startled him from his thoughts. "What? Oh, no, he's quite hale and hearty now, thank you for asking."

"And you? You are well?"

"As fit as ever."

Rosalind frowned, for the man had transferred his gaze to the embroidered design on the cushion of the chair and was following it aimlessly with his finger. Yes, something was definitely amiss.

"Have you seen Miss Weeton lately, Mr. Carlisle?"

"Miss Weeton?" He frowned, as if he did not know who she was talking about, before his brow cleared. "Ah, no. Not since Vauxhall I'm afraid."

Rosalind was shocked at the admission. "That was nearly a week ago now."

"Yes. Yes, it was."

"But Lord Kingston will have the upper hand," she blurted.

He stared at her, no doubt taken aback by her outburst. "Kingston? I seriously doubt it. Or perhaps you have not heard."

She shook her head. "What do you mean?"

"Kingston has set his sights elsewhere. Though it was not without reluctance."

She gaped at him. "How do you know all this?"

"I was there at White's the day Sir Tristan warned Kingston away from Miss Weeton. It seems the earl was not behaving honorably with the young lady."

Rosalind knew this fact quite well. She thought back on the last time she had seen the man, wrapped in some unknown woman's arms. His cocky assurance that he was doing nothing wrong.

But had Tristan learned of it? And how had he done so, for Grace was certainly in no shape that night to have been aware of what was going on.

But, more important than even that, if he knew of Lord Kingston's amorous pursuits *why* had he warned him away. For wasn't he cut from the same cloth? He would applaud such a way of thinking, not condemn it.

Wouldn't he?

"But," she said, frustration making her voice sharper than she intended, "I thought you cared for her. I had thought perhaps you might eventually offer for her."

Again that sigh, as if the weight of the world rested on his shoulders. "You recall me telling you, Miss Merriweather, that at one time many years ago I was in love?"

Well, she certainly hadn't expected that to come out of his mouth. She gave him a slow nod.

He frowned. It was the most troubled expression she had ever seen on his face. "What I failed to tell you at the time," he said haltingly, as if each word were causing him pain, "was the lady I loved was your sister."

The breath left Rosalind in a rush. She slumped back in her seat. "You loved Guinevere?"

A sad smile briefly lifted his lips. "With all my heart. How could I not? She was beautiful, and kind, and vivacious."

"I see." But she didn't, really. Why had he not spoken of this before now?

"I have so enjoyed our time together since your arrival," he continued. "Though learning of her passing has given me incredible grief, it has been such a pleasure reminiscing about her, remembering the times we shared. It was almost as if I got a piece of her back."

Despite her confusion, she could not help but smile at that. "I admit, I feel the same way. I have not been able to talk of her in so long, I feared for a time I had dreamed her up."

"Yes," he replied with feeling, sitting forward. "That is it exactly. I would that things had been different. I had thought, once, that I might have a chance with her, that she might be mine." His expression fell, and he seemed to deflate. "But I was mistaken. And then she left."

Rosalind thought then how different life would be if her sister had fallen in love with this man instead of with Mr. Lester. Guinevere's death had changed everything for them all. But if she had loved differently she would even now be with them. Their father would still live, ensconced in his country seat. Rosalind would not have been forced into service. She might have had a Season of her own, may have even married, had a child or two.

She tried mightily to imagine that never-to-be husband, those children that would never be born. Perhaps he might have been tall and thin, bookish and gentle. Their children would have been happy little things with dark hair and eyes.

Yet those images would not manifest. For all she could picture was Tristan by her side, a passel of rambunctious blond imps at her feet. And her heart ached for this thing she wanted so desperately.

She cleared her throat, overcome. "If only she had returned your feelings," she said, her voice gruff with unshed tears. "If only she had not chosen Mr. Lester as the recipient of her heart. You could have taken better care of her than he ever did."

Mr. Carlisle appeared stunned by her vehemence. Too late she forgot that he had considered Mr. Lester a friend. But even knowing this, she was astonished by his response.

"But Lester never meant to break her heart. It was beyond his control."

"Beyond his control?" Fury burned hot. For if Mr. Carlisle had loved Guinevere as he claimed he did, he should be outraged at his friend's treatment of her. "How can you say that, you who claims to have loved her so? Was it beyond his control to bed her, to ruin her?"

The words slipped out, fueled by outrage. In the next instant she wished she could recall them. For it was plain to see that Mr. Carlisle hadn't an inkling of the horrible thing Mr. Lester had done to Guinevere, the extent he had destroyed her.

"But Lester never took her to his bed," he said.

The man looked as if she had struck him. Regret washed over her, not only because she had revealed Guinevere's shame, but that she had hurt this man who had loved her sister and given Rosalind a much-needed friend. "I am sorry, I know Mr. Lester was your friend. And he is gone and cannot defend himself against my accusations. But I swear to you that what I say is true. Mr. Lester seduced her then abandoned her to the cruelties of fate."

"But Lester could not have done that to her." He was growing more agitated by the second.

It must be such a shock to him, to learn of what his friend did to the woman he loved. He could not comprehend it, it was so horrifying to him. She leaned forward and placed a comforting hand on his. "Mr. Carlisle I assure you, he did. She told me herself that she loved him. I heard it from her dearest friend, who she stayed with during her time in London, that she was seen going off alone with him, that later she reappeared quite distraught."

But Mr. Carlisle was shaking his head. "He could not have done it, I tell you."

Rosalind felt fury boil up again at his insistence in his friend's innocence. "And why not?"

He threw up his hands. "Because Lester preferred men," he blurted.

Silence fell over the room, so thick Rosalind thought she would drown in it.

It was that moment that a maid came in with the tea tray. She faltered as she came closer, sensing the tension. Depositing the tray on the low table between Rosalind and Mr. Carlisle, she bobbed a quick curtsy before rushing out.

"You are lying," Rosalind managed, her voice a hushed rasp. "You are protecting his memory."

Mr. Carlisle looked suddenly weary to the bone. "And how would telling you that protect his memory? For it is a criminal offense, and even in death he would be roasted over the coals should it ever get out."

"But it cannot be true."

"I assure you, it is. I am sorry you were misinformed. It was not well done of Guinevere's friend to implicate Lester, for he was a good man and did not deserve her disparagement."

"But she was ruined. I know she was."

"Because her friend told you she went off with Lester?" He shook his head mournfully. "Come now, Miss Merriweather, give your sister the benefit of the doubt."

"It was more than that," she insisted.

He ran a hand over his face. "What then? What could make you believe such a thing?"

Her fingers clasped around the locket at her throat. "Because there was a child."

The change in Mr. Carlisle was instantaneous. He blanched, went pale, then fairly collapsed against the back of his chair. "What?"

"There was a child," she repeated. Ah, God, she had not ever spoken those words. They clamored out of her now, clawing at her, breaking free with a violence that stunned her.

Mr. Carlisle gaped at her, disbelief and grief swirling in the usually mild depths of his eyes. Such pain there. And yet, she thought mournfully, she was not through with giving it out.

She reached for the ribbon that held the locket around her throat. Pulling the bow loose, she let the small gold circle fall into her palm. It gleamed dully, the delicate filigree work and inset turquoise worn down after years of being worried by her nervous fingers. His eyes fastened on it like a starving man. Wordlessly she held it out to him.

He reached for it with shaking fingers, as if already knowing what secrets it contained. After staring at it for long minutes he opened it.

Rosalind did not need to see the contents. She knew them by heart, the image of them burned into her mind. Inside the small compartment, behind a thin layer of glass, lay a curl of hair of the palest blond.

He gasped. For this was not Guinevere's hair. She'd had inky black hair, the very shade of a raven's wing.

"It was the tiniest babe you ever saw," she whispered, her mind filled with the memory of that small face. "So perfect, with the longest lashes, every finger and toe accounted for." She drew in a shuddering breath. "The babe did not survive the birth. My sister followed soon after. I think…" She cleared her throat and tried again. "I think, when we lost him, she simply gave up."

A low, involuntary moan escaped the white line his lips had become. "It was a boy?" His thumb caressed the glass window of the locket.

Looking on him, at the grief that etched his normally placid face, she knew. For this was no mere sadness one would expect at the knowledge of an unknown child's death, even if one knew and loved the mother. No, this was something more, much more.

"It was you," she gasped.

He nodded miserably.

She did not know she had risen, that her hand had shot out, until she heard the crack of her palm against his cheek. It echoed through the room, ringing in her ears.

He hardly flinched, though his cheek turned a bright red from the impact. "You may do it again," he said, his voice low and soaked with pain, "as many times as you like. I shall not stop you."

She shook, her rage was so great. She balled her hands into fists at her sides, ignoring the stinging pain of her palm, pressing her nails into her skin to keep herself from hurling the steaming teapot in his face. "How could you?" she demanded. "You claim to have loved her, pretended to be my friend, came around with your smiles and your memories of her. And all along you seduced her, destroyed her."

He squeezed his eyes shut, tears seeping from between his lids. "It wasn't like that. I never meant it to happen."

"And yet it did," she said coldly. "And she is dead because of it."

He looked as if he might be sick. "She swore to me nothing happened. If I had known, I never would have left. I would have begged her to marry me."

Rosalind frowned. "Explain yourself."

His hand closed around the locket, his head dropping as if in defeat. She thought he had not heard her. Finally, though, his voice reached her, so brittle, so thin she could hardly make out the words.

"I knew of her love for Lester, of course. She was not one to hide her feelings; rather she wore them on her sleeve proudly for all to see. It brought Lester incredible pain, for he liked her immensely yet knew he could never reciprocate her feelings.

"Then we were invited to a house party. I came upon her the last night. She was distraught, told me how she threw herself at Lester, how he refused her advances. I stayed to comfort her."

He swallowed hard and rubbed at the back of his neck. "If I had been any soberer I might have seen the folly in the plan. But I had been enjoying myself a bit too much, had more to drink than was good for me. And when Guinevere found the bottle of brandy in the cabinet I thought it would be the very thing to relax her."

He looked up then, his eyes begging Rosalind to understand. "I don't remember anything that followed. I swear it. One minute we were drinking and talking, the next I awoke to the morning sun in my eyes, a blinding headache nearly incapacitating me. Guinevere was gone, the only sign of her the empty glass she drank from on the table beside me." He flushed then, his eyes falling away from hers. "It was some minutes before I realized that my clothes were askew. I worried something might have happened between us. When next I saw her, in the front hall as everyone was departing back to London, I managed to pull her aside, asked her if I had…" He closed his eyes, drew in a shuddering breath. "She swore to me we hadn't. I confessed my love to her then, told her I wanted to marry her. But she refused me. She bid me farewell, told me she would see me back in London."

His gaze returned to Rosalind. "That was the last I saw of her. She returned home the very next day, and within the week I was off to the country at my father's orders. Had I known…"

He could be lying. He had kept this from her up until now; who was to say he wasn't spewing falsehoods to save his own skin?

Yet Rosalind knew, as sure as she knew her own name, that he was telling her nothing but the rawest truth. She stared into eyes of absolute desolation and knew without a doubt that this was what happened.

She hugged her middle, as if she could hold herself together by sheer force of will, and dropped heavily into her chair. Everything she had ever believed, everything that had driven her over the past years, was a lie.

She had been led to believe that a rake—for that was how Guinevere's friend had described Lester—had taken advantage of her sister. She thought he'd been a man with no care for Guinevere, who only wished to use her for his own pleasure and then had abandoned her.

Instead here was this gentle, kind man, who was utterly destroyed by the news of what he'd inadvertently done. A man who had loved her sister, who had been refused when he'd offered the protection of his name.

She felt as if she'd been told that up was down, that right was wrong. Nothing made sense any longer. The foundations of deep-seated beliefs had been stripped away.

Why had Guinevere refused this man? She had to have known what had happened. She could have held on to her honor, would have been loved and protected.

But even as she asked herself these things she knew. She remembered Guinevere calling Lester's name while overcome with the pain of her labor and knew. She had loved that man with everything in her, though he could not return it. She had been dramatic, and bold, and led by her emotions. And when she'd loved, it had been with her whole heart, her whole soul. She would have seen it as a betrayal to her very heart to marry another. Even if it could have saved her life.

"Damn it, Guinevere," she whispered.

"I am so sorry." Mr. Carlisle was back to staring at the locket, and Rosalind did not know if he was talking to her or the wisp of the child that still lived behind glass, a child he would never know.

But then he looked at her. "I am so sorry, for everything. If I could take it all back I would. What I did to her, what I have done to you…" He swallowed hard, and for a moment she thought he might begin to cry in earnest. Instead he gathered strength and said, "I shall never forgive myself for what I have done. I shall never, ever forget. But perhaps I can help you a bit. Please let me help you."

She frowned. "Help me?"

"I am not a rich man. But I can provide for you, give you independence."

Her frown deepened. "I don't understand."

But he was sitting forward, a new determination in his eyes. "I have a cottage. It's not grand, or large. But it is mine. It was left to me by my mother, came with her marriage portion. I can give it to you. You can live there in peace, without being beholden to anyone, without having to live a life of service for one more day." When she began to shake her head, confusion and hope and fear building in her, he rose, hurried around the low table, knelt in front of her. Taking up her hand, he pressed it to his heart.

"I loved your sister. So very much. She gave birth to my child, who never had a chance to live, and whom I shall never know. You are all I have left of both of them. Please, Rosalind, let me do this for you. Let me give you the life you deserve and that I took from you in one stupid, ill-conceived moment."

She stared into his agonized yet still gentle eyes, and a bud of hope began to bloom in her chest. She should accept what he offered. She should not have this life, after all, should have had a life quite different. And even though she had found a place with Grace, though she loved her like a sister, she was still in service and could lose this life any moment on a whim.

She imagined herself then in a home of her own, doing what she wanted when she wanted. Having to answer to no one. It was incredible and frightening all at once.

But something held her back from accepting this great gift. Because inside she felt empty. And she knew that filling the hole in her heart with the life he offered would not ease the ache of it.

"I can't," she whispered helplessly.

A look of sad understanding softened his face. "Is it Sir Tristan?" He must have seen the shock and agony that coursed through her. "I am so sorry. It is none of my business, of course. But please know that my offer still stands should you ever need it."

He sighed, opened his hand, looked down at the locket that still rested open in his palm. Rosalind, too, gazed down at it, taking in with new eyes the small curl of hair that she had worn so faithfully for nine long years. It was nearly the same hue as Mr. Carlisle's hair, she realized now.

He moved, faltered, then held it out to her, his jaw set. "Thank you for sharing this with me, for telling me what happened. Though it brings me more pain than I ever imagined, I am glad I know."

She reached for it, then at the last minute closed his fingers around it.

He gasped softly. "You are giving this to me?"

She smiled gently. "Have a good life, Mr. Carlisle. And try to forgive yourself. You deserve to be happy."

His throat worked for a time, his eyes shining. He leaned forward and placed a kiss on her forehead before rising. "Thank you, Rosalind. For everything."

With that he was gone.

Rosalind sat there for a moment, staring at the place he had been. After a time she reached out with shaking hands and poured herself a cup of tea. But it was cold and tasteless on her dry tongue, and she pushed it aside hardly touched. She rose. She would go to her room, finish packing. But when she reached the hall she found herself going, not to her own room, but to Tristan's.

She didn't know why. She had never been in his bedroom, had never passed the threshold, had never even looked inside. Yet she went in now, as if it was natural, as if she belonged. And a moment later she knew why. For he was here, in every bit of rich fabric, in every strong curve of the dark oak furniture, even in the scent of him that permeated the air.

She had thought men like him were the enemy. For years it had sat like a stone in her chest, affecting each decision she made, word she spoke.

But she had been wrong. At the bed she ran her fingers over the pillow and wondered what else she had been wrong about.

A noise sounded in the hall. She jumped. But it was only a maid passing by, soon gone. She should not be here. She would be gone in the morning, and he would be behind her, a memory that she would recall on cold Scottish nights to warm her. A lesson that she had learned.

For though Mr. Carlisle's revelations had rocked her to her very core, she must not forget that she had given herself to Tristan without him declaring himself, without him promising a future. That he had taken her innocence and never meant to marry her.

Even so, she found herself wandering about the room. She trailed her fingers over the table beside his bed, over the smooth surface of the desk in the corner, across the intricately carved doors of the armoire, imagining him using these pieces.

When she came to the mantle she paused. For there stood two miniatures, women both of them. One was Grace, albeit a much younger version. The other, though, was unknown to her, and depicted in clothing several decades out of fashion.

It was his mother, whom he said had died so young. It had to be. She could see now as she peered closely at the painting the same shape of the eyes as Tristan, the same golden hair. There was a wear mark near the edge of the frame, as if rubbed over and over. She could imagine Tristan standing here, mourning the mother he had lost so young, his thumb rubbing that spot until the varnish wore off. His grief wearing on him just as he wore down that small wooden frame.

As she'd worn down the delicate design on the locket she'd saved with the memory of Guinevere's son inside.

She cleared her throat of the lump that had formed in it. Taking a step back, she determined to leave as quickly as she could. This was doing her no good, only causing her more pain. But as she turned to go, a small inlaid box near the miniature caught her eye. Its lid was not fitted quite right, and the edge of a crumpled paper stuck out.

It was so out of place in a room that was neat as a pin. Curiosity momentarily overcoming her, she gingerly lifted the lid and extracted the paper.

It was twisted, crumpled, as if he had smashed it in his fist. If so, why had he kept it? And why was there weight to it? She should put it back. Of course she should. It was not meant to be seen.

But when had common sense stopped her? For if her tongue could not listen to reason and stay still, what made her think her fingers could?

The crackle of the paper was overloud in the hush of the room as she opened the small bundle. An item, small and shining, fell out. It bounced across the carpet, coming to rest under a nearby chair.

But she did not immediately follow it. For something on the paper had caught her eye: her name, written in an elegant script. Heart pounding in her ears, she smoothed the paper flat.

What she read stopped her breath. It was a special license, signed by the archbishop himself, proclaiming that Sir Tristan Artemis Douglas Crosby was to marry Miss Rosalind Merriweather.

He had meant to marry her? All along, he had meant to marry her? She searched the document, found the date. May the seventh. The day after their trip to Vauxhall.

That was where he had gone off to that morning, where he had traveled to after he had left her bed. He had not abandoned her. He had meant to marry her.

She thought then of how she had acted when he'd returned, how cold and cruel, to protect her heart from the pain that had taken her sister's life. And all the while he'd had this in his pocket.

"What have I done?" she moaned.

It was then she remembered the object that had fallen from the paper. She dropped to her knees, scrambling for the chair, reaching into the shadows. Her fingers brushed something hard and cold. She grabbed at it, bringing it into the light.

A gold ring lay in her palm, the metal formed into whimsical curlicues. And at the center, gleaming brilliant, a deep blue sapphire surrounded by seed pearls.

The breath left her in a soft exhale. He had meant to give this to her?

She had to find him, to take it all back, to tell him she was sorry for pushing him away. She scrambled to her feet, intending to do that very thing.

But he was gone, wasn't he? And he did not plan to return until she and Grace had departed. He had bid her farewell when last he'd seen her. It was over between them, for it appeared the words she had spewed in defense of her heart had worked all too well.

"Rosalind."

She gasped and looked up to find Grace in the doorway. The other woman's face was softened in understanding.

"You are staying, then?"

"No," Rosalind hurried to say. She frowned, holding the paper and ring close to her chest. "That is, I don't believe so. That is…"

Grace embraced her. "Darling, do what is in your heart," she murmured in her ear. "If you choose to stay, I shall not stop you. And if you wish to join me, I will gladly have you."

She pulled away, smiling encouragingly at Rosalind before walking out of the room. Leaving Rosalind with her battered heart and a frightening decision that would change the course of her very life. If she had the strength to make it.

Chapter 28

Tristan burst through the door of his Upper Grosvenor Street home early the following evening, eager after a day and a half on the road to find Rosalind.

He knew, even as he sprinted up the main staircase to the second floor and the family apartments, that something wasn't right. The house was too quiet, too empty.

Even so, he could not stop from rushing to her room and throwing open the door. He stood in the doorway, looking at the bed where they made love. It was as neatly made as it ever was. Everything was in its place. But it was more than that; it was as if her very presence had been stripped from the room. It felt barren, achingly so. Even her scent, the wonderful perfume of roses and lavender, was barely discernible.

Yet still he needed proof. He strode to the armoire, peered inside, went to the dressing table, the small table beside the bed. Everything was empty, stripped bare.

She was gone. She had left.

He was too late.

Desolation swept over him. Needing to escape the room and the memories that permeated the very walls, he left, walking blindly down the hall. At the doorway of his study, Danielson found him.

"Sir Tristan, welcome back. We did not expect you so soon."

"Good afternoon, Danielson. Lady Belham and Miss Merriweather have left, I see."

"Yes, just this morning."

"I don't…" He cleared his throat, tried again. "I don't suppose they left a letter or message for me?"

The butler's normally impassive expression faltered, a look of what appeared to be pity flaring in his eyes before his calm demeanor slid back into place. "No, sir, there was nothing." He paused. "Will there be anything else, sir?"

"No," Tristan mumbled, the brief hope that had flared snuffed out completely. "Not a thing."

The butler bowed and left. Tristan stood there for a time, utterly weary, before, with a sigh, he entered the study.

He sank into the chair behind the massive desk. He should go to the cabinet, pour himself a healthy glass of whiskey, drown himself in the stuff until he could no longer think or feel. It did seem like a sound plan. But he did not have even the energy for that, and so the next best thing it would be. He would drown himself in work.

He flipped listlessly through the large pile of letters that had accumulated on his desk. Several were from his steward back at Sainsly, one from his solicitor, a few from merchants on Bond Street. And one from Josephine.

The old anger tried to find purchase as he looked on his step-mother's delicate handwriting. The woman would not listen. He had told her time and again to go through the proper channels in reaching him. They had nothing to say to one another, not after the years of hurt that separated them.

He dug deep, found a shred of outrage to hold onto, and gripped the letter tight to rip it asunder.

At the last moment Rosalind's voice drifted to him, from that magical night at Vauxhall.

Perhaps it is time for you to heal from the pain your father caused you and reconcile with her. She could be lonely, could be wishing to make amends.

The outrage drained from him as quickly as it had come. How many letters had she sent in the past weeks? Three? Four? Perhaps Rosalind was right, and she was lonely. She had no other family, after all, from what he knew.

With a glance up to the heavens for guidance, he sighed and opened the letter.

It had been written nearly a week ago. The letter started off with talk of the local families, of births and deaths, repairs that had been made upon his orders. Everything he already knew from his steward's many letters. She must know that, he thought in frustration as the letter rambled on.

Finally he came to the end.

"I do not know if you are receiving my letters," it read. "I wish that things were different between us. I am for London to visit an old family friend, and should be there by the end of the week. I had hoped to see you while there. It has been too many years, Tristan. If you do not choose to see me I want you to know I understand. But I have enclosed the address, should you decide in favor of such a plan. I hope you do."

She signed it, "With love, Josephine."

He stared at it for a long moment, waiting for the anger, the bitterness, the hurt that had typically accompanied all thoughts of her to rear up. To his surprise they were muted. Instead a sadness enveloped him. Was she truly lonely as Rosalind had suggested?

But it was madness to think he could have a relationship with her after all this time. Damn it, she had never once fought his father on making sure Tristan was included. She had been more than happy with her little family, without her husband's heir coming in and mucking up everything.

As he looked over her carefully penned letter, however, he only saw the loneliness echoing within her words. She wrote as if she had penned him a hundred letters like it, speaking out into the void. Begging for a word back.

Without stopping to wonder if he was the greatest fool in Christendom for even considering going to her, he hurled himself from his chair, striding from his study and down the hall. "Danielson," he called, his voice echoing through the empty house.

The butler materialized as if out of the ether. "Yes, Sir Tristan?"

"I'm heading out. Have my horse saddled and readied before I change my bloody mind."

"Very good, sir."

• • •

Within a half hour he was standing in front of the little house on Green Street. The entire ride here he had not thought twice about his hasty decision. Now that he was faced with seeing Josephine, however, he found himself frozen, unable to even lift his hand to knock.

He did not have time to change his mind, however, for the front door was thrown wide. And there was Josephine, staring at him as if he was a ghost.

"Tristan," she breathed, her hands clasped before her breast. "How you've changed. I almost did not recognize you."

He could only stare at her, this woman he had hated for so long. She was much older than he remembered. How long had it been since he'd been home? Arthur's funeral? No, his father's, shortly after. That had to be eight years ago. He had not been back to Sainsly since.

Her hair had grayed and thinned from the thick mass of curls he remembered. She had lost weight, too, and her face was heavily lined. She no longer resembled the woman who had taken his mother's place, the elegant creature he had despised.

"Oh, but how rude of me," she said, her hands fluttering in agitation. "Please come in. My friend is out and so we may talk at our leisure."

Hesitating only a moment, he followed her into the house. His mind whirled. She was nothing like he expected, nothing like he remembered. She even moved differently, more nervous than before.

"Rose," she called to a maid who was hovering in the front hall, "please bring a tea tray in."

The maid bobbed a curtsy and disappeared, and Josephine showed him into a small front parlor done up in a riot of flowery fabrics and dainty furniture.

"Please, sit," she said, motioning to an overstuffed sofa. She perched nearby, barely resting her backside on the cushion, as if she might take flight at any moment.

She stayed silent as he settled himself, simply watching him with eyes that were full of all manner of emotion. He cleared his throat, shifted, and said, "I did not expect you to come to London."

"Nor did I." She laughed, a tentative, nervous thing. "Mrs. Curtis is an old school friend. Her goddaughter is marrying in a week's time. She asked me to come. I would not have presumed to otherwise."

He nodded, feeling more awkward than he had in his life. Where was that confident mask he was so used to showing to the world? Had Rosalind's ability to see through him pierced it beyond repair?

But no, it had always been thus with Josephine. He'd been only nine when she'd come into his life. His mother had become a distant memory, though he'd tried his damnedest to hold onto her. As much as his father would allow, anyway, having erased her from his home and life as much as he was able.

He had not wanted anyone to replace his mother. And that was how he saw Josephine, as a replacement, the final act of his father to eradicate the first Lady Crosby's very existence.

He could have been kinder to her, he knew now. But at the time he had been full of rage and thought that by denying Josephine's half-hearted initial attempts at befriending him, he was honoring his mother. Those attempts had not lasted long, and soon she ignored Tristan almost as totally as his father did. And then Arthur had come, and his feeling of being an outsider was made complete.

He was tired of it all in that moment, of the constant anger in his breast, of his battered confidence that kept him pretending that nothing was amiss. "What do you want, Josephine?" he asked, weariness coating the words.

She blinked. "I'm sorry?"

"I have asked you again and again to leave me be. Yet you will not honor my wishes. Why? What do you want from me?"

She swallowed hard, her throat working. To his shock her eyes filled with tears.

"I thought, perhaps, we might…"

"Might what, Josephine?" Tristan sighed and ran a hand over his face. "Might put the past behind us, have a relationship? Mother and son?"

"I wanted that from the very beginning," she whispered.

He narrowed his eyes. "Did you? I have very different memories of that time. I recall a woman who came into the home of a very hurt, very scared little boy and, after a very lukewarm attempt at making him feel at ease, she turned her back on him."

She appeared as if he'd struck her. "Is that what you think? Truly?"

The bitter taste of fury was making itself known, overriding the grief that had been his constant companion since Rosalind turned him away. "It is."

"But that is not what happened at all," she cried.

"Isn't it?" He sat forward, fire burning in his gut, loosening his tongue after over two decades of keeping silent. "I may have been difficult when you first arrived, but can you blame me? I lost my mother, and my father was doing everything in his power to destroy her memory. And then he brought you." His lip curled as she stared at him in wide-eyed shock. "And you never even tried. You gave up on me, like he did—"

His voice broke off, his throat closing. To his horror he felt the hot press of tears behind his eyes, something he had not felt since he was a boy. He turned, not wanting her to see how much it still hurt him.

There was silence for a time. From beyond the sitting room window the busy rattle of carriage wheels on the cobbles outside sounded, breaking the hush in the room. He fought to control his breathing, fighting down the sobs that lodged hard and painful in his chest. And then the rustle of fabric, the quiet patter of footsteps on the carpet. In the next moment the sofa dipped beside him, and a soft hand rubbed his back.

A sudden flash of memory hit him then, of a gentle hand on his back, rubbing away the hurt as he lay in his bed, exhausted after a bout of crying, sending him into the blessed peace of sleep.

He had thought it was a dream at the time, a memory of his mother. His immature imaginings had even chalked it up to her ghost, returning to comfort him in his darkest hours.

But now...

"I used to come to you at night." Josephine's voice was thick with tears as her hand continued its relaxing circle on his back. "I could hear you crying, though I know you tried to muffle it. I never told your father, of course. He would not have approved, would not have allowed me to comfort you. He was forever ordering me to leave you be, to keep my distance, that you had to be a man and deal with the way things were."

She paused, sniffled. "I did not agree with him, but what could I do? A wife's duty is to listen to her husband. As well, he was not an easy man to live with, forever losing his temper..." Her voice trailed off. She cleared her throat and continued. "And so I followed his orders, though it broke my heart to do so. I understood your hate for me, of course. I lost my own mother young and had to deal with my father's new wife before I was ready to let go of my mother's memory, what I deemed as her spot in our lives. And so I kept my distance, thinking you only needed time to come to terms with this new chapter in your life. I had hopes that eventually you would warm up to me.

"But when you cried as if your soul were being torn in two, I could not stay away. I knew, though, that you would push me away if you were aware of my presence. So I waited until your tears had nearly subsided, until I knew you were close to sleep. And I went to you, to give you what comfort I could. What little you would allow me to provide."

He turned, stunned, and she gave him a watery smile. "I would have given so much more if I could have."

She could be lying, of course. His memories of that time were so, so different.

But he had also been determined to protect his mother's memory. Thinking back, he knew now he had done everything in his power to push her away.

Too, there was that wisp of memory when she had rubbed his back, the recollection of many nights when he had been near sleep, then encouraged over the edge into dreamless slumber by a soft, gentle hand.

But years of hurt were hard to put aside. "Why did you never say anything?"

"I couldn't."

"Why?" The word was sharp, harsh. She flinched. He expected her to scurry away, but she kept her seat.

"I told you your father had a temper. You knew yourself how heavy-handed he could be. Do you think I did not escape him?"

That took him aback. He had been the victim of his father's fist more than once. But he had never even considered that the beautiful, poised woman his father married might also be the recipient of such cruelty.

And then a thought, horrifying to contemplate. "And...Arthur?"

A look of incredible pain flashed in her eyes. In the space of an instant she appeared a decade older. "It took everything in me to protect him. Your father was determined to make sure Arthur succeeded at everything he did. He wanted a perfect son, and if Arthur did something less than perfect he used force to 'fix' the problem."

Tristan felt sick. He knew of his father's use of punishment. But in the few times a year he returned home from school as a child, he had been faced with what appeared to be the ideal family. Arthur had been lauded as a genius boy, excelling at everything he put his hand to.

He had never thought for a moment of the price his half-brother had paid for such praise.

"I was glad you were in school and that your mother's cousin could take you in for much of the rest of the year. I could not protect you both, try as I might."

"Why didn't you leave him?" The question flew out of his mouth, truly an accusation. "Damn it, Josephine, why didn't you take us and leave? I would have been more than happy to go had you done so."

Agony such as he had never seen contorted her face. "Do you think I did not want to? I would have given my soul to be able to do such a thing. I even attempted it once, while you were away at school. He struck Arthur so hard he lost consciousness. A four-year-old child, can you imagine? And so I packed my boy up, and left in the dead of night, vowing to get you when I could. I went to my father's house."

She stopped on a gasp, gathered herself before continuing in a low, pained voice. "A woman is her husband's property when she weds him. You know that, I'm sure. And by law he may do as he wishes with her. Even beat her. So my father told me. Your father told me as well when he was summoned to fetch me and our child."

He could only stare in horror at her. "I didn't know," he whispered.

She gave him a small, sad smile. "I did not want you to know. You had enough heartache. You did not need mine and your brother's added on."

He shook his head, overcome. But there was one more question he had to ask.

"Arthur, he didn't…my father didn't…?" He could not even give voice to such a horrifying thought.

She seemed to understand immediately. "Not directly, no. But perhaps, if your father had been less harsh, Arthur might not have gone out to practice his riding, to perfect his skill. He forgot his jacket and scarf, the silly thing. He was forever forgetting them in the winter…" She gasped, her hand coming up to grasp the brooch at her breast. It reminded him so much of Rosalind, of the way she touched her locket when in distress.

So much this woman had gone through, and he, unaware, was thinking only what he had wished to think of her.

"How I lashed out at your father in my grief," she continued in a whisper. "He refused to acknowledge any blame, of course. But he was not the same after that. He never retaliated when I screamed at him, never raised another hand to me again. And then his health began to fail him; he seemed to give up on life. I know it is a sin to say so, but I was glad that he died so quickly after my Arthur. So very glad." A sob escaped her.

He did not know how she wound up in his arms. But she was there, and his hand was the one giving comfort, stroking her back as she let loose her grief. As she had done for him all those years ago.

Something in him loosened then, breaking away from the brittle ball that had sat in his chest for so long. He knew what it was in an instant: hope.

Chapter 29

Night had fallen by the time Tristan returned to his townhouse. The last several hours had been spent with Josephine. All the wounds of the past had not been completely healed. There was still much to do in that regard; Tristan's father had dug his claws too deep into the both of them, had damaged them too much for it to be accomplished in one meeting. But the great chasm between Tristan and Josephine had begun to seal.

He felt lighter than ever. And utterly exhausted. In the end he'd asked her to come stay with him for the remainder of her time in London. She had declined, saying her friend needed her. But that she would be happy to extend her stay, to come visit with him after the wedding, for as long as he liked.

He could hardly believe it. Josephine, his stepmother, the woman he had spent so long hating, was coming to stay with him. And he was glad for it.

Would wonders ever cease?

His bedchamber was dark when he shut himself inside. He had not entered since his return, and now the bed beckoned. After a day and a half of travelling, the grief over finding Rosalind gone with Grace and the revisited heartache of the past hours, he wanted nothing more than to fall into bed and the oblivion of sleep. Perhaps, he thought as he lit the lamp at his bedside, the light of day would bring a better understanding of the complete turn his life had taken. And a greater acceptance of what he had recently lost.

Sighing, for he knew the last would not be easy, he turned—and spied a lone figure seated by the cold hearth.

At first he could not make out who it was. But then the faint light from the lamp limned a pale cheek, glimmered in large brown eyes, threw shadows under the dark slash of brows drawn together in the middle.

"Rosalind?" he whispered.

A tentative smile flitted briefly over her face. "Hello, Tristan."

He looked her over like a starving man peering through a window at a great feast laid out. The faint orange glow gave her an otherworldly appearance, as if she did not belong here with him, a mortal man with too many flaws to count. He longed to pull her into his arms. It had been his intention upon returning to London to tell her of his feelings and to see if she would accept him. But her cold words haunted him still, holding him back, keeping his feet rooted to the floor.

"Danielson told me you left with Grace for Scotland this morning," he rasped.

"So I did."

He shook his head. "Then...what...?"

She rose at his confusion. It was then he noticed the bag she was carrying, the outerwear that she was still bundled in.

"I made a mistake," she whispered. "A horrible, stupid mistake. I believed it was too late to rectify, after the way I left things with you. But being in that carriage, knowing I was leaving you behind, I knew I had to at least try. And so I had Grace drop me off, came back."

Her hands were wringing the handle of the bag, holding it before her like a shield. Taking a steadying breath, she lowered the bag to the floor, reached into the pocket of her travelling cloak, and held out her hand. He stared mutely at what she offered. There lay the special license and the ring he had chosen with such care.

"Why did you never show these to me, Tristan?"

The sapphire glinted at him. He kept his gaze fastened to it, unable to look in her eyes for fear of seeing that same coldness from before. "I was told that marriage was the last thing you expected from me."

She sucked in a sharp breath. "I mucked everything up, didn't I?"

His eyes flew to her face. Her lip was trembling.

"I didn't mean a thing I said to you, Tristan, I swear it. But after Guinevere, and what she went through, and how love destroyed her, I had to protect myself. I had to…"

Her voice broke. He hurried to her then, took her face in his hands, his own hurt disappearing in the face of her own. "You silly, wonderful woman," he whispered. "You never have to worry about protecting your heart from me. For I swear, if you let me, I will cherish it for the rest of my days."

Tears filled her eyes. "You will?"

He smiled. "I will. I adore you, Miss Rosalind Merriweather, running at the mouth, bossy as can be, jumping to conclusions and all."

She gasped in mock outrage and laughter and tears. She made to speak but he held a finger up to her lips.

"For once, let me do the talking," he said with a chuckle, before his voice dipped low, thick with emotion. "I love you. So very much. I don't know how it came about, that the one woman who made me confront the very darkest places in myself was the one to capture my heart, but I am so grateful you did."

He reached for her hand, extracted the ring from her grip. And then, while she watched with huge eyes, he knelt before her.

"I should have done this before that night. If I had not been out of my mind with wanting you I would have, instead of leaving you in doubt as to my intentions. It is a week later than I wanted to, but now I ask, with all my heart, will you marry me, Rosalind?"

• • •

Rosalind stared down at this man, who had presented her with his heart even after she had trampled it, and wanted to weep.

Instead she knelt in front of him, taking hold of the hand that held the ring out to her, and pressed both to her heart. "I am so sorry for causing you grief, for doubting you. You are the kindest, best man I have ever known. I was blind not to see it. I love you, so very much. And I would be honored to be your wife."

Before the words were out, ringing through the air with their joy, his mouth was on hers, hard and hot and demanding.

They had come together before this. But now they knew what was in the other's heart. There was no doubt, no indecision. Most importantly, there was no fear of the future or the past. They belonged to each other, body and soul.

Rosalind felt tears seep from her eyes and trail down her cheek. His thumb was there in an instant, wiping them away.

"I love you," he murmured, his lips trailing where his thumb had been, a promise louder than words that he would be there to ease every grief, soothe every hurt. He pulled back, his eyes glittering like sapphires in the faint glow of the lamp. And then, taking up her hand, he removed her glove and slid the ring onto her finger.

The metal was cool on her heated skin. He brought her hand to his mouth and kissed the ring, the action as powerful as any vow.

"I'm yours," she whispered, knowing her eyes were as full as his and for once not caring that she wore her heart on her sleeve.

"Thank God," he groaned, the words a benediction as his lips found hers again.

There was no more room to talk after that. As he plundered her mouth, stealing her very breath, his hands found their way between them. He worked blindly at the fastenings of her cloak, his desperate need unhidden. Rosalind needed no further urging. She shrugged from her outerwear, began in on her dress, helped him as he made short work of her stays. His clothes did not escape their fumbling hands, either. Soon she was in her shift, he only in his trousers.

Her fingers slid greedily over the smooth expanse of his shoulders, reveling in the broadness of them, at the heat of his skin, and the way his muscles bunched under her touch. His hands found their way to her hips, pulling her flush against his arousal.

She tore her mouth free from his on a gasp. "Please, Tristan," she begged even as her lips found the corded length of his neck. "The bed. Now."

"I can't wait for the damn bed," he growled. In the next moment she was on her back, cushioned by the plush rug beneath her and the pile of their clothing. Her squeak of surprise quickly turned into a moan as his large hands found the hem of her chemise and dragged it up, his lips following in a searing hot path. Over her legs, her hips, her stomach, his lips adored every inch of her exposed skin. And then the shift was up and over her head, and his mouth found the straining tip of her breast, and Rosalind thought she would perish from the ecstasy of it.

He adored her breast, bringing her nipple into his mouth, doing wicked things with his teeth and tongue that had her panting and writhing beneath him. His hands were as busy, splaying across her lower belly before trailing between her thighs. He slid one finger inside her, his groan of satisfaction as he found her wet and ready for him vibrating against her breasts, driving her to new heights.

Rosalind's body went tight as a bow as his finger was joined by a second. His fingers moved within her, his thumb rubbing circles over her swollen flesh. She gasped, her body bowing. Her fingers dove into his hair, grasping tight, feeling as if she were in the midst of a maelstrom and he was the only safety in the storm.

"I want to feel you come around me," he gasped. Then his hand was gone, and Rosalind, nearly mad with desire, wanted to cry from the loss. But then his mouth was back on hers, and he was at the entrance of her. There was no hesitation, no resistance this time. In one smooth thrust he was seated to the hilt.

He growled low, the sound vibrating through her. And then he began to move. Slow at first, drawing nearly out of her before he slid inch by glorious inch into her again. Her arms came around him, her legs clasping about his lean flanks. She met each movement of his hips thrust for thrust. Their breaths mingled, coming in harsh pants as their movements quickened, taking her higher. The pleasure built until it was almost pain, until her breaths turned to sobs, begging him for release.

In answer his mouth found hers, swallowing her cries, and his movements became frenzied. She dug her fingers into his sweat-slicked backside, urging him on. Finally, with a hard thrust, she shattered around him. She was flying through the night sky, stars blinding in their brilliance all about her. And Tristan was with her, flying beside her. As he would for the rest of her life.

. . .

Later that night, bundled up in blankets and giggling like a pair of children, Rosalind followed Tristan down to the garden, her hand tight in his. The moonlight was full and fat in the sky, bathing the landscape in a bright, shining silver.

As they hurried down the garden path, the brilliant glint of her engagement ring in the moonlight caught her eye. She grinned, then laughed, the sound freer than it had been in years.

He answered it with a chuckle of his own. Stopping, he spun around, pulling her into his arms. And for the millionth time that night, he kissed her senseless, until she could hardly remember her own name.

When he raised his head, he gave her a lopsided smile. As dizzy as she was from his kisses, she was pleased to see he looked decidedly loopy himself.

"Now tell me," she said, breathless, "Why you had to come out in the garden in the middle of the night when we could be curled quite warm and cozy in bed."

"Oh, you may be assured, I have every intention of finding our way back there again, and with all haste." He grinned and kissed the tip of her nose. "But for now, I wished to return to where it all started."

He turned and, with a sweep of his arm, indicated the stone bench when she gave him a curious look. "The place of our first kiss."

She laid a hand on his cheek. "My, but you are a romantic, aren't you?"

"You've no idea."

A shiver of anticipation skittered up her spine. For she could not wait to find out how romantic he could be.

For now, however, she joined him on the cold bench, glad for the layers of blankets he had wrapped her in. She leaned into him, resting her head on his shoulder. The scent of roses enveloped them, and she recalled that long-ago day when she had wished to be a bee so that she could fly over the garden wall and away from him.

What a fool she had been.

They talked there in the garden, their voices low and intimate. Dreams and plans all coalesced in the cool summer night air, brought into being under the endless night sky: when they would marry, where they would live. The stars twinkled their approval from above in the cloudless, inky heavens.

Soon they turned to matters more immediate. Tristan told her of Josephine, how he had gone to her, what they had said. And she told him of Mr. Carlisle's revelation, of her sister's child. And that she had learned of Tristan's fight with Lord Kingston.

"And so poor Miss Weeton is without a beau after all we have put her through in the last weeks," he mused into the crown of her head. "I feel so horrible that she is alone. She deserves to be happy."

Rosalind snuggled closer into his warmth, and his arm tightened around her. "Oh, I don't know," she said, trying and failing to keep the amusement from her voice. "I do believe Miss Weeton will be fine."

He pulled back, eyeing her suspiciously. "What are you keeping from me, you minx?"

She did grin then. "Only that Grace and I learned right before we left that Miss Weeton shall not remain Miss Weeton for long. That cousin that she was going to be married to at the end of the Season should she fail to find a husband? He came to London when he learned of her sudden popularity. From all accounts it was love at first sight. They are to be married by the end of the month."

He gaped at her. "You must be joking."

"Not a bit. Although," she said, forcing her expression into one of concern, "this does pose a problem for us."

He cocked his head. "Does it now?"

"Oh, certainly. For we had agreed on the payments that must be made only if Miss Weeton should marry men of our choosing. We did not even consider her marrying a third option."

His lips turned up in a smile, his eyes growing heavy-lidded. "And what do you propose the remuneration should be?"

She pretended to consider but could not remain serious. Instead she melted against him, eyeing his mouth. "I do believe that making me happy all the days of your life would be ample payment."

"Well then, I'd best get started on that right away," he murmured with a smile before pulling her close and covering her mouth with his.

Epilogue

"I do believe we need another trunk," Josephine murmured with a chuckle a little over a week later.

Rosalind surveyed the piles of colorful dresses and delicate underthings, the hat boxes and shawls and gloves and shoes that had yet to be packed, with no small amount of embarrassment. "I told Tristan I did not need so much."

"He loves you, my dear." Josephine smiled and patted her arm. "Let the boy pamper you. I have never seen him as happy as he's been the last few days since his marriage to you."

"You have some part in that happiness as well," she replied with a gentle smile. "It means much for him to have you here."

Josephine looked at Rosalind with glowing eyes, pleasure in every line and curve of her face.

After sending one of the footmen into the attic for another trunk, the two women went back to work alongside the maids, gently folding away the newly acquired wardrobe between sheets of tissue paper, packing the items away for their coming journey. In a matter of days, they would be leaving London on a wedding trip. First, a visit to his friend Lord Willbridge in Northamptonshire, after which they would head north to visit Grace in Scotland. Only then would they make the trek to Tristan's childhood home, Sainsly. Once there, they would remain for the foreseeable future. Rosalind could not wait to create new memories with him there.

She cast an affectionate look at Josephine as the older woman guided one of the maids into packing some gloves. Tristan's step-mother had welcomed Rosalind into the family with open arms,

standing by their side during the quiet wedding ceremony that had
joined them forever as man and wife. She had been nothing but sup-
portive in the days afterward, too, as Rosalind and Tristan prepared
to depart for their new life together. Rosalind was glad Josephine
had agreed to go with them, for after nearly a week of having known
her, Rosalind could not now imagine life without her.

A short while later the butler appeared in the doorway. "Lady
Crosby, Sir Tristan has asked that you join him in the drawing room
presently."

It took Rosalind some moments to realize the man was talking to
her—her new title would take some getting used to. Her face warmed
as she gave the waiting butler an apologetic look. "Thank you, Danielson." She turned to Josephine. "I shall return momentarily."

"Take your time, my dear," the other woman said with a smile
before returning her attention to the maid.

Rosalind removed her apron, patting down her hair before hurrying out the door. She wondered what Tristan could want. Surely
nothing untoward. She blushed, for it was certainly not out of the
question. He seemed to find the most incredibly imaginative ways
to get her alone.

Their last encounter flashed in her mind then, memories of bared
limbs and soft sighs echoed back at them by the soaring walls of
books in the library.

So flustered by her musings, she very nearly lost her way to the
drawing room. Which, of course, brought to mind her first day at
the Upper Grosvenor Street house when she had thought Tristan
an intruder and had been bound and determined to put the man
in his place.

She smiled. How long ago that seemed. And how wrong she had
been about him.

Caught in her reverie, she was still smiling when she turned into
the drawing room. The sight that greeted her, however, stopped her
cold.

Tristan was not alone but had company. Several people sat about
him, one of whom was—

Mrs. Gladstow?

She stood in shock for a moment. The natural instinct in her from her months of service in the woman's household flared, bidding her to slink into the room, to sit quietly and await the curt orders the woman never failed to throw at her.

But she was no longer this woman's companion. She was, in fact, above Mrs. Gladstow in station now. Yet the urge was there to make herself small, to avoid detection. Utterly confused by the warring sides of herself, she stood stupidly, frozen in place.

"Ah, my dear, there you are," Tristan said, smiling as he stood.

He held out his hand and Rosalind thawed enough to gracelessly enter the room. As they sat, he slipped his arm about her and the world was righted.

"We have guests who have heard of our marriage and come to wish us well." He turned to the older woman. "Mrs. Gladstow, I'm sure you remember my wife. She was in your employ for a time, if I recall."

The woman looked as if she'd sucked on a lemon. "*You* are Sir Tristan's wife?" The implication was as blatant as it was insulting: she could not countenance her former companion having risen so far above her.

Anger boiled up, blotting out the numb shock that had taken over her. Rosalind opened her mouth to give the woman a scathing retort. Before she could, Tristan spoke up, his voice cool, the warning in it clear. "She is. Aren't you going to offer her the same congratulations you gave me, Mrs. Gladstow?"

The woman's mouth pinched tight until it was a thin line slashed across her face, holding her two pale, sunken cheeks together by sheer spite. With obvious distaste, she forced out, "Congratulations, Lady Crosby. You are lucky to have landed such a husband."

A horrified silence fell upon the room. But Tristan's voice pushed on. "I assure you, Mrs. Gladstow, I am the lucky one." He smiled down at Rosalind, his heart in his eyes. Rosalind melted into him, feeling the effects of it straight to her toes.

He seemed equally as moved. Until, that was, a gentle voice broke through their blissful moment.

"My fiancé and I also wish you congratulations, Lady Crosby."

Rosalind gasped and turned, for though she had not often heard that voice, she knew it well. Sure enough, Miss Gladstow was there, seated beside Mr. Marlow. Rosalind had not fully registered their presence until this moment, so focused had she been on the girl's mother. "Miss Gladstow. I did not expect to see you again."

The girl appeared a different person. Gone was the pale, anxious look that had been constant when Rosalind had been in their employ. Now Miss Gladstow's skin held the healthy blush of a true happiness of heart. To Rosalind's everlasting surprise, the girl leaned forward and embraced her.

"I was so very sad that you left us with such haste so many weeks ago," she said, releasing Rosalind and giving her mother a faintly censorious look. "When I learned of your new position as Lady Belham's companion," she continued, smiling gently at Rosalind once more, "I was so very relieved. But hearing you are the new Lady Crosby gave me great joy."

"You knew of this before we came?" Mrs. Gladstow's voice was shrill as she eyed her daughter in outrage.

"Of course, Mama." Miss Gladstow replied. "Sir Tristan sent word of it himself. He knew we would want to know."

As Rosalind watched Miss Gladstow and Tristan exchange small smiles, she knew exactly what this strange visit was about: Tristan was giving her the opportunity to close this still painful part of her past for good. He was bringing Mrs. Gladstow to her like a gift, to punish as she wished. And as she gazed into his blue eyes, patience and love clear in their depths, she knew he would be behind her whatever path she chose to take. She could rail at the woman, could ruin her, and he would support her.

The temptation was there, so strong she could taste it. How many times had she sat helpless as this woman reproached her? How many sleepless nights had she spent terrified that the next day would see her on the street without food or a roof over her head?

Rosalind turned to Mrs. Gladstow and took a deep breath, finding strength in Tristan at her side.

As he would be for the rest of her life.

Her breath caught in her throat. For it was in that moment that it truly hit her: Tristan would be there always. She never again had to walk through life alone and frightened.

Any animosity or bitterness she had toward this woman melted away in an instant. She smiled and sat forward, taking Mrs. Gladstow's hand. The woman froze and blinked in shock.

"Mrs. Gladstow, I want to thank you," Rosalind said. "If you had not freed me from your employ I would not now be married to the best, most loving, most wonderful husband. Because of your actions all those weeks ago, I was able to carve a new path for myself and find the greatest happiness imaginable in the process." She squeezed the woman's cold fingers before releasing them. "Thank you so very much."

Mrs. Gladstow paled even further, all manner of emotions flooding her face from incredulity to fury to horror to guilt. There was a time Rosalind would have waited with bated breath for the woman's reaction. No more. She turned with a smile to Miss Gladstow. "When do you wed?"

"In a month's time. We are for home at the end of the week."

Mr. Marlow took Miss Gladstow's hand, placing a kiss on her knuckles before looking to Tristan. "It is our especial wish that you and your bride attend. You would be our guests of honor, you see, considering how instrumental you were in bringing us together in the first place."

Tristan smiled sheepishly. "Ah, you know about that then, do you?"

"Sarah and I do not keep anything from each other," Mr. Marlow said with a loving look for his fiancé. "Not any longer."

Tristan looked to Rosalind, who nodded happily. "I do believe a short detour in our travel plans can be managed. We would love to attend," he said with a grin, shaking the other man's hand.

It seemed with the revelation of Tristan's interference in her daughter's engagement, however, Mrs. Gladstow was breaking free from her stupor. She sputtered, gaping at all parties involved.

Miss Gladstow and Mr. Marlow stood, bidding their farewells with hugs and handshakes before ushering Mrs. Gladstow from the house. After the sounds of their retreating footsteps and the closing of the front door faded, Tristan took Rosalind in his arms and gazed down at her. Rosalind couldn't be sure, but she thought there was a new respect in his eyes.

"Why, Lady Crosby," he murmured, "you surprise me more every day."

"Do I?"

He nodded. "I thought you would jump at the chance to give that horrid woman her comeuppance. And yet you *thanked* her." He shook his head, all amazement. "How did I ever deserve the love of such a woman?"

"You have always deserved everything your heart could ever desire, you silly man," she murmured, twining her arms about his neck.

His eyes softened. "Then it is lucky I have you. For you are all I ever want," he said before claiming her mouth with his own.

It was some time later—and with fewer clothes on than before—when Rosalind laid her head on her husband's bare chest. With the steady beat of his heart beneath her ear, she asked the question that had been on her mind for the past week.

"Except for that one last hiccup, you were quite a successful matchmaker. Do you see any more matchmaking in your future?"

His arms tightened about her. "What need have I for more matchmaking, when I have been so happily matched myself?"

Rosalind rose up on her elbow, staring down into Tristan's beloved face. "Oh, I don't know," she said, tracing her finger over the hard planes of his chest. "There may come a time when your talents for matchmaking are needed. You would not want to deny the world of your talents, would you?"

He raised one golden eyebrow. "Why, Rosalind, never tell me you have got a taste for it yourself."

She shrugged, trying to hide her smile and failing spectacularly. "You never know. It may come in handy one day."

He growled, rolling her onto her back. "Woman, I dearly hope you never stop surprising me."

She grinned. "I think it is safe to say I never shall," she said before pulling him down for a kiss.

Acknowledgments

I have been so blessed that these characters I've created, once mere wisps of an idea in my head, have been embraced so wonderfully. Thank you to the readers for taking them into your hearts and showing them such love.

Thank you so very much to everyone at EverAfter Romance, especially my fabulous editor Kayla Park, as well as Shannon, Michelle, Laura and many more. I've loved working on this series with you; you have made writing these books a joy.

A huge thank you to my agent Kim Lionetti. I love having you in my corner.

Thank you to the wonderful ladies who read this book when it was a raw, unfinished thing and gave me such incredible feedback. Maria and Silvi, you ladies are angels.

There are so many fabulous, crazy talented people who cheer me on daily. From fellow members in the RWA and my chapter SVRWA, to my Le Bou Crew, to my wonderful 2017 Golden Heart Rebelles, to the other Patronesses in The Drawing Room, to the Authors 18 group, and so many more: I am blown away by the support and love that you all have given me. Thank you.

And, last but certainly not least, I cannot forget to thank my own personal muses, my husband and my children. You have made sure to never leave any doubt that you believe in me, utterly and completely. Even though, yet again, I have failed to add a sword with a secret compartment in the hilt. I love you, my amazing family, so very much.

CHRISTINA BRITTON developed a passion for writing romance novels shortly after buying her first at the tender age of thirteen. Though for several years she turned to art and put brush instead of pen to paper, she has returned to her first love and is now writing full time. She spends her days dreaming of corsets and cravats and noblemen with tortured souls.

She lives with her husband and two children in the San Francisco Bay Area. A member of Romance Writers of America, she also belongs to her local chapter, Silicon Valley RWA, and is a 2017 RWA® Golden Heart® Winner. You can find her on the web at **www.christinabritton.com**, Twitter as **@cbrittonauthor**, or **facebook.com/ChristinaBrittonAuthor**.

AUG   2019

$15.99

Massapequa Public Library
523 Central Avenue
Massapequa, NY 11758
(516) 798-4607

CPSIA information can be obtained
at www.ICGtesting.com
Printed in the USA
BVHW031456050719
552685BV00005B/5/P